PENGUIN ENGLISH LIBRARY

FOUR JACOBEAN CITY COMEDIES

Gāmini Salgādo is a Reader in the School of English and American Studies in the University of Sussex. In addition to editing *Three Jacobean Tragedies*, *Three Restoration Comedies* and *Cony-Catchers and Bawdy Baskets* for the Penguin English Library, he has written a short study of *Sons and Lovers* and edited a collection of essays on the same novel.

FOUR JACOBEAN CITY COMEDIES

Marston
THE DUTCH COURTESAN

Middleton
A MAD WORLD, MY MASTERS

Jonson
THE DEVIL IS AN ASS

Massinger
A NEW WAY TO PAY OLD DEBTS

Edited with an Introduction and Notes
by Gāmini Salgādo

PENGUIN BOOKS

Penguin Books Ltd, Harmondsworth, Middlesex, England
Penguin Books Inc., 7110 Ambassador Road, Baltimore, Maryland 21207, U.S.A.
Penguin Books Australia Ltd, Ringwood, Victoria, Australia
Penguin Books Canada Ltd, 41 Steelcase Road West, Markham, Ontario, Canada
Penguin Books (N.Z.) Ltd, 182-190 Wairau Road, Auckland 10, New Zealand

—

This collection published in Penguin Books 1975
Introduction and Notes copyright © Gāmini Salgādo, 1975

—

Made and printed in Great Britain by
Hazell Watson & Viney Ltd, Aylesbury, Bucks
Set in Monotype Plantin

To
MELANIE

for her twenty-first

CONTENTS

INTRODUCTION

THE phrase 'Jacobean City Comedy', like all such phrases, is no more than a convenient label for the editor and critic. It does not describe so much as point to a body of drama whose main features are fairly clear, although its edges are blurred. But, as applied to this volume, the phrase does have the advantage of offering us three different ways of looking at the plays, depending on which of its three components we choose to stress.

We could, for instance, think of the plays as chiefly Jacobean – that is, as not only very different from anything produced in the Elizabethan period, but also as specifically related to the court of King James and its way of life. (The fact that this relationship is mainly a hostile one makes it stand out in sharper relief.) Of course, nothing comes out of nothing, especially where the drama is concerned, and Jacobean City Comedy has its roots in the last decade of Elizabeth's reign, in the literature of Eliza-bethan low-life (collected in *Cony-Catchers and Bawdy Baskets*, Penguin Books), in the satirical verse of Hall, Marston and others, and more immediately in such plays as Dekker's *The Shoe-maker's Holiday* and Heywood's *Four Prentices of London*. But to turn from either of these plays to any in this collection is to become aware of a different world, and the awareness of differ-ence is all the more forcible because outwardly the world is recognizably similar. That world is generally London, or a part of the country temporarily invaded by Londoners bringing with them their own tempo and outlook on life. More particularly it is the world of moneymaking, legitimate, doubtfully legitimate or downright crooked, along with the pursuit of women for purposes legitimate, doubtfully legitimate or downright crooked. But the light in which these activities are presented is altogether sharper and the response which they evoke in us is harsher and less genial. The dramatic objectives of Dekker and Heywood are as simple and straightforward as the responses they wish to evoke.

Their plays celebrate the honest tradesman and his apprentice and present with simple relish the variety and excitement of London life in its middle and lower reaches. If they sometimes suggest that the tradesman and his prentices are every bit as good as their blue-blooded betters, they do it in a spirit of naïve hyperbole, in no way seriously questioning the gradations of the ordered Elizabethan social framework. Nothing could be further from the spirit of these plays than satire in either of its extreme moods: savage indignation or ironic detachment.

With Chapman's *An Humorous Day's Mirth*, first performed three years before the end of the sixteenth century, we are appreciably closer to later city comedy. Chapman's play can fairly claim the distinction of being the first dramatized satire in an urban setting, and the character of the presenter, standing in an intermediate relation between the audience and the main action, is one that this type of comedy uses over and over again. But the satire is still mild and the plot is little more than a series of episodic sketches, very different from the often rigidly schematic arrangements of the later comedy. Not until *Eastward Ho!*, written by Jonson, Chapman and Marston and first performed in 1605, do we find a city comedy in which London life is looked at with emotions other than affectionate pride or genial amusement. The harsher colours and more strident tones found in the city plays of the new century may be conveniently labelled Jacobean, because they are fairly closely related to the accession of James I and the changed atmosphere and attitudes brought about by that event.

It is a commonplace that the new king did not have anything like the personal popularity of his predecessor, but the change of sovereign had effects which cut far more deeply than differences of personality. At the level of social hierarchy, Elizabeth was more serious in her conception of 'degree', as is shown by her rebuke to Sir Philip Sidney when he quarrelled at the tennis court with the Earl of Oxford. Elizabeth was sparing in bestowing titles (there had been no dukes in England since Norfolk's execution in 1572, a fact alluded to in *The Devil is an Ass*) precisely because she had some regard for them. For James on the other hand, in spite of, or perhaps because of, his insistence on his own divinity, the bestowing of honours and titles was little more than a handy way of replenishing the depleted royal coffers. He began his lavish dispensation of knighthoods on his progress from Edinburgh to London early in 1603, at the very beginning of his reign, and thereafter never lost an opportunity to brandish the royal sword and increase the ranks of the nobility. In the first year of his reign the new king revived the decree that all landowners whose income exceeded forty pounds a year should either accept knighthoods (and pay for them) or pay a fine. (This is the point of Follywit's remark in *A Mad World, My Masters* that his uncle, Sir Bounteous Progress, 'is a knight of thousands, and therefore no knight since one thousand six hundred'.) Not surprisingly, the upshot of this rash of instant honours was that the whole idea of nobility and social rank was brought into question and became a constant target for satire in city comedy. In *The Devil is an Ass*, for instance, Jonson manages to get a good deal of satirical mileage out of Fitzdottrel's ambition to become the Duke of Drown'dland by financing the reclamation of submerged land; while, in a much darker mood, Massinger pours scorn on the new-made knight Sir Giles Overreach's consuming ambition to have his daughter 'write honourable, right honourable'.* To us today it may seem that the whole issue of titles for sale is nothing but rank snobbery, to be treated with the same kind of tolerant disregard with which we read of birthday honours or life peerages. But in the carefully graded society to which, though it was crumbling here and there, the early seventeenth century still paid more than lip-service, the pollution of 'honour' at the source was neither trivial nor irrelevant. It seemed to threaten, as Massinger saw it, the very foundation of social order, and thereby of morality itself. This is how Lady Alworth, one of the positive points of reference in *A New Way to Pay Old Debts*, characterizes another character intended to be equally sympathetic, the noble Lord Lovell:

> As you are noble (howe'er common men
> Make sordid wealth the object and sole end

* It was only in the sixteenth century that anything like precise genealogical information was available to many families; much of it was manufactured.

> Of their industrious aims) 'twill not agree
> With those of eminent blood (who are engag'd
> More to prefer their honours than to increase
> The state left to 'em by their ancestors)
> To study large additions to their fortunes
> And quite neglect their births.

She then attempts to dissuade Lovell from marrying the daughter of the *nouveau riche* Overreach; far from raising his wife's station by this match, he would only degrade his own:

> ... so all wealth
> (I mean if ill acquir'd) cemented to honour
> By virtuous ways achiev'd, and bravely purchas'd,
> Is but as rubbage pour'd into a river
> (Howe'er intended to make good the bank)
> Rend'ring the water that was pure before
> Polluted and unwholesome.

The metaphor of the river suggests not so much the particular defilement of one family or individual as a general contamination. For his part, Lord Lovell disclaims any intention of marrying Overreach's daughter with a vehemence in which concern for rank is mingled with something like moral outrage:

> Were Overreach's 'states thrice centupl'd, his daughter
> Millions of degrees much fairer than she is,
> (Howe'er I might urge precedents to excuse me)
> I would not so adulterate my blood
> By marrying Margaret, and so leave my issue
> Made up of several pieces, one part scarlet
> And the other London blue. In my own tomb
> I will inter my name first.

To which Lady Alworth replies (aside, as she well may), 'I am glad to hear this.' Massinger's play is not strictly a city comedy, being set in Nottinghamshire, and having been written in the 1620s, when the vogue for this type of comedy had passed. But its preoccupation with the phenomenon of social rank and social climbing is representative; only the uncompromising firmness of its standpoint is untypical. For Massinger, the attempt to take short-cuts to nobility (and he makes, revealingly, no distinction between social and moral nobility) is not a matter for detached amusement; it is, quite literally, a form of madness, as the progress of his hero-villain clearly demonstrates.

The sale of titles and its repercussions on those who sell and buy them, as well as on society at large, is probably the most striking 'Jacobean' motif in these plays, but it is by no means the only one. The court itself is never directly presented, as by definition the plays are concerned with city life, but there is a pervasive sense that the court is at best tawdry and trivial, at worst squalid and corrupt. (Many courtiers were heavily in debt and this fact of course heightened the tendency to financial corruption.) This can be seen in the farcical transvestite episode in *The Devil is an Ass* where Wittipol is presented as a lady lately returned from Spain 'come from your great friends at court'. The hypocrisy and obsequiousness of Lady Tailbush and Lady Eitherside, as well as their obsession with the latest fashions and cosmetics, provide a picture of court life at one remove which, for all its farcical exaggeration, is etched with acid. It is the comic counterpart to the vision of courtly corruption found in the tragedies of Webster and Tourneur.

Another feature which places these comedies very firmly in their own time is the central importance given to money and moneymaking. Of course love and money (in that order for 'romantic' comedy, in the reverse order for 'realistic' comedy) have always been the staple of comic drama, but in these plays, money is not simply the reward the hero gets at the end along with the girl. It is a much more fluid and indeterminate quantity, as potentially powerful and often as delusory as the philosopher's stone. (It is not accidental that the finest of all city comedies, not included here, is called *The Alchemist*. Jonson sees an almost literal connection between alchemical transformations and some of the newer and wilder ways of making money, as well as their solvent effects on social relationships, so that 'projecting' can be said, in Jonson's terms, to be alchemy come true.) Even to us today, who are well used to smooth operators who sell shares in non-existent mines or make a small fortune by juggling funds from one holding company to another, the sheer variety and zany inventiveness of some of Meercraft's fund-raising ventures in *The Devil is an Ass* are exhilarating (though some of them, like the project for the wholesale manufacture and distribution of toothpicks, seem oddly practical today). The impulse to get rich quick is of course one shared by all of us who have ever pricked crosses with a pin on a football pools coupon. But when the impulse is widespread, concentrated and accelerated, when there is a general tendency to take the building of castles in the air as a serious architectural pursuit, we may fairly look for an explanation somewhat firmer than that of ordinary human cupidity. Such an explanation for the interest in fantastic money-making schemes which prevailed in the early years of the Jacobean era is provided by a phenomenon with which we are all too familiar today, that of inflation.

The one hundred and fifty odd years before the outbreak of the Civil War may be seen as a single phase of continual inflation. By the beginning of the seventeenth century, prices were more than five times what they had been a hundred years earlier. The steepest rise in prices came towards the close of the sixteenth century. (Naturally enough, James's sale of honours had a good deal to do with inflation; as the greatest spender in the country, inflation hit the monarch hardest.) As a means of softening the crippling effect of inflation on fixed incomes, new 'ventures' appealed to gentry and the wealthier citizenry alike. Though the Industrial Revolution was still a century and more away, there was a good deal of opportunity to make large profits from many manufacturing and raw material industries, such as cloth, coal, salt and glass. (In passing, we may note that many of the chief investors in the new ventures were aristocrats.) The risks were high, the capital required might be considerable, but the rewards could be rapid and handsome. In this respect, the fantastic money-raising schemes and plain swindles depicted in the city comedies are a fairground mirror which throws a distorted but recognizable picture of the flurry of new economic activity which marked the Jacobean period.

The sense of the debasement of ancient honours and the loosening of traditional ties, of a court at once remote from the people's affections and corrupt, financially and otherwise, and of a society where many of the worst seemed to be full of a passionate intensity in their devotion to the amassing of wealth – all these contribute to give the particular flavour to these plays which the epithet 'Jacobean' points to. When we think of them as *city* comedies – that is, as comedies which derive their life from the life of London – the first thing that strikes us is that London is no mere background or setting for these plays, any more than England is merely the background to Shakespeare's history plays. Indeed, it is almost true to say that London is, for Jonson and Marston, one of the chief characters. By a slight extension, we can say the same of Middleton's *A Mad World, My Masters*, for although the play is set in the country mansion of Sir Bounteous Progress, it is almost entirely concerned with the activities of Follywit and his London-based consorts, activities which clearly belong to the world of sharpers, rogues and con-men so devotedly observed and chronicled by Robert Greene and others in the metropolis. And even Massinger's play, insofar as one of its leading themes is the conflict between London blue and aristocratic scarlet, has some claim to be described as looking towards London and its society.

Though overcrowding had begun somewhat earlier, seventeenth century London was still 'the flower of cities all' rather than the great wen. Foreign visitors remarked on its size, its variety and the magnificence of its buildings and the aspect of its citizens. A few years before the beginning of the century one of the most observant of foreign travellers, Frederick Duke of Württemberg, recorded his impressions:

London is a large, excellent and mighty city of business, and the most important in the whole kingdom; most of the inhabitants are employed in buying and selling merchandize, and trading in almost every corner of the world . . . It is a very populous city, so that one can scarcely pass along the streets, on account of the throng.
The inhabitants are magnificently apparelled, and are extremely proud and overbearing . . . The women have much more liberty than perhaps in any other place; they also know well how to make use of it, for they go dressed out in exceedingly fine clothes, and give all their attention to their ruffs and stuffs.*

*W. B. Rye (ed.), *England as Seen by Foreigners in the Days of Elizabeth and James the First*, 1865.

Most of the points touched on by the visiting duke figure prominently in the plays. The sheer hustle and bustle of London life fascinates Jonson, and in the opening of *The Devil is an Ass*, Iniquity, like the chorus of *Henry V*, seems to invite the audience to 'behold/In the quick forge and workinghouse of thought/ How London doth pour out her citizens':

> I will fetch thee a leap
> From the top of Paul's steeple to the Standard in Cheap . . .
> We will survey the suburbs, and make forth our sallies
> Down Petticoat Lane, and up the Smock-alleys,
> To Shoreditch, Whitechapel, and so to Saint Kather'n's,
> To drink with the Dutch there, and take forth their patterns.
> From thence we will put in at Custom-house quay there,
> And see how the factors and prentices play there . . .
> Nay, boy, I will bring thee to the bawds and the roysters
> At Billingsgate, feasting with claret-wine and oysters;
> From thence shoot the Bridge, child, to the Cranes i' the Vintry,
> And see there the gimblets, how they make their entry!
> Or, if thou hadst rather, to the Strand down to fall,
> 'Gainst the lawyers come dabbled from Westminster hall,
> And mark how they cling, with their clients together,
> Like ivy to oak, so velvet to leather.

The jog-trot rhythm which Jonson took from the older moral plays is the perfect vehicle for the hither-and-thithering glimpses of the city and its inhabitants. It is worth noting how, at the end of the play, the satirist's point, namely that London is a city much like hell – only more so – is almost completely submerged in the Londoner's pride that 'hell is a grammar school to this'.

The civic pride of Jonson and Marston finds expression in the loving attention to geographical detail which is evident everywhere in their plays. But more interesting and important is their response to the style of life which the city encourages and often enforces. Cocledemoy and Mulligrub, the wily trickster and the hypocritical vintner in *The Dutch Courtesan*, are inconceivable outside Jacobean London, while Freevill's eloquent defence of whores reeks of the city stews in every line:

Alas, good creatures, what would you have them do? Would you have them get their living by the curse of man, the sweat of their brows? So they do; every man must follow his trade, and every woman her occupation. A poor decayed mechanical man's wife, her husband is laid up; may not she lawfully be laid down, when her husband's only rising is by his wife's falling? A captain's wife wants means; her commander lies in open field abroad; may not she lie in civil arms at home? A waiting gentlewoman that had wont to take say to her lady, miscarries or so: the court misfortune throws her down; may not the city courtesy take her up? Do you know no alderman would pity such a woman's case? Why is charity grown a sin? Or relieving the poor and impotent an offence?

We are a good way here from anything like the direct expression of civic sentiment; but one cannot help feeling, as with Jonson, that the moralist's censure is softened by the awareness of the richness and variety of city life; London may be dirty, but it is alive, and comedy characteristically embraces life, dirt and all, with a warmth and wholeheartedness that leaves little room for discrimination.

London was of course a much smaller place then than it is now. Islington and Tottenham Court, Highgate, Hampstead and Kentish Town were all country places where, we are told, one could still rise early on May Day morning to gather fresh dew for the complexion. Nevertheless London lived by money-making and it is this aspect which attracts the attention of the playwrights. In fact, with only a very slight oversimplification, it could be said that Elizabethan city comedy celebrates honest moneymaking while Jacobean city comedy anatomizes, and often comes very near celebrating, dishonest moneymaking. (St Paul's, where Jonson begins *Every Man in His Humour*, was the centre of this latter activity, being thieves' club, information centre, labour market and place of assignation combined – as much a den of thieves as a house of prayer.) The gulling of dupes and the seduction of women often appear as almost interchangeable forms of exploitation where the dramatist's sympathies are by no means unequivocally on the side of the victims. This is one reason why a speech of repentance or remorse, such as Penitent Brothel's towards the end of *A Mad World, My Masters*, falls on the ear with a dull and unconvincing sound; whatever lesson the moralist may want to teach us, the dramatist can scarcely conceal his approval, or at least condonation, of the body's desires.

In language and action too these plays catch the rhythm of the city's life. Whether it is in the nimble verse of *The Devil is an Ass* or the supple prose of *The Dutch Courtesan* and *A Mad World, My Masters*, the idiom is everywhere that of the bustling and bawdy metropolis. Listen to Follywit chaffing his companions:

Call me your forecast, you whoresons. When you come drunk out of a tavern, 'tis I must cast your plots into form still; 'tis I must manage the prank, or I'll not give a louse for the proceeding; I must let fly my civil fortunes, turn wild-brain, lay my wits upo' th' tenters, you rascals, to maintain a company of villains whom I love in my very soul and conscience.

And where plot is concerned too – though in comedy of intrigue events tend to move faster than in other kinds of drama – there is an especially frenetic acceleration of incident which seems to catch the tempo of city life. There are differences between the plays here and elsewhere, but in all of them, except perhaps *A New Way to Pay Old Debts*, we get a feeling of action speeded up and bolting headlong downhill to disaster.

London, then, gave to these plays their sights and sounds, the behaviour and accents of their characters, and the rhythm and patterns of their plot. And it did so because its size, variety and restless energy made it appear to these dramatists a striking and comprehensive image of human appetite and human folly.

Appetite and folly bring us conveniently to the consideration of these plays as comedies, though neither pure nor simple. Comedy has traditionally based its outlook on life on a clear recognition of the body's imperfections, or rather the body's desires and their imperiousness, the urgency of appetite, and the 'catastrophonical' (Cocledemoy's word) folly of flouting or ignoring these imperatives. This frank avowal of physical needs is one of the things we might mean by calling these comedies 'realistic'; but the resolute concentration of such a play as *The Dutch Courtesan* on man as a creature the chief good and market of whose time is but to sleep, feed and defecate makes it plain that this kind of realism is very different from an unselective rendering – assuming this was possible – of a slice of contemporary life. It is much nearer to what we mean when we call a novel or a film 'realistic' in the sense that it is about something which we all recognize to be true but choose to ignore because it is unpleasant. Marston, who had cut his satirical teeth in the late 1590s in the ten fierce verse diatribes comprising *The Scourge of Villainy*, has his eye so firmly fixed on man's genital and excretory activities that he comes dangerously close in this play to a kind of indecent exposure whose main significance we might be tempted to call pathological rather than literary or dramatic. But this is not quite fair. No doubt a good many of the obscenities with which Cocledemoy freely bespatters his speech are there because of the professional dramatist's shrewd calculation that his audience could stomach this kind of thing with relish (a comparison with certain current developments in films suggests itself almost automatically). And perhaps the titillatory effect was heightened by the fact that this play, like Middleton's *A Mad World, My Masters*, was first performed by a children's company, a group of those 'little eyases' whose activities so annoyed the players in *Hamlet*. Bawdy talk and gesture would acquire a further dimension when uttered and performed by wide-eyed lads with piping treble voices. Making every allowance for all this, however, one can fairly claim that the obscenity of *The Dutch Courtesan* is more closely related to the play as a whole than is the case with most comedies of the time. For the play is an inquiry into the extent to which the physical appetites and functions of man can be ignored or suppressed in the supposed interest of 'higher' or more 'spiritual' activities. It conducts this inquiry by juxtaposing three couples. At the centre of the main action are Freevill and Beatrice. The latter is very much the starry-eyed heroine of romantic comedy, but the relationship is anchored in psychological reality by Freevill's experience of prostitution (he had earlier had a liaison with the Dutch courtesan, Franceschina) and his frank recognition of it as a necessary step in his approach to marriage. With the easy air of one outlining a thoroughly reasonable sequence of events,

Freevill says of his relationship with Franceschina: 'I loved her with my heart until my soul showed me the imperfection of my body, and placed my affection on a lawful love, my modest Beatrice.' And nothing that is said or done in the play makes his viewpoint seem anything other than reasonable. On the other hand, the actual love scene between Freevill and Beatrice does not impress us as a meeting between sensible and mature individuals, but rather as a stereotyped exercise in romantic lyricism. This is the soft underside of Cocledemoy's bawdy talk, but its more immediate place is as one extreme of sexual relationship, as the tempestuous love scenes between Malheureux and Franceschina are the other. Malheureux, as his name signifies, is unfortunate because he is so totally unaware of his own nature. He thinks himself 'a man of snow', totally impervious to the temptations of the flesh, and especially to those offered by professional purveyors. The nemesis that inevitably falls upon such total self-delusion could, in another key, yield the sombre near-tragic predicament of an Angelo in *Measure for Measure* (a play which belongs to the same period as Marston's). But here any tragic possibilities in the situation are very firmly excluded by the parody of Malheureux's imminent execution by that of Mulligrub in the sub-plot and the ludicrous 'Dutch' accent inflicted by Marston on Franceschina which cripples any effort on her part to reach tragic stature (though Billie Whitelaw, in the Chichester Festival Theatre production some years ago, almost outmanoeuvred Marston). Between these two pairs stand Tysefew and Crispinella (Marston's own addition to his principal narrative source), whose relationship reminds us, as we see it unfolding, of nothing so much as that of Benedick and Beatrice in *Much Ado About Nothing*. Crispinella lacks the lightness and radiance of Beatrice and Tysefew has more of the 'blunt gallant' aspect of Benedick's character than of his ready wit; nevertheless their relationship is based on a true understanding of each other's physical selves and can therefore find room both for romantic sentiment and fierce passion. Neither of these qualities emerges 'neat' in their courtship, which is full of earthy banter, but we sense their presence as we respond to the undoubted genuineness of their feelings for each other. So, like most good comedies, *The Dutch Courtesan* reminds us that man is also an animal, and that he forgets this at his peril, even in his most exalted relationships. And there is a sub-plot, concerned with jowls of salmon, drinking goblets and invitations to non-existent dinners, in which the master of ceremonies, Cocledemoy, by his single-minded assumption that man is *only* an animal, helps us to remember that he is not.

In *A Mad World, My Masters* the obscenity is, though less obvious, more pervasive than in Marston's play, because it is not so closely identified with a single character. It is also less easy to justify in terms of the play's theme. Follywit's machinations are directed mainly towards acquiring what would become lawfully his by unlawful means. He knows his grandsire, Sir Bounteous Progress, has made him his heir but is impatient to come into his inheritance forthwith: 'Then, since he has no will to do me good as long as he lives, by mine own will I'll do myself good before he dies.' Follywit's triumph over Sir Bounteous remains ambiguous to the end. Not only are his robberies discovered, but in the end he finds that he has unwittingly married his grandfather's whore. In the other part of the plot, concerned with Penitent Brothel's attempts to get into bed with Mistress Harebrain, we have the more overt moralizing of the play, with Penitent's quite implausible last-minute change of heart. But of all these plays this one seems least concerned to drive home a moral lesson. It is far too closely involved in admiration for the virtuosity of its villain-heroes. The scene where Follywit is disguised as a courtesan, for example, keeps our attention constantly focused on the adroitness of the performance, not on its somewhat dubious purpose. This delight in deft performance appears in the innumerable transformations which Follywit undergoes during the action, culminating in a final scene of Pirandellian cross-perspective, where Follywit is compelled to play a 'real' and a 'fake' Justice of the Peace simultaneously to two separate audiences, with only us, the real audience, able to take in both performances together.

A distinctive feature of Middleton's play is the way in which action and language combine the apparently contradictory attributes of genial celebration and ironic detachment. Thus there is the happy ending with a marriage and a feast. But it is marriage to a whore, and the host at the feast is not so much the master of ceremonies as their victim. There is a dimension of irony even in Sir Bounteous's realization that he may be the prey of parasites, for though he utters this as a general truth he is totally unaware of its precise application: 'a man knows not till he make a feast how many varlets he feeds.' No indeed – not even long afterwards. Similarly, in the other plot, Harebrain's reconciliation with Penitent, who has been attempting to seduce his wife, projects an image of his wife which may be literally true but is totally incompatible with the sentiments and activities of the Mistress Harebrain we have seen throughout the play:

> Let me embrace thee, sir, whom I will love
> Even next unto my soul, and that's my wife;
> Two dear rare gems this hour presents me with,
> A wife that's modest, and a friend that's right!
> Idle suspect and fear, now take your flight.

The last lines spoken by Sir Bounteous neatly combine the celebratory and ironic aspects of the play precisely because they seem to have a range of application in the audience's mind which is beyond the speaker's own experience:

> Come, gentlemen, to th' feast, let not time waste;
> We have pleas'd our ear, now let us please our taste.
> Who lives by cunning, mark it, his fate's cast;
> When he has gull'd all, then is himself the last.

Jonson is a much more consistent moralist in his comedy than either Marston or Middleton, but in *The Devil is an Ass* we find him in a more expansive mood than he is in, say, *Volpone*. I have already noted the way in which satire is not necessarily the dominant note in such pronouncements as that of Satan on the importance of London as a potential recruiting centre for the infernal regions:

> The state of Hell must care
> Whom it employs, in point of reputation,
> Here, about London.

Jonson provides his own variation on the play-within-a-play device when we encounter Fitzdottrel, the self-important dupe who is the target for most of the play's trickery, all dressed up and ready to go to see a play called *The Devil is an Ass*. No particular moral point is being made; the aptness of the device consists in the fact that seeing plays, and being seen at them, is an important part of Fitzdottrel's mode of life.

Even what appears to be didactic utterance, such as 'This man defies the devil and all his works', takes on a different local colouring from its context and becomes a tactical rather than a moral maxim. It is instructive to compare the near-hysterical scorn with which Massinger portrays Overreach's passion for social climbing with the way Jonson looks at Gilthead's ambition to make his son a gentleman. Jonson's tone is one of cool amusement, but the laughter is by no means entirely at the expense of Gilthead senior and junior. The father knows full well how 'gentlemen' are made:

> We citizens never trust, but we do cozen:
> For if our debtors pay, we cozen them,
> And if they do not, then we cozen ourselves.
> But that's a hazard everyone must run
> That hopes to make his son a gentleman!

And the son has the dramatist's own awareness of how gentlemen come to be unmade:

> I do not wish to be one, truly, father.
> In a descent or two we come to be
> Just i' their state, fit to be cozen'd, like 'em.

Some of the satirist's sharpest barbs are aimed at the court ladies Tailbush and Eitherside, and especially at their obsession with cosmetics. But in the scene where Wittipol, disguised as a lady lately returned from the Spanish court, holds forth on the most effective preparations, the sheer delight in the diversity and sonorousness of the ingredients seems to blunt the edge of the satire:

> They have
> Water of gourds, of radish, the white beans,
> Flowers of glass, of thistles, rose-marine,

> Raw honey, mustard-seed, and bread dough-bak'd,
> The crumbs o' bread, goat's milk, and whites of eggs,
> Camphire, and lily roots, the fat of swans,
> Marrow of veal, white pigeons, and pine-kernels,
> The seeds of nettles, purseline, and hare's gall,
> Lemons, thin-skinn'd –

The effect is not unlike the contrast between the lyrical delight expressed in the list of dainties which Volpone offers to Celia and the evident moral censure of the purpose (seduction) for which he offers them.

Perhaps the moralist's farthest reach is displayed in the part of the plot concerned with Wittipol's efforts to seduce Fitzdottrel's wife. It begins with a witty variation on the 'cuckolding scene' in which Wittipol continues to pay court to Mistress Fitzdottrel in full view of her husband. And we are left in no real doubt, in the subsequent development of the action, that if his wife succumbs to the hero's blandishments, it will be no more than Fitzdottrel deserves for his total insensitivity to her existence as an individual. But when it comes to the point Mistress Fitzdottrel draws a clear distinction between appreciation of Wittipol's ingenuity and yielding to his sexual importunity, and Wittipol himself rises to it. Thus in spite of the delicious irony of Fitzdottrel practically pushing his wife into Wittipol's arms (when the latter is disguised as the 'Spanish' lady), Mistress Fitzdottrel remains virtuous to the end and the claims of moral orthodoxy are met in full.

As for the more than dubious activities of Meercraft, Trains and company, almost everything conspires to arouse in the spectator or reader something very close to undisguised admiration. There is, to begin with, the fact already noted that Fitzdottrel is a fool of such awesome proportions that we feel his whole reason for being is to be gulled; we cannot imagine his existence except as a dupe. Secondly, there is the fact that at one point Meercraft and his crew join forces with Wittipol, the nearest thing to a hero in the play, and thereby receive a kind of implicit endorsement from him. And finally, there is the delightful fantasy of Meercraft's schemes – dog-skin bottles, wine from raisins and so on – and the dexterity with which he manipulates his various fraudulent schemes. When we first see him he is despatching attendants as today's slick operators arrange for international telephone calls to impress prospective clients. And the pace and zest of their frauds continue almost unabated while they run through the repertoire of situations – important personages who need to be complimented with gifts, trifling sums urgently needed, imminent elevation to high office – and costumes – double-sided cloaks, false beards – with which the cony-catching pamphlets have made us familiar. In the end, of course, their schemes misfire, for it is an essential part of the comic effect that we, the audience, should feel superior to the professional schemers by witnessing their exposure. But in the end the important point seems to be that no one is punished for his misdeeds, and while the celebratory feast referred to in the last lines is that which the players propose to give the playwright if the piece has been well received, and is thus outside the world of the play, the final note struck within the play-world itself is that of tolerant recognition of human weakness:

> It is not manly to take joy or pride
> In human errors; we do all ill things;
> They do 'em worst that love 'em, and dwell there
> Till the plague comes.

And it is, as I have argued, wholly typical of these plays that the explicit moral should be slightly tangential to the implicit one, which seems to be something much more like 'Be good if you can, but be clever anyway'.

Massinger's *A New Way to Pay Old Debts* is strikingly different from the other three plays, and not only because it is set well away from London. It is, to begin with, much more resolutely moralistic in its approach than any of the others. In Massinger's view of the criminal folly of social climbing and the private and public iniquities of Overreach, there is no place for any attitude other than violent condemnation. We are clearly intended to feel far more sympathetic towards Margaret in her plot to outwit her rapacious father than Shakespeare intends us to feel for Jessica in a somewhat similar situation. Again, Massinger has nothing but admiration for Lovell, Lady Alworth and Welborne as they cheat, lie and brazen their way through the plot. Massinger uses the chorus of domestics to underline the anticipated response at key points throughout the play. And this response is, in the main, single and simple. It is significant but not surprising that there is hardly any emphasis here on the ingenuity of the various means whereby Overreach is foiled. Significant because the dramatist's interest is in the moral and social implications of his theme; not surprising because, by comparison with the 'practices' in the other plays, there is no ingenuity here to speak of.

Secondly, the body's appetites, here seen mainly in the insatiable hunger and thirst of Justice Greedy, are a matter not for acceptance and, within limits, enjoyment, but for the fiercest contempt. Very occasionally the itemization of the various good things to eat achieves a kind of Jonsonian relish, but the spectre of the deadly sin of gluttony is never very far from the feast. (It is perhaps worth noting that Massinger has a different standard by which to judge the self-indulgence, past and present, of his hero Welborne and the gluttony of his minor villain, Greedy.)

Another notable difference between *A New Way to Pay Old Debts* and the other three plays is that Massinger lacks the sheer verbal exuberance of the others, especially Jonson; this may help to remind us how closely that exuberance was related to the London scene. Not that Massinger is lacking in eloquence. But his eloquence is at its highest when the play is farthest from comedy, in the magnificent outbursts of Sir Giles Overreach, in and out of his frenzy:

> How? Forsake thee?
> Do I wear a sword for fashion? Or is this arm
> Shrunk up, or wither'd? Does there live a man,
> Of that large list I have encounter'd with,
> Can truly say I e'er gave inch of ground
> Not purchas'd with his blood that did oppose me?
> Forsake thee when the thing is done? He dares not.

And this leads to the last point of difference, which is that the force of Overreach's corrupt and powerful personality is too vast to be contained within the comic framework, and very nearly shatters it. The play ends, in the best Jacobean manner, with one wedding celebrated and another imminent, but the sound of wedding bells is all but drowned by the furious ravings of the demented father; it is as if, while watching the last scene of *Much Ado About Nothing*, we were to catch faint echoes from a rehearsal of the heath scenes in *King Lear*.

But while perhaps no definition of city comedy would be sufficiently elastic to be able to include *A New Way to Pay Old Debts*, it does share some of the concerns of the other plays and the contrasts it offers with them are instructive rather than merely incidental. And it is Massinger's best play.

GĀMINI SALGĀDO

University of Sussex,
9 November 1973

FURTHER READING

UNA ELLIS-FERMOR, *The Jacobean Drama*, 1936.
L. C. KNIGHTS, *Drama and Society in the Age of Jonson*, 1937.
M. C. BRADBROOK, *The Growth and Structure of Elizabethan Comedy*, 1955.
BRIAN GIBBONS, *Jacobean City Comedy*,* 1968.

*I am especially indebted to this book, although it uses the term 'Jacobean City Comedy' in a more extended sense than I do.

A NOTE ON THE TEXTS

The texts are based on the Bodleian Library copies of the earliest quartos: *The Dutch Courtesan* (1605), *A Mad World, My Masters* (1608), *The Devil is an Ass* (1631) and *A New Way to Pay Old Debts* (1633). An occasional reading (as well as the list of characters for Middleton's play) has been silently adopted from a later edition, though important changes are usually noted. Spelling and punctuation have been modernized, and editorial interpolations or emendations put in square brackets. I have also, in some instances, followed the line-divisions of later editors.

I am much indebted to various editors of these plays, particularly to A. H. Bullen, Martin Wine and Peter Davison's editions of *The Dutch Courtesan*, Standish Henning's edition of *A Mad World, My Masters* (including the references given in it to G. J. Eberle's unpublished critical edition), and the editions of *A New Way to Pay Old Debts* by A. H. Cruickshank and T. W. Craik. For *The Devil is an Ass* my chief debt is of course to the monumental Herford and Simpson edition.

Grateful thanks are due to my colleague Michael Hawkins for his comments on my Introduction and to Anna Johnston and Cecilia Benjamin for their help in the preparation of the typescript.

THE
Dutch Courtezan.

AS

IT WAS PLAYD IN THE
Blacke-Friars, by the Children
of her Maiesties Reuels.

VVritten
BY IOHN MARSTON.

AT LONDON,
¶ Printed by T.P. for *Iohn Hodgets,*
and are to be sould at his shop in
Paules Church-yard. 1605.

Facsimile of the title-page of the first edition, the quarto of 1605.

THE DUTCH COURTESAN

by

John Marston

DRAMATIS PERSONAE

FRANCESCHINA, a Dutch courtesan
MARY FAUGH, an old woman
SIR LIONEL FREEVILL ⎱ two old knights
SIR HUBERT SUBBOYS ⎰
YOUNG FREEVILL, Sir Lionel's son
BEATRICE ⎱ Sir Hubert's daughters
CRISPINELLA ⎰
PUTIFER, their nurse
TYSEFEW, a blunt gallant
CAQUETEUR, a prattling gull
MALHEUREUX, young Freevill's unhappy friend
COCLEDEMOY, a knavishly witty city companion
MASTER MULLIGRUB, a vintner
MISTRESS MULLIGRUB, his wife
MASTER BURNISH, a goldsmith
LIONEL, his man
HOLIFERNES REINSCURE, a barber's boy
THREE WATCHMEN
[PAGES, GENTLEMEN]

Putifer: lit. 'bearer of rottenness'.
Tysefew: ? Fr. tison = firebrand, and feu = fire.
Caqueteur: Fr. 'prattler'.
Malheureux: Fr. 'unhappy'.
Mulligrub: mulligrubs = intestinal pains.
Reinscure: reins = kidneys.

PROLOGUE

Slight hasty labours in this easy play
Present not what you would, but what we may:
For this vouchsafe to know, the only end
Of our now study is not to offend.
Yet think not, but like others, rail we could,
(Best art presents not what it can, but should)
And if our pen in this seem over-slight,
We strive not to instruct but to delight.
As for some few, we know of purpose here
To tax, and scout: know, firm art cannot fear   10
Vain rage: only the highest grace we pray
Is, you'll not tax, until you judge our play.
Think and then speak; 'tis rashness, and not wit
To speak what is in passion, and not judgment, fit.
Sit then, with fair expectance, and survey
Nothing but passionate man in his slight play,
Who hath this only ill, to some deem'd worst,
A modest diffidence, and self-mistrust.

FABULAE ARGUMENTUM

The difference betwixt the love of a courtesan and a wife is the
full scope of the play, which, intermixed with the deceits of a
witty city jester, fills up the comedy.

Turpe est difficiles habere nugas

16–18. *Nothing . . . self-mistrust*: referring to Malheureux.
Turpe . . . nugas: 'It is disgraceful to arrive at difficult nonsense' (Martial,
Epigrams, II, xxxvi, 9).

ACT ONE

SCENE ONE

(*Enter three pages with lights.* MULLIGRUB, FREEVILL, MALHEUREUX, TYSEFEW *and* CAQUETEUR.)

FREEVILL: Nay comfort, my good host Shark, my good Mulligrub.

MALHEUREUX: Advance thy snout; do not suffer thy sorrowful nose to drop on thy Spanish leather jerkin, most hardly honest Mulligrub.

FREEVILL: What, cogging Cocledemoy is run away with a nest of goblets? True, what then? They will be hammer'd out well enough, I warrant you.

MULLIGRUB: Sure, some wise man would find them out presently.

FREEVILL: Yes, sure, if we could find out some wise man 10 presently.

MALHEUREUX: How was the plate lost? How did it vanish?

FREEVILL: In most sincere prose thus: that man of much money, some wit, but less honesty, cogging Cocledemoy, comes this night late into mine host Mulligrub's tavern here, calls for a room; the house being full, Cocledemoy consorted with his movable chattel, his instrument of fornication, the bawd Mistress Mary Faugh, are inparlour'd next the street. Good poultry was their food, blackbird, lark, woodcock; and mine host here comes in, cries 'God bless you!' and departs. 20 A blind harper enters, craves audience, uncaseth, plays. The drawer, for female privateness' sake, is nodded out, who knowing that whosoever will hit the mark of profit must, like those that shoot in stone-bows, wink with one eye, grows blind o' the right side and departs.

5. *cogging*: swindling.
22. *drawer*: tapster, waiter.
24. *stone-bows*: catapults or crossbows for shooting stones.

CAQUETEUR: He shall answer for that winking with one eye at the last day.

MALHEUREUX: Let him have day till then, and he will wink with both his eyes.

30 FREEVILL: Cocledemoy perceiving none in the room but the blind harper (whose eyes heaven had shut up from beholding wickedness) unclasps a casement to the street very patiently, pockets up three bowls unnaturally, thrusts his wench forth the window, and himself most preposterously with his heels forward follows. The unseeing harper plays on, bids the empty dishes and the treacherous candles much good do them. The drawer returns, but out alas, not only the birds, but also the nest of goblets were flown away. Laments are rais'd –

TYSEFEW: Which did not pierce the heavens.

40 FREEVILL: The drawers moan, mine host doth cry, the bowls are gone.

MULLIGRUB: *Hic finis Priami!*

MALHEUREUX: Nay, be not jaw-fall'n, my most sharking Mulligrub.

FREEVILL: 'Tis your just affliction; remember the sins of the seller, and repent, repent!

MULLIGRUB: I am not jaw-fall'n, but I will hang the cony-catching Cocledemoy, and there's an end of't. (*Exit.*)

CAQUETEUR: Is it a right stone? It shows well by candlelight.

50 TYSEFEW: So do many things that are counterfeit, but I assure you this is a right diamond.

CAQUETEUR: Might I borrow it of you? It will not a little grace my finger in visitation of my mistress.

TYSEFEW: Why, use it most sweet Caqueteur, use it.

CAQUETEUR: Thanks, good sir. 'Tis grown high night. Gentles, rest to you. (*Exit.*)

TYSEFEW: A torch! Sound wench, soft sleep and sanguine dreams to you both. On, boy. [*Exit with a Page.*]

---

28. *Let . . . day*: let him postpone.

34. *preposterously*: in literal sense, 'backside first'.

42. *Hic . . . Priami*: for *Haec finis Priami fatorum*, 'such was the fate of Priam' (Virgil, *Aeneid*, II, 554).

47-8. *cony-catching*: swindling.

FREEVILL: Let me bid you good rest.

MALHEUREUX: Not so, trust me, I must bring my friend home: 60
I dare not give you up to your own company; I fear the
warmth of wine and youth will draw you to some common
house of lascivious entertainment.

FREEVILL: Most necessary buildings, Malheureux; ever since
my intention of marriage, I do pray for their continuance.

MALHEUREUX: Lov'd sir, your reason?

FREEVILL: Marry, lest my house should be made one. I would
have married men love the stews, as Englishmen lov'd the
Low Countries: wish war should be maintain'd there, lest it
should come home to their own doors. What, suffer a man to 70
have a hole to put his head in, though he go to the pillory for
it! Youth and appetite are above the club of Hercules.

MALHEUREUX: This lust is a most deadly sin, sure.

FREEVILL: Nay, 'tis a most lively sin, sure.

MALHEUREUX: Well, I am sure 'tis one of the head sins.

FREEVILL: Nay, I am sure it is one of the middle sins.

MALHEUREUX: Pity, 'tis grown a most daily vice.

FREEVILL: But a more nightly vice, I assure you.

MALHEUREUX: Well, 'tis a sin.

FREEVILL: Ay, or else few men would wish to go to heaven; and 80
not to disguise with my friend, I am now going the way of all
flesh.

MALHEUREUX: Not to a courtesan?

FREEVILL: A courteous one.

MALHEUREUX: What, to a sinner?

FREEVILL: A very publican.

MALHEUREUX: Dear my lov'd friend, let me be full with you:
Know, sir, the strongest argument that speaks
Against the soul's eternity is lust,
That wise man's folly, and the fool's wisdom: 90
But to grow wild in loose lasciviousness,
Given up to heat and sensual appetite,

68–70. *Englishmen . . . doors*: Elizabeth supported the Dutch against the
Spanish to postpone the latter's attack on the English mainland.
72. *club of Hercules*: symbol of strength.
87. *full*: frank.

Nay, to expose your health and strength and name,
Your precious time, and with that time the hope
Of due preferment, advantageous means
Of any worthy end to the stale use,
The common bosom of a money creature,
One that sells human flesh, a mangonist!

FREEVILL: Alas, good creatures, what would you have them do?
100 Would you have them get their living by the curse of man, the
sweat of their brows? So they do; every man must follow his
trade, and every woman her occupation. A poor decayed
mechanical man's wife, her husband is laid up; may not she
lawfully be laid down, when her husband's only rising is by
his wife's falling? A captain's wife wants means; her commander lies in open field abroad; may not she lie in civil
arms at home? A waiting gentlewoman that had wont to take
say to her lady, miscarries or so: the court misfortune throws
her down; may not the city courtesy take her up? Do you
110 know no alderman would pity such a woman's case? Why is
charity grown a sin? Or relieving the poor and impotent an
offence? You will say beasts take no money for their fleshly
entertainment; true, because they are beasts, therefore
beastly. Only men give to lose, because they are men, therefore manly; and indeed, wherein should they bestow their
money better? In land, the title may be crack'd; in houses,
they may be burnt; in apparel, 'twill wear; in wine, alas for
pity, our throat is but short. But employ your money upon
women, and a thousand to nothing some one of them will
120 bestow that on you which shall stick by you as long as you
live. They are no ungrateful persons; they will give quit for
quo: do ye protest, they'll swear; do you rise, they'll fall; do
you fall, they'll rise, do you give them the French crown,

98. *mangonist*: patcher-up of inferior goods for sale.
103. *mechanical man's*: manual worker's.
106. *civil*: (i) civilian, (ii) courteous.
107–8. *take say*: say = (i) fine cloth, (ii) test (assay).
108. *miscarries*: (i) comes to grief, (ii) has miscarriage.
110. *case*: (i) predicament, (ii) kaze (female sex organ) (Bullen).
121–2. *quit for quo*: tit for tat.
123. *French crown*: (i) French coin of Henri IV, (ii) baldness caused
by pox.

they'll give you the French – *O justus justa justum*! They sell
their bodies; do not better persons sell their souls? Nay,
since all things have been sold – honour, justice, faith, nay,
even God himself –
Aye me, what base ignobleness is it
To sell the pleasure of a wanton bed?
Why do men scrape, why heap to full heaps join?   130
But for his mistress, who would care for coin?
For this I hold to be denied of no man –
All things are made for man, and man for woman.
Give me my fee!

MALHEUREUX: Of ill you merit well. My heart's good friend,
Leave yet at length, at length; for know this ever,
'Tis no such sin to err, but to persever.

FREEVILL: Beauty is woman's virtue; love the life's music and
woman the daintiness or second course of heaven's curious
workmanship. Since, then, beauty, love and woman are good,   140
how can the love of woman's beauty be bad? And, *Bonum,
quo communius, eo melius*; wilt then go with me?

MALHEUREUX: Whither?

FREEVILL: To a house of salvation.

MALHEUREUX: Salvation?

FREEVILL: Yes, 'twill make thee repent. Wilt go to the Family
of Love? I will show thee my creature: a pretty, nimble-
ey'd Dutch Tanakin; an honest soft-hearted impropriation, a
soft plump, round cheek'd froe that has beauty enough for her
virtue, virtue enough for a woman, and woman enough for   150
any reasonable man in my knowledge. Wilt pass along with me?

MALHEUREUX: What, to a brothel, to behold an impudent
prostitution? Fie on't, I shall hate the whole sex to see her!
The most odious spectacle the earth can present is an immodest vulgar woman.

124. *O . . . justum*: declension of Lat. adj. 'just'.
139. *curious*: well wrought.
141–2. *Bonum . . . melius*: 'If good, the commoner the better'.
148. *Tanakin*: diminutive of Ann or Anna, applied to Dutch or German
girl.
149. *froe*: Dutchwoman (*frow*).
153. *prostitution*: prostitute.

FREEVILL: Good still; my brain shall keep't. You must go, as you love me.

MALHEUREUX: Well, I'll go to make her loathe the shame she's in;

The sight of vice augments the hate of sin.

160 FREEVILL: The sight of vice augments the hate of sin! Very fine, perdy!

(*Exeunt.*)

SCENE TWO

(*Enter* COCLEDEMOY *and* MARY FAUGH.)

COCLEDEMOY: Mary, Mary Faugh!

MARY FAUGH: Hem!

COCLEDEMOY: Come, my worshipful, rotten, rough-bellied bawd! Ha, my blue-tooth'd patroness of natural wickedness, give me the goblets.

MARY FAUGH: By yea and by nay, Master Cocledemoy, I fear you'll play the knave and restore them.

COCLEDEMOY: No, by the Lord, aunt; restitution is Catholic, and thou know'st we love –

10 MARY FAUGH: What?

COCLEDEMOY: Oracles are ceas'd: *Tempus preteritum.* Dost hear, my worshipful glister-pipe, thou ungodly fire that burnt Diana's temple? Dost hear, bawd?

MARY FAUGH: In very good truthness, you are the foulest-mouth'd profane railing brother! Call a woman the most ungodly names. I must confess we all eat of the forbidden fruit; and for mine own part, tho' I am one of the Family of Love and, as they say, a bawd that covers the multitude of sins, yet I trust I am none of the wicked that eat fish o'
20 Fridays.

161. *perdy !*: Fr. *par Dieu,* 'by God!'
8. *aunt*: whore.
11. *Tempus preteritum*: the time is past.
12. *glister-pipe*: clyster-pipe, suppository-tube.
13. *Diana's temple*: Diana = Roman goddess of chastity.

COCLEDEMOY: Hang toasts! I rail at thee, my worshipful organ
bellows that fills the pipes, my fine rattling phlegmy cough
o'the lungs and cold with a pox? I rail at thee? What, my
right precious pandress, supportress of barber-surgeons and
inhauntress of lotium and diet-drink! I rail at thee, necessary
damnation? I'll make an oration, I, in praise of thy most
courtly-in-fashion, and most pleasureable function, I.

MARY FAUGH: I prithee do, I love to hear myself prais'd, as
well as any old lady, I.

COCLEDEMOY: List then: a bawd, first for her profession or 30
vocation it is most worshipful of all the twelve companies; for
as that trade is most honourable that sells the best com-
modities, as the draper is more worshipful than the pointmaker, the silkman more worshipful than the draper, and the
goldsmith more honourable than both, little Mary, so the
bawd above all. Her shop has the best ware, for where these
sell but cloth, satins and jewels, she sells divine virtues, as
virginity, modesty and such rare gems, and those not like a
petty chapman, by retail, but like a great merchant by wholesale. Wa, ha, ho! And who are her customers? Not base corn 40
cutters or sowgelders, but most rare wealthy knights, and
most rare bountiful lords are her customers. Again, whereas
no trade or vocation profiteth but by the loss and displeasure
of another – as the merchant thrives not but by the licen-
tiousness of giddy and unsettled youth, the lawyer but by the
vexation of his client, the physician but by the maladies of his
patient – only my smooth gumm'd bawd lives by others'
pleasure, and only grows rich by others' rising. O merciful
gain, O righteous income! So much for her vocation, trade
and life. As for their death, how can it be bad, since their 50

21. *Hang toasts*: spiced toasts dipped in liquor were a delicacy at this
time.
24. *barber-surgeons*: often one and the same; they shared one guild.
25. *lotium*: stale wine, used as 'lye' for hair by barbers.
25. *diet-drink*: treatment for pox.
31. *twelve companies*: the major London Livery Guilds.
33-4. *pointmaker*: points = laces for fastening garments.
39. *petty chapman*: small trader or pedlar.
40-41. *corn cutters*: chiropodists.

wickedness is always before their eyes, and a death's-head most commonly on their middle finger? To conclude, 'tis most certain they must needs both live well and die well, since most commonly they live in Clerkenwell, and die in Bridewell. *Dixi*, Mary.

(*Enter* FREEVILL *and* MALHEUREUX [*attended by a page*].)

FREEVILL: Come along! Yonder's the preface or exordium to my wench, the bawd. Fetch, fetch!

[*Exit Mary Faugh.*]

What, Master Cocledemoy, is your knaveship yet stirring? Look to it, Mulligrub lies for you.

60 COCLEDEMOY: The more fool he; I can lie for myself, worship-ful friend. Hang toasts! I vanish? Ha, my fine boy, thou art a scholar and hast read Tully's *Offices*, my fine knave. Hang toasts!

FREEVILL: The vintner will toast you an he catch you.

COCLEDEMOY: I will draw the vintner to the stoop, and when he runs low tilt him. Ha, my fine knave, art going to thy recreation?

FREEVILL: Yes, my capricious rascal.

COCLEDEMOY: Thou wilt look like a fool then, by and by.

70 FREEVILL: Look like a fool? Why?

COCLEDEMOY: Why, according to the old saying. A beggar when he is lousing of himself looks like a philosopher, a hard bound philosopher when he is on the stool looks like a tyrant, and a wise man, when he is in his belly act, looks like a fool. God give your worship good rest, grace and mercy. Keep your syringe straight, and your lotium unspilt.

[*Exit* COCLEDEMOY.]

51. *death's-head*: ring with figure of skull, often worn by bawds.
54. *Clerkenwell*: then a notorious quarter.
55. *Bridewell*: house of correction.
55. *Dixi*: 'I have spoken' (Roman legal term).
59. *lies for*: lies in wait for.
62. *Tully's Offices*: Cicero's *De officiis*, a widely used school text.
68. *capricious*: (i) lively, witty, (ii) lecherous (Lat. *caper* = goat, symbol of lechery).
72–3. *hard bound*: constipated.
74. *belly act*: copulation.

(*Enter* FRANCESCHINA.)

FREEVILL: See, sir, this is she.

MALHEUREUX: This?

FREEVILL: This.

MALHEUREUX: A courtesan? [*Aside*] Now cold blood defend   80
me! What a proportion afflicts me!

FRANCESCHINA: O mine aderliver love, vat sall me do to
requit dis your mush affection?

FREEVILL: Marry, salute my friend, clip his neck and kiss him
welcome.

FRANCESCHINA: O mine 'eart, sir, you bin very velcome.

FREEVILL: Kiss her, man, with a more familiar affection!
[*Kisses her*.] So! Come, what entertainment? Go to your
lute.

(*Exit* FRANCESCHINA.)

And how dost approve my sometimes elected? She's none of   90
your ramping cannibals that devour man's flesh, nor any of
your Curtian gulfs that will never be satisfied until the best
thing a man has be thrown into them. I lov'd her with my
heart until my soul showed me the imperfection of my body
and placed my affection on a lawful love, my modest Beatrice,
which if this short-heels knew, there were no being for me
with eyes before her face. But faith, dost thou not somewhat
excuse my sometimes incontinency with her enforcive
beauties? Speak.

MALHEUREUX: Hah! She is a whore, is she not?   100

FREEVILL: Whore? Fie, whore! You may call her a courtesan, a
cockatrice, or (as that worthy spirit of an eternal happiness
said) a suppository. But whore? Fie, 'tis not in fashion to call
things by their right names. Is a great merchant a cuckold?
You must say he is one of the livery. Is a great lord a fool?

81. *proportion*: ? imbalance of physical elements, hence agitation.
82. *aderliver*: Dutch *alderliefest* = dearest.
84. *clip*: embrace.
89. *sometimes*: former.
95. *short-heels*: wanton (? easily tipped backwards).
97. *enforcive*: compelling.
102. *cockatrice*: prostitute (lit. basilisk, a serpent which killed with its
glance). The 'worthy spirit' is Ariosto, author of *I Suppositi*.

You must say he is weak. Is a gallant pocky? You must say he
has the court scab. Come, she's your mistress, or so.

    (*[Re-]enter* FRANCESCHINA *with her lute.*)

– Come siren, your voice.

FRANCESCHINA: Vill not you stay in mine bosom tonight, love?

110 FREEVILL: By no means, sweet breast; this gentleman has
vow'd to see me chastely laid.

FRANCESCHINA: He shall have a bed too, if dat it please him.

FREEVILL: Peace, you tender him offence; he is one of a professed abstinence. Siren, your voice and away!

    (*She sings to her lute.*)

[FRANCESCHINA]: The dark is my delight,
             So 'tis the nightingale's.
        My music's in the night,
             So is the nightingale's.
        My body is but little,
120   So is the nightingale's.
        I love to sleep 'gainst prickle,
             So doth the nightingale.

FREEVILL: Thanks, Buss, so! The night grows old; good rest.

FRANCESCHINA: Rest to mine dear love, rest, and no long
absence.

FREEVILL: Believe me not long.

FRANCESCHINA: Sall ick not believe you long.

    [*Exit* FRANCESCHINA.]

FREEVILL: O yes. Come, *via*, away boy, on!

    (*Exit, his Page lighting him.*)

    (*[Re-]enter* FREEVILL *and seems to overhear* MALHEUREUX.)

MALHEUREUX: Is she unchaste? Can such a one be damn'd?

130 O love and beauty, ye two eldest seeds

Of the vast chaos, what strong right you have,

Even in things divine, our very souls!

FREEVILL [*aside*]: Wha, ha, ho! Come, bird, come! Stand, peace!

MALHEUREUX: Are strumpets then such things, so delicate?

Can custom spoil what nature made so good,

      106. *pocky*: poxed.
      123. *Buss*: kiss.
      128. *via*: away!
      135. *custom*: (i) convention, (ii) (sexual) usage.

Or is their custom bad? Beauty's for use;
I never saw a sweet face vicious, –
It might be proud, inconstant, wanton, nice,
But never tainted with unnatural vice.
Their worst is, their best art is love to win.   140
O, that to love should be or shame, or sin!

FREEVILL [*aside*]: By the Lord, he's caught! Laughter eternal!

MALHEUREUX: Soul, I must love her. Destiny is weak
To my affection. A common love!
Blush not, faint breast!
That which is ever loved of most is best.
Let colder eld the strong'st objections move,
No love's without some lust, no life without some love.

FREEVILL: Nay come on, good sir. What though the most
odious spectacle the world can present be an immodest vulgar   150
woman? Yet sir, for my sake –

MALHEUREUX: Well sir, for your sake I'll think better of them.

FREEVILL: Do, good sir and pardon me that have brought you
in. You know the sight of vice augments the hate of sin.

MALHEUREUX: Hah! Will you go home, sir? 'Tis high bed
time.

FREEVILL: With all my heart, sir; only do not chide me. I must
confess.

MALHEUREUX: A wanton lover you have been.

FREEVILL: 'O, that to love should be or shame, or sin!'   160

MALHEUREUX: Say ye?

FREEVILL: 'Let colder eld the strong'st objections move!'

MALHEUREUX: How's this?

FREEVILL: 'No love's without some lust, no life without some
love!' Go your ways for an *apostata*! I believe my cast garment
must be let out in the seams for you when all is done.
Of all the fools that would all man out-thrust,
He that 'gainst Nature would seem wise is worst.
   (*Exeunt.*)

138. *nice*: (i) fussy, (ii) wanton.
147. *eld*: old age.
165. *apostata*: apostate, renegade.

ACT TWO

SCENE ONE

(*Enter* FREEVILL, *Pages with torches, and Gentlemen with music.*)

FREEVILL: The morn is yet but young. Here, gentlemen,
    This is my Beatrice' window, this the chamber
    Of my betrothed dearest, whose chaste eyes,
    Full of lov'd sweetness, and clear cheerfulness,
    Have gag'd my soul to her enjoyings,
    Shredding away all those weak under-branches
    Of base affections, and unfruitful heats.
    Here bestow your music to my voice. [*He sings.*]
      (*Enter* BEATRICE *above.*)
    Always a virtuous name to my chaste love!
10 BEATRICE: Lov'd sir, the honour of your wish return to you.
    I cannot with a mistress' compliment,
    Forced discourses, or nice art of wit,
    Give entertain to your dear wished presence;
    But safely thus: what hearty gratefulness,
    Unsullen silence, unaffected modesty,
    And an unignorant shamefastness can express,
    Receive as your protested due. Faith, my heart,
    I am your servant.
    O let not my secure simplicity breed your mislike,
20   As one quite void of skill;
    'Tis grace enough in us not to be ill.
    I can some good, and faith, I mean no hurt.
    Do not then, sweet, wrong sober ignorance;

---

12. *nice art*: subtlety.
16. *shamefastness*: modesty.
17. *protested*: solemnly declared.
19. *secure*: unsuspecting.
21. *ill*: sinful.

I judge you all of virtue, and our vows
Should kill all fears that base distrust can move.
My soul, what say you? Still you love?

FREEVILL: Still?
My vow is up above me, and like time,
Irrevocable. I am sworn all yours,
No beauty shall untwine our arms, no face
In my eyes can or shall seem fair,   30
And would to God only to me you might
Seem only fair! Let others disesteem
Your matchless graces, so might I safer seem.
Envy I covet not; far, far be all ostent,
Vain boasts of beauties, soft joys and the rest;
He that is wise pants on a private breast.
So could I live in desert most unknown,
Yourself to me enough were populous.
Your eyes shall be my joys, my wine that still
Shall drown my often cares. Your only voice   40
Shall cast a slumber on my list'ning sense,
You with soft lip shall only ope mine eyes,
And suck their lids asunder. Only you
Shall make me wish to live and not fear death,
So on your cheeks I might yield latest breath.
O he that thus may live and thus shall die,
May well be envied of a deity!

BEATRICE: Dear my lov'd heart be not so passionate;
Nothing extreme lives long.

FREEVILL: But not to be
Extreme – nothing in love's extreme! – my love   50
Receives no mean.

BEATRICE: I give you faith, and prithee,
Since, poor soul, I am so easy to believe thee,
Make it much more pity to deceive me.
Wear this slight favour in my remembrance.
        (Throweth down a ring to him.)

                34. *ostent*: ostentation, show.
                39. *still*: always.
                40. *only*: unique, matchless.

FREEVILL: Which when I part from, hope, the best of life,
  Ever part from me.

BEATRICE: I take you and your word, which may ever live your
  servant. – See, day is quite broke up; the best of hours.

FREEVILL: Good morrow, graceful mistress. Our nuptial day
60 holds.

BEATRICE: With happy constancy, a wished day. (*Exit.*)
    (*Enter* MALHEUREUX.)

FREEVILL: Myself and all content rest with you!

MALHEUREUX: The studious morn with paler cheek draws on,
  The day's bold light. Hark, how the free-born birds
  Carol their unaffected passions!
    (*The nightingales sing.*)
  Now sing they sonnets; thus they cry, 'We love!'
  O breath of heaven! Thus they harmless souls
  Give entertain to mutual affects.
  They have no bawds, no mercenary beds,
70 No politic restraints, no artificial heats,
  No faint dissemblings. No custom makes them blush,
  No shame afflicts their name. O you happy beasts,
  In whom an inborn heat is not held sin,
  How far transcend you wretched, wretched man
  Whom national custom, tyrannous respects
  Of slavish order, fetters; lames his power,
  Calling that sin in us which in all things else
  Is nature's highest virtue.
    (*O miseri quorum gaudia crimen habent!*)
80 Sure nature against virtue cross doth fall,
  Or virtue's self is oft unnatural; –
  That I should love a strumpet! I, a man of snow!
  Now shame forsake me, whither am I fallen!
  A creature of a public use! My friend's love, too!
  To live to be a talk to men, a shame
  To my professed virtue! O accursed reason,

63. *studious*: conscientious.
66. *sonnets*: songs.
68. *affects*: affections, feelings.
69–81. *They . . . unnatural*: cf. Ovid, *Amores*, I, x, 25–36.

How many eyes hast thou to see thy shame,
And yet how blind once to prevent defame!

FREEVILL: *Diaboli virtus in lumbis est!* Morrow, my friend.
Come, I could make a tedious scene of this now but, what? 90
Pah! Thou art in love with a courtesan. Why sir, should we
loathe all strumpets, some men should hate their own mothers
or sisters – a sin against kind, I can tell you.

MALHEUREUX: May it beseem a wise man to be in love?

FREEVILL: Let wise men alone, 'twill beseem thee and me well
enough.

MALHEUREUX: Shall I not offend the vow-band of our friendship?

FREEVILL: What, to affect that which thy friend affected? By
heaven, I resign her freely; the creature and I must grow off. 100
By this time she has assurely heard of my resolved marriage,
and no question swears, 'God's Sacrament, ten tousand
Divels!' I'll resign, i'faith.

MALHEUREUX: I would but embrace her, hear her speak, and
at the most but kiss her.

FREEVILL: O friend, he that could live with the smoke of
roast meat might live at a cheap rate.

MALHEUREUX: I shall ne'er prove heartily received;
A kind of flat ungracious modesty,
An insufficient dullness, stains my 'haviour. 110

FREEVILL: No matter, sir. Insufficiency and sottishness are
much commendable in a most discommendable action. Now
could I swallow thee, and thou hadst wont to be so harsh and
cold! I'll tell thee, Hell and the prodigies of angry Jove are not
so fearful to a thinking mind as a man without affection. Why
friend, philosophy and nature are all one; love is the centre in
which all lines close the common bond of being.

---

88. *defame*: disgrace.
89. *Diaboli . . . est*: 'The devil's strong point is in our loins' (St Jerome).
Also quoted by Montaigne.
93. *kind*: nature.
99. *affect*: love.
110. *insufficient*: crass.
110. *dullness*: stupidity, with possible hint of sexual insufficiency.

MALHEUREUX: O, but a chaste, reserved privateness, a modest continence!

120 FREEVILL: I'll tell thee what – take this as firmest sense:
Incontinence will force a continence;
Heat wasteth heat, light defaceth light;
Nothing is spoiled but by his proper might.
This is something too weighty for thy floor.

MALHEUREUX: But howsoe'er you shade it, the world's eye
Shines hot and open on't.
Lying, malice, envy are held but slidings,
Errors of rage, when custom and the world
Calls lust a crime spotted with blackest terrors.

130 FREEVILL: Where errors are held crimes, crimes are but errors.
Along sir, to her. She is an arrant strumpet, and a strumpet is a serpigo, venom'd gonorrhy to man – things actually possessed: yet since thou art in love –

(*Offers to go out and suddenly draws back.*)

And again as good make use of a statue,
A body without a soul, a carcass three months dead – yet since thou art in love –

MALHEUREUX: Death, man, my destiny I cannot choose.

FREEVILL: Nay, I hope so. Again, they sell but only flesh, no jot affection, so that even in the enjoying *Absentem mar-*
140 *moreamque putes.* Yet since you needs must love –

MALHEUREUX: Unavoidable, though folly worse than madness.

FREEVILL: It's true, but since you needs must love, you must know this,
He that must love, a fool and he must kiss.

(*Enter* COCLEDEMOY.)

Master Cocledemoy, *ut vales, domine!*

123. *proper*: own.
124. *floor*: i.e. brain.
127. *slidings*: slips, small faults.
132. *serpigo*: skin-disease.
139–40. *Absentem . . . putes*: 'Of marble you would think she were/Or that she were not present there' (Martial, *Epigrams*, XI, lx, 8). From Florio's Montaigne again.
145. *ut . . . domine!*: Greetings, sir!

COCLEDEMOY: *Ago tibi gratias*, my worshipful friend! How does your friend?

FREEVILL: Out, you rascal!

COCLEDEMOY: Hang toasts, you are an ass. Much o' your worship's brain lies in your calves. Bread o' God, boy, I was at supper last night with a new-wean'd bulchin, bread o' God, drunk, horribly drunk, horribly drunk! There was a wench, one Frank Frailty, a punk, an honest pole-cat, of a clean instep, sound leg, smooth thigh, and the nimble devil in her buttock. Ah, fist o' grace, when saw you Tysefew, or Master Caqueteur, that prattling gallant of a good draught, common customs, fortunate impudence and sound fart? 150

FREEVILL: Away, rogue!

COCLEDEMOY: Hang toasts, my fine boy, my companions are worshipful! 160

MALHEUREUX: Yes, I hear you are taken up with scholars and churchmen.

(*Enter* HOLIFERNES *the Barber*.)

COCLEDEMOY: *Quanquam te Marce fili*, my fine boy. [*To* FREEVILL] Does your worship want a barber-surgeon?

FREEVILL: Farewell knave! Beware the Mulligrubs!

(*Exeunt* FREEVILL *and* MALHEUREUX.)

COCLEDEMOY: Let the Mulligrubs beware the knave. – What, a barber-surgeon, my delicate boy?

HOLIFERNES: Yes sir, an apprentice to surgery.

COCLEDEMOY: 'Tis my fine boy. To what bawdy house doth your master belong? What's thy name? 170

HOLIFERNES: Holifernes Reinscure.

COCLEDEMOY: Reinscure? Good Master Holifernes, I desire your further acquaintance. Nay, pray ye be covered, my fine

---

147. *Ago . . . gratias*: Thank you.
152. *new-wean'd bulchin*: new-fledged bull-calf, i.e. young gallant.
154. *Frank*: short for Frances (china).
154. *punk; pole-cat*: whore.
156. *fist*: fart.
157. *draught*: drinking capacity (lit. drinking without taking breath).
164. *Quanquam . . . fili*: 'Although, son Marcus' – opening words of Cicero's *De officiis*. cf. note to I, ii, 62.
174. *pray . . . covered*: Holifernes doffs his hat respectfully.

boy. Kill thy itch and heal thy scabs. Is thy master rotten?

HOLIFERNES: My father forsooth is dead.

COCLEDEMOY: *And laid in his grave.*
Alas, what comfort shall Peggy then have?

HOLIFERNES: None but me, sir, that's my mother's son, I
180 assure you.

COCLEDEMOY: Mother's son? A good witty boy; would live to
read an homily well. And to whom are you going now?

HOLIFERNES: Marry, forsooth, to trim Master Mulligrub the
vintner.

COCLEDEMOY: Do you know Master Mulligrub?

HOLIFERNES: My godfather, sir.

COCLEDEMOY: Good boy! Hold up thy chops. I pray thee do
one thing for me. My name is Gudgeon.

HOLIFERNES: Good Master Gudgeon.

190 COCLEDEMOY: Lend me thy basin, razor, and apron.

HOLIFERNES: O Lord, sir!

COCLEDEMOY: Well spoken; good English! But what's thy
furniture worth?

HOLIFERNES: O Lord, sir, I know not.

COCLEDEMOY: Well spoken; a boy of a good wit. Hold this
pawn. Where dost dwell?

HOLIFERNES: At the sign of the Three Razors, sir.

COCLEDEMOY: A sign of good shaving, my catastrophonical fine
boy. I have an odd jest to trim Master Mulligrub for a wager.
200 A jest boy, a humour. I'll return thy things presently. Hold!

HOLIFERNES: What mean you, good Master Gudgeon?

COCLEDEMOY: Nothing, faith, but a jest, boy. Drink that. [*Gives
him money.*] I'll recoil presently.

HOLIFERNES: You'll not stay long?

COCLEDEMOY: As I am an honest man. The Three Razors?

HOLIFERNES: Ay, sir. (*Exit* HOLIFERNES.)

COCLEDEMOY: Good! And if I shave not Master Mulligrub,
my wit has no edge, and I may go cack in my pewter. Let me

182. *homily*: sermon.
193. *furniture*: equipment.
196. *pawn*: pledge.
208. *cack*: defecate.

see, a barber ... my scurvy tongue will discover me; must dissemble, must disguise ... for my beard, my false hair; for my tongue, Spanish, Dutch, or Welsh – no, a Northern barber! Very good. Widow Reinscure's man, well; newly entertain'd, right. So, hang toasts! All cards have white backs, and all knaves would seem to have white breasts. So proceed now, worshipful Cocledemoy.

(*Exit* COCLEDEMOY *in his barber's furniture.*)

[SCENE TWO]

(*Enter* MARY FAUGH *and* FRANCESCHINA *with her hair loose, chafing.*)

MARY FAUGH: Nay, good sweet daughter, do not swagger so. You hear your love is to be married, true; he does cast you off, right; he will leave you to the world. What then? Tho' blue and white, black and green leave you, may not red and yellow entertain you? Is there but one colour in the rainbow?

FRANCESCHINA: Grand grincome on your sentences! God's sacrament, ten tousand divels take you! You ha' brought mine love, mine honour, mine body all to noting!

MARY FAUGH: To nothing! I'll be sworn I have brought them to all the things I could. I ha' made as much o' your maidenhead – an you had been mine own daughter, I could not ha' sold your maidenhead oft'ner than I ha' done. I ha' sworn for you, God forgive me! I have made you acquainted with the Spaniard Don Skirtoll, with the Italian Master Beieroane, with the Irish lord Sir Patrick, with the Dutch merchant Haunce Herkin Glukin Skellam Flapdragon, and specially with the greatest French, and now lastly with this English (yet in my conscience) an honest gentleman. And am I now grown one of the accursed with you for my labour? Is this my reward? Am I call'd bawd? Well, Mary Faugh, go thy ways, Mary Faugh; thy kind heart will bring thee to the hospital.

213. *entertain'd*: taken on.
6. *grincome*: syphilis.
6. *sentences*: moralizings.

FRANCESCHINA: Nay, good naunt, you'll help me to anoder love, vil you not?

MARY FAUGH: Out, thou naughty belly! Wouldst thou make me thy bawd? Thou'st best make me thy bawd; I ha' kept counsel for thee. Who paid the apothecary? Wast not honest Mary Faugh? Who redeem'd thy petticoat and mantle? Wast not honest Mary Faugh? Who helped thee to thy custom, not of swaggering Ireland captains, nor of two-shilling Inns o' Court
30 men, but with honest flat-caps, wealthy flat-caps that pay for their pleasure the best of any men in Europe, nay, which is more, in London? And dost thou defy me, vile creature?

FRANCESCHINA: Foutra 'pon you, vitch, bawd, polecat! Paugh! Did not you praise Freevill to mine love?

MARY FAUGH: I did praise, I confess, I did praise him; I said he was a fool, an unthrift, a true whoremaster, I confess, a constant drab-keeper, I confess. But what, the wind is turn'd!

FRANCESCHINA: It is, it is, vile woman, reprobate woman,
40 naughty woman it is! Vat sal become of mine poor flesh now, mine body must turn Turk for twopence! O Divela, life o' mine 'eart, ick sall be reveng'd! Do ten thousand hell damn me, ick sall have the rogue troat cut, and his love, and his friend, and all his affinity sall smart, sall die, sall hang! Now legion of devil seize him, de gran pest, St Anthony's fire, and de hot Neopolitan poc rot him!

(*Enter* FREEVILL *and* MALHEUREUX.)

FREEVILL: Franceschina!

FRANCESCHINA: O mine seet, dear'st, kindest, mine loving, O mine tousand, ten tousand, delicated, petty seetart! Ah, mine
50 aderlievest affection!

FREEVILL: Why monkey, no fashion in you? Give entertain to my friend.

FRANCESCHINA: Ick sall make de most of you, dat courtesy

---

22. *naunt*: 'aunt' = prostitute.
30. *flat-caps*: citizens and tradesmen (apprentices wore woollen caps).
41. *turn Turk*: turn infidel.
44. *affinity*: kith and kin.
45. *St Anthony's fire*: erysipelas.

may; – Aunt Mary! Mettre Faugh! Stools, stools for dese
gallants.

(*Sings fast*)
    Mine mettre sing non oder song –
  Frolic, frolic, sir,
    But still complain me do her wrong,
  Lighten your heart, sir,
    For me did but kiss her,   60
    For me did but kiss her,
      And so let go.
Your friend is very heavy; ick sall ne'er like such sad company.

FREEVILL: No, thou delightest only in light company.

FRANCESCHINA: By mine trot, he been very sad – Vat ail you,
sir?

MALHEUREUX: A toothache, lady, a paltry rheum.

FRANCESCHINA: De diet is very goot for de rheum.

FREEVILL: How far off dwells the house-surgeon, Mary Faugh?

MARY FAUGH: You are a profane fellow i' faith. I little thought   70
to hear such ungodly terms come from your lips.

FRANCESCHINA: Pridee now, 'tis but a toy, a very trifle.

FREEVILL: I care not for the value, Frank, but i' faith –

FRANCESCHINA: I'fait, me must needs have it. [*Aside*] Dis is
Beatrice' ring; oh, could I get it! [*To* FREEVILL] Seet,
pridee now, as ever you have embraced me with a hearty
arm, a warm thought, or a pleasing touch, as ever you will
profess to love me, as ever you do wish me life, give me dis
ring, dis little ring.

FREEVILL: Prithee be not uncivilly importunate; sha' not ha't.   80
Faith, I care not for thee nor thy jealousy. Sha' not ha't,
i' faith.

FRANCESCHINA: You do not love me. I hear of Sir Hubert
Subboys' daughter, Mistress Beatrice. God's sacrament, ick
could scratch out her eyes and suck the holes!

FREEVILL: Go, y'are grown a punk rampant!

FRANCESCHINA: So! Get thee gone! Ne'er more behold min
eyes, by thee made wretched!

FREEVILL: Mary Faugh, farewell; farewell, Frank.

FRANCESCHINA: Shall I not ha' de ring?   90

FREEVILL: No, by the Lord.

FRANCESCHINA: By te Lord?

FREEVILL: By the Lord.

FRANCESCHINA: Go to your new blowze, your unprov'd sluttery, your modest Mettre, forsooth!

FREEVILL: Marry, will I, forsooth.

FRANCESCHINA: Will you marry, forsooth?

FREEVILL: Do not turn witch before thy time. [*To* MALHEUREUX] With all my heart sir, you will stay.

100 MALHEUREUX: I am no whit myself. *Video meliora proboque*,
But raging lust my fate all strong doth move:
The Gods themselves cannot be wise and love.

FREEVILL: Your wishes to you. [*Exit* FREEVILL.]

MALHEUREUX: Beauty entirely choice –

FRANCESCHINA: Pray ye, prove a man of fashion and neglect the neglected.

MALHEUREUX: Can such a rarity be neglected? Can there be measure or sin in loving such a creature?

FRANCESCHINA: O min poor forsaken heart!

110 MALHEUREUX: I cannot contain; he saw thee not that left thee.
If there be wisdom, reason, honour, grace
Or any foolishly esteemed virtue,
In giving o'er possession of such beauty,
Let me be vicious, so I may be lov'd.
Passion, I am thy slave! Sweet, it shall be my grace,
That I account thy love, my only virtue;
Shall I swear I am thy most vow'd servant?

FRANCESCHINA: Mine vow'd? Go, go, go, I can no more of love. No, no, no, you bin all unconstant. O unfaithful men,
120 tyrants, betrayers! De very enjoying us loseth us; and when you only ha' made us hateful, you only hate us. O mine forsaken heart!

MALHEUREUX: I must not rave; silence and modesty, two customary virtues. Will you be my mistress?

FRANCESCHINA: Mettress? Ha, ha, ha!

MALHEUREUX: Will you lie with me?

94. *blowze*: wench.

FRANCESCHINA: Lie with you? Oh no! You men will out-lie any woman. Fait, me no more can love.

MALHEUREUX: No matter, let me enjoy your bed.

FRANCESCHINA: O vile man, vat do you tink on me? Do you 130
take me to be a beast, a creature that for sense only will entertain love, and not only for love, love? O brutish abomination!

MALHEUREUX: Why then, I pray thee, love, and with thy love enjoy me.

FRANCESCHINA: Give me reason to affect you. Will you swear you love me?

MALHEUREUX: So seriously, that I protest no office so dangerous, no deed so unreasonable, no cost so heavy, but I vow to the utmost tentation of my best being to effect it. 140

FRANCESCHINA: Sall I, or can I trust again? O fool,
How natural 'tis for us to be abus'd!
Sall ick be sure that no satiety,
No enjoying, nor time, shall languish your affection?

MALHEUREUX: If there be ought in brain, heart or hand,
Can make you doubtless, I am your vowed servant.

FRANCESCHINA: Will you do one ting for me?

MALHEUREUX: Can I do it?

FRANCESCHINA: Yes, yes, but – ick do not love dis same Free- 150
vill.

MALHEUREUX: Well.

FRANCESCHINA: Nay, I do hate him.

MALHEUREUX: So?

FRANCESCHINA: By this kiss, I hate him. [*Kisses him.*]

MALHEUREUX: I love to feel such oaths; swear again.

FRANCESCHINA: No, no. Did you ever hear of any that lov'd at the first sight?

MALHEUREUX: A thing most proper.

FRANCESCHINA: Now fait, I judge it all incredible until this
hour I saw you, pretty fair-eyed yout. Would you enjoy me? 160

MALHEUREUX: Rather than my breath, even as my being.

FRANCESCHINA: Vel, had ick not made a vow –

131. *sense*: sensual pleasure.
140. *tentation*: effort.

MALHEUREUX: What vow?

FRANCESCHINA: O, let me forget it; it makes us both despair.

MALHEUREUX: Dear soul, what vow?

FRANCESCHINA: Hah! Good morrow, gentle sir; endeavour to forget me, as I must be enforced to forget all men. Sweet mind rest in you.

170 MALHEUREUX: Stay! Let not my desire burst me. O, my impatient heat endures no resistance, no protraction. There is no being for me but your sudden enjoying.

FRANCESCHINA: I do not love Freevill.

MALHEUREUX: But what vow, what vow?

FRANCESCHINA: So long as Freevill lives, I must not love.

MALHEUREUX: Then he –

FRANCESCHINA: Must –

MALHEUREUX: Die.

FRANCESCHINA: Ay. – No, there is no such vehemence in your affects. Would I were anything, so he were not!

180 MALHEUREUX: Will you be mine when he is not?

FRANCESCHINA: Will I? Dear, dear breast, by this most zealous kiss – but I will not persuade you: but if you hate him that I loathe most deadly – yet as you please, I'll persuade noting.

MALHEUREUX: Will you be only mine?

FRANCESCHINA: Vill I? How hard 'tis for true love to dissemble! I am only yours.

MALHEUREUX: 'Tis as irrevocable as breath, he dies. Your love –

190 FRANCESCHINA: My vow, not until he be dead,
Which that I may be sure not to infringe,
Dis token of his death sall satisfy:
He has a ring, as dear as the air to him,
His new love's gift; tat got and brought to me,
I shall assured your possessed rest.

MALHEUREUX: To kill a man?

FRANCESCHINA: O, done safely; a quarrel sudden pick'd,
With an advantage, strike, then bribe, a little coin,

> 171. *your sudden enjoying*: enjoying you immediately.
> 179. *affects*: temperament.

All's safe, dear soul – but I'll not set you on.

MALHEUREUX: Nay, he is gone. The ring – well, come, little 200
more liberal of thy love.

FRANCESCHINA: Not yet; my vow.

MALHEUREUX: O heaven, there is no hell
But love's prolongings! Dear, farewell.

FRANCESCHINA: Farewell. [*Aside.*] Now does my heart swell
high, for my revenge
Has birth and form. First, friend sall kill his friend.
He dat survives, I'll hang; besides, de chaste
Beatrice I'll vex. Only de ring;
Dat got, the world sall know the worst of evils:
Woman corrupted is the worst of devils. 210

(*Exit* FRANCESCHINA.)

MALHEUREUX: To kill my friend! O 'tis to kill myself!
Yet man's but man's excrement, man breeding man,
As he does worms, or this (*he spits*) to spoil this nothing!
The body of a man is of the selfsame soul,
As ox or horse; no murder to kill these.
As for that only part which makes us man,
Murder wants power to touch't. O wit, how vile,
How hellish art thou when thou raisest nature
'Gainst sacred faith! Think more, to kill a friend
To gain a woman, to lose a virtuous self 220
For appetite and sensual end, whose very having
Loseth all appetite and gives satiety
That corporal end, remorse and inward blushings,
Forcing us loathe the steam of our own heats,
Whilst friendship clos'd in virtue, being spiritual,
Tastes no such languishings and moments' pleasure,
With much repentance, but like rivers flow,
And further that they run, they bigger grow!
Lord, how was I misgone! How easy 'tis to err
When passion will not give us leave to think! 230
A learn'd, that is an honest man may fear,

212. *excrement*: outgrowth.
217. *wit*: judgment.
229. *misgone*: gone astray.

And lust, and rage, and malice, and anything,
When he is taken uncollected suddenly:
'Tis sin of cold blood, mischief with wak'd eyes
That is the damnéd and the truly vice.
Not he that's passionless, but he 'bove passion's wise.
My friend shall know it all. (*Exit.*)

SCENE THREE

(*Enter* MASTER MULLIGRUB *and* MISTRESS MULLIGRUB,
she with bag of money.)

MISTRESS MULLIGRUB: It is right, I assure you, just fifteen
pounds.

MULLIGRUB: Well Cocledemoy, 'tis thou put'st me to this
charge, but an I catch thee, I'll charge thee with as many
irons! Well, is the barber come? I'll be trim'd and then to
Cheapside to buy a fair piece of plate to furnish the loss. Is
the barber come?

MISTRESS MULLIGRUB: Truth, husband, surely heaven is not
pleas'd with our vocation; we do wink at the sins of our
10 people, our wines are Protestants, and – I speak it to my grief,
and to the burden of my conscience – we fry our fish with salt
butter.

MULLIGRUB: Go look to your business, mend the matter and
score false with a vengeance.

[*Exit* MISTRESS MULLIGRUB.]

(*Enter* COCLEDEMOY *like a barber.*)

Welcome friend. Whose man?

COCLEDEMOY: Widow Reinscure's man, an't shall please your
good worship; my name's Andrew Shark.

MULLIGRUB: How does my godson, good Andrew?

COCLEDEMOY: Very well. He's gone to trim Master Quicquid,

232. *malice*: used as verb.
6. *the loss*: the goblets stolen by Cocledemoy.
14. *score false*: cook the books.
17. *Andrew*: cf. merryandrew, a mountebank's assistant.
19. *Quicquid*: 'Whoever', 'What-you-may-call-'em'.

our parson. Hold up your head. 20

MULLIGRUB: How long have you been a barber, Andrew?

COCLEDEMOY: Not long sir; this two year.

MULLIGRUB: What, and a good workman already? I dare scarce
trust my head to thee.

COCLEDEMOY: O, fear not, we ha' poll'd better men than you.
We learn the trade very quickly. Will your good worship be
shaven or cut?

MULLIGRUB: As you will. What trade didst live by before thou
turnedst barber, Andrew?

COCLEDEMOY: I was a pedlar in Germany, but my countrymen 30
thrive better by this trade.

MULLIGRUB: Wha's the news, barber? Thou art sometimes at
court?

COCLEDEMOY: Sometimes poll a page or so, sir.

MULLIGRUB: And what's the news? How do all my good
lords and all my good ladies, and all the rest of my acquaintance?

COCLEDEMOY [aside]: What an arrogant knave's this! I'll
acquaintance ye! (He spieth the bag.) 'Tis cash! [To MULLI-
GRUB.] Say ye, sir? 40

MULLIGRUB: And what news? What news, good Andrew?

COCLEDEMOY: Marry sir, you know the Conduit at Greenwich
and the under-holes that spouts up water?

MULLIGRUB: Very well. I was wash'd there one day, and so was
my wife; you might have wrung her smock, i' faith. But what
o' those holes?

COCLEDEMOY: Thus sir: out of those little holes, in the midst
of the night, crawl'd out twenty-four huge, horrible, monstrous, fearful devouring –

MULLIGRUB: Bless us! 50

COCLEDEMOY: Serpents, which no sooner were beheld, but they
turn'd to mastiffs, which howl'd; those mastiffs instantly
turn'd to cocks which crowed; those cocks in a moment were
chang'd to bears which roar'd; which bears are at this hour to
be yet seen in Paris Garden, living upon nothing but toasted
cheese and green onions.

25. *poll'd*: trimmed, sheared.

MULLIGRUB: By the Lord, an this may be, my wife and I will go see them; this portends something.

COCLEDEMOY [*aside*]: Yes, worshipful fist, thoul't feel what
60 portends by and by.

MULLIGRUB: And what more news? You shave the world, especially you barber-surgeons. You know the ground of many things, you are cunning privy searchers. By the Mass, you scour all! What more news?

COCLEDEMOY: They say, sir, that twenty-five couple of Spanish jennets are to be seen hand in hand dance the old measures, whilst six goodly Flanders mares play to them on a noise of flutes.

MULLIGRUB: O monstrous! This is a lie o' my word. Nay, an
70 this be not a lie – I am no fool, I warrant – nay, make an ass of me once –

COCLEDEMOY: Shut your eyes close, wink. Sure sir, this ball will make you smart.

MULLIGRUB: I do wink.

COCLEDEMOY: Your head will take cold.

(COCLEDEMOY *puts on a coxcomb on* MULLIGRUB'S *head*.)
I will put on your good worship's nightcap whilst I shave you, so. [*Aside*] Mum. Hang toasts! Faugh! *Via!* Sparrows must peck and Cocledemoy munch. [*Exit.*]

MULLIGRUB: Ha, ha, ha! Twenty-five couple of Spanish jen-
80 nets to dance the old measures. Andrew makes my worship laugh, i' faith. Dost take me for an ass, Andrew? Dost know one Cocledemoy in town? He made me an ass last night, but I'll ass him! Art thou free, Andrew? Shave me well, I shall be one of the Common Council shortly, and then Andrew – why Andrew, Andrew, dost leave me in the suds? (*Sings.*) Why, Andrew, I shall be blind with winking. Ha, Andrew! Wife! Andrew! What means this? Wife! My money! Wife!

(*Enter* MISTRESS MULLIGRUB.)

63. *privy searchers*: (i) appointed investigators, (ii) searchers of toilets and (iii) of genitals.

67. *noise*: band of musicians.

72. *ball*: i.e. of soap.

75. Stage direction. *coxcomb*: fool's cap.

MISTRESS MULLIGRUB: What's the noise with you? What ail you?

MULLIGRUB: Where's the barber?

MISTRESS MULLIGRUB: Gone. I saw him depart long since. 90
Why, are not you trim'd?

MULLIGRUB: Trim'd! O wife, I am shav'd! Did you take hence
the money?

MISTRESS MULLIGRUB: I touch'd it not, as I am religious.

MULLIGRUB: O Lord, I have wink'd fair!
(*Enter* HOLIFERNES.)

HOLIFERNES: I pray, godfather, give me your blessing.

MULLIGRUB: O Holifernes! O where's thy mother's Andrew?

HOLIFERNES: Blessing, godfather!

MULLIGRUB: The devil choke thee! Where's Andrew, thy
mother's man? 100

HOLIFERNES: My mother hath none such, forsooth.

MULLIGRUB: My money – fifteen pounds! Plague of all
Andrews! Who was't trim'd me?

HOLIFERNES: I know not, godfather. Only one met me as I was
coming to you and borrowed my furniture, as he said, for a
jest sake.

MULLIGRUB: What kind of fellow?

HOLIFERNES: A thick elderly stub-bearded fellow.

MULLIGRUB: Cocledemoy, Cocledemoy! Raise all the wise men
in the street! I'll hang him with mine own hands! O wife, 110
some *rosa solis*!

MISTRESS MULLIGRUB: Good husband, take comfort in the
Lord. I'll play the devil, but I'll recover it. Have a good
conscience, 'tis but a week's cutting in the Term.

MULLIGRUB: O wife, O wife! O Jack! How does thy mother?
Is there any fiddlers in the house?

MISTRESS MULLIGRUB: Yes, Master Creak's noise.

MULLIGRUB: Bid 'em play, laugh, make merry. Cast up my
accounts, for I'll go hang myself presently. I will not curse –
but a pox on Cocledemoy! He has poll'd and shav'd me, he 120
has trim'd me!
(*Exeunt.*)

108. *stub-bearded*: short-bearded.
111. *rosa solis*: spiced cordial.

ACT THREE

SCENE ONE

(*Enter* BEATRICE, CRISPINELLA, *and* NURSE PUTIFER.)

PUTIFER: Nay good child o' love, once more Master Freevill's sonnet o' the kiss you gave him!

BEATRICE: Sh'a't, good nurse. [*Reads*]
>   Purest lips, soft banks of blisses,
>   Self alone deserving kisses
>   O give me leave to, etc.

CRISPINELLA: Pish, sister Beatrice, prithee read no more! My stomach o' late stands against kissing extremely.

BEATRICE: Why, good Crispinella?

10 CRISPINELLA: By the faith and trust I bear to my face, 'tis grown one of the most unsavoury ceremonies. Body o' beauty, 'tis one of the most unpleasing injurious customs to ladies. Any fellow that has but one nose on his face, and standing collar and skirts also lin'd with taffety sarcenet, must salute us on the lips as familiarly – soft skins save us! There was a stub-bearded John-a-stile with a ployden's face saluted me last day, and stroke his bristles through my lips; I ha' spent ten shillings in pomatum since to skin them again! Marry, if a nobleman or a knight with one lock visit us; though his
20 unclean goose-turd-green teeth ha' the palsy, his nostrils smell worse than a putrified maribone, and his loose beard drops into our bosom, yet we must kiss him with a cursy; a curse! For my part, I had as lief they would break wind in my lips.

BEATRICE: Fie, Crispinella, you speak too broad.

---

2. *sonnet*: short love poem.
14. *taffety sarcenet*: soft silk stuff.
16. *John-a-stile*: fictitious name for legal personage (cf. John Doe).
16. *ployden's*: lawyer's (see also Additional Notes).
22. *cursy*: courtesy, bow.

CRISPINELLA: No jot, sister. Let's ne'er be ashamed to speak what we be not asham'd to think. I dare as boldly speak venery, as think venery.

BEATRICE: Faith, sister, I'll be gone if you speak so broad.

CRISPINELLA: Will you so? Now bashfulness seize you! We 30 pronounce boldly robbery, murder, treason, which deeds must needs be far more loathsome than an act which is so natural, just and necessary as that of procreation. You shall have an hypocritical vestal virgin speak that with close teeth publicly which she will receive with open mouth privately. For my own part I consider nature without apparel, without disguising of custom or compliment. I give thoughts words, and words truth, and truth boldness. She whose honest freeness makes it her virtue to speak what she thinks will make it her necessity to think what is good. I love no prohibited things, 40 and yet I would have nothing prohibited by policy but by virtue. For as in the fashion of time, those books that are call'd in are most in sale and request, so in nature those actions that are most prohibited are most desired.

BEATRICE: Good quick sister, stay your pace. We are private, but the world would censure you, for truly, severe modesty is women's virtue.

CRISPINELLA: Fie, fie! Virtue is a free pleasant buxom quality. I love a constant countenance well, but this froward ignorant coyness, sour austere lumpish uncivil privateness, that 50 promises nothing but rough skins and hard stools, ha, fie on't! good for nothing but for nothing – Well nurse, and what do you conceive of all this?

PUTIFER: Nay faith, my conceiving days be done. Marry, for kissing, I'll defend that, that's within my compass. But for my own part here's Mistress Beatrice is to be married with the grace of God. A fine gentleman he is shall have her, and I warrant a strong; he has a leg like a post, a nose like a lion, a brow like a bull, and a beard of most fair expectation. This week you must marry him, and I now will read a lecture to you 60 both, how you shall behave yourselves to your husbands the

48. *buxom*: tolerant, engaging.

first month of your nuptial. I ha' broke my skull about it, I can tell you, and there is much brain in it.

CRISPINELLA: Read it to my sister, good nurse, for I assure you I'll ne'er marry.

PUTIFER: Marry, God forfend! What will you do then?

CRISPINELLA: Faith, strive against the flesh. Marry? No, faith. Husbands are like lots in the lottery: you may draw forty blanks before you find one that has any prize in him. A hus-
70   band generally is a careless, domineering thing that grows like coral, which as long as it is under water is soft and tender, but as soon as it has got his branch above the waves is presently hard stiff, not to be bowed but burst; so when your husband is a suitor and under your choice, Lord how supple he is, how obsequious, how at your service sweet lady! Once married, got up his head above, a stiff, crooked, knobby, inflexible, tyrannous creature he grows. Then they turn like water, more you would embrace the less you hold. I'll live my own woman, and if the worst come to the worst, I had rather prove
80   a wag than a fool.

BEATRICE: O, but a virtuous marriage –

CRISPINELLA: Virtuous marriage? There is no more affinity betwixt virtue and marriage than betwixt a man and his horse. Indeed, virtue gets up upon marriage sometimes and mana-geth it in the right way, but marriage is of another piece. For as a horse may be without a man, and a man without a horse, so marriage you know is often without virtue, and virtue I am sure more oft without marriage. But thy match, sister – by my troth, I think 'twill do well. He's a well-shap'd clean-lipp'd
90   gentleman of a handsome, but not affected fineness, a good faithful eye and a well-humour'd cheek. Would he did not stoop in the shoulders for thy sake. See, here he is.

(*Enter* FREEVILL *and* TYSEFEW.)

FREEVILL: Good day, sweet.

72. *his branch*: perhaps a glancing allusion to cuckold's horns.
80. *wag*: wit.
90. *fineness*: elegant appearance.
91. *well-humour'd*: with 'humours' well-balanced, i.e. equable.

CRISPINELLA: Good morrow, brother. Nay, you shall have my lip. – Good morrow, servant.

TYSEFEW: Good morrow, sweet life.

CRISPINELLA: Life? Dost call thy mistress life?

TYSEFEW: Life, yes, why not life?

CRISPINELLA: How many mistresses hast thou?   100

TYSEFEW: Some nine.

CRISPINELLA: Why then, thou hast nine lives, like a cat.

TYSEFEW: Mew! You would be taken up for that.

CRISPINELLA: Nay, good, let me still sit. We low statures love still to sit, lest when we stand we may be supposed to sit.

TYSEFEW: Dost not wear high cork shoes – chopines?

CRISPINELLA: Monstrous ones. I am as many other are, piec'd above and piec'd beneath –

TYSEFEW: Still the best part in the –

CRISPINELLA: – And yet all will scarce make me so high as one   110
of the giants' stilts that stalks before my Lord Mayor's pageant.

TYSEFEW: By the Lord, so, I thought 'twas for something Mistress Joyce jested at thy high insteps.

CRISPINELLA: She might well enough, and long enough, before I would be ashamed of my shortness. What I made or can mend myself I may blush at, but what nature put upon me, let her be ashamed for me, I ha' nothing to do with it. I forget my beauty.

TYSEFEW: Faith, Joyce is a foolish bitter creature.   120

CRISPINELLA: A pretty mildewed wench she is.

TYSEFEW: And fair.

CRISPINELLA: As myself.

TYSEFEW: O, you forget your beauty now.

CRISPINELLA: Troth, I never remember my beauty, but as some men do religion, for controversy's sake.

BEATRICE: A motion, sister –

CRISPINELLA: *Nineveh, Julius Caesar, Jonas,* or *The Destruction of Jerusalem?*

107-8. *piec'd above*: i.e. with a false hair-piece on top.

127. *motion*: (i) suggestion, (ii) puppet-show: Crispinella names some popular shows.

130 BEATRICE: My love here –

CRISPINELLA: Prithee call him not love, 'tis the drab's phrase, nor sweet honey, nor my cunny, nor dear duckling, 'tis the citizen terms, but call me him –

BEATRICE: What?

CRISPINELLA: Anything. What's the motion?

BEATRICE: You know this night our parents have intended solemnly to contract us; and my love, to grace the feast, hath promised a masque.

FREEVILL: You'll make one, Tysefew, and Caqueteur shall fill
140 up a room.

TYSEFEW: 'Fore heaven, well rememb'red! He borrowed a diamond of me last night to grace his finger in your visitation. The lying creature will swear some strange thing on it now.

(*Enter* CAQUETEUR.)

CRISPINELLA: Peace, he's here; stand close, lurk.

[TYSEFEW *withdraws*.]

CAQUETEUR: Good morrow, most dear, and worthy to be most wise. How does my mistress?

CRISPINELLA: Morrow, sweet servant, you glister. Prithee, let's see that stone.

CAQUETEUR: A toy, lady, I bought to please my finger.

150 CRISPINELLA: Why, I am more precious to you than your finger.

CAQUETEUR: Yes, or than all my body, I swear.

CRISPINELLA: Why, then, let it be bought to please me. Come, I am no professed beggar.

CAQUETEUR: Troth, mistress, zoons! Forsooth, I protest!

CRISPINELLA: Nay, if you turn Protestant for such a toy –

CAQUETEUR: In good deed la, another time I'll give you a –

CRISPINELLA: Is this yours to give?

CAQUETEUR: O God, forsooth! Mine, quoth you? Nay, as for
160 that –

CRISPINELLA: Now I remember, I ha' seen this on my servant Tysefew's finger.

131. *drab's*: whore's.
132. *cunny*: rabbit.
155. *zoons !*: God's wounds!
161. *servant*: admirer.

CAQUETEUR: Such another.

CRISPINELLA: Nay, I am sure this is it.

CAQUETEUR: Troth 'tis, forsooth. The poor fellow wanted money to pay for supper last night, and so pawn'd it to me. 'Tis a pawn i' faith, or else you should have it.

TYSEFEW [*stepping forward; aside to* CAQUETEUR]: Hark ye, thou base lying – How dares thy impudence hope to prosper? Wer't not for the privilege of this respected company, I 170 would so bang thee!

CRISPINELLA: Come hither, servant. What's the matter betwixt you two?

CAQUETEUR: Nothing. [*Aside to* CRISPINELLA] But (hark you) he did me some uncivil discourtesies last night, for which, because I should not call him to account, he desires to make me any satisfaction. The coward trembles at my very presence, but I ha' him on the hip; I'll take the forfeit on his ring.

TYSEFEW: What's that you whisper to her? 180

CAQUETEUR: Nothing, sir, but satisfy her that the ring was not pawn'd, but only lent by you to grace my finger, and so told her I crav'd your pardon for being too familiar, or indeed overbold with your reputation.

CRISPINELLA: Yes, indeed he did. He said you desired to make him any satisfaction for an uncivil discourtesy you did him last night, but he said he had you o' the hip and would take the forfeit of your ring.

TYSEFEW: How now, ye base poltroon!

CAQUETEUR: Hold, hold! My mistress speaks by contraries. 190

TYSEFEW: Contraries?

CAQUETEUR: She jests, faith, only jests.

CRISPINELLA: Sir, I'll no more o' your service. You are a child, I'll give you to my nurse.

PUTIFER: An he come to me, I can tell you as old as I am, what to do with him.

CAQUETEUR: I offer my service, forsooth.

TYSEFEW: Why, so. Now every dog has his bone to gnaw on.

FREEVILL: The mask holds, Master Caqueteur.

199. *holds*: is about to take place.

200 CAQUETEUR: I am ready, sir. [*To* PUTIFER] Mistress, I'll
   dance with you, ne'er fear. I'll grace you.

PUTIFER: I tell you I can my singles and my doubles and my
   trick o' twenty, my carantapace, my traverse forward, and my
   falling back yet, i' faith.

BEATRICE: Mine, the provision for the night is ours.
   Much must be our care; till night we leave you.
   I am your servant; be not tyrannous,
   Your virtue won me; faith, my love's not lust.
   Good, wrong me not; my most fault is much trust.

210 FREEVILL: Until night only. My heart be with you! [*To*
   CRISPINELLA] Farewell, sister.

CRISPINELLA: Adieu, brother. Come on, sister, for these sweetmeats.

FREEVILL: Let's meet and practise presently.

TYSEFEW: Content, we'll but fit our pumps. – Come, ye per-
   nicious vermin!

   (*Exeunt* [*all but* FREEVILL.])
   (*Enter* MALHEUREUX.)

FREEVILL: My friend, wished hours! What news from Babylon?
   How does the woman of sin and natural concupiscence?

MALHEUREUX: The eldest child of nature ne'er beheld
220   So damn'd a creature.

FREEVILL: What! *In nova fert animus mutatas dicere formas!*
   Which way bears the tide?

MALHEUREUX: Dear loved sir, I find a mind courageously
   vicious may put on a desperate security, but can never be
   blessed with a firm enjoying and self-satisfaction.

FREEVILL: What passion is this, my dear Lindabrides?

MALHEUREUX: 'Tis well, we both may jest. I ha' been tempted
   to your death.

FREEVILL: What? Is the rampant cockatrice grown mad for the
230   loss of her men?

MALHEUREUX: Devilishly mad.

FREEVILL: As most assured of my second love?

   202–4. *singles . . . back*: dance steps, with pun on sexual sense of 'falling
   back'.
   224. *desperate security*: heedless rashness.

MALHEUREUX: Right.

FREEVILL: She would have had this ring.

MALHEUREUX: Ay, and this heart; and in true proof you were slain, I should bring her this ring, from which she was assured you would not part, until from life you parted. For which deed, and only for which deed, I should possess her sweetness.

FREEVILL: O bloody villainess! Nothing is defamed but by his 240 proper self. Physicians abuse remedies, lawyers spoil the law, and women only shame women. You ha' vow'd my death?

MALHEUREUX: My lust, not I, before my reason would; yet I must use her. That I, a man of sense, should conceive endless pleasure in a body whose soul I know to be so hideously black!

FREEVILL: That a man at twenty-three should cry, 'O sweet pleasure!' and at forty-three should sigh, 'O sharp pox!' But consider man furnished with omnipotency and you overthrow him. Thou must cool thy impatient appetite. 'Tis fate, 'tis 250 fate!

MALHEUREUX: I do malign my creation that I am subject to passion. I must enjoy her.

FREEVILL: I have it! Mark; I give a masque tonight
To my love's kindred. In that thou shalt go:
In that we two make show of falling out,
Give seeming challenge, instantly depart,
With some suspicion to present fight.
We will be seen as going to our swords
And after meeting, this ring only lent, 260
I'll lurk in some obscure place till rumour
(The common bawd to loose suspicions)
Have feigned me slain, which (in respect myself
Will not be found, and our late seeming quarrel)
Will quickly sound to all as earnest truth.
Then to thy wench; protest me surely dead.
Show her this ring, enjoy her, and, blood cold,
We'll laugh at folly.

241. *proper*: own.
266. *protest*: proclaim.

MALHEUREUX: O but think of it!

270 FREEVILL: Think of it. Come away! Virtue, let sleep thy
passions;

What old times held as crimes are now but fashions.

(*Exeunt.*)

SCENE TWO

(*Enter* MASTER BURNISH *and* LIONEL: MASTER MULLI-
GRUB, *with a standing cup in his hand, and an obligation in
the other.* COCLEDEMOY *stands at the other door disguised
like a French pedlar, and overhears them.*)

MULLIGRUB: I am not at this time furnished, but there's my
bond for your plate.

BURNISH: Your bill had been sufficient; y'are a good man. A
standing cup parcel-gilt, of thirty-two ounces, eleven pound,
seven shillings, the first of July. Good plate, good man, good
day – good all!

MULLIGRUB: 'Tis my hard fortune. I will hang the knave; no,
first he shall half rot in fetters in the dungeon, his conscience
made despairful. I'll hire a knave o' purpose shall assure him

10   he is damn'd, and after see him with mine own eyes, hanged
without singing any psalm. Lord, that he has but one neck!

BURNISH: You are too tyrannous. You'll use me no further?

MULLIGRUB: No, sir. Lend me your servant, only to carry the
plate home. I have occasion of an hour's absence.

BURNISH: With easy consent, sir. [*To Lionel*] Haste, and be
careful. (*Exit* BURNISH.)

MULLIGRUB: Be very careful I pray thee – to my wife's own
hands.

LIONEL: Secure yourself, sir.

Stage direction. *standing cup*: cup with base and stem.
Stage direction. *obligation*: bond.
1. *furnished*: supplied with money.
4. *parcel-gilt*: partly gilded.
11. *without ... psalm*: without a psalm sung for him.
19. *Secure yourself*: rest assured.

MULLIGRUB: To her own hand.   20

LIONEL: Fear not, I have delivered greater things than this to a woman's own hand.

COCLEDEMOY: Monsieur, please you to buy a fine delicate ball, sweet ball, a camphor ball?

MULLIGRUB: Prithee, away!

COCLEDEMOY: [Or] a ball to scour, a scouring ball, a ball to be shaved?

MULLIGRUB: For the love of God, talk not of shaving! I have been shaved, mischief and a thousand devils seize him! I have been shaved. (*Exit* MULLIGRUB.)   30

COCLEDEMOY: The fox grows fat when he is cursed. I'll shave ye smoother yet. Turd on a tile-stone! My lips have a kind of rheum at this bowl – I'll hav't! I'll gargalize my throat with this vintner, and when I have done with him, spit him out. I'll shark; conscience does not repine. Were I to bite an honest gentleman, a poor grogaran poet, or a penurious parson, that had but ten pigs' tails in a twelvemonth and for want of learning had but one good stool in a fortnight, I were damn'd beyond the works of supererogation. But to wring the withers of my gouty, barm'd, spigot-frigging jumbler of   40 elements, Mulligrub, I hold it as lawful as sheep-shearing, taking eggs from hens, caudles from asses, or butter'd shrimps from horses – they make no use of them, were not provided for them. And therefore, worshipful Cocledemoy, hang toasts! On, in grace and virtue to proceed! Only beware, beware degrees. There be rounds in a ladder and knots in a halter; 'ware carts. Hang toasts! The Common Council has decreed it; I must draw a lot for the great goblet. (*Exit.*)

32–3. *My lips . . . rheum*: my mouth waters.
33. *gargalize*: gargle.
36. *grogaran*: grogran, coarse, stiff cloth.
40. *barm'd*: fermented.
40. *spigot-frigging*: frig = tamper. Hence 'drink-adulterating'.
42. *caudles*: warm drinks of sweetened and spiced gruel and ale or wine.
46. *degrees*: steps, i.e. to scaffold, with pun on 'proceeding' to academic degree.
47. *'ware carts*: criminals were carted to execution.

SCENE THREE

(*Enter* MISTRESS MULLIGRUB, *and* LIONEL *with a goblet.*)

MISTRESS MULLIGRUB: Nay, I pray you stay and drink. And
how does your mistress? I know her very well. I have been
inward with her, and so has many more. She was ever a good
patient creature i' faith. With all my heart I'll remember your
master, an honest man; he knew me before I was married. An
honest man he is, and a crafty. He comes forward in the world
well, I warrant him, and his wife is a proper woman, that she
is. Well, she has been as proper a woman as any in Cheap;
she paints now, and yet she keeps her husband's old customers
10 to him still. In troth, a fine fac'd wife in a wainscot carved
seat is a worthy ornament to a tradesman's shop, and an
attractive, I warrant. Her husband shall find it in the custom
of his ware, I'll assure him. God be with you, good youth, I
acknowledge the receipt.

(*Exit* LIONEL.)

'I acknowledge all the receipt.' Sure, 'tis very well spoken!
'I acknowledge the receipt.' Thus 'tis to have good education
and to be brought up in a tavern! I do keep as gallant and as
good company, though I say it, as any she in London. Squires,
gentlemen and knights diet at my table, and I do lend some of
20 them money, and full many fine men go upon my score, as
simple as I stand here, and I trust them; and truly they very
knightly and courtly promise fair, give me very good words,
and a piece of flesh when time of year serves. Nay, though my
husband be a citizen and's cap's made of wool, yet I ha' wit,
and can see my good as soon as another, for I have all the
thanks. My silly husband, alas, he knows nothing of it; 'tis
I that bear, 'tis I that must bear a brain for all.

[*Enter* COCLEDEMOY.]

COCLEDEMOY: Fair hour to you, mistress!

3. *inward*: intimate, with sexual innuendo in next phrase.
8. *Cheap*: Cheapside.
9. *paints*: i.e. her face.
20. *score*: accounts, i.e. on credit.

MISTRESS MULLIGRUB [*aside*]: Fair hour! Fine term, faith; I'll score it up anon. [*To* COCLEDEMOY] A beautiful thought to you, sir.   30

COCLEDEMOY: Your husband and my master, Master Burnish, has sent you a jowl of fresh salmon, and they both will come to dinner to season your new cup with the best wine; which cup your husband entreats you to send back by me, that his arms may be grav'd o' the side, which he forgot before it was sent.

MISTRESS MULLIGRUB: By what token are you sent? By no token? Nay, I have wit.

COCLEDEMOY: He sent me by the same token, that he was dry-   40
shaved this morning.

MISTRESS MULLIGRUB: A sad token, but true. Here, sir; [*Gives cup*] I pray you, commend me to your master, but especially to your mistress, tell them they shall be most sincerely welcome. (*Exit.*)

COCLEDEMOY: Shall be most sincerely welcome! Worshipful Cocledemoy, lurk close. Hang toasts! Be not ashamed of thy quality! Every man's turd smells well in's own nose. Vanish, foist! (*Exit.*)

([*Re-*]*enter* MISTRESS MULLIGRUB, *with servants and furniture for the table.*)

MISTRESS MULLIGRUB: Come, spread these table diaper nap-   50
kins and do you hear? – perfume! This parlour does so smell of profane tobacco. I could never endure this ungodly tobacco since one of our elders assured me upon his knowledge tobacco was not used in the congregation of the Family of Love. – Spread, spread handsomely! Lord, these boys do things arsy-varsy! You show your bringing up. I was a gentlewoman by my sister's side, I can tell ye so methodically. Methodically! I wonder where I got that word. O! Sir Aminadab Ruth bade me kiss him methodically; I had it somewhere, and I had it indeed.   60

33. *jowl*: head parts.
40–41. *dry-shaved*: gulled.
49. *foist*: (i) rogue, (ii) stink.
50. *diaper*: figured.

(*Enter* MASTER MULLIGRUB.)

MULLIGRUB: Mind, be not desperate, I'll recover all.
　All things with me shall seem honest, that can be profitable.
　He must ne'er wince, that would or thrive or save,
　To be call'd niggard, cuckold, cut-throat, knave.

MISTRESS MULLIGRUB: Are they come, husband?

MULLIGRUB: Who? What? How now? What feast towards in
　my private parlour?

MISTRESS MULLIGRUB: Pray leave your foolery. What, are
　they come?

70 MULLIGRUB: Come? Who come?

MISTRESS MULLIGRUB: You need not mak't so strange!

MULLIGRUB: Strange?

MISTRESS MULLIGRUB: Ay, strange. You know no man that
　sent me word that he and his wife would come to dinner to
　me, and sent this jowl of fresh salmon beforehand?

MULLIGRUB: Peace, not I! Peace, the messenger hath mistaken
　the house, let's eat it up quickly, before it be enquir'd for.
　Sit to it! Some vinegar, quick! Some good luck yet. Faith, I
　never tasted salmon relish'd better. Oh, when a man feeds at
80 　other men's cost!

MISTRESS MULLIGRUB: Other men's cost? Why, did not you
　send this jowl of salmon?

MULLIGRUB: No.

MISTRESS MULLIGRUB: By Master Burnish' man?

MULLIGRUB: No.

MISTRESS MULLIGRUB: Sending me word that he and his wife
　would come to dinner to me?

MULLIGRUB: No, no!

MISTRESS MULLIGRUB: To season my new bowl?

90 MULLIGRUB: Bowl?

MISTRESS MULLIGRUB: And withal will'd me to send the bowl
　back?

MULLIGRUB: Back?

MISTRESS MULLIGRUB: That you might have your arms grav'd
　on the side?

MULLIGRUB: Ha?

66. *towards*: in preparation.

MISTRESS MULLIGRUB: By the same token you were dry-shaven this morning before you went forth?

MULLIGRUB: Pah! How this salmon stinks!

MISTRESS MULLIGRUB: And thereupon sent the bowl back, 100 prepar'd dinner – nay, an I bear not a brain!

MULLIGRUB: Wife, do not vex me. Is the bowl gone, is it deliver'd?

MISTRESS MULLIGRUB: Delivered! Yes sure, 'tis delivered.

MULLIGRUB: I will never more say my prayers. Do not make me mad; 'tis common. Let me not cry like a woman – is it gone?

MISTRESS MULLIGRUB: Gone? God is my witness, I delivered it with no more intention to be cozen'd on't than the child new born; and yet – 110

MULLIGRUB: Look to my house, I am haunted with evil spirits. Hear me, do; hear me! If I have not my goblet again, heaven, I'll to the devil! I'll to a conjurer. Look to my house! I'll raise all the wise men i' the street.

(*Exit* MULLIGRUB.)

MISTRESS MULLIGRUB: Deliver us! What words are these? I trust in God he is but drunk, sure.

([*Re-*]enter COCLEDEMOY.)

COCLEDEMOY [*aside*]: I must have the salmon too, worship: Cocledemoy, now for the masterpiece! God bless thy neck-piece, and fowtra! Fair mistress, my master –

MISTRESS MULLIGRUB: Have I caught you? – What, Roger! 120

COCLEDEMOY: Peace, good mistress, I'll tell you all. A jest, a very mere jest. Your husband only took sport to fright you. The bowl's at my master's, and there is your husband, who sent me in all haste, lest you should be over-frighted with his feigning, to come to dinner to him. –

MISTRESS MULLIGRUB: Praise heaven it is no worse!

COCLEDEMOY: And desired me to desire you to send the jowl of salmon before, and yourself to come after to them; my mistress would be right glad to see you.

MISTRESS MULLIGRUB: I pray carry it; now thank them 130

118–19. *neck-piece*: neck.
122. *took sport*: pretended.

entirely. Bless me, I was never so out of my skin in my life!
Pray thank your mistress most entirely.

COCLEDEMOY [*aside*]: So now, figo! worshipful Moll Faugh and
I will munch. Cheaters and bawds go together like washing
and wringing. (*Exit.*)

MISTRESS MULLIGRUB: Beshrew his heart for his labour! How
everything about me quivers! [*To servant*] What, Christian,
my hat and apron. Here, take my sleeves. – And how I
tremble! So. I'll gossip it now for't, that's certain; here has
140 been revolutions and false fires indeed!

([*Re-*]*enter* MULLIGRUB.)

MULLIGRUB: Whither now? What's the matter with you now?
Whither are you a-gadding?

MISTRESS MULLIGRUB: Come, come, play the fool no more.
Will you go?

MULLIGRUB: Whither, in the rank name of madness, whither?

MISTRESS MULLIGRUB: Whither? Why, to Master Burnish, to
eat the jowl of salmon. Lord, how strange you make it!

MULLIGRUB: Why so, why so?

MISTRESS MULLIGRUB: Why so? Why, did not you send the
150 self-same fellow for the jowl of salmon that had the cup?

MULLIGRUB: 'Tis well, 'tis very well!

MISTRESS MULLIGRUB: And will'd me to come and eat it with
you at the goldsmith's.

MULLIGRUB: O ay, ay, ay! Art in thy right wits?

MISTRESS MULLIGRUB: Do you hear? Make a fool of somebody
else! An you make an ass of me, I'll make an ox of you, do
you see?

MULLIGRUB: Nay wife, be patient; for look you, I may be mad,
or drunk, or so; for my own part, though you can bear more
160 than I, yet I can do well. I will not curse nor cry, but heaven

132. *entirely*: heartily.
133. *figo !*: expression referring to contemptuous gesture of thumb and
fingers.
138. *apron*: decorative wear in this period.
138. *sleeves*: detachable items of dress.
139. *gossip*: (i) take part, (ii) make oneself at home (*O.E.D.*).
156. *an ox of you*: the obligatory cuckold's horn joke.
160. *cry*: Q – 'cary'.

knows what I think. Come, let's go hear some music. I will never more say my prayers. Let's go hear some doleful music. Nay, if heaven forget to prosper knaves, I'll go no more to the synagogue. Now I am discontented, I'll turn sectary; that is fashion.

(*Exeunt.*)

164. *synagogue*: Puritan term for church.
164. *sectary*: member of sect, dissenter.

ACT FOUR

SCENE ONE

(*Enter* SIR HUBERT SUBBOYS, SIR LIONEL FREEVILL, CRISPINELLA, *servants with lights.*)

SIR HUBERT: More lights! Welcome, Sir Lionel Freevill – brother Freevill shortly. – Look to your lights.

SERVANT: The masquers are at hand.

SIR LIONEL: Call down our daughter: hark, they are at hand. Rank handsomely.

(*Enter the Masquers [including* FREEVILL, TYSEFEW *and* CAQUETEUR; FREEVILL *dances with* BEATRICE, *who has just entered*]; *they dance. Enter* MALHEUREUX *and take* BEATRICE *from* FREEVILL. *They draw.*)

FREEVILL: Know sir, I have the advantage of the place. You are not safe. I would deal even with you.

MALHEUREUX: So!

(*They exchange gloves as pledges.*)

FREEVILL: So!

10 BEATRICE: I do beseech you sweet, do not for me provoke your fortune.

SIR LIONEL: What sudden flaw is risen?

SIR HUBERT: From whence comes this?

FREEVILL: An ulcer long time lurking now is burst.

SIR HUBERT: Good sir, the time and your designs are soft.

BEATRICE: Ay, dear sir, counsel him, advise him; 'twill relish well from your carving. – Good my sweet, rest safe.

FREEVILL: All's well, all's well; this shall be ended straight.

SIR HUBERT: The banquet stays; there we'll discourse more large.

20 FREEVILL: Marriage must not make men cowards.

---

5. *Rank handsomely*: arrange yourselves elegantly for dance.
7. *even*: fairly.
17. *straight*: straight away.

SIR LIONEL: Nor rage fools.   20

SIR HUBERT: 'Tis valour not where heat, but reason rules.

> ([*Exeunt.*] *Only* TYSEFEW *and* CRISPINELLA *stay.*)

TYSEFEW: But do you hear lady, you proud ape, you,
What was the jest you brake of me even now?

CRISPINELLA: Nothing; I only said you were all mettle, that
you had a brazen face, a leaden brain and a copper beard.

TYSEFEW: Quicksilver! Thou little more than a dwarf and
something less than a woman!

CRISPINELLA: A wisp, a wisp, a wisp! Will you go to the
banquet?

TYSEFEW: By the Lord I think thou wilt marry shortly too;   30
thou growest somewhat foolish already.

CRISPINELLA: O i' faith, 'tis a fair thing to be married, and a
necessary. To hear this word 'must'! If our husbands be
proud we must bear his contempt, if noisome we must bear
with the goat under his armholes, if a fool we must bear his
babble, and which is worse, if a loose liver, we must live upon
unwholesome reversions. Where, on the contrary side, our
husbands, because they *may* and we *must*, care not for us.
Things hop'd with fear and got with strugglings are men's
high pleasures, when duty pales and flats their appetite.   40

TYSEFEW: What a tart monkey is this! By heaven, if thou hadst
not so much wit I could find in my heart to marry thee. Faith,
bear with me for all this.

CRISPINELLA: Bear with thee! I wonder how thy mother could
bear thee ten months in her belly, when I cannot endure thee
two hours in mine eye.

TYSEFEW: Alas for you, sweet soul! By the Lord you are grown
a proud, scurvy, apish, idle, disdainful, scoffing – God's foot!
because you have read *Euphues and his England, Palmerin de
Oliva,* and the *Legend of Lies*!   50

CRISPINELLA: Why, i' faith; yet, servant, you of all others
should bear with my known unmalicious humours. I have

---

28. *wisp*: ? cf. proverbial expression, 'as wise as a wisp' (Wine).

36. *babble*: (i) childish prattle, (ii) fool's sceptre (bauble, often spelt
'bable').

40. *pales*: weakens.

always in my heart given you your due respect; and heaven may be sworn, I have privately given fair speech of you, and protested –

TYSEFEW: Nay look you, for my own part, if I have not as religiously vow'd my heart to you, been drunk to your health, swallow'd flap-dragons, ate glasses, drunk urine, stabb'd arms and done all the offices of protested gallantry for your sake!
60 And yet you tell me I have a brazen face, a leaden brain and a copper beard! Come yet, an it please you.

CRISPINELLA: No, no, you do not love me!

TYSEFEW: By – but I do now, and whosoever dares say that I do not love you, nay honour you, and if you would vouchsafe to marry –

CRISPINELLA: Nay, as for that, think on't as you will, but God's my record – and my sister knows I have taken drink and slept upon't – that if ever I marry it shall be you – and I will marry – and yet I hope I do not say it shall be you
70 neither.

TYSEFEW: By heaven I shall be as soon weary of health as of your enjoying. Will you cast a smooth cheek upon me?

CRISPINELLA: I cannot tell; I have no crump'd shoulders, my back needs no mantle, and yet marriage is honourable. Do you think ye shall prove a cuckold?

TYSEFEW: No, by the Lord, not I!

CRISPINELLA: Why, I thank you, i' faith. Heigh ho! I slept on my back this morning and dreamt the strangest dreams. Good Lord, how things will come to pass! Will you go to the
80 banquet?

TYSEFEW: If you will be mine, you shall be your own. My purse, my body, my heart is yours; only be silent in my house, modest at my table, and wanton in my bed, and the Empress of Europe cannot content, and shall not be contented, better.

CRISPINELLA: Can any kind heart speak more discreetly affectionately! My father's consent, and as for mine –

58. *flap-dragons*: resins in flaming brandy.
58. *stabb'd arms*: i.e. to obtain blood to mix with wine.
73. *crump'd*: curved.
74. *back ... mantle*: to conceal hump.

TYSEFEW [*kissing her*]: Then thus, and thus, so Hymen should
begin,
Sometimes a falling out proves falling in.
[*Exeunt.*]

[SCENE TWO]

(*Enter* FREEVILL, *speaking to some within;* MALHEUREUX
at the other door.)

FREEVILL: As you respect my virtue, give me leave
To satisfy my reason, though not blood:
So, all runs right; our feigned rage hath ta'en
To fullest life; they are much possess'd
Of force most, most all quarrel. Now, my right friend,
Resolve me with open breast, free and true heart;
Cannot thy virtue, having space to think
And fortify her weakened powers with reason,
Discourses, meditations, discipline,
Divine ejaculatories, and all those aids against devils,   10
Cannot all these curb thy low appetite
And sensual fury?
MALHEUREUX: There is no God in blood, no reason in desire.
Shall I but live? Shall I not be forc'd to act
Some deed whose very name is hideous?
FREEVILL: No.
MALHEUREUX: Then I must enjoy Franceschina.
FREEVILL: You shall:
I'll lend this ring; show it to that fair devil,
It will resolve me dead;
Which rumour, with my artificial absence,   20
Will make most firm. Enjoy her suddenly!
MALHEUREUX: But if report go strong that you are slain,
And that by me, whereon I may be seiz'd,
Where shall I find your being?

> 87. *Hymen*: Greek god of marriage (hence marriage itself).
> 3-4. *ta'en . . . life*: succeeded completely.
> 10. *ejaculatories*: ejaculations, short prayers.
> 21. *suddenly*: at once.

FREEVILL: At Master Shatewe's the jeweller's, to whose breast
    I'll trust our secret purpose.

MALHEUREUX: Ay, rest yourself;
    Each man hath follies.

FREEVILL: But those worst of all,
    Who with a willing eye do, seeing, fall.

MALHEUREUX: 'Tis true, but truth seems folly in madness'
30   spectacles.
    I am not now myself, no man. Farewell.

FREEVILL: Farewell.

MALHEUREUX: When woman's in the heart, in the soul hell.
    (*Exit* MALHEUREUX.)

FREEVILL: Now repentance, the fool's whip, seize thee!
    Nay, if there be no means I'll be thy friend,
    But not thy vice's; and with greatest sense
    I'll force thee feel thy errors to the worst.
    The vildest of dangers thou shalt sink into.
    No jeweller shall see me; I will lurk
    Where none shall know or think; close I'll withdraw,
40   And leave thee with two friends, a whore and knave.
    But is this virtue in me? No, not pure;
    – Nothing extremely best with us endures –
    No use in simple purities; the elements
    Are mix'd for use. Silver without alloy
    Is all too eager to be wrought for use:
    Nor precise virtues ever purely good
    Holds useful size with temper of weak blood.
    Then let my course be borne, tho' with side-wind,
    The end being good, the means are well assign'd. (*Exit.*)

> 37. *vildest*: vilest.
> 45. *eager*: imperfectly tempered (*O.E.D.*).
> 46. *precise*: (i) rigid, (ii) Puritanical.

[SCENE THREE]

(*Enter* FRANCESCHINA *melancholy*, COCLEDEMOY *leading her.*)

COCLEDEMOY: Come catafugo Frank o' Frank Hall! Ho, ho, ho!
  Excellent! Ha, here's a plump-rump'd wench, with a breast
  Softer than a courtier's tongue, an old lady's gums,
  Or an old man's *mentula*. My fine rogue –

FRANCESCHINA: Pah, you poltroon!

COCLEDEMOY: Goody fist, flumpum pumpum! Ah, my fine
  wagtail,
  Thou art as false, as prostituted and adulcerate
  As some translated manuscript. Buss, fair whore, buss!

FRANCESCHINA: God's sacrament! Pox!

COCLEDEMOY: *Hadamoy key,* dost thou frown *medianthon
  teukey?*
  Nay look here: *Numeron key* silver *blithefor cany os cany*
  goblet: 10
  Us key ne moy blegefoy oteeston, pox on you, gosling!

FRANCESCHINA: By me fait, dis bin very fine langage. Ick
  sall bush ye now! Ha, be garzon, vare had you dat plate?

COCLEDEMOY: *Hedemoy key,* get you gone, punk rampant, *key,*
  common up-tail!

  (*Enter* MARY FAUGH, *in haste.*)

MARY FAUGH: O daughter, cousin, niece, servant, mistress!

COCLEDEMOY: Humpum, plumpum squat, I am gone!

  (*Exit* COCLEDEMOY.)

MARY FAUGH: There is one Master Malheureux at the door
  desires to see you; he says he must not be denied, for he hath
  sent you this ring and withal says 'tis done.   20

FRANCESCHINA: Vat sall me do now, God's sacrament! Tell
  him two hours hence he sall be most affectionately velcome.
  Tell him (vat sall me do?) tel him ick am bin in my bate, and

---

1. *catafugo*: cacafuego; Lat. *cacare*, to defecate, and Spanish *fuego*, fire.
3. *mentula*: Lat. 'penis'.
7. *translated*: ? transported (across Channel, hence Catholic).
15. *common up-tail*: i.e. whore.

ick sall perfume my feets, mak-a mine body so delicate for his arm, two hours hence.

MARY FAUGH: I shall satisfy him; two hours hence, well.

(*Exit* MARY FAUGH.)

FRANCESCHINA: Now ick sall revange! Hay, begar, me sal tartar de whole generation! Mine brain vork it. Frevill is daad, Malheureux sall hang, and mine rival Beatrice, ick sall
30 make run mad.

([*Re-*]*enter* MARY FAUGH.)

MARY FAUGH: He's gone, forsooth, to eat a caudle of cock-stones, and will return within this two hours.

FRANCESCHINA: Very vel. Give monies to some fellow to squire me. Ick sall go abroad.

MARY FAUGH: There's a lusty bravo beneath; a stranger, but a good stale rascal; he swears valiantly, kicks a bawd right virtuously, and protests with an empty pocket right desperately. He'll squire you.

FRANCESCHINA: Very velcome. Mine fan; ick sall retorn
40 presently.

[*Exit* MARY FAUGH.]

Now sal me be revange Ten tousant devla! Der sall be no Got in me but passion, no tought but rage, no mercy but blood, no spirit but Divla in me. Dere sal noting tought good for me, but dat is mischievous for others. (*Exit.*)

[SCENE FOUR]

(*Enter* SIR HUBERT, SIR LIONEL, BEATRICE, CRISPINELLA, *and* NURSE, TYSEFEW *following*.)

SIR LIONEL: Did no one see him since? Pray God – nay, all is well. A little heat, what? He is but withdrawn? And yet I would to God – But fear you nothing.

---

28. *tartar*: torture.
31-2. *cock-stones*: kidney beans, an aphrodisiac.
35. *stranger*: foreigner.
36. *stale*: ? experienced.

BEATRICE: Pray God that all be well, or would I were not!

TYSEFEW: He's not to be found, sir, anywhere.

SIR LIONEL: You must not make a heavy face presage an ill
event. I like your sister well; she's quick and lively. Would
she would marry, faith.

CRISPINELLA: Marry! Nay, an I would marry – methinks an
old man's a quiet thing.   10

SIR LIONEL: Ha, Mass, and so he is.

CRISPINELLA: You are a widower.

SIR LIONEL: That I am, i' faith, fair Crisp; and I can tell you,
would you affect me, I have it in me yet, i' faith.

CRISPINELLA: Troth, I am in love. Let me see your hand.
Would you cast yourself away upon me willingly?

SIR LIONEL: Will I? Ay, by the –

CRISPINELLA: Would you be a cuckold willingly? By my troth,
'tis a comely, fine, and handsome sight for one of my years
to marry an old man; truth, 'tis restorative. What a com-   20
fortable thing it is to think of her husband, to hear his
venerable cough o' the everlastings, to feel his rough skin, his
summer hands and winter legs, his almost no eyes, and
assuredly no teeth! And then to think what she must dream
of, when she considers others' happiness and her own want!
'Tis a worthy and notorious comfortable match.

SIR LIONEL: Pish, pish! Will you have me?

CRISPINELLA: Will you assure me –

SIR LIONEL: Five-hundred pound jointure.

CRISPINELLA: That you will die within this fortnight?   30

SIR LIONEL: No, by my faith, Cris[p].

CRISPINELLA: Then Crisp, by her faith, assures you she'll have
none of you.

(*Enter* FREEVILL *disguised like a pander, and* FRANCES-
CHINA.)

FREEVILL: By'r leave, gentles and men of nightcaps, I would
speak, but that here stands one is able to express her own tale
best.

FRANCESCHINA: Sir, mine speech is to you; you had a son,
Matre Freevill?

SIR LIONEL: Had? Ha, and have.

40 FRANCESCHINA: No, point; me am come to assure you dat one
Mestre Malheureux hath killed him.

BEATRICE: O me! Wretched, wretched!

SIR HUBERT: Look to our daughter.

SIR LIONEL: How art thou informed?

FRANCESCHINA: If dat it please you to go vid me, ick sall bring
you where you sall hear Malheureux vid his own lips confess
it; and dere ye may apprehend him, and revenge your and
mine love's blood.

SIR HUBERT: Your love's blood, mistress? Was he your love?

50 FRANCESCHINA: He was so, sir. Let your daughter hear it. Do
not veep, lady, de yong man dat be slain did not love you, for
he still lovit me ten tousant tousant times more dearly.

BEATRICE: O my heart! I will love you the better; I cannot hate
what he affected. O passion! O my grief! Which way wilt
break, think and consume?

CRISPINELLA: Peace!

BEATRICE: Dear woes cannot speak.

FRANCESCHINA: For look you, lady, dis your ring he gave me,
vid most bitter jests at your scorn'd kindness.

60 BEATRICE: He did not ill not to love me, but sure he did not
well to mock me: gentle minds will pity though they cannot
love. Yet peace, and my love sleep with him! – Unlace, good
nurse. – Alas, I was not so ambitious of so supreme an happiness that he should only love me; 'twas joy enough for me,
poor soul, that I might only love him.

FRANCESCHINA: O, but to be abus'd, scorn'd, scoff'd at! O,
ten tousand divla, by such a one, and unto such a one!

BEATRICE: I think you say not true. Sister, shall we know one
another in the other world?

70 CRISPINELLA: What means my sister?

BEATRICE: I would fain see him again. O my tortur'd mind!
Freevill is more than dead, he is unkind.

([*Exeunt*] BEATRICE *and* CRISPINELLA *and* NURSE.)

SIR HUBERT: Convey her in, and so, sir, as you said,
Set a strong watch.

SIR LIONEL:　　　　Ay, sir, and so pass along

40. *No, point*: not at all.

With this same common woman.

[*To* FRANCESCHINA] You must make it good.

FRANCESCHINA: Ick sall, or let me pay for his mine blood.

SIR HUBERT: Come then, along all, with quiet speed.

SIR LIONEL: O Fate!

TYSEFEW: O sir, be wisely sorry, but not passionate.

(*Exeunt.*] FREEVILL [*remains.*])

FREEVILL: I will go and reveal myself. Stay! No, no,
  Grief endears love. Heaven! To have such a wife   80
  Is happiness to breed pale envy in the saints.
  Thou worthy dove-like virgin without gall,
  Cannot (that woman's evil) jealousy,
  Despite disgrace, nay which is worst, contempt,
  Once stir thy faith? O Truth, how few sisters hast thou!
  Dear memory, with what a suff'ring sweetness, quiet modesty,
  Yet deep affection she receiv'd my death,
  And then with what a patient, yet oppressed kindness
  She took my lewdly intimated wrongs! O, the dearest of
    heaven!
  Were there but three such women in the world,   90
  Two might be saved. Well, I am great
  With expectation to what devilish end
  This woman of foul soul will drive her plots:
  But providence all wicked art o'er-tops.
  And impudence must know, tho' stiff as ice,
  That fortune doth not alway dote on vice. (*Exit.*)

[SCENE FIVE]

(*Enter* SIR HUBERT, SIR LIONEL, TYSEFEW, FRAN-
CESCHINA *and three with halberds.*)

SIR HUBERT: Plant a watch there. Be very careful, sirs; the rest
  with us.

TYSEFEW: The heavy night grows to her depth of quiet; 'tis
  about mid-darkness.

---

78. *passionate*: excessively moved.
89. *lewdly*: ignorantly.

FRANCESCHINA: Mine shambre is hard by. Ick sall bring you to it presantment.

SIR LIONEL: Deep silence! On.

(*Exeunt.*)

COCLEDEMOY (*within*): Wa, ha, ho!

(*Enter* MULLIGRUB.)

MULLIGRUB: It was his voice; 'tis he. He sups with his cupping-
10   glasses. 'Tis late; he must pass this way. I'll ha' him, I'll ha' my fine boy, my worshipful Cocledemoy. I'll moy him! He shall be hang'd in lousy linen. I'll hire some sectary to make him an heretic before he die. And when he is dead, I'll piss on his grave.

(*Enter* COCLEDEMOY.)

COCLEDEMOY: Ah, my fine punks, good night. Frank Frailty, Frail o' Frail Hall, *Bonus noches*, my *ubiquitari*!

MULLIGRUB: 'Ware polling and shaving, sir!

COCLEDEMOY: A wolf, a wolf, a wolf!

(*Exit* COCLEDEMOY, *leaving his cloak behind him.*)

MULLIGRUB: Here's something yet! A cloak, a cloak! Yet I'll
20   after, he cannot 'scape the watch. I'll hang him if I have any mercy! I'll slice him! (*Exit.*)

([*Re-*]*enter* COCLEDEMOY [*and Constables.*])

1 CONSTABLE: Who goes there? Come before the constable.

COCLEDEMOY: Bread o' God, constable, you are a watch for the devil! Honest men are robb'd under your nose. There's a false knave in the habit of a vintner set upon me; he would have had my purse, but I took me to my heels. Yet he got my cloak – a plain stuff cloak, poor, yet 'twill serve to hang him. 'Tis my loss, poor man that I am! (*Exit.*)

2 CONSTABLE: Masters, we must watch better. Is't not strange
30   that knaves, drunkards and thieves should be abroad, and yet we of the watch, scriveners, smiths, and tailors, never stir?

([*Re-*]*enter* MULLIGRUB *running, with* COCLEDEMOY'S *cloak.*)

9–10. *cupping-glasses*: vessels used in drawing blood – here, drinking glasses.

16. *ubiquitari*: people found everywhere, gadabouts.

2 CONSTABLE: Hark, who goes there?

MULLIGRUB: An honest man and a citizen.

2 CONSTABLE: Appear, appear. What are you?

MULLIGRUB: A simple vintner.

1 CONSTABLE: A vintner ha? and simple? Draw nearer, nearer. Here's the cloak!

2 CONSTABLE: Ay, Master Vintner, we know you. A plain stuff cloak – 'tis it.   40

1 CONSTABLE: Right, come! Oh thou varlet, dost not thou know that the wicked cannot 'scape the eyes of the constable?

MULLIGRUB: What means this violence? As I am an honest man I took the cloak –

1 CONSTABLE: As you are a knave you took the cloak. We are your witnesses for that.

MULLIGRUB: But hear me, hear me! I'll tell you what I am.

2 CONSTABLE: A thief you are.

MULLIGRUB: I tell you, my name is Mulligrub.

1 CONSTABLE: I will grub you. In with him to the stocks! There   50 let him sit till tomorrow morning that Justice Quodlibet may examine him.

MULLIGRUB: Why, but I tell thee –

2 CONSTABLE: Why but I tell thee, we'll tell thee now.
    [*They put him in stocks.*]

MULLIGRUB: Am I not mad, am I not an ass? Why, scabs, God's foot, let me out!

2 CONSTABLE: Ay, ay, let him prate, he shall find matter in us scabs, I warrant. God's-so, what good members of the commonwealth do we prove!

1 CONSTABLE: Prithee, peace, let's remember our duties, and   60 let go sleep, in the fear of God.
    (*Exeunt, having left* MULLIGRUB *in the stocks.*)

MULLIGRUB: Who goes there? Illo, ho, ho! Zounds, shall I run mad, lose my wits? Shall I be hang'd? Hark, who goes there? Do not fear to be poor, Mulligrub, thou hast a sure stock now.

51. *Quodlibet*: lit. 'wherever you please'; term for scholastic debate.
64. *stock*: (i) store, (ii) stocks (for prisoners).

93

([*Re-*]*enter* COCLEDEMOY *like a bellman.*)

COCLEDEMOY: The night grows old,
And many a cuckold
Is now – Wha, ha, ha, ho!
Maids on their backs
70   Dream of sweet smacks,
And warm – Wo, ho, ho, ho!

I must go comfort my venerable Mulligrub; I must fiddle him
till he fist. Fough!

Maids in your night-rails,
Look well to your light –
Keep close your locks,
And down your smocks,
Keep a broad eye,
And a close thigh.

80 Excellent, excellent! Who's there? Now Lord, Lord Master
Mulligrub! Deliver us! What does your worship in the stocks?
I pray come out, sir.

MULLIGRUB: Zounds, man, I tell thee I am lock'd!

COCLEDEMOY: Lock'd? O world! O men! O time! O night!
that canst not discern virtue and wisdom, and one of the
Common Council! What is your worship in for?

MULLIGRUB: For – a plague on't! – suspicion of felony.

COCLEDEMOY: Nay, an it be but such a trifle, Lord, I could
weep to see your good worship in this taking. Your worship
90   has been a good friend to me, and tho' you have forgot me,
yet I knew your wife before she was married, and since; I
have found your worship's door open and I have knock'd,
and God knows what I have saved; and do I live to see your
worship stock'd?

MULLIGRUB: Honest bellman, I perceive thou knowst me. I
prithee call the Watch. Inform the constable of my reputation,
that I may no longer abide in this shameful habitation, and
hold thee all I have about me.

(*Gives him his purse.*)

Stage direction. *bellman*: night watchman.
74. *night-rails*: night gowns.
94. *stock'd*: put in stocks.

COCLEDEMOY: 'Tis more than I deserve, sir. Let me alone for
your delivery.   100

MULLIGRUB: Do, and then let me alone with Cocledemoy. I'll
moy him!

COCLEDEMOY: Maids in your –
  [*Re-enter Constables.*]
  Master Constable, whose that i' th' stocks?

1 CONSTABLE: One for a robbery; one Mulligrub, he calls
himself. Mulligrub? Bellman, know'st thou him?

COCLEDEMOY: Know him? O master Constable, what good
service have you done! Know him? He's a strong thief; his
house has been suspected for a bawdy tavern a great while,
and a receipt for cut-purses, 'tis most certain. He has been   110
long in the black book; and is he ta'en now?

2 CONSTABLE: By'r Lady, my masters, we'll not trust the stocks
with him. We'll have him to the justices, get a *mittimus* to
Newgate presently. Come sir, come on sir!

MULLIGRUB: Ha! Does your rascalship yet know my worship
in the end?

1 CONSTABLE: Ay, the end of your worship we know.

MULLIGRUB: Ha, goodman constable, here's an honest fellow
can tell you what I am.

2 CONSTABLE: 'Tis true sir; y'are a strong thief, he says on his 120
own knowledge. Bind fast, bind fast. We know you. We'll
trust no stocks with you. Away with him to the jail instantly!

MULLIGRUB: Why, but dost hear? Bellman! Rogue! Rascal!
God's – why, but –
  (*The constable drags away* MULLIGRUB.)

COCLEDEMOY: Why, but! Wha, ha, ha, excellent, excellent!
Ha, my fine Cocledemoy, my vintner fists! I'll make him fart
crackers before I ha' done with him; tomorrow is the day of
judgement. Afore the Lord God, my knavery grows unperegal!
'Tis time to take a nap, until half an hour hence: God give   130
your worship music, content, and rest.
  (*Exeunt.*)

----

99. *Let me alone*: rely on me.
110. *receipt*: receiving place.
113. *mittimus*: J.P.'s warrant for commitment.
128. *unperegal*: without equal.

ACT FIVE

SCENE ONE

(*Enter* FRANCESCHINA, SIR LIONEL, TYSEFEW, [FREE-VILL *in disguise*] *with Officers.*)

FRANCESCHINA: You bin very velcom to mine shambra.

SIR LIONEL: But how know ye, how are ye assur'd both of the deed and of his sure return?

FRANCESCHINA: O mynheer, ick sall tell you. Mettre Mal-heureux came all breatless running a' my shambra, his sword all bloody: he tell-a me he had kill Freevill, and pray'd-a me to conceal him. Ick flatter him, bid bring monies, he should live and lie vid me. He went whilst ick (me hope vidout sins) out of mine mush love to Freevill betray him.

10 SIR LIONEL: Fear not, 'tis well: good works get grace for sin.
    (*She conceals them behind the curtain.*)

FRANCESCHINA: Dere, peace, rest dere; so softly, all go in.
    [*Aside*] De net is lay, now sall ick be revenge.
    If dat me knew a dog dat Freevill love,
    Me would puisson him; for know de deepest hell
    As a revenging woman's naught so fell.
    (*Enter* MARY FAUGH.)

MARY FAUGH: Ho, Cousin Frank, the party you wot of, Master Malheureux.

FRANCESCHINA: Bid him come up, I pride.
    (*She sings and dances to cittern.*)
    (*Enter* MALHEUREUX.)

FRANCESCHINA: O mynheer man, aderliver love,
20 Mine ten tousant times velcom love!
    Ha, by mine trat, you bin de just – vat sall me say?
    Vat seet honey name sall I call you?

MALHEUREUX: Any from you is pleasure. Come, my loving prettiness,

15. *fell*: terrible.

96

Where's thy chamber? I long to touch your sheets.

FRANCESCHINA: No, no, not yet, mine seetest soft-lipped love:
You sall not gulp down all delights at once.
Be min trat, dis all-fles-lovers, dis ravenous wenchers
Dat sallow all down whole, vill have all at one bit!
Fie, fie, fie! Be min fait, dey do eat comfits vid spoons.
No, no, I'll make you chew your pleasure vit love,   30
De more degrees and steps, de more delight,
De more endeared is de pleasure height.

MALHEUREUX: What, you're a learned wanton, and proceed by art?

FRANCESCHINA: Go, little vag! Pleasure should have a crane's long neck,
To relish de Ambrosia of delight.
And ick pridee tell me, for me loves to hear
Of manhood very mush, i' fait: Ick pridee –
Vat vas me a-saying – Oh, ick pridee tell-a me
How did you kill a Mettre Freevill?

MALHEUREUX: Why, quarrel'd o' set purpose, drew him out,   40
Singled him, and having th' advantage of my sword and might,
Ran him through and through.

FRANCESCHINA: Vat did you vid him van he was sticken?

MALHEUREUX: I dragg'd him by the heels to the next wharf
And spurn'd him in the river.

(*Those in ambush rusheth forth and take him.*)

SIR LIONEL: Seize, seize him! O monstrous! O ruthless villain!

MALHEUREUX: What mean you gentlemen? By heaven –

TYSEFEW: Speak not of anything that's good.

MALHEUREUX: Your errors gives you passion: Freevill lives.

SIR LIONEL: Thy own lips say thou liest.

MALHEUREUX: Let me die,   50
If at Shatewe's the jeweller he lives not safe untouch'd.

TYSEFEW: Meantime to strictest guard, to sharpest prison.

MALHEUREUX: No rudeness, gentlemen: I'll go undragg'd.
O wicked, wicked devil! (*Exit [guarded].*)

SIR LIONEL: Sir, the day
Of trial is this morn. Let's prosecute

29. *comfits*: sweetmeats.

The sharpest rigour, and severest end:
Good men are cruel, when they're vice's friend.

SIR HUBERT: Woman, we thank thee with no empty hand.
[*Gives money.*]
Strumpets are fit – fit for something. Farewell.
(*All save* FREEVILL *depart.*)

60 FREEVILL: Ay, for hell! O thou unreprievable, beyond all
Measure of grace damn'd immediately!
That things of beauty created for sweet use,
Soft comfort, and as the very music of life,
Custom should make so unutterably hellish!
O heaven, what difference is in women and their life!
What man, but worthy name of man, would leave
The modest pleasures of a lawful bed,
The holy union of two equal hearts
Mutually holding either dear as health,
70 The undoubted issues, joys of chaste sheets,
The unfeigned embrace of sober ignorance,
To twine the unhealthful loins of common loves,
The prostituted impudence of things.
Senseless like those by cataracts of Nile,
Their use so vile takes away sense! How vile
To love a creature made of blood and hell,
Whose use makes weak, whose company doth shame,
Whose bed doth beggar, issue doth defame!
(*Enter* FRANCESCHINA.)

FRANCESCHINA: Mettre Freevill live! Ha, ha! Live at Mestre
80 Shatewe's! Mush at Mettre Shatewe's! Freevill is dead; Malheureux sall hang. And sweet divel, dat Beatrice would but
run mad, dat she would but run mad, den me would dance and
sing. [*To* FREEVILL] Mettre Don Dubon, me pray ye now, go
to Mestress Beatrice, tell her Freevill is sure dead, and dat he
curse herself especially, for dat he was sticked in her quarrel,
swearing in his last gasp, dat if it had bin in mine quarrels,
'twould never have grieved him.

FREEVILL: I will.

FRANCESCHINA: Pridee do, and say anyting dat vil vex her.

90 FREEVILL: Let me alone to vex her.

FRANCESCHINA: Vill you? Vill you mak-a her run mad? Here, take dis ring; see me scorn to wear anyting dat was hers, or his: I pridee torment her. Ick cannot love her; she honest and virtuous, forsooth!

FREEVILL: Is she so? O vile creature! Then let me alone with her.

FRANCESCHINA: Vat, vill you mak-a her mad? Seet, by min trat, be pretta servan! Bush! Ick sall go to bet now. [Exit.]

FREEVILL: Mischief, whither wilt thou?
O thou tearless woman!   100
How monstrous is thy devil!
The end of hell as thee. How miserable
Were it to be virtuous, if thou couldst prosper?
I'll to my love, the faithful Beatrice,
She has wept enough, and faith, dear soul, too much.
But yet how sweet it is to think how dear
One's life was to his love: how mourn'd his death!
'Tis joy not to be express'd with breath.
But, O, let him that would such passion drink
Be quiet of his speech, and only think. (Exit.)   110

[SCENE TWO]

(Enter BEATRICE and CRISPINELLA.)

BEATRICE: Sister, cannot a woman kill herself? Is it not lawful to die when we should not live?

CRISPINELLA: O sister, 'tis a question not for us; we must do what God will.

BEATRICE: What God will? Alas, can torment be his glory, or our grief his pleasure? Does not the nurse's nipple, juic'd over with wormwood, bid the child it should not suck? And does not heaven, when it hath made our breath bitter unto us, say we should not live? O my best sister,
To suffer wounds when one may 'scape this rod   10
Is against nature, that is against God.

98. *Bush!*: ? Buss! = Kiss!

CRISPINELLA: Good sister, do not make me weep. Sure, Free-
    vill was not false:
  I'll gage my life that strumpet, out of craft
  And some close second end, hath malic'd him.
BEATRICE: O sister, if he were not false, whom have I lost!
  If he were, what grief to such unkindness!
  From head to foot I am all misery;
  Only in this, some justice I have found:
  My grief is like my love, beyond all bound.
    (*Enter* NURSE [PUTIFER.])
20 PUTIFER: My servant, Master Caqueteur, desires to visit you.
CRISPINELLA: For grief's sake, keep him out! His discourse is
  like the long word, Honorificabilitudinitatibus; a great deal of
  sound and no sense. His company is like a parenthesis to a
  discourse: you may admit it, or leave it out, it makes no
  matter.
    (*Enter* FREEVILL *in his* [*disguise.*])
FREEVILL: By your leave, sweet creatures.
CRISPINELLA: Sir, all I can yet say of you, is, you are uncivil.
FREEVILL: You must deny it. [*To* BEATRICE] By your sorrow's
  leave,
  I bring some music to make sweet your grief.
30 BEATRICE: Whate'er you please. O break, my heart!
  Canst thou yet pant? O, dost thou yet survive?
  Thou didst not love him, if thou now canst live.
FREEVILL [*sings*]: O Love, how strangely sweet
          Are thy weak passions,
      That love and joy should meet
          In selfsame fashions.
      O who can tell
          The cause why this should move?
      But only this,
40   No reason ask of Love!
  [BEATRICE *swoons.*]
CRISPINELLA: Hold, peace, the gentlest soul is swooned! O my
  best sister!

---

22. *Honorificabilitudinitatibus*: from Lat. 'honourableness' (cf. *Love's
Labour's Lost*, V, ii.)

FREEVILL: Ha, get you gone! Close the doors. My Beatrice!
    (*Discovers himself.*)
  Curs'd be my indiscreet trials. O my immeasurably loving!

CRISPINELLA: She stirs; give air, she breathes!

BEATRICE: Where am I, ha? How have I slipp'd off life?
  Am I in heaven? O my Lord, though not loving,
  By our eternal being, yet give me leave
  To rest by this dear side. Am I not in heaven?

FREEVILL: O eternally much loved, recollect your spirits.   50

BEATRICE: Ha, you do speak, I do see you, I do live!
  I would not die now: let me not burst with wonder.

FREEVILL: Call up your blood; I live to honour you,
  As the admired glory of your sex.
  Nor ever hath my love been false to you –
  Only I presum'd to try your faith too much,
  For which I most am grieved.

CRISPINELLA: Brother, I must be plain with you; you have
    wrong'd us.

FREEVILL: I am not so covetous to deny it;   60
  But yet, when my discourse hath stay'd your quaking,
  You will be smoother-lipp'd; and the delight
  And satisfaction which we all have got
  Under these strange disguisings, when you know,
  You will be mild and quiet, forget at last.
  It is much joy to think on sorrows past.

BEATRICE: Do you then live? And are you not untrue?
  Let me not die with joy! Pleasure's more extreme
  Than grief; there's nothing sweet to man but mean.

FREEVILL: Heaven cannot be too gracious to such goodness. I   70
shall discourse to you the several chances, but hark I must yet
rest disguis'd.
  The sudden close of many drifts now meet;
  Where pleasure hath some profit, art is sweet.
    (*Enter* TYSEFEW.)

TYSEFEW: News, news, news, news!

CRISPINELLA: Oysters, oysters, oysters, oysters!

69. *mean*: moderation.
73. *drifts*: plots.

TYSEFEW: Why, is not this well now? Is not this better than
louring and pouting and puling, which is hateful to the living,
and vain to the dead? Come, come, you must live by the quick,
80   when all is done; and for my own part, let my wife laugh at
me when I am dead, so she'll smile upon me whilst I live. But
to see a woman whine, and yet keep her eyes dry; mourn, and
yet keep her cheeks fat; nay, to see a woman claw her husband
by the feet when he is dead, that would have scratch'd him by
the face when he was living – this now is somewhat ridiculous.

CRISPINELLA: Lord, how you prate!

TYSEFEW: And yet I was afraid, i' faith, that I should ha' seen
a garland on this beauty's hearse; but time, truth, experience,
and variety are great doers with women.

90 CRISPINELLA: But what's the news? The news, I pray you.

TYSEFEW: I pray you? Ne'er pray me, for by your leave, you
may command me. This 'tis:
The public sessions which this day is past,
Hath doom'd to death ill-fortun'd Malheureux.

CRISPINELLA: But sir, we heard he offer'd to make good
That Freevill liv'd at Shatewe's the jeweller's.

BEATRICE: And that 'twas but a plot betwixt them two.

TYSEFEW: O, ay, ay, he gag'd his life with it; but know,
When all approach'd the test, Shatewe denied
100   He saw or heard of any such complot,
Or of Freevill; so that his own defence,
Appear'd so false that, like a madman's sword,
He struck his own heart. He hath the course of law
And instantly must suffer: but the jest –
If hanging be a jest, as many make it –
Is to take notice of one Mulligrub, a sharking vintner.

FREEVILL: What of him, sir?

TYSEFEW: Nothing but hanging. The whoreson slave is mad
before he hath lost his senses.

110 FREEVILL: Was his fact clear and made apparent, sir?

TYSEFEW: No, faith, suspicions; for 'twas thus protested:
A cloak was stol'n, that cloak he had; he had it

94. *ill-fortun'd*: i.e. Fr. 'Malheureux'.
110. *fact*: crime.

Himself confess'd by force. The rest of his defence
The choler of a justice wrong'd in wine,
Join'd with malignance of some hasty jurors,
Whose wit was lighted by the justice' nose. The knave was
    cast;
But Lord, to hear his moan, his prayers, his wishes,
His zeal ill-tim'd and his words unpitied,
Would make a dead man rise and smile,
Whilst he observed how fear can make men vile.   120
CRISPINELLA: Shall we go meet the execution?
BEATRICE: I shall be rul'd by you.
TYSEFEW: By my troth, a rare motion. You must haste,
For malefactors goes like the world upon wheels.
BEATRICE: Will you man us? [*To* FREEVILL.] You shall be our
    guide.
FREEVILL: I am your servant.
TYSEFEW: Ha, servant? Zounds, I am no companion for pan-
    ders! You're best make him your love.
BEATRICE: So will I, sir; we must live by the quick, you say.   130
TYSEFEW: 'Sdeath o' virtue! What a damn'd thing's this?
Who'll trust fair faces, tears, and vows? 'Sdeath, not I,
She is a woman, that is, she can lie.
CRISPINELLA: Come, come, turn not a man of time, to make
    all ill,
Whose goodness you conceive not, since the worst of chance
Is to crave grace for heedless ignorance.
    (*Exeunt.*)

[SCENE THREE]

(*Enter* COCLEDEMOY *like a Sergeant.*)
COCLEDEMOY: So, I ha' lost my sergeant in an ecliptic mist.
Drunk, horrible drunk. He is fine; so now will I fit myself.
I hope this habit will do me no harm. I am an honest man
already. Fit, fit, fit as a punk's tail, that serves everybody. By

        123. *motion*: (i) proposal, (ii) movement.
        125. *man*: escort.
        1. *ecliptic*: obscuring.

this time my vintner thinks of nothing but hell and sulphur;
he farts fire and brimstone already. Hang toasts! The execution approacheth.

 (*Enter* SIR LIONEL, SIR HUBERT, MALHEUREUX *pinioned,*
 TYSEFEW, BEATRICE, FREEVILL, CRISPINELLA, FRAN-
 CESCHINA, *and* [*officers with*] *halberds.*)

MALHEUREUX: I do not blush, although condemn'd by laws.
 No kind of death is shameful but the cause,
10 Which I do know is none. And yet my lust
 Hath made the one (although not cause) most just.
 May I not be reprieved? Freevill is but mislodg'd,
 Some lethargy hath seiz'd him – no, much malice.
 Do not lay blood upon your souls with good intents,
 Men may do ill and law sometime repents.

 (COCLEDEMOY *picks* MALHEUREUX'S *pocket of his purse.*)

SIR LIONEL: Sir, sir, prepare; vain is all lewd defence.
MALHEUREUX: Conscience was law, but now law's conscience.
 My endless peace is made, and to the poor –
 My purse, my purse!
20 COCLEDEMOY: Ay, sir, an it shall please you, the poor has your
 purse already.
MALHEUREUX: You are a wily man.
 [*To* FRANCESCHINA] But now, thou source of devils, oh, how
 I loathe
 The very memory of that I ador'd!
 He that's of fair blood, well mean'd, of good breeding,
 Best fam'd, of sweet acquaintance and true friends,
 And would with desperate impudence lose all these,
 And hazard landing at this fatal shore,
 Let him ne'er kill nor steal, but love a whore!
30 FRANCESCHINA: De man does rave. Tink o' Got, tink o' Got,
 and bid de flesh, de world, and the dible farewell!
MALHEUREUX: Farewell!
FREEVILL: Farewell! (FREEVILL *discovers himself.*)
FRANCESCHINA: Vat is't you see, ha?
FREEVILL: Sir, your pardon, with my this defence:
 Do not forget protested violence

   16. *lewd defence*: i.e. pleading ignorance.

Of your low affections; no requests,
No arguments of reason, no known danger,
No assured wicked bloodiness,
Could draw your heart from this damnation.   40
MALHEUREUX: Why, stay —
FRANCESCHINA: Unprosperous divel! Vat sall me do now?
FREEVILL: Therefore to force you from the truer danger,
  I wrought the feigned, suffering this fair devil
  In shape of woman to make good her plot,
  And knowing that the hook was deeply fast
  I gave her line at will, till with her own vain strivings
  See here she's tired. O, thou comely damnation!
  Dost think that vice is not to be withstood?
  O, what is woman merely made of blood!   50
SIR LIONEL: You maze us all; let us not be lost in darkness.
FREEVILL: All shall be lighted; but this time and place
  Forbids longer speech. Only what you can think
  Has been extremely ill is only hers.
SIR LIONEL: To severest prison with her.
  With what heart canst live? What eyes behold a face?
FRANCESCHINA: Ick vil not speak. Torture, torture your fill,
  For me am worse than hang'd; me ha' lost my will.
        (*Exit* FRANCESCHINA *with the guard.*)
SIR LIONEL: To the extremest whip and jail!
FREEVILL: Frolic, how is it, sirs?   60
MALHEUREUX: I am myself. How long wast ere I could
  Persuade my passion to grow calm to you?
  Rich sense makes good bad language, and a friend
  Should weigh no action, but the action's end.
  I am now worthy yours, when before
  The beast of man, loose blood, distemper'd us,
  He that lust rules cannot be virtuous.
        (*Enter* MULLIGRUB, MISTRESS MULLIGRUB *and officers.*)
OFFICER: On afore there, room for the prisoner!
MULLIGRUB: I pray you do not lead me to execution through
  Cheapside. I owe Master Burnish the goldsmith money, and   70
  I fear he'll set a sergeant on my back for it.

51. *maze*: bewilder.

COCLEDEMOY: Trouble not your sconce, my Christian brother, but have an eye unto the main chance. I will warrant your shoulders; as for your neck, Plinius Secundus, or Marcus Tullius Cicero, or somebody it is, says that a three-fold cord is hardly broken.

MULLIGRUB: Well, I am not the first honest man that hath been cast away, and I hope shall not be the last.

COCLEDEMOY: O sir, have a good stomach and maws, you shall
80 have a joyful supper.

MULLIGRUB: In troth, I have no stomach to it. And it please you, take my trencher; I use to fast at nights.

MISTRESS MULLIGRUB: O husband, I little thought you should have come to think on God thus soon! Nay, an you had been hang'd deservedly, it would never have griev'd me – I have known of many honest innocent men have been hang'd deservedly – but to be cast away for nothing!

COCLEDEMOY: Good woman, hold your peace, your prittles and your prattles, your bibbles and your babbles, for I pray
90 you, hear me in private. I am a widower, and you are almost a widow. Shall I be welcome to your houses, to your tables, and your other things?

MISTRESS MULLIGRUB: I have a piece of mutton and a feather-bed for you at all times. [*To* MULLIGRUB] I pray, make haste.

MULLIGRUB: I do here make my confession. If I owe any man anything, I do heartily forgive him; if any man owe me anything, let him pay my wife.

COCLEDEMOY: I will look to your wife's payment, I warrant you.

100 MULLIGRUB: And now, good yoke-fellow, leave thy poor Mulligrub.

MISTRESS MULLIGRUB: Nay, then I were unkind, i' faith. I will not leave you until I have seen you hang.

COCLEDEMOY: But brother, brother, you must think of your sins and iniquities. You have been a broacher of profane

72. *sconce*: noddle, head.
79. *maws*: jaws.
105. *broacher*: opener, piercer.
105–6. *profane vessels*: Puritan cant for 'wine casks'.

vessels; you have made us drink of the juice **of** the whore of Babylon. For whereas good ale, perrys, bragets, ciders and metheglins was the true ancient British and Troyan drinks, you ha' brought in Popish wines, Spanish wines, French wines, *tam Marti quam Mercurio*, both muscadine and malmsey, to 110 the subversion, staggering, and sometimes overthrow of many a good Christian. You ha' been a great jumbler. O remember the sins of your nights, for your night works ha' been unsavoury in the taste of your customers.

MULLIGRUB: I confess, I confess, and I forgive as I would be forgiven. Do you know one Cocledemoy?

COCLEDEMOY: O, very well. Know him? An honest man he is, and a comely, an upright dealer with his neighbours, and their wives speak good things of him.

MULLIGRUB: Well, wheresoe'er he is, or whatsoe'er he is, I'll 120 take it on my death he's the cause of my hanging. I heartily forgive him, and if he would come forth he might save me, for he only knows the why and the wherefor.

COCLEDEMOY: You do from your hearts, and midriffs and entrails, forgive him then? You will not let him rot in rusty irons, procure him to be hang'd in lousy linen without a song, and after he is dead piss on his grave?

MULLIGRUB: That hard heart of mine has procur'd all this, but I forgive as I would be forgiven.

COCLEDEMOY: Hang toasts, my worshipful Mulligrub! Behold 130 thy Cocledemoy, my fine vintner, my castrophomical fine boy! Behold and see! [*Reveals himself.*]

TYSEFEW: Bliss o' the blessed, who would but look for two knaves here!

COCLEDEMOY: No knave, worshipful friend, no knave; for observe, honest Cocledemoy restores whatsoever he has got, to make you know, that whatsoe'er he has done, has been only

---

107. *bragets*: fermented honey and ale.
108. *metheglins*: strong drink made of herbs and honey.
108. *Troyan*: New Troy = another name for London.
110. *tam . . . Mercurio*: as much for Mars (war) as for Mercury (commerce).
112. *jumbler*: adulterator.
126. *song*: psalm.

euphoniae gratia, for wit's sake. I acquit this vintner as he has acquitted me. All has been done for emphasis of wit, my fine
140 boy, my worshipful friends.

TYSEFEW: Go, you are a flatt'ring knave.

COCLEDEMOY: I am so; 'tis a good thriving trade. It comes forward better than the seven liberal sciences or the nine cardinal virtues, which may well appear in this: you shall never have flattering knave turn courtier, and yet I have read of many courtiers that have turned flatt'ring knaves.

SIR HUBERT: Was't even but so? Why then, all's well!

MULLIGRUB: I could even weep for joy!

MISTRESS MULLIGRUB: I could weep too, but God knows for
150 what!

TYSEFEW: Here's another tack to be given: your son and daughter.

SIR HUBERT: Is't possible? Heart, ay, all my heart! Will you be joined here?

TYSEFEW: Yes, faith, father; marriage and hanging are spun both in one hour.

COCLEDEMOY: Why then, my worshipful good friends, I bid myself most heartily welcome to your merry nuptials and wanton jigga-joggies. [*Addresses audience*]
160 And now, my very fine Heliconian gallants, and you, my worshipful friends in the middle region:
  If with content our hurtless mirth hath been,
  Let your pleas'd minds as our much care [be seen].
  For he shall find, that slights such trivial wit,
  'Tis easier to reprove than better it.
  We scorn to fear, and yet we fear to swell;
  We do not hope 'tis best: 'tis all, if well.
    (*Exeunt.*)

138. *euphoniae gratia*: lit. 'for the sake of pleasant sound'.
160. *Heliconian gallants*: Mount Helicon was the seat of the muses.
161. *middle region*: ? galleries (of theatre).

FINIS

A
MAD WORLD,
MY
MASTERS.

As it hath bin lately in Action by the
Children of Paules.

Composed by T. M.

LONDON,
Printed by *H. B.* for WALTER BVRRE, and are to
be sold in Paules Church-yard, at the signe of
the Crane. 1608.

Facsimile of the title-page of the first edition, the quarto of 1608.

A MAD WORLD, MY MASTERS

by

Thomas Middleton

THE ACTORS IN THE COMEDY

SIR BOUNTEOUS PROGRESS, an old rich knight
RICHARD FOLLYWIT, nephew to Sir Bounteous Progress
MASTER PENITENT BROTHEL, a country gentleman
MAWWORM, a lieutenant ⎫
HOBOY, an ancient ⎭ comrades to Follywit
MASTER INESSE ⎫
MASTER POSSIBILITY ⎭ two brothers
MASTER HAREBRAIN, a citizen
GUNWATER, Sir Bounteous' steward
JASPER, Penitent's man
RAFE, Master Harebrain's man
TWO KNIGHTS
ONE CONSTABLE
A SUCCUBUS
WATCHMEN
A FOOTMAN
AN OLD GENTLEWOMAN, mother to the courtesan
MISTRESS HAREBRAIN, the citizen's wife
FRANK GULLMAN, the courtesan
ATTENDANTS

Hoboy, an ancient: Hoboy = hautboy, oboe; ancient = ensign, standard-bearer.
Inesse: In being. See also Additional Notes.
Frank: short for Frances.

ACT ONE

SCENE ONE

(*Enter* DICK FOLLYWIT, *and his consorts*, LIEUTENANT
MAWWORM, ANCIENT HOBOY, *and others his comrades.*)

MAWWORM: Oh Captain, regent, principal!

HOBOY: What shall I call thee? The noble spark of bounty, the
lifeblood of society!

FOLLYWIT: Call me your forecast, you whoresons; when you
come drunk out of a tavern, 'tis I must cast your plots into
form still; 'tis I must manage the prank, or I'll not give a
louse for the proceeding; I must let fly my civil fortunes, turn
wild-brain, lay my wits upo' th' tenters, you rascals, to maintain a company of villains whom I love in my very soul and
conscience.   10

MAWWORM: Aha, our little forecast!

FOLLYWIT: Hang you, you have bewitched me among you, I
was as well given till I fell to be wicked, my grandsire had
hope of me, I went all in black, swore but o' Sundays, never
came home drunk but upon fasting nights to cleanse my
stomach; 'slid now I'm quite altered, blown into light colours,
let out oaths by th' minute, sit up late till it be early, drink
drunk till I am sober, sink down dead in a tavern, and rise in
a tobacco shop. Here's a transformation; I was wont yet to
pity the simple, and leave 'em some money; 'slid, now I gull   20
'em without conscience. I go without order, swear without
number, gull without mercy, and drink without measure.

MAWWORM: I deny the last, for if you drink ne'er so much, you
drink within measure.

FOLLYWIT: How prove you that, sir?

---

4. *forecast*: (i) prudence, (ii) astrologer.
8. *tenters*: frame for stretching cloth.
14. *all in black*: i.e. sober-suited.
16. *'slid*: God's (eye-) lid.

113

MAWWORM: Because the drawers never fill their pots.

FOLLYWIT: Mass, that was well found out; all drunkards may lawfully say, they drink within measure by that trick. And now I'm put i' th' mind of a trick, can you keep your counten-
30 ance, villains? Yet I am a fool to ask that, for how can they keep their countenance that have lost their credits?

HOBOY: I warrant you for blushing, captain.

FOLLYWIT: I easily believe that, ancient, for thou lost thy colours once. Nay faith, as for blushing, I think there's grace little enough amongst you all, 'tis Lent in your cheeks, the flag's down. Well, your blushing face I suspect not, nor indeed greatly your laughing face, unless you had more money in your purses. Then thus compendiously now. You all know the possibilities of my hereafter fortunes, and the humour of my
40 frolic grandsire Sir Bounteous Progress, whose death makes all possible to me: I shall have all, when he has nothing, but now he has all, I shall have nothing. I think one mind runs through a million of 'em; they love to keep us sober all the while they're alive, that when they're dead we may drink to their healths; they cannot abide to see us merry all the while they're above ground; and that makes so many laugh at their fathers' funerals. I know my grandsire has his will in a box, and has bequeath'd all to me, when he can carry nothing away; but stood I in need of poor ten pounds now, by his will
50 I should hang myself ere I should get it; there's no such word in his will I warrant you, nor no such thought in his mind.

MAWWORM: You may build upon that, captain.

FOLLYWIT: Then since he has no will to do me good as long as he lives, by mine own will, I'll do myself good before he dies. And now I arrive at the purpose. You are not ignorant, I'm sure, you true and necessary implements of mischief, first, that my grandsire Sir Bounteous Progress is a knight of thousands, and therefore no knight since one thousand six
60 hundred; next, that he keeps a house like his name, bounteous, open for all comers; thirdly and lastly, that he stands much

39. *humour*: whim, temperament.

upon the glory of his complement, variety of entertainment, together with the largeness of his kitchen, longitude of his buttery, and fecundity of his larder, and thinks himself never happier than when some stiff lord or great countess alights to make light his dishes. These being well mixed together, may give my project better encouragement, and make my purpose spring forth more fortunate: to be short, and cut off a great deal of dirty way, I'll down to my grandsire like a lord.

MAWWORM: How, captain?   70

FOLLYWIT: A French ruff, a thin beard, and a strong perfume will do't: I can hire blue coats for you all by Westminster clock and that colour will be soonest believed.

MAWWORM: But prithee, captain –

FOLLYWIT: Push, I reach past your fathoms; you desire crowns.

MAWWORM: From the crown of our head to the sole of our foot, bully.

FOLLYWIT: Why, carry yourselves but probably, and carry away enough with yourselves.

(*Enter* MASTER PENITENT BROTHEL.)

HOBOY: Why, there spoke a Roman captain. Master Penitent   80
Brothel!

[*Exeunt all but Penitent.*]

PENITENT: Sweet Master Follywit –

Here's a mad-brain o' th' first, whose pranks scorn to have precedents, to be second to any, or walk beneath any madcap's intentions; h'as played more tricks than the cards can allow a man, and of the last stamp too; hating imitation, a fellow whose only glory is to be prime of the company, to be sure of which he maintains all the rest: he's the carrion and they the kites that gorge upon him.

But why in others do I check wild passions,   90
And retain deadly follies in myself?

62. *complement*: retinue, household personnel.

71. *French ruff*: deep ruff, hanging from a high stock and fastened at the chin.

72. *blue coats*: servants (from their traditional livery).

75. *fathoms*: grasp.

75. *crowns*: coins.

86. *last stamp*: latest minting.

I tax his youth of common receiv'd riot, –
Time's comic flashes, and the fruits of blood –
And in myself soothe up adulterous motions,
And such an appetite that I know damns me,
Yet willingly embrace it. Love, too, Harebrain's wife,
Over whose hours and pleasures her sick husband,
With a fantastick but deserv'd suspect,
Bestows his serious time in watch and ward.
100 And therefore I'm constrain'd to use the means
Of one that knows no mean, a courtesan,
(One poison for another) whom her husband
Without suspicion innocently admits
Into her company, who with tried art
Corrupts and loosens her most constant powers,
Making his jealousy more than half a wittol,
Before his face plotting his own abuse,
To which himself gives aim,
 (*Enter* COURTESAN.)
Whilst the broad arrow with the forkéd head
110 Misses his brow but narrowly. See, here she comes,
The close courtesan, whose mother is her bawd.
COURTESAN: Master Penitent Brothel!
PENITENT: My little pretty Lady Gullman, the news, the comfort?
COURTESAN: Y'are the fortunate man, Sir Knight o' th' holland shirt; there wants but opportunity and she's wax of your own fashioning. She had wrought herself into the form of your love before my art set finger to her.
PENITENT: Did our affections meet? Our thoughts keep time?
120 COURTESAN: So it should seem by the music. The only jar is in the grumbling base viol her husband.
PENITENT: Oh, his waking suspicion!

98. *suspect*: suspicion, jealousy.
106. *wittol*: acquiescent cuckold.
109. *broad . . . head*: the cuckold's horn joke blows again.
111. *close*: secret.
115–16. *Sir Knight o' th' holland shirt*: i.e. Sir Penitent (holland = coarse, unbleached linen, i.e. hair-shirt). (Q – 'skirt'.)

COURTESAN: Sigh not, Master Penitent, trust the managing of the business with me; 'tis for my credit now to see't well finished. If I do you no good, sir, you shall give me no money, sir.

PENITENT [*aside*]: I am arriv'd at the court of conscience; a courtesan! O admirable times! Honesty is removed to the common place. [*To her*] Farewell, Lady. (*Exit* PENITENT.)

(*Enter* MOTHER.)

MOTHER: How now, daughter?

COURTESAN: What news, mother?   130

MOTHER: A token from thy keeper.

COURTESAN: Oh, from Sir Bounteous Progress? He's my keeper indeed, but there's many a piece of venison stol'n that my keeper wots not on; there's no park kept so warily, but loses flesh one time or other; and no woman kept so privately, but may watch advantage to make the best of her pleasure. And in common reason one keeper cannot be enough for so proud a park as a woman.

MOTHER: Hold thee there, girl!

COURTESAN: Fear not me, mother.   140

MOTHER: Every part of the world shoots up daily into more subtlety. The very spider weaves her cauls with more art and cunning, to entrap the fly.
The shallow ploughman can distinguish now
'Twixt simple truth and a dissembling brow.
Your base mechanic fellow can spy out
A weakness in a lord and learns to flout.
How does't behoove us then that live by sleight
To have our wits wound up to their stretched height!
Fifteen times thou know'st I have sold thy maidenhead,   150
To make up a dowry for thy marriage, and yet
There's maidenhead enough for old Sir Bounteous still,
He'll be all his lifetime about it yet,
And be as far to seek when he has done.

126. *court of conscience*: Court of Requests, set up in 1517 to deal with small claims.

128. *common place*: Dyce suggests a pun on (Court of) 'Common pleas', one of the three major law courts.

142. *cauls*: webs.

146. *mechanic fellow*: labourer.

The sums that I have told upon thy pillow!
I shall once see those golden days again;
Tho' fifteen, all thy maidenheads are not gone;
The Italian is not serv'd yet, nor the French;
The British men come for a dozen at once,
160 They engross all the market. Tut, my girl,
'Tis nothing but a politic conveyance,
A sincere carriage, a religious eyebrow
That throws their charms over the worldlings' senses.
And when thou spiest a fool that truly pities
The false springs of thine eyes,
And honourably dotes upon thy love,
If he be rich, set him by for a husband.
Be wisely tempered and learn this, my wench,
Who gets th' opinion for a virtuous name
170 May sin at pleasure, and ne'er think of shame:
COURTESAN: Mother, I am too deep a scholar grown
To learn my first rules now.
MOTHER: 'Twill be thy own,
I say no more; peace, hark – remove thyself.
Oh, the two elder brothers.
      [*Exit* COURTESAN.]
      (*Enter* INESSE *and* POSSIBILITY.)
POSSIBILITY: A fair hour, sweet lady.
MOTHER: Good morrow gentlemen, Master Inesse, and Master
   Possibility.
INESSE: Where's the little sweet lady your daughter?
MOTHER: Even at her book, sir.
180 POSSIBILITY: So religious?
MOTHER: 'Tis no new motion, sir, sh'as took it from an infant.
POSSIBILITY: May we deserve a sight of her, lady?
MOTHER: Upon that condition you will promise me, gentlemen,
   to avoid all profane talk, wanton compliments, undecent

155. *told*: reckoned.
160. *engross*: buy up, monopolize.
161. *politic conyevance*: tactful behaviour (with the pun on conveyance =
cheating).
181. *motion*: bias of mind.

phrases, and lascivious courtings, which I know my daughter will sooner die than endure, I am contented your suits shall be granted.

POSSIBILITY: Not a bawdy syllable, I protest.

190 INESSE: Syllable was [well]-plac'd there, for indeed your one syllables are your bawdiest words; prick that down.

   (*Exeunt.*)

[SCENE TWO]

(*Enter* MASTER HAREBRAIN.)

HAREBRAIN: She may make nightwork on't, 'twas well recovered.

He-cats and courtesans stroll most i' th' night;

Her friend may be receiv'd and convey'd forth nightly.

I'll be at charge for watch and ward, for watch and ward i' faith;

And here they come.

   (*Enter two or three* [*watchmen*].)

FIRST WATCHMAN: Give your worship good even.

HAREBRAIN: Welcome, my friends. I must deserve your diligence in an employment serious. The truth is, there is a cunning plot laid, but happily discovered, to rob my house; the night uncertain when, but fix'd within the circle of this   10 month.

Nor does this villainy consist in numbers:

Or many partners; only someone

Shall, in the form of my familiar friend,

Be receiv'd privately into my house,

By some perfidious servant of mine own,

Address'd fit for the practice.

FIRST WATCHMAN: O abominable!

HAREBRAIN: If you be faithful watchmen, show your goodness,

And with these angels shore up your eyelids.   20

1. *recovered*: ? discovered (Dyce).
17. *Address'd . . . practice*: (Bribed) ready for the deception.
20. *angels*: gold coins worth about fifty pence.

Let me not be purloin'd – [*Aside*] purloin'd indeed; the merry
Greeks conceive me – there is a gem I would not lose, kept by
the Italian under lock and key; we Englishmen are careless
creatures. Well, I have said enough.

SECOND WATCHMAN: And we will do enough, sir.

   (*Exeunt.*)

HAREBRAIN: Why well said, watch me a good turn now; so, so, so.
Rise villainy with the lark, why, 'tis prevented.
Or steal't by with the leather-winged bat,
The evening cannot save it. Peace –

   [*Enter* COURTESAN.]

30 Oh, Lady Gullman, my wife's only company, welcome! And
how does the virtuous matron, that good old gentlewoman thy
mother? I persuade myself if modesty be in the world she
has part on't; a woman of an excellent carriage all her lifetime,
in court, city and country.

COURTESAN: Sh'as always carried it well in those places, sir.
[*Aside*] Witness three bastards apiece – How does your sweet
bedfellow, sir? You see I'm her boldest visitant.

HAREBRAIN: And welcome, sweet virgin, the only companion
my soul wishes for her. I left her within at her lute, prithee
40 give her good counsel.

COURTESAN: Alas, she needs none, sir.

HAREBRAIN: Yet, yet, yet, a little of thy instructions will not
come amiss to her.

COURTESAN: I'll bestow my labour, sir.

HAREBRAIN: Do labour her, prithee; I have convey'd away all
her wanton pamphlets, as *Hero and Leander*, *Venus and
Adonis* – oh, two luscious mary-bone pies for a young married
wife. Here, here, prithee take the *Resolution*, and read to her a
little.

50 COURTESAN: Sh'as set up her resolution already, sir.

---

21. *purloin'd*: (i) robbed, (ii) pur = knave in card-game; loin = copulate
Hence loined by a knave (Henning, quoting Eberle).
21–2. *merry Greeks*: witty fellows.
22–3. *kept . . . key*: i.e. marital chastity.
27. *prevented*: forestalled.
47. *mary-bone*: marrow bone, one of the innumerable alleged aphrodisiacs.

HAREBRAIN: True, true, and this will confirm it the more.
There's a chapter of hell 'tis good to read this cold weather.
Terrify her, terrify her; go, read to her the horrible punishments for itching wantonness, the pains allotted for adultery;
tell her her thoughts, her very dreams are answerable; say so,
rip up the life of a courtesan, and show how loathsome 'tis.

COURTESAN [*aside*]: The gentleman would persuade me in time
to disgrace myself and speak ill of mine own function. (*Exit.*)

HAREBRAIN: This is the course I take. I'll teach the married
man   60
A new selected strain; I admit none
But this pure virgin to her company;
Puh, that's enough; I'll keep her to her stint,
I'll put her to her pension;
She gets but her allowance, that's [a] bare one,
Few women but have that beside their own.
Ha, ha, ha, nay, I'll put her hard to't.
    (*Enter wife* [MISTRESS HAREBRAIN] *and* COURTESAN.)

MISTRESS HAREBRAIN: Fain would I meet the gentleman.

COURTESAN: Push, fain would you meet him! Why, you do not
take the course.   70

HAREBRAIN: How earnestly she labours her, like a good wholesome sister of the Family! She will prevail, I hope.

COURTESAN: Is that the means?

MISTRESS HAREBRAIN: What is the means? I would as gladly
to enjoy his sight, embrace it as the –

COURTESAN: Shall I have hearing? Listen –

HAREBRAIN: She's round with her i' faith.

COURTESAN: When husbands in their rank'st suspicions dwell,
Then 'tis our best art to dissemble well.
Put but these notes in use that I'll direct you,   80
He'll curse himself that e'er he did suspect you.
Perhaps he will solicit you, as in trial,
To visit such and such: still give denial.
Let no persuasions sway you; they are but fetches

72. *Family*: Family of Love, a religious sect which advocated sexual love
for religious reasons.
84. *fetches*: traps.

Set to betray you, jealousies, slights and reaches.
Seem in his sight to endure the sight of no man,
Put by all kisses, till you kiss in common;
Neglect all entertain; if he bring in
Strangers, keep you your chamber, be not seen;
90   If he chance steal upon you, let him find
Some book lie open 'gainst an unchaste mind,
And coted Scriptures, tho' for your own pleasure,
You read some stirring pamphlet, and convey it
Under your skirt, the fittest place to lay it.
This is the course, my wench, to enjoy thy wishes.
Here you perform best when you most neglect;
The way to daunt is to outvie suspect.
Manage these principles but with art and life,
Welcome all nations, thou'rt an honest wife.
100 HAREBRAIN: She puts it home i' faith, ev'n to the quick;
From her elaborate action I reach that;
I must requite this maid. Faith, I'm forgetful. [*Withdraws.*]
MISTRESS HAREBRAIN: Here, lady, convey my heart unto him
  in this jewel.
Against you see me next you shall perceive
I have profited; in the mean season, tell him
I am a prisoner yet, o' th' master's side,
My husband's jealousy,
That masters him, as he doth master me;
And as a keeper that locks prisoners up
110 Is himself prison'd under his own key,
Even so my husband, in restraining me,
With the same ward bars his own liberty.
COURTESAN: I'll tell him how you wish it, and I'll wear
My wits to the third pile, but all shall clear.
MISTRESS HAREBRAIN: I owe you more than thanks, but that
  I hope
My husband will requite you.
COURTESAN: Think you so, lady? He has small reason for't.

92. *coted*: quoted.
93. *stirring*: titillating.
97. *suspect*: suspicion.

HAREBRAIN: What, done so soon? Away, to't again, to't again, good wench, to't again; leave her not so. Where left you? Come –   120

COURTESAN: Faith, I am weary, sir.
I cannot draw her from her strict opinion
With all the arguments that sense can frame.

HAREBRAIN: No? Let me come. Fie, wife, you must consent; what opinion is't? Let's hear.

COURTESAN: Fondly and wilfully she retains that thought,
That every sin is damn'd.

HAREBRAIN: Oh fie, fie, wife! Pea, pea, pea, pea, how have you lost your time? For shame, be converted. There's a diabolical opinion indeed; then you may think that usury were damn'd; 130 you're a fine merchant i' faith; or bribery? You know the law well; or sloth? Would some of the clergy heard you, i' faith; or pride? You come at court; or gluttony? You're not worthy to dine at an alderman's table:
Your only deadly sin's adultery,
That villainous ringworm, woman's worst requital.
'Tis only lechery that's damn'd to th' pit-hole;
Ah, that's an arch-offence, believe it, squall,
All sins are venial but venereal.

COURTESAN: I've said enough to her.   140

HAREBRAIN: And she will be rul'd by you.

COURTESAN: Fah!

HAREBRAIN: I'll pawn my credit on't. Come hither, lady,
I will not altogether rest ingrateful;
Here, wear this ruby for thy pains and counsel.

COURTESAN: It is not so much worth, sir. I am a very ill counsellor, truly.

HAREBRAIN: Go to, I say.

COURTESAN: Y'are to blame, i' faith, sir; I shall ne'er deserve it.

HAREBRAIN: Thou hast done't already. Farewell, sweet virgin; 150 prithee, let's see thee oft'ner.

123. *sense*: (i) reasonableness, (ii) sensuality.
126. *Fondly*: foolishly.
136. *requital*: (i) repayment, (ii) revenge.
138. *squall*: i.e. 'pet'.

COURTESAN [*aside*]: Such gifts will soon entreat me. (*Exit.*)

HAREBRAIN: Wife, as thou lov'st the quiet of my breast
    Embrace her counsel, yield to her advices;
    Thou wilt find comfort in 'em in the end;
    Thou'lt feel an alteration; prithee think on't;
    Mine eyes can scarce refrain.

MISTRESS HAREBRAIN: Keep in your dew, sir, lest when you
    would, you want it.

HAREBRAIN: I've pawn'd my credit on't. Ah, didst thou know
160   The sweet fruit once, thou'dst never let it go.

MISTRESS HAREBRAIN: 'Tis that I strive to get.

HAREBRAIN: And still do so.
    (*Exeunt.*)

ACT TWO

[SCENE ONE]

(*Enter* SIR BOUNTEOUS *with two Knights.*)

FIRST KNIGHT: You have been too much like your name, Sir
Bounteous.

SIR BOUNTEOUS: Oh not so, good knights, not so, you know my
humour; most welcome, good Sir Andrew Polcut, Sir Aqui-
taine Colewort, most welcome!

BOTH: Thanks, good Sir Bounteous.

(*Exeunt at one door.*)

(*At the other, enter in haste a footman.*)

FOOTMAN: Oh, cry your worship heartily mercy, sir.

SIR BOUNTEOUS: How now, linen stockings, and threescore
mile a day, whose footman art thou?

FOOTMAN: Pray can your worship tell me – Hoh, hoh, hoh – if   10
my lord be come in yet?

SIR BOUNTEOUS: Thy lord? What lord?

FOOTMAN: My Lord Owemuch, sir.

SIR BOUNTEOUS: My Lord Owemuch! I have heard much
speech of that lord; h'as great acquaintance i' th' city. That
lord has been much followed.

FOOTMAN: And is still, sir; he wants no company when he's in
London; he's free of the mercers, and there's none of 'em all
dare cross him.

SIR BOUNTEOUS: An they did, he'd turn over a new leaf with   20
'em; he would make 'em all weary on't i' th' end. Much fine
rumour have I heard of that lord, yet had I never the fortune
to set eye upon him. Art sure he will alight here, footman? I am
afraid thou'rt mistook.

FOOTMAN: Thinks your worship so, sir? By your leave, sir.
[*Prepares to leave.*]

17. *wants*: lacks.

SIR BOUNTEOUS: Puh! Passion of me, footman! Why, pumps, I say, come back!

FOOTMAN: Does your worship call?

SIR BOUNTEOUS: Come hither, I say! I am but afraid on't;
30 would it might happen so well. How dost know? Did he name the house with the great turret o' th' top?

FOOTMAN: No faith, did he not, sir.

SIR BOUNTEOUS: Come hither, I say! Did he speak of a cloth o' gold chamber?

FOOTMAN: Not one word, by my troth, sir.

SIR BOUNTEOUS: Come again, you lousy seven-mile-an-hour!

FOOTMAN: I beseech your worship, detain me not.

SIR BOUNTEOUS: Was there no talk of a fair pair of organs, a great gilt candlestick, and a pair of silver snuffers?

40 FOOTMAN: 'Twere sin to belie my lord; I heard no such words, sir.

SIR BOUNTEOUS: A pox confine thee! Come again! Puh!

FOOTMAN: Your worship will undo me, sir.

SIR BOUNTEOUS: Was there no speech of a long dining room, a huge kitchen, large meat and a broad dresser board?

FOOTMAN: I have a greater maw to that indeed, an't please your worship.

SIR BOUNTEOUS: Whom did he name?

FOOTMAN: Why, one Sir Bounteous Progress.

50 SIR BOUNTEOUS: Ahaa! I am that Sir Bounteous, you progressive round-about rascal.

FOOTMAN [laughs]: Puh!

SIR BOUNTEOUS: I knew I should have him i' th' end; there's not a lord will miss me, I thank their good honours; 'tis a fortune laid upon me, they can scent out their best entertainment. I have a kind of complimental gift given me above ordinary country knights, and how soon 'tis smelt out! I warrant ye there's not one knight i' th' shire able to entertain a lord i' th' cue, or a lady i' th' nick like me, like me. There's a

26. *pumps*: i.e. footwear.
38. *pair of organs*: (musical) organ.
45. *dresser board*: kitchen table.
50–51. *progressive*: i.e. long-winded.
59. *lord . . . nick*: ? at short notice (with possible sexual innuendo).

kind of grace belongs to't, a kind of art which naturally slips   60
from me. I know not on't, I promise you, 'tis gone before I'm
aware on't. Cuds me, I forget myself. Where!

[*Enter* FIRST SERVANT.]

FIRST SERVANT: Does your worship call?

SIR BOUNTEOUS: Run, sirrah, call in my chief gentleman i' th'
chain of gold, expedite.

[*Exit* FIRST SERVANT.]

And how does my good lord? I never saw him before in my
life. A cup of bastard for this footman!

FOOTMAN: My lord has travel'd this five year, sir.

SIR BOUNTEOUS: Travail'd this five year? How many children
has he? Some bastard, I say!   70

FOOTMAN: No bastard, an't please your worship.

SIR BOUNTEOUS: A cup of sack to strengthen his wit, the footman's a fool.

[*Enter* GUNWATER.]

Oh, come hither Master Gunwater, come hither. – Send
presently to Master Pheasant for one of his hens; there's
partridge i' th' house.

GUNWATER: And wild duck, an't please your worship.

SIR BOUNTEOUS: And woodcock, an't please thy worship.

GUNWATER: And woodcock, an't please your worship. I had
thought to have spoke before you.   80

SIR BOUNTEOUS: Remember the pheasant, down with some
plover, clap down six woodcocks, my Lord's coming. Now,
sir?

GUNWATER: An't please your worship, there's a lord and his
followers newly alighted.

SIR BOUNTEOUS: Dispatch I say, dispatch. Why, where's my
music? He's come indeed.

[*Enter* FOLLYWIT *like a lord, with his comrades in blue
coats.*]

65. *chain of gold*: steward's emblem of office.
67. *bastard*: sweet Spanish wine.
68–9. *travel'd*: ... *Travail'd*: travail = labour of childbirth. A common
pun.
72. *sack ... wit*: cf. Falstaff's celebrated encomium.
Stage direction. *blue coats*: servants' dress.

FOLLYWIT: Footman.

FOOTMAN: My Lord?

90 FOLLYWIT: Run swiftly with my commendations to Sir Jasper
Topaz;

We'll ride and visit him i' th' morning, say.

FOOTMAN: Your lordship's charge shall be effected. [*Exit.*]

FOLLYWIT: That courtly, comely form should present to me
Sir Bounteous Progress.

SIR BOUNTEOUS: Y'ave found me out, my lord; I cannot hide
myself.

Your honour is most spaciously welcome.

FOLLYWIT: In this forgive me, sir, that being a stranger to your
houses,

And you, I make my way so bold, and presume

100 Rather upon your kindness than your knowledge;
Only your bounteous disposition
Fame hath divulg'd, and is to me well known.

SIR BOUNTEOUS: Nay, an your lordship know my disposition,
you know me better than they that know my person; your
honour is so much the welcomer for that.

FOLLYWIT: Thanks, good Sir Bounteous.

SIR BOUNTEOUS: Pray pardon me, it has been often my ambition, my lord, both in respect of your honourable presence,
and the prodigal fame that keeps even stroke with your un-

110 bounded worthiness,
To have wish'd your lordship where your lordship is,
A noble guest in this unworthy seat –
Your lordship ne'er heard my organs?

FOLLYWIT: Heard of 'em, Sir Bounteous, but never heard 'em.

SIR BOUNTEOUS: They're but double gilt my lord; some
hundred and fifty pound will fit your lordship with such
another pair.

FOLLYWIT: Indeed, Sir Bounteous?

SIR BOUNTEOUS: O my lord, I have a present suit to you.

120 FOLLYWIT: To me, Sir Bounteous? And you could ne'er speak
at fitter time, for I'm here present to grant you.

SIR BOUNTEOUS: Your lordship has been a traveller?

100. *knowledge*: acquaintance.

FOLLYWIT: Some five year, sir.

SIR BOUNTEOUS: I have a grandchild, my lord. I love him, and when I die I'll do somewhat for him. I'll tell your honour the worst of him: a wild lad he has been.

FOLLYWIT: So we have been all, sir.

SIR BOUNTEOUS: So we have been all indeed, my lord. I thank your lordship's assistance. Some comic pranks he has been guilty of, but I'll pawn my credit for him, an honest, trusty 130 bosom.

FOLLYWIT: And that's worth all, sir.

SIR BOUNTEOUS: And that's worth all indeed, my lord, for he's like to have all when I die. *Imberbis iuvenis*, his chin has no more prickles yet than a midwife's; there's great hope of his wit, his hair's so long a-coming. Shall I be bold with your honour, to prefer this aforesaid Ganymede to hold a plate under your lordship's cup?

FOLLYWIT: You wrong both his worth and your bounty, an you call that boldness. Sir, I have heard much good of that 140 young gentleman.

SIR BOUNTEOUS: Nay, h'as a good wit, i' faith, my lord.

FOLLYWIT: H'as carried himself always generously.

SIR BOUNTEOUS: Are you advis'd of that, my lord? H'as carried many things cleanly. I'll show your lordship my will. I keep it above in an outlandish box. The whoreson boy must have all; I love him, yet he shall ne'er find it as long as I live.

FOLLYWIT: Well sir, for your sake, and his own deserving, I'll reserve a place for him nearest to my secrets.

SIR BOUNTEOUS: I understand your good lordship, you'll make 150 him your secretary. My music, give my lord a taste of his welcome.

(*A strain played by the consort;* SIR BOUNTEOUS *makes a courtly honour to that lord and seems to foot the tune.*)

---

134. *Imberbis iuvenis*: 'beardless youth'.
135. *midwife*: sometimes signifying an effeminate man.
135–6. *there's . . . a-coming*: cf. proverb 'More hair than wit' (Bullen).
137. *Ganymede*: beautiful youth who was Jove's cup-bearer.
Stage direction. *consort*: band of musicians.
Stage direction. *courtly honour*: dance figure.

SIR BOUNTEOUS: So, how like you our airs, my lord? Are they
  choice?
FOLLYWIT: They're seldom match'd, believe it.
SIR BOUNTEOUS: The consort of mine own household.
FOLLYWIT: Yea, sir?
SIR BOUNTEOUS: The musicians are in ordinary, yet no ordinary
  musicians; your lordship shall hear my organs now.
160 FOLLYWIT: Oh I beseech you, Sir Bounteous.
SIR BOUNTEOUS: My organist.
  (*The organs play, and cover'd dishes march over the stage.*)
  Come, my lord, how does your honour relish my organ?
FOLLYWIT: A very proud air, i' faith, sir.
SIR BOUNTEOUS: Oh, how can't choose? A Walloon plays upon
  'em, and a Welshman blows wind in their breech.
  (*Exeunt.*)
              (*A song to the organs.*)

[SCENE TWO]

  (*Enter* SIR BOUNTEOUS *with* FOLLYWIT *and his consorts
  towards his lodging.*)
SIR BOUNTEOUS: You must pardon us, my lord, hasty cates.
  Your honour has had ev'n a hunting meal on't, and now I am
  like to bring your lordship to as mean a lodging, a hard down
  bed i' faith, my lord, poor cambric sheets, and a cloth o' tissue
  canopy. The curtains indeed were wrought in Venice, with
  the story of the prodigal child in silk and gold; only the swine
  are left out, my lord, for spoiling the curtains.
FOLLYWIT: 'Twas well prevented, sir.
SIR BOUNTEOUS: Silken rest, harmonious slumbers, and
10 venereal dreams to your lordship.

  158. *in ordinary*: part of regular staff.
  164. *Walloon*: ? boldly, emphatically (The Walloons were noted for
fighting spirit).
  165. *Welshman*: reputedly great braggers.
Stage direction. *consorts*: companions.
  1. *hasty cates*: i.e. 'pot luck'.
  10. *venereal*: i.e. inspired by Venus, goddess of love.

FOLLYWIT: The like to kind Sir Bounteous.

SIR BOUNTEOUS: Fie, not to me, my lord. I'm old, past dreaming
of such vanities.

FOLLYWIT: Old men should dream best.

SIR BOUNTEOUS: Their dreams indeed, my lord, y'ave gi'n t'us.
Tomorrow your lordship shall see my cocks, my fish ponds,
my park, my champaign grounds; I keep champers in my
house can show your lordship some pleasure.

FOLLYWIT: Sir Bounteous, you ev'n whelm me with
delights.   20

SIR BOUNTEOUS: Once again a musical night to your honour;
I'll trouble your lordship no more. (*Exit*.)

FOLLYWIT: Good rest, Sir Bounteous. – So, come the vizards;
where be the masking suits?

MAWWORM: In your lordship's portmantua.

FOLLYWIT: Peace, lieutenant.

MAWWORM: I had rather have war, captain.

FOLLYWIT: Puh, the plot's ripe. Come, to our business, lad;
Tho' guilt condemns, 'tis gilt must make us glad.

MAWWORM: Nay, an' you be at your distinctions, captain, I'll   30
follow behind no longer.

FOLLYWIT: Get you before then, and whelm your nose with
your vizard, go.

    [*Exit* MAWWORM.]

Now grandsire, you that hold me at hard meat,
And keep me out at the dag's end, I'll fit you;
Under his lordship's leave, all must be mine –
He and his will confesses. What I take, then,
Is but a borrowing of so much beforehand;
I'll pay him again when he dies, in so many blacks,
I'll have the church hung round with a noble a yard,   40

17. *champaign grounds*: open meadows.
17. *champers*: ? eaters, horses.
23. *vizards*: masks.
29. *gilt*: gelt, money.
35. *dag's end*: i.e. 'arm's length'; dag = heavy pistol.
39. *blacks*: funeral hangings.
40. *noble*: coin worth about forty pence.

Or requite him in scutcheons. Let him trap me
In gold, and I'll lap him in lead; *quid pro quo.* I
Must look none of his angels in the face, forsooth,
Until his face be not worth looking on. Tut, lads,
Let sires and grandsires keep us low, we must
Live when they're flesh, as well as when they're dust.
    [*Exeunt.*]

[SCENE THREE]

    (*Enter* COURTESAN *with her man.*)

COURTESAN: Go, sirrah, run presently to Master Penitent
  Brothel; you know his lodging, knock him up, I know he can-
  not sleep for sighing.
  Tell him I've happily bethought a mean,
  To make his purpose prosper in each limb,
  Which only rests to be approv'd by him:
  Make haste, I know he thirsts for't.
    (*Exeunt.*)

[SCENE FOUR]

WITHIN: Oh!
    (*Enter in a masking suit with a vizard in his hand,* FOLLY-
    WIT.)
FOLLYWIT: Hark, they're at their business.
WITHIN: Thieves, thieves!
FOLLYWIT: Gag that gaping rascal, tho' he be my grandsire's
  chief gentleman i' th' chain of gold, I'll have no pity of him.
  How now, lads?
    (*Enter the rest [of* FOLLYWIT's *crew] vizarded.*)

41. *scutcheons*: plaques with armorial bearings of deceased fixed at the
entrance to his house.
  41. *trap*: equip.
  42. *lap . . . lead*: encase corpse for burial.
  42. *quid pro quo*: 'tit for tat'.
  43. *angels*: see note to I, ii, 20.

MAWWORM: All's sure and safe; on with your vizard, sir; the
servants are all bound.

FOLLYWIT: There's one care past then. Come, follow me, lads,
I'll lead you now to th'point and top of all your fortunes; yon   10
lodging is my grandsire's.

MAWWORM: So, so, lead on, on.

HOBOY: Here's a captain worth the following, and a wit worth a
man's love and admiring!

([*Exeunt and re-*]*enter with* SIR BOUNTEOUS *in his night-
gown.*)

SIR BOUNTEOUS: Oh gentlemen, an' you be kind gentlemen,
what countrymen are you?

FOLLYWIT: Lincolnshire men, sir.

SIR BOUNTEOUS: I am glad of that i' faith.

FOLLYWIT: And why should you be glad of that?

SIR BOUNTEOUS: Oh, the honestest thieves of all come out of   20
Lincolnshire, the kindest natur'd gentlemen; they'll rob a man
with conscience; they have a feeling of what they go about, and
will steal with tears in their eyes: ah, pitiful gentlemen.

FOLLYWIT: Push! Money, money, we come for money.

SIR BOUNTEOUS: Is that all you come for? Ah what a beast was
I to put out my money t'other day; alas, good gentlemen,
what shift shall I make for you? Pray come again another time.

FOLLYWIT: Tut, tut, sir, money!

SIR BOUNTEOUS: Oh not so loud, sir, you're too shrill a gentleman. I have a lord lies in my house; I would not for the world   30
his honour should be disquieted.

FOLLYWIT: Who, my Lord Owemuch? We have took order
with him beforehand; he lies bound in his bed – and all his
followers.

SIR BOUNTEOUS: Who, my lord? Bound my lord? Alas, what
did you mean to bind my lord? He could keep his bed well
enough without binding. Y'ave undone me in't already, you
need rob me no farther.

FOLLYWIT: Which is the key, come?

SIR BOUNTEOUS: Ah, I perceive now y'are no true Lincolnshire   40

23. *pitiful*: i.e. full of pity.
26. *put out*: invest.

133

spirits; you come rather out of Bedfordshire; we cannot lie quiet in our beds for you. So, take enough, my masters; spur a free horse, my name's Sir Bounteous. A merry world, i' faith; what knight but I keep open house at midnight? Well, there should be a conscience, if one could hit upon't.

FOLLYWIT: Away now, seize upon him, bind him.

SIR BOUNTEOUS: Is this your court of equity? Why should I be bound for mine own money? But come, come, bind me, I have need on't; I have been too liberal tonight. Keep in my hands,
50 nay, as hard as you list, I am too good to bear my lord company. You have watch'd your time, my masters; I was knighted at Westminster, but many of these nights will make me a knight of Windsor; y'ave deserv'd so well, my masters. I bid you all to dinner tomorrow. I would I might have your companies, i' faith, I desire no more.

FOLLYWIT: Oh ho, sir!

SIR BOUNTEOUS: Pray meddle not with my organs, to put 'em out of tune.

FOLLYWIT: Oh no, here's better music, sir.

60 SIR BOUNTEOUS: Ah, pox feast you!

FOLLYWIT: Dispatch with him, away.

[SIR BOUNTEOUS *is taken off.*]

So, thank you, good grandsire; this was bounteously done of him i' faith. It came somewhat hard from him at first, for indeed nothing comes stiff from an old man but money, and he may well stand upon that when he has nothing else to stand upon. Where's our portmantua?

MAWWORM: Here, bully captain.

FOLLYWIT: In with the purchase, 'twill lie safe enough, there under's nose, I warrant you.

(*Enter* HOBOY.)

70 What, is all sure?

HOBOY: All's sure, captain.

48. *bound . . . money*: with pun on legal sense.

50. *I am too good*: ? (i) I too am good, (ii) good = financially sound, (iii) how good of me (Henning).

53. *knight of Windsor*: gentleman pensioner.

68. *purchase*: loot.

FOLLYWIT: You know what follows now; one villain binds his
fellows. Go, we must be all bound for our own securities,
rascals, there's no dallying upo' th' point. You conceit me?
There is a lord to be found bound in the morning, and all his
followers; can you pick out that lord now?

MAWWORM: O admirable spirit!

FOLLYWIT: You ne'er plot for your safeties, so your wants be
satisfied.

HOBOY: But if we bind one another, how shall the last man be   80
bound?

FOLLYWIT: Pox on't, I'll have the footman 'scape.

FOOTMAN: That's I, I thank you, sir.

FOLLYWIT: The footman, of all other, will be suppos'd to
'scape, for he comes in no bed all night, but lies in's clothes,
to be first ready i' th' morning. The horse and he lies in litter
together, that's the right fashion of your bonny footman; and
his freedom will make the better for our purpose, for we must
have one i' th' morning to unbind the knight, that we may
have our sport within ourselves. We now arrive at the most   90
ticklish point: to rob, and take our ease, to be thieves and lie
by't. Look to't, lads, it concerns every man's gullet; I'll not have
the jest spoil'd, that's certain, tho' it hazard a windpipe. I'll
either go like a lord as I came, or be hang'd like a thief as I am;
and that's my resolution.

MAWWORM: Troth, a match, captain, of all hands.

(*Exeunt.*)

[SCENE FIVE]

(*Enter* COURTESAN *with* MASTER PENITENT BROTHEL.)

COURTESAN: Oh Master Penitent Brothel!

PENITENT: What is't, sweet Lady Gullman, that so seizes on
thee with rapture and admiration?

73. *bound . . . securities*: see note to II, iv, 48.
74. *conceit*: understand.
91–2. *lie by't*: (i) remain alongside booty, (ii) brazen it out.
93. *hazard a windpipe*: i.e. run risk of being hanged.

COURTESAN: A thought, a trick, to make you sir, especially
happy, and yet I myself a saver by it.

PENITENT: I would embrace that lady with such courage, I
would not leave you on the losing hand.

COURTESAN: I will give trust to you, sir, the cause then why I
rais'd you from your bed so soon, wherein I know sighs would
10   not let you sleep; thus understand it:
   You love that woman, Master Harebrain's wife,
   Which no invented means can crown with freedom
   For your desires and her own wish but this,
   Which in my slumbers did present itself.

PENITENT: I'm covetous, lady.

COURTESAN: You know her husband, ling'ring in suspect,
   Locks her from all society, but mine.

PENITENT: Most true.

COURTESAN: I only am admitted, yet hitherto that has done you
20   no real happiness; by my admittance I cannot perform that
deed that should please you, you know: wherefore thus I've
convey'd it; I'll counterfeit a fit of violent sickness.

PENITENT: Good.

COURTESAN: Nay, 'tis not so good, by my faith, but to do you
good.

PENITENT: And in that sense I call'd it. But take me with you,
lady; would it be probable enough to have a sickness so
suddenly violent?

COURTESAN: Puh, all the world knows women are soon down;
30   we can be sick when we have a mind to't, catch an ague with
the wind of our fans, surfeit upon the rump of a lark, and
bestow ten pound in physic upon't; we're likest ourselves
when we're down. 'Tis the easiest art and cunning for our sect
to counterfeit sick, that are always full of fits when we are
well; for since we were made for a weak, imperfect creature,
we can fit that best that we are made for. I thus translated, and
yourself slipp'd into the form of a physician –

5. *saver*: a winning card in certain games (cf. 'trick').
15. *covetous*: desirous (to hear).
26. *But . . . you*: let me understand you.
33. *sect*: sex.
36. *translated*: transformed.

PENITENT: I a physician, lady? Talk not on't I beseech you; I shall shame the whole college.

COURTESAN: Tut, man, any quacksalving terms will serve for this purpose; for I am pitifully haunted with a brace of elder brothers, new perfum'd in the first of their fortunes, and I shall see how forward their purses will be to the pleasing of my palate and restoring of my health. Lay on load enough upon 'em and spare 'em not, for they're good plump fleshly asses, and may well enough bear it. Let gold, amber and dissolved pearl be common ingredients, and that you cannot compose a cullis without 'em; put but this cunningly in practice, it shall be both a sufficient recompense for all my pains in your love and the ready means to make Mistress Harebrain way, by the visiting of me, to your mutual desired company.

PENITENT: I applaud thee, kiss thee, and will constantly embrace it.

(*Exeunt.*)

[SCENE SIX]

(*Voices within.*)

SIR BOUNTEOUS: Ho, Gunwater!

FOLLYWIT: Singlestone!

WITHIN: Jenkin, wa, ha, ho!

WITHIN: Ewen!

WITHIN: Simcod!

FOLLYWIT: Footman! whewe –!

FOOTMAN: Oh, good your worship, let me help your good old worship.

(*Enter* SIR BOUNTEOUS *with a cord half unbound, footman with him.*)

SIR BOUNTEOUS: Ah, poor honest footman, how didst thou 'scape this massacre?

FOOTMAN: E'en by miracle, and lying in my clothes, sir.

39. *college*: College of Physicians.
48. *cullis*: nourishing broth.
2. *Singlestone*: eunuch.

SIR BOUNTEOUS: I think so. I would I had lain in my clothes too, footman, so I had 'scap'd 'em; I could have but risse like a beggar then, and so I do now, till more money come in. But nothing afflicts me so much, my poor geometrical footman, as that the barbarous villains should lay violence upon my lord. Ah, the binding of my lord cuts my heart in two pieces! So, so, 'tis well, I thank thee; run to thy fellows, undo 'em, undo 'em, undo 'em.

20 FOOTMAN: Alas, if my lord should miscarry, they're unbound already sir; they have no occupation but sleep, feed, and fart. (*Exit*.)

SIR BOUNTEOUS: If I be not asham'd to look my lord i' th' face, I'm a Saracen. My lord –

FOLLYWIT [*within curtains*]: Who's that?

SIR BOUNTEOUS: One may see he has been scar'd, a pox on 'em for their labours.

FOLLYWIT: Singlestone!

SIR BOUNTEOUS: Singlestone? I'll ne'er answer to that, i' faith.

FOLLYWIT: Suchman!

30 SIR BOUNTEOUS: Suchman? Nor that neither i' faith; I am not brought so low, tho' I be old.

FOLLYWIT: Who's that i' th' chamber?

SIR BOUNTEOUS: Good morrow, my lord, 'tis I.

FOLLYWIT: Sir Bounteous, good morrow. I would give you my hand, sir, but I cannot come at it. Is this the courtesy o' th' country, Sir Bounteous?

SIR BOUNTEOUS: Your Lordship grieves me more than all my loss;
'Tis the unnatural'st sight that can be found,
40 To see a noble gentleman hard bound.

FOLLYWIT: Trust me, I thought you had been better belov'd, Sir Bounteous; but I see you have enemies, sir, and your friends fare the worse for 'em: I like your talk better than

13. *risse*: risen.
15. *geometrical*: 'ground-measuring' (cf. 'threescore-mile-a-day' and 'seven-mile-an-hour').
Stage direction. *within curtains*: i.e. in the inner stage area.
29. *Suchman*: i.e. such a one as 'Singlestone'.

your lodging; I ne'er lay harder in a bed of down; I have had
a mad night's rest on't. Can you not guess what they should
be, Sir Bounteous?

SIR BOUNTEOUS: Faith, Lincolnshire men, my lord.

FOLLYWIT: How? Fie, fie, believe it not, sir, these lie not far
off, I warrant you.

SIR BOUNTEOUS: Think you so, my lord? 50

FOLLYWIT: I'll be burnt an they do; some that use to your
house, sir, and are familiar with all the conveyances.

SIR BOUNTEOUS: This is the commodity of keeping open house,
my lord, that makes so many shut their doors about dinner
time.

FOLLYWIT: They were resolute villains. I made myself known
to 'em, told 'em what I was, gave 'em my honourable word
not to disclose 'em.

SIR BOUNTEOUS: O saucy unmannerly villains!

FOLLYWIT: And think you the slaves would trust me upon my 60
word?

SIR BOUNTEOUS: They would not?

FOLLYWIT: Forsooth no, I must pardon 'em. They told me
lords' promises were mortal, and commonly die within half
an hour after they are spoken; they were but gristles, and not
one amongst a hundred come to any full growth or perfection,
and therefore tho' I were a lord, I must enter into bond.

SIR BOUNTEOUS: Insupportable rascals!

FOLLYWIT: Troth, I'm of that mind, Sir Bounteous. You far'd
the worse for my coming hither. 70

SIR BOUNTEOUS: Ah good my lord, but I'm sure your lordship
far'd the worse.

FOLLYWIT: Pray pity not me, sir.

SIR BOUNTEOUS: Is not your honour sore about the brawn of
the arm? A murrain meet 'em, I feel it.

FOLLYWIT: About this place, Sir Bounteous?

SIR BOUNTEOUS: You feel as it were a twinge, my lord?

52. *conyeyances*: (i) passages, (ii) trickeries.
53. *commodity*: profit.
65. *gristles*: infants (whose bones are gristly).
75. *murrain*: cattle-disease (here, as usually, an oath).

FOLLYWIT: I, e'en a twinge, you say right.

SIR BOUNTEOUS: A pox discover 'em, that twinge I feel too.

80 FOLLYWIT: But that which disturbs me most, Sir Bounteous, lies here.

SIR BOUNTEOUS: True, about the wrist, a kind of tumid numbness.

FOLLYWIT: You say true, sir.

SIR BOUNTEOUS: The reason of that, my lord, is the pulses had no play.

FOLLYWIT: Mass, so I guess'd it.

SIR BOUNTEOUS: A mischief swell 'em, for I feel that too.

(*Enter* MAWWORM.)

MAWWORM: 'Slid, here's a house haunted indeed.

90 SIR BOUNTEOUS: A word with you, sir.

FOLLYWIT: How now, Singlestone?

MAWWORM: I'm sorry, my lord, your lordship has lost –

SIR BOUNTEOUS: Pup, pup, pup, pup, pup!

FOLLYWIT: What have I lost? Speak.

SIR BOUNTEOUS: A good night's sleep, say.

FOLLYWIT: Speak, what have I lost, I say?

MAWWORM: A good night's sleep, my lord, nothing else.

FOLLYWIT: That's true. My clothes, come.

(*Curtains drawn.*)

MAWWORM: My lord's clothes! His honour's rising.

100 SIR BOUNTEOUS: Hist, well said. Come hither, what has my lord lost, tell me; speak softly.

MAWWORM: His lordship must know that, sir.

SIR BOUNTEOUS: Hush, prithee tell me.

MAWWORM: 'Twill do you no pleasure to know't, sir.

SIR BOUNTEOUS: Yet again? I desire it, I say.

MAWWORM: Since your worship will needs know't, they have stol'n away a jewel in a blue silk riband of a hundred pound price, beside some hundred pounds in fair spur-royals.

SIR BOUNTEOUS: That's some two hundred i' th' total.

110 MAWWORM: Your worship's much about it, sir.

108. *spur-royal*: gold coin worth about seventy-five pence.
110. *much about it*: 'about right'.

SIR BOUNTEOUS: Come, follow me. I'll make that whole again in so much money. Let not my lord know on't.

MAWWORM: Oh pardon me, Sir Bounteous, that were a dishonour to my lord. Should it come to his ear, I should hazard my undoing by it.

SIR BOUNTEOUS: How should it come to his ear? If you be my lord's chief man about him, I hope you do not use to speak, unless you be paid for't, and I had rather give you a councillor's double fee to hold your peace. Come, go to, follow me, I say.

MAWWORM: There will be scarce time to tell it, sir, my lord will away instantly.

SIR BOUNTEOUS: His honour shall stay dinner by his leave; I'll prevail with him so far; and now I remember a jest; I bade the whoreson thieves to dinner last night, I would I might have their companies. A pox poison 'em! (*Exit.*)

MAWWORM: Faith, and you are like to have no other guests, Sir Bounteous, if you have none but us; I'll give you that gift, i' faith.

(*Exeunt.*)

ACT THREE

[SCENE ONE]

(*Enter* MASTER HAREBRAIN *with two elder brothers,* MASTER INESSE *and* MASTER POSSIBILITY.)

POSSIBILITY: You see bold guests, Master Harebrain.

HAREBRAIN: You're kindly welcome to my house, good Master Inesse and Master Possibility.

INESSE: That's our presumption, sir.

HAREBRAIN: Rafe!

RAFE: Here, sir.

HAREBRAIN: Call down your mistress to welcome these two gentlemen my friends.

RAFE: I shall, sir. (*Exit.*)

10 HAREBRAIN [*aside*]: I will observe her carriage, and watch
The slippery revolutions of her eye,
I'll lie in wait for every glance she gives,
And poise her words i' th' balance of suspect;
If she but swag she's gone, either on this hand
Overfamiliar, or this, too neglectful;
It does behove her carry herself even.

POSSIBILITY: But Master Harebrain –

HAREBRAIN: True, I hear you, sir; was't you said?

POSSIBILITY: I have not spoke it yet, sir.

20 HAREBRAIN: Right, so I say.

POSSIBILITY: Is it not strange, that in so short a time, my little Lady Gullman should be so violently handled?

HAREBRAIN: Oh, sickness has no mercy, sir;
It neither pities ladies' lip, nor eye,
It crops the rose out of the virgin's cheek,
And so deflowers her that was ne'er deflower'd;
Fools then are maids to lock from men that treasure

---

13. *poise*: weigh.
14. *swag*: sink down.

142

Which death will pluck, and never yield 'em pleasure.
Ah gentlemen, tho' I shadow it, that sweet virgin's sickness
grieves me not lightly; she was my wife's only delight and   30
company;
Did you not hear her gentlemen, i' th' midst
Of her extremest fit, still how she call'd upon my wife,
Remember'd still my wife, sweet Mistress Harebrain?
When she sent for me, o' one side of her bed stood the
physician, the scrivener on the other; two horrible objects,
but mere opposites in the course of their lives, for the scrivener
binds folks, and the physician makes them loose.

POSSIBILITY: But not loose of their bonds, sir?

HAREBRAIN: No, by my faith, sir, I say not so. If the physician   40
could make 'em loose of their bonds, there's many a one would
take physic that dares not now for poisoning. But as I was
telling of you, her will was fashioning,
Wherein I found her best and richest jewel,
Given as a legacy unto my wife.
When I read that, I could not refrain weeping. Well, of all
other, my wife has most reason to visit her; if she have any
good nature in her, she'll show it there.
    [*Enter* RAFE.]
Now sir, where's your mistress?

RAFE: She desires you, and the gentlemen your friends, to hold   50
her excused; sh'as a fit of an ague now upon her, which begins
to shake her.

HAREBRAIN: Where does it shake her most?

RAFE: All over her body, sir.

HAREBRAIN: Shake all her body? 'Tis a saucy fit; I'm jealous of
that ague. Pray walk in, gentlemen, I'll see you instantly.
    [*Exeunt* INESSE *and* POSSIBILITY.]

RAFE: Now they are absent, sir, 'tis no such thing.

HAREBRAIN: What?

RAFE: My mistress has her health, sir,
But 'tis her suit, she may confine herself   60
From sight of all men, but your own dear self, sir,
For since the sickness of that modest virgin,

       36. *scrivener*: notary (to record her will).

Her only company, she delights in none.

HAREBRAIN: No; visit her again, commend me to her,
Tell her they're gone, and only I myself
Walk here to exchange a word or two with her.

RAFE: I'll tell her so, sir. (*Exit.*)

HAREBRAIN: Fool that I am, and madman, beast! What worse?
Suspicious o'er a creature that deserves
70   The best opinion and the purest thought;
Watchful o'er her that is her watch herself;
To doubt her ways, that looks too narrowly
Into her own defects. I, foolish-fearful,
Have often rudely, out of giddy flames,
Barr'd her those objects which she shuns herself.
Thrice I've had proof of her most constant temper.
Come I at unawares by stealth upon her,
I find her circled in with divine writs
Of heavenly meditations; here and there
80   Chapters with leaves tuck'd up, which when I see
They either tax pride or adultery.
Ah, let me curse myself, that could be jealous
Of her whose mind no sin can make rebellious.
And here the unmatched comes.

[*Enter* MISTRESS HAREBRAIN.]

                    Now wife, i' faith, they're gone;
Push, see how fearful 'tis, will you not credit me? They're
gone, i' faith; why, think you I'll betray you? Come, come,
thy delight and mine, thy only virtuous friend, thy sweet
instructress is violently taken, grievous sick, and which is
worse, she mends not.

90 MISTRESS HAREBRAIN: Her friends are sorry for that, sir.

HAREBRAIN: She calls still upon thee, poor soul, remembers thee
still, thy name whirls in her breath. 'Where's Mistress Harebrain?' says she.

MISTRESS HAREBRAIN: Alas, good soul!

HAREBRAIN: She made me weep thrice, sh'as put thee in a
jewel in her will.

MISTRESS HAREBRAIN: E'en to th' last gasp a kind soul.

80. *tuck'd up*: i.e. with corners folded.

HAREBRAIN: Take my man, go, visit her.

MISTRESS HAREBRAIN: Pray pardon me, sir, alas my visitation
cannot help her.   100

HAREBRAIN: Oh, yet the kindness of a thing, wife. – [*Aside*] –
Still she holds the same rare temper – take my man, I say.

MISTRESS HAREBRAIN: I would not take your man, sir, tho' I
did purpose going.

HAREBRAIN: No? Thy reason?

MISTRESS HAREBRAIN: The world's condition is itself so vild,
sir,
'Tis apt to judge the worst of those deserve not,
'Tis an ill-thinking age and does apply
All to the form of it[s] own luxury.
This censure flies from one, that, from another;   110
That man's her squire, says he; her pimp, the t'other;
She's of the stamp, a third; fourth, I ha' known her.
I've heard this, not without a burning cheek.
Then our attires are tax'd, our very gait
Is call'd in question, where a husband's presence
Scatters such thoughts, or makes 'em sink for fear
Into the hearts that breed 'em. Nay, surely, if I went, sir,
I would entreat your company.

HAREBRAIN: Mine? Prithee, wife, I have been there already.

MISTRESS HAREBRAIN: That's all one; altho' you bring me but 120
to th' door, sir, I would entreat no farther.

HAREBRAIN: Thou'rt such a wife! Why, I will bring thee thither
then, but not go up, I swear.

MISTRESS HAREBRAIN: I' faith you shall not, I do not desire
it, sir.

HAREBRAIN: Why then, content.

MISTRESS HAREBRAIN: Give me your hand you will do so, sir.

HAREBRAIN: Why there's my lip I will. [*Kisses her.*]

MISTRESS HAREBRAIN: Why then I go, sir.

HAREBRAIN [*aside*]: With me or no man! Incomparable, such a 130
woman!

    (*Exeunt.*)

      106. *vild*: vile.
      109. *luxury*: lasciviousness.
      112. *of the stamp*: i.e. generally recognized as 'current' (available).

[SCENE TWO]

(*Viols, gallipots, plate, and an hourglass by her, the* COUR-
TESAN *on a bed, for her counterfeit fit. To her,* MASTER
PENITENT BROTHEL, *like a doctor of physic.*)

PENITENT: Lady?

COURTESAN: Ha, what news?

PENITENT: There's one Sir Bounteous Progress newly alighted
from his foot-cloth, and his mare waits at door, as the fashion is.

COURTESAN: 'Slid, 'tis the knight that privately maintains me!
A little short old spiny gentleman in a great doublet?

PENITENT: The same; I know'm.

COURTESAN: He's my sole revenue, meat, drink, and raiment.
My good physician, work upon him, I'm weak.

10 PENITENT: Enough.

    [*Enter* SIR BOUNTEOUS.]

SIR BOUNTEOUS: Why, where be these ladies, these plump soft
delicate creatures, ha?

PENITENT: Who would you visit, sir?

SIR BOUNTEOUS: Visit, who? What are you with the plague in
your mouth?

PENITENT: A physician, sir.

SIR BOUNTEOUS: Then you are a loose liver, sir; I have put you
to your purgation.

PENITENT [*aside*]: But you need none, you're purg'd in a worse
20   fashion.

COURTESAN: Ah, Sir Bounteous.

SIR BOUNTEOUS: How now? What art thou?

COURTESAN: Sweet Sir Bounteous.

SIR BOUNTEOUS: Passion of me, what an alteration's here!
Rosamund sick, old Harry? Here's a sight able to make an old
man shrink! I was lusty when I came in, but I am down now,
i' faith. Mortality, yea? This puts me in mind of a hole seven

Stage direction. *gallipots*: glazed medicine jars.
4. *foot-cloth*: large ornamented cloth laid over horse's back; sign of rank.
17. *loose liver*: physicians were reputedly impious.
18. *purgation*: (i) proof, trial, (ii) movement of bowels.

foot deep, my grave, my grave, my grave. Hist, master doctor, a word, sir; hark, 'tis not the plague, is't?

PENITENT: The plague, sir? No!   30

SIR BOUNTEOUS: Good.

PENITENT [aside]: He ne'er asks whether it be the pox or no, and of the twain that had been more likely.

SIR BOUNTEOUS: How now, my wench? How dost?

COURTESAN [coughing]: Huh. Weak, knight. Huh.

PENITENT [aside]: She says true, he's a weak knight indeed.

SIR BOUNTEOUS: Where does it hold thee most, wench?

COURTESAN: All parts alike, sir.

PENITENT [aside]: She says true still, for it holds her in none.

SIR BOUNTEOUS: Hark in thine ear, thou'rt breeding of young   40
bones; I am afraid I have got thee with child, i' faith.

COURTESAN: I fear that much, sir.

SIR BOUNTEOUS: Oh, oh, if it should! A young Progress, when all's done!

COURTESAN: You have done your good will, sir.

SIR BOUNTEOUS: I see by her, 'tis nothing but a surfeit of Venus i' faith, and tho' I be old, I have gi'n't her. But since I had the power to make thee sick, I'll have the purse to make thee whole, that's certain. – Master doctor.

PENITENT: Sir?   50

SIR BOUNTEOUS: Let's hear, I pray, what is't you minister to her?

PENITENT: Marry sir, some precious cordial, some costly refocillation, a composure comfortable and restorative.

SIR BOUNTEOUS: Ay, ay, that, that, that.

PENITENT: No poorer ingredients than the liquor of coral, clear amber, or *succinum*; unicorn's horn, six grains; *magisterium perlarum*, one scruple.

SIR BOUNTEOUS: Ah!

PENITENT: *Ossis de corde cervi*, half a scruple; *aurum potabile* or   60
his tincture –

54. *refocillation*: cordial.
57–8. *magisterium perlarum*: dog-Latin 'chief of pearls'.
58. *scruple*: one-third of a dram.
60. *Ossis . . . cervi*: little bones of female deer.
60. *aurum potabile*: liquid gold.

SIR BOUNTEOUS: Very precious, sir.

PENITENT: All which being finely contunded and mixed in a stone or glass mortar, with the spirit of diamber –

SIR BOUNTEOUS: Nay, pray be patient, sir.

PENITENT: That's impossible, I cannot be patient and a physician too, sir.

SIR BOUNTEOUS: Oh, cry you mercy, that's true, sir.

PENITENT: All which aforesaid –

70 SIR BOUNTEOUS: Ay, there you left, sir.

PENITENT: When it is almost exsiccate or dry, I add thereto *olei succini*, *olei masi*, and *cinamoni*.

SIR BOUNTEOUS: So, sir, *olei masi*, that same oil of mace is a great comfort to both the Counters.

PENITENT: And has been of a long time, sir.

SIR BOUNTEOUS: Well, be of good cheer, wench; there's gold for thee. – Huh, let her want for nothing, master doctor; a poor kinswoman of mine, nature binds me to have a care of her. – [*Aside*] There I gull'd you, master doctor. – Gather up a

80 good spirit, wench, the fit will away, 'tis but a surfeit of gristles. Ha, ha, I have fitted her; an old knight and a cock o' th' game still; I have not spurs for nothing, I see.

PENITENT: No, by my faith, they're hatch'd; they cost you an angel, sir.

SIR BOUNTEOUS: Look to her good, master doctor, let her want nothing. I've given her enough already, ha, ha, ha! (*Exit.*)

COURTESAN: So, is he gone?

PENITENT: He's like himself, gone.

COURTESAN: Here's somewhat to set up with. How soon he

90 took occasion to slip into his own flattery, soothing his own

63. *contunded*: pounded.

64. *diamber*: cordial containing ambergris.

72. *olei succini*: oil of amber.

72. *olei masi*: oil of mace; with pun on mace carried by sergeants when arresting debtors.

74. *Counters*: two debtors' prisons.

81. *gristles*: see note to II, vi, 65.

83. *hatch'd*: inlaid; with possible pun on spur-royal 'hatching' angel (coin).

88. *gone*: (i) departed, (ii) out of his wits.

defects! He only fears he has done that deed, which I ne'er
fear'd to come from him in my life. This purchase came
unlook'd for.

PENITENT: Hist, the pair of sons and heirs.

COURTESAN: Oh, they're welcome, they bring money.

    (*Enter* MASTER[S] INESSE *and* POSSIBILITY.)

POSSIBILITY: Master doctor –.

PENITENT: I come to you, gentlem[e]n.

POSSIBILITY: How does she now?

PENITENT: Faith, much after one fashion, sir.

INESSE: There's hope of life, sir? 100

PENITENT: I see no signs of death of her.

POSSIBILITY: That's some comfort; will she take anything yet?

PENITENT: Yes, yes, yes, she'll take still: sh'as a kind of facility
in taking. How comes your band bloody, sir?

INESSE: You may see I met with a scab, sir.

PENITENT: *Diversa genera scabierum*, as Pliny reports, there are
divers kind of scabs.

INESSE: Pray let's hear 'em, sir.

PENITENT: An itching scab, that is your harlot; a sore scab,
your usurer; a running, your promoter; a broad scab, your 110
intelligencer; but a white scab, that's a scald knave and a
pander: but to speak truth, the only scabs we are nowadays
troubled withal, are new officers.

INESSE: Why now you come to mine, sir, for I'll be sworn one
of them was very busy about my head this morning, and he
should be a scab by that, for they are ambitious and covet the
head.

PENITENT: Why, you saw I deriv'd him, sir.

INESSE: You physicians are mad gentlemen.

PENITENT: We physicians see the most sights of any men 120
living. Your astronomers look upward into th' air, we look
downward into th' body, and indeed we have power upward
and downward.

                92. *purchase*: profit.
              104. *band*: wide collar.
              110. *promoter*: informer.
              111. *intelligencer*: spy.
              118. *deriv'd*: traced his ancestry.

INESSE: That you have, i' faith, sir.

POSSIBILITY: Lady, how cheer you now?

COURTESAN: The same woman still – huh.

POSSIBILITY: That's not good.

COURTESAN: Little alteration. Fie, fie, you have been too lavish, gentlemen.

130 INESSE: Puh, talk not of that, lady, thy health's worth a million. Here, master doctor, spare for no cost.

POSSIBILITY: Look what you find there, sir.

COURTESAN: What do you mean, gentlemen? Put up, put up; you see I'm down and cannot strive with you; I would rule you else. You have me at advantage, but if ever I live, I will requite it deeply.

INESSE: Tut, an't come to that once, we'll requite ourselves well enough.

POSSIBILITY: Mistress Harebrain, lady, is setting forth to
140 visit you too.

COURTESAN: Hah, huh!

PENITENT [*aside*]: There struck the minute that brings forth the birth of all my joys and wishes. But see the jar now, how shall I rid these from her?

COURTESAN: Pray, gentlem[e]n, stay not above an hour from my sight.

INESSE: S'foot, we are not going, lady.

PENITENT [*aside*]: Subtly brought about, yet 'twill not do, they'll stick by't. – A word with you, gentlemen.

150 BOTH: What says master doctor?

PENITENT: She wants but settling of her sense with rest; one hour's sleep, gentlemen, would set all parts in tune.

POSSIBILITY: He says true, i' faith.

INESSE: Get her to sleep, master doctor, we'll both sit here and watch by her.

PENITENT [*aside*]: Hell's angels watch you! No art can prevail with 'em. What with the thought of joys, and sight of crosses, my wits are at Hercules' Pillars, *non plus ultra*.

133. *Put up*: i.e. put away your purses.
143. *jar*: obstacle.
158. *non plus ultra*: 'no further'.

COURTESAN: Master doctor, master doctor!

PENITENT: Here, lady. 160

COURTESAN: Your physic works; lend me your hand.

POSSIBILITY: Farewell, sweet lady.

INESSE: Adieu, master doctor.

[*Exeunt* INESSE *and* POSSIBILITY.]

COURTESAN: So.

PENITENT: Let me admire thee,
The wit of man wanes and decreases soon,
But women's wit is ever at full moon.
(*Enter* MISTRESS HAREBRAIN.)
There shot a star from heaven.
I dare not yet behold my happiness,
The splendour is so glorious and so piercing. 170

COURTESAN: Mistress Harebrain, give my wit thanks hereafter;
your wishes are in sight, your opportunity spacious.

MISTRESS HAREBRAIN: Will you but hear a word from me?

COURTESAN: Wha-a-?

MISTRESS HAREBRAIN: My husband himself brought me to th'
door, walks below for my return. Jealousy is prick-ear'd, and
will hear the wagging of a hair.

COURTESAN: Pish, y'are a faint-liver! Trust yourself with your
pleasure and me with your security. Go.

PENITENT: The fullness of my wish!

MISTRESS HAREBRAIN: Of my desire! 180

PENITENT: Beyond this sphere I never will aspire.

[*Exeunt* PENITENT *and* MISTRESS HAREBRAIN.]

(*Enter* MASTER HAREBRAIN, *listening.*)

HAREBRAIN: I'll listen, now the flesh draws nigh her end;
At such a time women exchange their secrets,
And ransack the close corners of their hearts;
What many years hath whelm'd, this hour imparts.

COURTESAN: Pray, sit down, there's a low stool. Good Mistress
Harebrain, this was kindly done; huh, give me your hand; huh,
alas how cold you are. Ev'n so is your husband, that worthy
wise gentleman; as comfortable a man to woman in my case
as ever trod – huh – shoe-leather. Love him, honour him, stick 190

Stage direction. *Harebrain, listening*: see Additional Notes.

by him, he lets you want nothing that's fit for a woman; and
to be sure on't, he will see himself that you want it not.

HAREBRAIN: And so I do i' faith, 'tis right my humour.

COURTESAN: You live a lady's life with him, go where you will,
ride when you will, and do what you will.

HAREBRAIN: Not so, not so neither, she's better look'd to.

COURTESAN: I know you do, you need not tell me that; 'twere
e'en pity of your life, i' faith, if ever you should wrong such an
innocent gentleman. Fie, Mistress Harebrain, what do you
200 mean? Come you to discomfort me? Nothing but weeping
with you?

HAREBRAIN: She's weeping, 'tas made her weep; my wife shows
her good nature already.

COURTESAN: Still, still weeping? Huff, huff, huff, why, how
now, woman? Hey, hy, hy, for shame, leave. Suh, suh, she
cannot answer me for snobbing.

HAREBRAIN: All this does her good. Beshrew my heart and I
pity her; let her shed tears till morning, I'll stay for her. She
shall have enough on't by my goodwill, I'll not be her hin-
210 drance.

COURTESAN: O no, lay your hand here, Mistress Harebrain; ay,
there, oh, there, there lies my pain, good gentlewoman. Sore?
Oh, ay, I can scarce endure your hand upon't.

HAREBRAIN: Poor soul, how she's tormented.

COURTESAN: Yes, yes, I ate a cullis an hour since.

HAREBRAIN: There's some comfort in that yet; she may 'scape
it.

COURTESAN: Oh, it lies about my heart much!

HAREBRAIN: I'm sorry for that, i' faith, she'll hardly 'scape it.

220 COURTESAN: Bound? No, no, I'd a very comfortable stool this
morning.

HAREBRAIN: I'm glad of that i' faith, that's a good sign, I smell
she'll 'scape it now.

COURTESAN: Will you be going then?

HAREBRAIN: Fall back, she's coming.

COURTESAN: Thanks, good Mistress Harebrain, welcome sweet

---

193. *humour*: (i) temperament, (ii) desire.
206. *snobbing*: sobbing.

Mistress Harebrain; pray commend me to the good gentleman
your husband.

HAREBRAIN: I could do that myself now.

COURTESAN: And to my uncle Winchcombe, and to my Aunt 230
Lipsalve, and to my cousin Falsetop, and to my cousin Lickit,
and to my cousin Horseman, and to all my good cousins in
Clerkenwell and St John's.

(*Enter* MISTRESS HAREBRAIN *with* MASTER PENITENT.)

MISTRESS HAREBRAIN: At three days' end my husband takes
a journey.

PENITENT: Oh, thence I derive a second meeting.

MISTRESS HAREBRAIN: May it prosper still;
Till then I rest a captive to his will.
Once again health, rest, and strength to thee, sweet lady.
Farewell, you witty squall. Good master doctor, have a care 240
to her body if you stand her friend. I know you can do her
good.

COURTESAN: Take pity of your waiter, go. Farewell, sweet
Mistress Harebrain. [*Exit.*]

HAREBRAIN: Welcome sweet wife, alight upon my lip, never
was hour spent better.

MISTRESS HAREBRAIN: Why, were you within the hearing,
sir?

HAREBRAIN: Ay, that I was, i' faith, to my great comfort; I
deceiv'd you there, wife, ha, ha!   250
I do entreat thee, nay, conjure thee, wife
Upon my love, or what can more be said,
Oft'ner to visit this sick, virtuous maid.

MISTRESS HAREBRAIN: Be not so fierce, your will shall be
obey'd.

HAREBRAIN: Why then, I see thou lov'st me.
[*Exeunt* HAREBRAIN *and his wife.*]

PENITENT: Art of ladies!
When plots are e'en past hope and hang their head,
Set with a woman's hand, they thrive and spread. (*Exit.*)

243. *waiter*: servant, admirer.

[SCENE THREE]

(*Enter* FOLLYWIT *with* LIEUTENANT MAWWORM,
ANCIENT HOBOY *and the rest of his consorts.*)

FOLLYWIT: Was't not well manag'd, you necessary mischiefs?
Did the plot want either life or art?

MAWWORM: 'Twas so well, captain, I would you could make
such another muss at all adventures.

FOLLYWIT: Dost call't a muss? I am sure my grandsire ne'er
got his money worse in his life than I got it from him. If ever
he did cozen the simple, why I was born to revenge their
quarrel; if ever oppress the widow, I, a fatherless child, have
done as much for him. And so 'tis through the world either in
10   jest or earnest. Let the usurer look for't, for craft recoils in the
end, like an overcharg'd musket, and maims the very hand
that puts fire to't; there needs no more but a usurer's own
blow to strike him from hence to hell, 'twill set him forward
with a vengeance. But here lay the jest, whoresons: my grandsire, thinking in his conscience that we had not robb'd him
enough o'ernight, must needs pity me i' th' morning, and
give me the rest.

MAWWORM: Two hundred pounds in fair rose-nobles, I protest!

FOLLYWIT: Push, I knew he could not sleep quietly till he had
20   paid me for robbing of him too; 'tis his humour, and the
humour of most of your rich men in the course of their lives;
for you know, they always feast those mouths that are least
needy and give them more that have too much already. And
what call you that, but robbing of themselves a courtlier way?
Oh!

MAWWORM: Cuds me, how now, captain?

FOLLYWIT: A cold fit that comes over my memory, and has a
shrewd pull at my fortunes.

MAWWORM: What's that, sir?

4. *muss*: row, scramble.
18. *rose-nobles*: gold coins, worth about eighty pence each.
28. *shrewd*: sharp.

FOLLYWIT: Is it for certain, lieutenant, that my grandsire keeps 30
    an uncertain creature, a quean?

MAWWORM: Ay, that's too true, sir.

FOLLYWIT: So much the more preposterous for me. I shall hop
    shorter by that trick; she carries away the thirds at least. 'Twill
    prove entail'd land, I am afraid, when all's done, i' faith.
    Nay, I have known a vicious, old, thought-acting father,
    Damn'd only in his dreams, thirsting for game,
    (When his best parts hung down their heads for shame)
    For his blanch'd harlot dispossess his son,
    And make the pox his heir; 'twas gravely done. – 40
    How had'st thou first knowledge on't, lieutenant?

MAWWORM: Faith, from discourse, yet all the policy
    That I could use, I could not get her name.

FOLLYWIT: Dull slave, that ne'er couldst spy it!

MAWWORM: But the manner of her coming was describ'd to me.

FOLLYWIT: How is the manner, prithee?

MAWWORM: Marry sir, she comes most commonly coach'd.

FOLLYWIT: Most commonly coach'd indeed, for coaches are as
    common nowadays as some that ride in 'em. She comes most
    commonly coach'd –? 50

MAWWORM: True, there I left, sir, guarded with some leash of
    pimps.

FOLLYWIT: Beside the coachman?

MAWWORM: Right, sir; then alighting, she's privately receiv'd
    by Master Gunwater.

FOLLYWIT: That's my grandsire's chief gentleman i' th' chain
    of gold. That he should live to be a pander, and yet look upon
    his chain and his velvet jacket!

MAWWORM: Then is your grandsire rounded i' th' ear, the key,

31. *quean*: slut.

33. *preposterous*: in etymological sense 'placing last what should come
first' (Henning). Cf. *The Dutch Courtesan*, I, i, 34.

35. *entail'd*: with restrictions on transference (with pun on 'tail').

36. *thought-acting*: capable of (sex) act only in imagination.

39. *blanch'd*: artificially whitened.

40. *gravely*: with the usual pun.

48. *coach'd*: by coach.

59. *rounded*: whispered.

60   given after the Italian fashion, backward, she closely convey'd
into his closet, there remaining till either opportunity smile
upon his credit, or he send down some hot caudle to take
order in his performance.

FOLLYWIT: Peace, 'tis mine own i' faith, I ha't!

MAWWORM: How now, sir?

FOLLYWIT: Thanks, thanks to any spirit,
That mingled it 'mong my inventions!

HOBOY: Why, Master Follywit?

ALL: Captain?

FOLLYWIT: Give me scope and hear me,

70   I have begot that means which will both furnish me,
And make that quean walk under his conceit.

MAWWORM: That were double happiness, to put thyself into
money and her out of favour.

FOLLYWIT: And all at one dealing!

HOBOY: 'Sfoot, I long to see that hand play'd!

FOLLYWIT: And thou shalt see't quickly, i' faith; nay, 'tis in
grain, I warrant it hold colour. Lieutenant, step behind yon
hanging; if I mistook not at my entrance, there hangs the
lower part of a gentlewoman's gown, with a mask and a chin-

80   clout; bring all this way. Nay, but do't cunningly now, 'tis a
friend's house, and I'd use it so – there's a taste for you.

    [*Exit* MAWWORM.]

HOBOY: But prithee what wilt thou do with a gentlewoman's
lower part?

FOLLYWIT: Why, use it.

HOBOY: Y'ave answered me indeed in that, I can demand no
farther.

    [*Re-enter* MAWWORM.]

FOLLYWIT: Well said. Lieutenant –

MAWWORM: What will you do now, sir?

FOLLYWIT: Come, come, thou shalt see a woman quickly made

90   up here.

---

62. *caudle*: warm, spiced cordial.
71. *walk . . . conceit*: sink in his opinion.
76–7. *in grain*: colour-fast (grain = cochineal dye).
79–80. *chin-clout*: scarf.

MAWWORM: But that's against kind, captain, for they are always long a-making ready.

FOLLYWIT: And is not most they do against kind, I prithee? To lie with their horse-keeper, is not that against kind? To wear half-moons made of another's hair, is not that against kind? To drink down a man, she that should set him up, pray is not that monstrously against kind now? Nay, over with it, lieutenant, over with it; ever while you live put a woman's clothes over her head; Cupid plays best at blind-man['s] buff.

MAWWORM: You shall have your will, maintenance. I love mad   100
tricks as well as you for your heart, sir. But what shift will you make for upper bodies, captain?

FOLLYWIT: I see now thou'rt an ass, why I'm ready.

MAWWORM: Ready?

FOLLYWIT: Why, the doublet serves as well as the best, and is most in fashion; we're all male to th' middle, mankind from the beaver to th' bum. 'Tis an Amazonian time, you shall have women shortly tread their husbands. I should have a couple of locks behind, prithee, lieutenant, find 'em out for me, and wind 'em about my hatband. Nay, you shall see, we'll   110
be in fashion to a hair, and become all with probability; the most musty-visage critic shall not except against me.

MAWWORM: Nay, I'll give thee thy due behind thy back, thou art as mad a piece of clay –

FOLLYWIT: Clay! Dost call thy captain clay? Indeed, clay was made to stop holes, he says true. Did not I tell you, rascal, you should see a woman quickly made up?

HOBOY: I'll swear for't, captain.

FOLLYWIT: Come, come, my mask and my chin-clout – come into th' clout.   120

MAWWORM: Nay, they were both i' th' court long ago, sir.

FOLLYWIT: Let me see, where shall I choose two or three for pimps now? But I cannot choose amiss amongst you all, that's

91. *kind*: nature (i.e. of their sex).

102. *upper bodies*: bodices; from the 1580s, these closely resembled men's doublets.

107. *beaver . . . bum*: hat to waist. (Bum = roll of stiffened fabric placed around hips.)

the best. Well, as I am a quean, you were best have a care of me, and guard me sure, I give you warning beforehand, 'tis a monkey-tail'd age. Life, you shall go nigh to have half a dozen blithe fellows surprise me cowardly, carry me away with a pair of oars, and put in at Putney.

MAWWORM: We should laugh at that i' faith.

130 FOLLYWIT: Or shoot in upo' th' coast of Cue.

MAWWORM: Two notable fit landing places for lechers, P. and C., Putney and Cue.

FOLLYWIT: Well, say you have fair warning on't. The hair about the hat is as good as a flag upo' th' pole at a common playhouse to waft company, and a chin-clout is of that powerful attraction I can tell you, 'twill draw more linen to't.

MAWWORM: Fear not us, captain, there's none here but can fight for a whore as well as some Inns o' Court man.

FOLLYWIT: Why then, set forward; and as you scorn two
140 shilling brothel, twelvepenny panderism, and such base bribes, guard me from bonny scribs and bony scribes.

MAWWORM: Hang 'em, pensions, and allowances, fourpence half-penny a meal, hang 'em!

(*Exeunt.*)

126. *monkey-tail'd*: lecherous.
136. *draw . . . to't*: ? (i) attract gallants in fine clothes, (ii) draw gifts of clothes.
139–40. *two shilling brothel*: somewhat less than the standard fee of half a crown.
141. *scribs*: misers.

ACT FOUR

[SCENE ONE]

(Enter in his chamber out of his study, MASTER PENITENT
BROTHEL, *a book in his hand, reading.)*
PENITENT: Ha! Read that place again, *Adultery*
Draws the divorce 'twixt heaven and the soul.
Accursed man that stand'st divorc'd from heaven!
Thou wretched unthrift, that has play'd away
Thy eternal portion at a minute's game,
To please the flesh, hast blotted out thy name,
Where were thy nobler meditations busied
That they durst trust this body with itself,
This natural drunkard that undoes us all
And makes our shame apparent in our fall?   10
Then let my blood pay for't and vex and boil,
My soul I know would never grieve to th' death
The eternal spirit that feeds her with his breath;
Nay, I that knew the price of life and sin,
What crown is kept for continence, what for lust,
The end of man, and glory of that end
As endless as the giver,
To dote on weakness, slime, corruption, woman!
What is she, took asunder from her clothes?
Being ready, she consists of hundred pieces,   20
Much like your German clock, and near allied
Both are so nice, they cannot go for pride.
Beside a greater fault, but too well known,
They'll strike to ten when they should stop at one.
Within these three days the next meeting's fix'd;
If I meet then, hell and my soul be mix'd.
My lodging I know constantly, she not knows.
Sin's hate is the best gift that sin bestows;

I'll ne'er embrace her more; never, better witness, never.
(*Enter the devil in her shape, claps him on the shoulder.*)

30 SUCCUBUS: What, at a stand? The fitter for my company!

PENITENT: Celestial soldiers guard me!

SUCCUBUS: How now, man? Life, did the quickness of my
presence fright thee?

PENITENT: Shield me, you ministers of faith and grace!

SUCCUBUS: Leave, leave; are you not asham'd to use such
words to a woman?

PENITENT: Th'art a devil.

SUCCUBUS: A devil? Feel, feel, man! Has a devil flesh and bone?

40 PENITENT: I do conjure thee by that dreadful power –

SUCCUBUS: The man has a delight to make me tremble;
Are these the fruits of thy adventurous love?
Was I entic'd for this, to be soon rejected?
Come, what has chang'd thee so, delight?

PENITENT: Away!

SUCCUBUS: Remember –

PENITENT: Leave my sight!

SUCCUBUS: Have I this meeting wrought with cunning,
Which when I come I find thee shunning?

50 Rouse thy amorous thoughts and twine me,
All my interest I resign thee.
Shall we let slip this mutual hour,
Comes so seldom in her power?
Where's thy lip, thy clip, thy fathom?
Had women such loves, would't not mad 'em?
Art a man? Or dost abuse one?
A love, and know'st not how to use one?
Come, I'll teach thee –

PENITENT: Do not follow!

60 SUCCUBUS: Once so firm and now so hollow?
When was place and season sweeter?
Thy bliss in sight and dar'st not meet her?

Stage direction. *her*: i.e. Mistress Harebrain's.
30. *Succubus*: female demon alleged to cohabit with men.
30. *at a stand*: (i) idle, (i) sexually ready.
54. *clip . . . fathom*: embrace.

Where's thy courage, youth and vigour?
Love's best pleas'd when't's seiz'd with rigour:
Seize me then with veins most cheerful,
Women love no flesh that's fearful.
'Tis but a fit. Come, drink't away,
And dance and sing, and kiss and play.
Fa le la, le la, fa le la, le la la;
Fa le la, fa la le, la le la!   70

PENITENT: Torment me not!

SUCCUBUS: Fa le la, fa le la, fa la la, loh!

PENITENT: Fury!

SUCCUBUS: Fa le la, fa le la, fa la la loh!

PENITENT: Devil! I do conjure thee once again,
By that soul-quaking thunder, to depart,
And leave this chamber, freed from thy damn'd art.
    [SUCCUBUS *stamps and exit.*]

PENITENT: It has prevail'd. Oh my sin-shaking sinews!
What should I think? Jasper! Why, Jasper!
    [*Enter* JASPER.]

JASPER: Sir? How now? What has disturb'd you, sir?   80

PENITENT: A fit, a qualm – is Mistress Harebrain gone?

JASPER: Who, sir? Mistress Harebrain?

PENITENT: Is she gone, I say?

JASPER: Gone? Why, she was never here yet.

PENITENT: No?

JASPER: Why no, sir.

PENITENT: Art sure on't?

JASPER: Sure on't? If I be sure I breathe, and am myself!

PENITENT: I like it not – where kept'st thou?

JASPER: I' th' next room, sir.   90

PENITENT: Why, she struck by thee, man.

JASPER: You'd make one mad, sir. That a gentlewoman should
steal by me and I not hear her! 'Sfoot, one may hear the
ruffling of their bums almost an hour before we see 'em.

PENITENT: I will be satisfied, altho' to hazard.
What though her husband meet me? I am honest.
When men's intents are wicked, their guilt haunts 'em,

64–5. *seiz'd . . . Seize*: Q – 'seard . . . Ceare'.

But when they're just, they're arm'd and nothing daunts 'em.

JASPER [*aside*]: What strange humour call you this? He dreams
100   of women and both his eyes broad open!

(*Exeunt.*)

[SCENE TWO]

(*Enter at one door* SIR BOUNTEOUS, *at another* GUNWATER.)

SIR BOUNTEOUS: Why how now, Master Gunwater? What's the
news with your haste?

GUNWATER: I have a thing to tell your worship.

SIR BOUNTEOUS: Why, prithee tell me; speak, man.

GUNWATER: Your worship shall pardon me, I have better
bringing up than so.

SIR BOUNTEOUS: How, sir?

GUNWATER: 'Tis a thing made fit for your ear, sir.

SIR BOUNTEOUS: Oh-o-o, cry you mercy; now I begin to taste
10   you. Is she come?

GUNWATER: She's come, sir.

SIR BOUNTEOUS: Recover'd, well and sound again?

GUNWATER: That's to be fear'd, sir.

SIR BOUNTEOUS: Why, sir?

GUNWATER: She wears a linen cloth about her jaw.

SIR BOUNTEOUS: Ha, ha, haw! Why, that's the fashion, you
whoreson Gunwater.

GUNWATER: The fashion, sir?

Live I so long time to see that a fashion,
20   Which rather was an emblem of dispraise?

It was suspected much in Monsieur's days.

SIR BOUNTEOUS: Ay, ay, in those days; that was a queasy time.
Our age is better harden'd now, and put oft'ner in the fire;
we are tried what we are. Tut, the pox is as natural now, as an
ague in the springtime, we seldom take physic without it.
Here, take this key, you know what duties belong to't. Go,
give order for a cullis; let there be a good fire made i' th'
matted chamber, do you hear, sir?

9. *taste*: (i) understand, (ii) appreciate.
15. *linen* . . . *jaw*: i.e. to hide effect of syphilis.

GUNWATER: I know my office, sir. (*Exit.*)

SIR BOUNTEOUS: An old man's venery is very chargeable, my   30
masters; there's much cookery belongs to't. (*Exit.*)

[SCENE THREE]

(*Enter* GUNWATER *with* FOLLYWIT *in* COURTESAN'S
disguise, and mask'd.)

GUNWATER: Come, lady, you know where you are now?

FOLLYWIT: Yes, good Master Gunwater.

GUNWATER: This is the old closet, you know.

FOLLYWIT: I remember it well, sir.

GUNWATER: There stands a casket. I would my yearly revenue
were but worth the wealth that's lock'd in't, lady; yet I have
fifty pound a year, wench.

FOLLYWIT: Beside your apparel, sir?

GUNWATER: Yes, faith, have I.

FOLLYWIT: But then you reckon your chain, sir.   10

GUNWATER: No, by my troth do I not, neither; faith, an you
consider me rightly, sweet lady, you might admit a choice
gentleman into your service.

FOLLYWIT: Oh, pray, away, sir.

GUNWATER: Pusha, come, come, you do but hinder your fortunes, i' faith. I have the command of all the house, I can
tell you. Nothing comes into th' kitchen, but comes through
my hands.

FOLLYWIT: Pray do not handle me, sir.

GUNWATER: Faith y'are too nice, lady; and as for my secrecy,   20
you know I have vow'd it often to you.

FOLLYWIT: Vow'd it? No, no, you men are fickle.

GUNWATER: Fickle? 'Sfoot, bind me, lady –

FOLLYWIT: Why, I bind you by virtue of this chain to meet me
tomorrow at the Flower de luce yonder, between nine and ten.

30. *venery*: (i) lechery, (ii) hunting.
30. *chargeable*: expensive.
12–13. *admit . . . service*: i.e. as a lover.
20. *nice*: fastidious.

GUNWATER: And if I do not, lady, let me lose it, thy love and
my best fortunes.

FOLLYWIT: Why, now I'll try you. Go to!

GUNWATER: Farewell, sweet lady. (*Kisses her [and] exit.*)

30 FOLLYWIT: Welcome sweet cockscomb; by my faith, a good
induction. I perceive by his overworn phrase, and his action
toward the middle region, still there has been some saucy
nibbling motion, and no doubt the cunning quean waited
but for her prey, and I think 'tis better bestow'd upon me for
his soul's health – and his body's too. I'll teach the slave to be
so bold yet, as once to offer to vault into his master's saddle,
i' faith. Now casket, by your leave, I have seen your outside
oft, but that's no proof. Some have fair outsides that are
nothing worth. Ha! Now, by my faith, a gentlewoman of very
40 good parts, Diamond, Ruby, Sapphire, *onyx cum prole
silexque*. If I do not wonder how the quean 'scap'd tempting,
I'm an hermaphrodite. Sure she could lack nothing but the
devil to point to't – and I wonder that he should be missing.
Well, 'tis better as it is; this is the fruit of old-grunting-venery.
Grandsire, you may thank your drab for this; oh fie, in your
crinkling days, grandsire, keep a courtesan to hinder your
grandchild! 'Tis against nature, i' faith, and I hope you'll be
weary on't. Now to my villains that lurk close below.
Who keeps a harlot tell him this from me,
50 He needs nor thief, disease, nor enemy. (*Exit.*)
  (*Enter* SIR BOUNTEOUS.)

SIR BOUNTEOUS: Ah, sirrah, methinks I feel myself well toasted,
bumbasted, rubb'd and refresh'd; but i' faith, I cannot forget
to think how soon sickness has altered her to my taste. I gave
her a kiss at bottom o' th' stairs, and by th' mass, methought
her breath had much ado to be sweet, like a thing compounded
methought of wine, beer and tobacco; I smelt much pudding
in't.

33. *quean*: harlot.
46. *crinkling*: wrinkled.
52. *bumbasted*: (i) beaten, (ii) stuffed.
56. *pudding*: kind of tobacco.

It may be but my fancy, or her physic,
For this I know, her health gave such content,
The fault rests in her sickness, or my scent.   60
How dost thou now, sweet girl, what, well recover'd? Sickness
quite gone, ha? Speak. Ha? Wench? Frank Gullman, why,
body of me, what's here? My casket wide open, broke open,
my jewels stol'n! Why, Gunwater!

GUNWATER [within]: Anon, anon, sir.

SIR BOUNTEOUS: Come hither, Gunwater!

GUNWATER [within]: That were small manners sir, i' faith, I'll
find a time anon. Your worship's busy yet.

SIR BOUNTEOUS: Why, Gunwater!

GUNWATER [within]: Foh, nay then, you'll make me blush i'   70
faith, sir –

SIR BOUNTEOUS: Where's this creature?

GUNWATER: What creature is't you'd have, sir?

SIR BOUNTEOUS: The worst that ever breathes.

GUNWATER: That's a wild boar, sir.

SIR BOUNTEOUS: That's a vild whore, sir. Where didst thou
leave her, rascal?

GUNWATER: Who, your recreation, sir?

SIR BOUNTEOUS: My execration, sir.

GUNWATER: Where I was wont, in your worship's closet.   80

SIR BOUNTEOUS: A pox engross her, it appears too true. See
you this casket, sir?

GUNWATER: My chain, my chain, my chain, my one and only
chain! (Exit.)

SIR BOUNTEOUS: Thou run'st to much purpose now, Gunwater,
yea? Is not a quean enough to answer for, but she must join
a thief to't? A thieving quean! Nay, I have done with her, i'
faith, 'tis a sign sh'as been sick o' late, for she's a great deal
worse than she was. By my troth, I would have pawn'd my
life upon't.   90
Did she want anything? Was she not supplied?
Nay and liberally, for that's an old man's sin,
We'll feast our lechery though we starve our kin.
Is not my name Sir Bounteous? Am I not express'd there?

Ah fie, fie, fie, fie, fie, but I perceive
Tho' she have never so complete a friend,
A strumpet's love will have a waft i' th' end,
And distaste the vessel. I can hardly bear this;
But say I should complain, perhaps she has pawn'd 'em,
100 'Sfoot the judges will but laugh at it and bid her borrow more
money of 'em, make the old fellow pay for's lechery, that's all
the 'mends I get. I have seen the same case tried at Newbury
the last 'sizes.
Well, things must slip and sleep; I will dissemble it,
Because my credit shall not lose her lustre,
But whilst I live I'll neither love nor trust her.
I ha' done, I ha' done, I ha' done with her, i' faith. (*Exit.*)

[SCENE FOUR]

(MASTER PENITENT BROTHEL *knocking within; enter a
Servant.*)
SERVANT: Who's that knocks?
PENITENT [*within*]: A friend.
(*Enter* MASTER PENITENT.)
SERVANT: What's your will, sir?
PENITENT: Is Master Harebrain at home?
SERVANT: No, newly gone from it, sir.
PENITENT: Where's the gentlewoman his wife?
SERVANT: My mistress is within, sir.
PENITENT: When came she in, I pray?
SERVANT: Who, my mistress? She was not out these two days to
10 my knowledge.
PENITENT: No? Trust me, I'd thought I'd seen her. I would
request a word with her.
SERVANT: I'll tell her, sir.
PENITENT: I thank you – It likes me worse and worse –
(*Enter* MISTRESS HAREBRAIN.)

96. *friend*: as in 'we're just good friends'.
97. *waft*: bad taste or odour.

MISTRESS HAREBRAIN: Why, how now, sir? 'Twas desperately
  adventur'd; I little look't for you until the morrow.

PENITENT: No? Why, what made you at my chamber then,
  even now?

MISTRESS HAREBRAIN: I, at your chamber?

PENITENT: Puh, dissemble not; come, come, you were there.   20

MISTRESS HAREBRAIN: By my life, you wrong me, sir.

PENITENT: What?

MISTRESS HAREBRAIN: First y'are not ignorant what watch
  keeps o'er me,
  And for your chamber, as I live I know't not.

PENITENT: Burst into sorrow then, and grief's extremes,
  Whilst I beat on this flesh.

MISTRESS HAREBRAIN: What is't disturbs you, sir?

PENITENT: Then was the devil in your likeness there.

MISTRESS HAREBRAIN: Ha?

PENITENT: The very devil assum'd thee formally,
  That face, that voice, that gesture, that attire,   30
  E'en as it sits on thee, not a pleat alter'd,
  That beaver band, the colour of that periwig,
  The farthingale above the navel, all
  As if the fashion were his own invention.

MISTRESS HAREBRAIN: Mercy defend me!

PENITENT: To beguile me more,
  The cunning succubus told me that meeting
  Was wrought o' purpose by much wit and art,
  Wept to me, laid my vows before me, urg'd me,
  Gave me the private marks of all our love,
  Woo'd me in wanton and effeminate rhymes,   40
  And sung and danc'd about me like a fairy,
  And had not worthier cogitations blest me,
  Thy form and his enchantments had possess'd me.

MISTRESS HAREBRAIN: What shall become of me? My own
  thoughts doom me!

PENITENT: Be honest; then the devil will ne'er assume thee.
  He has no pleasure in that shape to abide,

29. *assumed . . . formally*: took your form.
32. *beaver band*: beaver-skin hat-band.

Where these two sisters reign not, lust or pride.
He as much trembles at a constant mind
As looser flesh at him. Be not dismay'd;
50 Spring souls for joy, his policies are betray'd.
Forgive me, Mistress Harebrain, on whose soul
The guilt hangs double,
My lust and thy enticement; both I challenge,
And therefore of due vengeance it appear'd
To none but me, to whom both sins inher'd.
What knows the lecher when he clips his whore
Whether it be the devil his parts adore?
They're both so like, that in our natural sense
I could discern no change nor difference.
60 No marvel then times should so stretch and turn:
None for religion, all for pleasure burn.
Hot zeal into hot lust is now transform'd,
Grace into painting, charity into clothes,
Faith into false hair, and put off as often.
There's nothing but our virtue knows a mean,
He that kept open house now keeps a quean.
He will keep open still that he commends,
And there he keeps a table for his friends;
And she consumes more than his sire could hoard,
70 Being more common than his house or board.
    (*Enter* HAREBRAIN.)
Live honest, and live happy, keep thy vows,
She's part a virgin whom but one man knows.
Embrace thy husband, and beside him none,
Having but one heart, give it but to one.
MISTRESS HAREBRAIN: I vow it on my knees, with tears true
    bred
No man shall ever wrong my husband's bed.
PENITENT: Rise, I'm thy friend for ever.
HAREBRAIN: And I thine for ever and ever.

---

50. *his*: used as masculine and feminine possessive.
51. *whose*: i.e. the speaker's.
53. *challenge*: claim.
67. *that*: that which.

Let me embrace thee, sir, whom I will love
Even next unto my soul, and that's my wife; 80
Two dear rare gems this hour presents me with,
A wife that's modest, and a friend that's right.
Idle suspect and fear, now take your flight.

PENITENT: A happy inward peace crown both your joys.

HAREBRAIN: Thanks above utterance to you.

[*Enter* SERVANT.]

Now, the news?

SERVANT: Sir Bounteous Progress, sir,
Invites you and my mistress to a feast,
On Tuesday next; his man attends without.

HAREBRAIN: Return both with our willingness and thanks.
I will entreat you, sir, to be my guest. 90

PENITENT: Who, I, sir?

HAREBRAIN: Faith, you shall.

PENITENT: Well, I'll break strife.

HAREBRAIN: A friend's so rare, I'll sooner part from life.

[*Exeunt.*]

[SCENE FIVE]

(*Enter* FOLLYWIT, *the* COURTESAN *striving from him.*)

FOLLYWIT: What, so coy, so strict? Come, come.

COURTESAN: Pray change your opinion, sir, I am not for that use.

FOLLYWIT: Will you but hear me?

COURTESAN: I shall hear that I would not. (*Exit.*)

FOLLYWIT: 'Sfoot, this is strange. I've seldom seen a wench
stand upon stricter points; life, she will not endure to be
courted. Does she e'er think to prosper? I'll ne'er believe that
tree can bring forth fruit that never bears a blossom; courtship's a blossom, and often brings forth fruit in forty weeks.
'Twere a mad part in me now to turn over; if ever there were 10
any hope on't, 'tis at this instant; shall I be madder now than
ever I have been? I'm in the way, i' faith.
Man's never at high height of madness full,

83. *suspect*: suspicion.
93. *strife*: striving, strong effort.

Until he love and prove a woman's gull.
I do protest in earnest I ne'er knew
At which end to begin to affect a woman;
Till this bewitching minute, I ne'er saw
Face worth my object, till mine eye met hers.
I should laugh an' I were caught, i' faith. I'll see her again,
20   that's certain, what e'er comes on't – by your favour, ladies.
    (*Enter the* MOTHER.)

MOTHER: You're welcome, sir.

FOLLYWIT: Know you the young gentlewoman that went in
lately?

MOTHER: I have best cause to know her; I'm her mother, sir.

FOLLYWIT: Oh, in good time. I like the gentlewoman well; a
pretty, contriv'd beauty.

MOTHER: Ay, nature has done her part, sir.

FOLLYWIT: But she has one uncomely quality.

MOTHER: What's that, sir?

30 FOLLYWIT: 'Sfoot, she's afraid of a man.

MOTHER: Alas, impute that to her bashful spirit; she's fearful
of her honour.

FOLLYWIT: Of her honour? 'Slid, I'm sure I cannot get her
maidenhead with breathing upon her, nor can she lose her
honour in her tongue.

MOTHER: True, and I have often told her so, but what would
you have of a foolish virgin, sir? A wilful virgin, I tell you, sir.
I need not have been in that solitary estate that I am, had she
had grace and boldness to have put herself forward. Always
40   timorsome, always backward; ah, that same peevish honour of
hers has undone her and me both, good gentleman. The suitors,
the jewels, the jointures that has been offer'd her! We had
been made women for ever, but what was her fashion? She
could not endure the sight of a man, forsooth, but run and hole
herself presently, so choice of her honour, I am persuaded,
whene'er she has husband
She will e'en be a precedent for all married wives,
How to direct their actions, and their lives.

43. *made*: wealthy, successful.

FOLLYWIT: Have you not so much power with her to command
her presence? 50

MOTHER: You shall see straight what I can do, sir. (*Exit.*)

FOLLYWIT: Would I might be hang'd if my love do not stretch
to her deeper and deeper; those bashful maiden humours take
me prisoner. When there comes a restraint on't, upon flesh,
we are always most greedy upon't, and that makes your
merchant's wife oftentimes pay so dear for a mouthful. Give
me a woman as she was made at first, simple of herself, without sophistication, like this wench; I cannot abide them when
they have tricks, set speeches and artful entertainments. You
shall have some so impudently aspected, they will outcry the 60
forehead of a man, make him blush first and talk him into
silence, and this is counted manly in a woman. It may hold
so, sure; womanly it is not, no,

If e'er I love, or anything move me,
'Twill be a woman's simple modesty.

(*Enter* MOTHER *bringing in strivingly the* COURTESAN.)

COURTESAN: Pray let me go! Why, mother, what do you mean?
I beseech you, mother, is this your conquest now? Great glory
'tis, to overcome a poor and silly virgin.

FOLLYWIT: The wonder of our time sits in that brow,
I ne'er beheld a perfect [maid] till now. 70

MOTHER: Thou childish thing, more bashful than thou'rt wise,
Why dost thou turn aside, and drown thine eyes?
Look, fearful fool, there's no temptation near thee,
Art not asham'd that any flesh should fear thee?
Why, I durst pawn my life the gentleman means no other but
honest and pure love to thee. How say you, sir?

FOLLYWIT: By my faith, not I, lady.

MOTHER: Hark you there, what think you now forsooth? What
grieves your honour now?
Or what lascivious breath intends to rear 80

58. *sophistication*: adulteration.
60–61. *outcry . . . man*: outrage a man's modesty.
68. *silly*: innocent.
70. *maid*: Q – 'man'.
72. *drown*: drop.
74. *fear*: frighten.

Against that maiden organ your chaste ear?
Are you resolv'd now better of men's hearts?
Their faiths and their affections? With you none,
Or at most, few, whose tongues and minds are one.
Repent you now of your opinion past,
Men love as purely as you can be chaste.
To her yourself, sir, the way's broke before you.
You have the easier passage.

FOLLYWIT: Fear not, come.
90   Erect thy happy graces in thy look.
I am no curious wooer, but in faith
I love thee honourably.

COURTESAN: How mean you that, sir?

FOLLYWIT: 'Sfoot, as one loves a woman for a wife.

MOTHER: Has the gentleman answered you, troth?

FOLLYWIT: I do confess it truly to you both,
My estate is yet but sickly, but I've a grandsire
Will make me lord of thousands at his death.

MOTHER: I know your grandsire well; she knows him better.

FOLLYWIT: Why then, you know no fiction; my state then will
100   be a long day's journey 'bove the waste, wench.

MOTHER: Nay, daughter, he says true.

FOLLYWIT: And thou shalt often measure it in thy coach,
And with the wheel's tract make a girdle for't.

MOTHER: Ah, 'twill be a merry journey.

FOLLYWIT: What, is't a match? If't be, clap hands and lips.

MOTHER: 'Tis done, there's witness on't.

FOLLYWIT: Why then, mother, I salute you.

MOTHER: Thanks, sweet son. Son Follywit, come hither; if I
might counsel thee, we'll e'en take her while the good mood's
110   upon her. Send for a priest and clap't up within this hour.

FOLLYWIT: By my troth, agreed, mother.

MOTHER: Nor does her wealth consist all in her flesh,
Tho' beauty be enough wealth for a woman,
She brings a dowry of three hundred pound with her.

FOLLYWIT: 'Sfoot, that will serve till my grandsire dies; I
warrant you, he'll drop away at fall o' th' leaf. If ever he reach
to All Hollantide, I'll be hang'd.

MOTHER: O yes, son, he's a lusty old gentleman.

FOLLYWIT: Ah pox, he's given to women; he keeps a quean at this present. 120

MOTHER: Fie!

FOLLYWIT: Do not tell my wife on't.

MOTHER: That were needless, i' faith.

FOLLYWIT: He makes a great feast upon the 'leventh of this month, Tuesday next, and you shall see players there. I have one trick more to put upon him. My wife and yourself shall go thither before as my guests, and prove his entertainment. I'll meet you there at night. The jest will be here: that feast which he makes will, unknown to him, serve fitly for our wedding dinner. We shall be royally furnish'd and get some 130 charges by't.

MOTHER: An excellent course, i' faith, and a thrifty. Why, son, methinks you begin to thrive before y'are married.

FOLLYWIT: We shall thrive one day, wench, and clip enough, Between our hopes there's but a grandsire's puff. (*Exit.*)

MOTHER: So, girl, here was a bird well caught.

COURTESAN: If ever, here; but what for's grandsire? 'Twill scarce please him well.

MOTHER: Who covets fruit ne'er cares from whence it fell. Thou'st wedded youth and strength, and wealth will fall: 140 Last thou'rt made honest.

COURTESAN: And that's worth 'em all.
    (*Exeunt.*)

ACT FIVE

[SCENE ONE]

(*Enter busily* SIR BOUNTEOUS PROGRESS *for the feast* [*with* GUNWATER *and servants.*])

SIR BOUNTEOUS: Have a care, blue-coats! Bestir yourself, Master Gunwater, cast an eye into th' kitchen, o'erlook the knaves a little. Every Jack has his friend today, this cousin and that cousin puts in for a dish of meat; a man knows not till he make a feast how many varlets he feeds; acquaintances swarm in every corner like flies at Bartholomewtide that come up with drovers. 'Sfoot, I think they smell my kitchen seven mile about.

[*Enter* MASTER *and* MISTRESS HAREBRAIN *and* PENITENT BROTHEL.]

Master Harebrain and his sweet bedfellow, y'are very copi-
10 ously welcome.

HAREBRAIN: Sir, here's an especial dear friend of ours; we were bold to make his way to your table.

SIR BOUNTEOUS: Thanks for that boldness ever, good Master Harebrain. Is this your friend, sir?

HAREBRAIN: Both my wife's friend and mine, sir.

SIR BOUNTEOUS: Why then, compendiously, sir, y'are welcome.

PENITENT: In octavo I thank you, sir.

SIR BOUNTEOUS: Excellently retorted, i' faith; he's welcome for's wit. I have my sorts of salutes, and know how to place
20 'em courtly. Walk in, sweet gentlemen, walk in, there's a good fire i' th' hall. You shall have my sweet company instantly.

HAREBRAIN: Ay, good Sir Bounteous.

SIR BOUNTEOUS: You shall indeed, gentlemen.

[*Enter* SERVANT.]

How now, what news brings thee in stumbling now?

SERVANT: There are certain players come to town, sir, and desire to interlude before your worship.

SIR BOUNTEOUS: Players? By the mass, they are welcome, they'll grace my entertainment well. But for certain players, there thou liest, boy; they were never more uncertain in their lives; now up and now down, they know not when to play, where to play, nor what to play. Not when to play for fearful fools, where to play for Puritan fools, nor what to play for critical fools. Go, call 'em in. 30

[*Exit* SERVANT.]

How fitly the whoresons come upo' th' feast; troth, I was e'en wishing for 'em.

[*Enter* FOLLYWIT, MAWWORM, HOBOY *and others, disguised as players.*]

Oh welcome, welcome my friends!

FOLLYWIT: The month of May delights not in her flowers,
More than we joy in that sweet sight of yours.

SIR BOUNTEOUS: Well acted, o' my credit, I perceive he's your best actor. 40

SERVANT: He has greatest share, sir, and may live of himself, sir.

SIR BOUNTEOUS: What, what? Put on your hat, sir, pray, put on. Go to, wealth must be respected; let those that have least feathers stand bare. And whose men are you, I pray? Nay, keep on your hat still.

FOLLYWIT: We serve my Lord Owemuch, sir.

SIR BOUNTEOUS: My Lord Owemuch? By my troth, the welcom'st men alive! Give me all your hands at once. That honourable gentleman? He lay at my house in a robbery once, and took all quietly, went away cheerfully. I made a very good feast for him. I never saw a man of honour bear things braevelier away. Serve my Lord Owemuch? Welcome, i' faith. Some bastard for my lord's players; where be your boys? 50

FOLLYWIT: They come along with the waggon, sir.

SIR BOUNTEOUS: Good, good. And which is your politician among'st you? Now, i' faith, he that works out restraints, makes best legs at court, and has a suit made of purpose for

51–2. *bear . . . away*: (i) conduct himself better. With obvious pun on (ii) steal more boldly.

57. *restraints*: restrictions on acting.

the company's business, which is he? Come, be not afraid of
60   him.

FOLLYWIT: I am he, sir.

SIR BOUNTEOUS: Art thou he? Give me thy hand. Hark in
    thine ear, thou rollest too fast to gather so much moss as thy
    fellow there; champ upon that. Ah, and what play shall we
    have, my masters?

FOLLYWIT: A pleasant witty comedy, sir.

SIR BOUNTEOUS: Ay, ay, ay, a comedy in any case, that I and
    my guests may laugh a little. What's the name on't?

FOLLYWIT: 'Tis call'd *The Slip*.

70 SIR BOUNTEOUS: *The Slip*? By my troth, a pretty name, and a
    glib one! Go all and slip into't as fast as you can. – Cover a
    table for the players. First, take heed of a lurcher, he cuts
    deep, he will eat up all from you. Some sherry for my lord's
    players there, sirrah! Why, this will be a true feast, a right
    Mitre supper, a play and all. More lights –

    [*Exeunt* FOLLYWIT *and others.*]

    I call'd for light, here come in two are light enough for a
    whole house, i' faith.

    (*Enter* MOTHER *and* COURTESAN.)

    Dare the thief look me i' th' face? O impudent times! Go to,
    dissemble it.

80 MOTHER: Bless you, Sir Bounteous.

SIR BOUNTEOUS: O welcome, welcome, thief, quean and bawd,
    welcome all three.

MOTHER: Nay, here's but two on's, sir.

SIR BOUNTEOUS: O' my troth, I took her for a couple; I'd
    have sworn there had been two faces there.

MOTHER: Not all under one hood, sir.

SIR BOUNTEOUS: Yes, faith, would I, to see mine eyes bear
    double.

MOTHER: I'll make it hold, sir, my daughter is a couple. She
90   was married yesterday.

SIR BOUNTEOUS: Buz!

69. *slip*: counterfeit coin.
72. *lurcher*: (i) one who grabs unfair share of food, (ii) swindler.
75. *Mitre*: well-known London tavern.

MOTHER: Nay, to no buzzard neither, a right hawk
Whene'er you know him.

SIR BOUNTEOUS: Away, he cannot be but a rascal. Walk in,
walk in, bold guests that come unsent for – post.
[*Exit* MOTHER.]
I perceive how my jewels went now – to grace her marriage.

COURTESAN: Would you with me, sir?

SIR BOUNTEOUS: Ay, how happ'd it, wench, you put the slip
upon me,
Not three nights since? I name it gently to you,
I term it neither pilfer, cheat, nor shark.   100

COURTESAN: Y'are past my reach.

SIR BOUNTEOUS: I'm old and past your reach, very good; but
you will not deny this, I trust.

COURTESAN: With a safe conscience, sir.

SIR BOUNTEOUS: Yea? Give me thy hand; fare thee well. I have
done with her.

COURTESAN: Give me your hand, sir; you ne'er yet begun with
me. (*Exit.*)

SIR BOUNTEOUS: Whew, whew! O audacious age,
She denies me and all, when on her fingers   110
I spied the ruby sit that does betray her,
And blushes for her face. Well, there's a time for't,
For all's too little now for entertainment.
Feast, mirth, ay, harmony, and the play to boot.
A jovial season.
[*Enter* FOLLYWIT.]
How now, are you ready?

FOLLYWIT: Even upon readiness, sir. (*Takes [hat] off.*)

SIR BOUNTEOUS: Keep you your hat on.

FOLLYWIT: I have a suit to your worship.

SIR BOUNTEOUS: Oh, cry you mercy, then you must stand bare.

FOLLYWIT: We could do all to the life of action, sir, both for   120
the credit of your worship's house, and the grace of our
comedy.

SIR BOUNTEOUS: Cuds me, what else, sir?

FOLLYWIT: And for some defects, as the custom is, we would
be bold to require your worship's assistance.

SIR BOUNTEOUS: Why, with all my heart. What is't you want? Speak.

FOLLYWIT: One's a chain for a Justice's hat, sir.

130 SIR BOUNTEOUS: Why here, here, here, here whoreson, will this serve your turn? What else lack you?

FOLLYWIT: We should use a ring with a stone in't.

SIR BOUNTEOUS: Nay, whoop, I have given too many rings already, talk no more of rings, I pray you. Here, here, here, make this jewel serve for once.

FOLLYWIT: Oh, this will serve, sir.

SIR BOUNTEOUS: What, have you all now?

FOLLYWIT: All now, sir – only Time is brought i' th' middle of the play, and I would desire your worship's watch-time.

140 SIR BOUNTEOUS: My watch? With all my heart, only give Time a charge that he be not fiddling with it.

FOLLYWIT: You shall ne'er see that, sir.

SIR BOUNTEOUS: Well now you are furnish'd, sir, make haste away. [*Exit.*]

FOLLYWIT: E'en as fast as I can, sir. I'll set my fellows going first, they must have time and leisure, or they're dull else. I'll stay and speak a prologue, yet o'ertake 'em. I cannot have conscience, i' faith, to go away and speak ne'er a word to 'em. My grandsire has given me three shares here; sure I'll do somewhat for 'em. (*Exit.*)

[SCENE TWO]

(*Enter* SIR BOUNTEOUS *and all the guests.*)

SIR BOUNTEOUS: More lights, more stools! Sit, sit, the play begins.

HAREBRAIN: Have you players here, Sir Bounteous?

SIR BOUNTEOUS: We have 'em for you, sir, fine nimble comedians, proper actors most of them.

PENITENT: Whose men, I pray you, sir?

SIR BOUNTEOUS: Oh, there's their credit sir, they serve an honourable popular gentleman, yclipped my Lord Owemuch.

HAREBRAIN: My Lord Owemuch? He was in Ireland lately.

8. *yclipped*: called.

SIR BOUNTEOUS: O, you ne'er knew any of the name but were   10
   great travellers.

HAREBRAIN: How is the comedy call'd, Sir Bounteous?

SIR BOUNTEOUS: Marry, sir, *The Slip*.

HAREBRAIN: *The Slip*?

SIR BOUNTEOUS: Ay, and here the prologue begins to slip in
   upon's.

HAREBRAIN: 'Tis so indeed, Sir Bounteous.

   (*Enter, for a Prologue,* FOLLYWIT.)

                Prologue

FOLLYWIT: We sing of wand'ring knights, what them betide,
   Who nor in one place, nor one shape abide;
   They're here now, and anon no scouts can reach 'em,   20
   Being every man well-hors'd like a bold Beacham.
   The play which we present, no fault shall meet
   But one, you'll say 'tis short, we'll say 'tis sweet.
   'Tis given much to dumb shows, which some praise,
   And like the Term, delights much in delays.
   So to conclude, and give the name her due,
   The play being call'd *The Slip*, I vanish too. (*Exit.*)

SIR BOUNTEOUS: Excellently well acted, and a nimble conceit.

HAREBRAIN: The Prologue's pretty, i' faith.

PENITENT: And went off well.   30

SIR BOUNTEOUS: Ay, that's the grace of all, when they go away
   well, ah!

COURTESAN: O' my troth, an' I were not married, I could find
   in my heart to fall in love with that player now, and send for
   him to a supper. I know some i' th' town that have done as
   much, and there took such a good conceit of their parts into
   th' two-penny room that the actors have been found i' th'
   morning in a less compass than their stage, tho' 'twere ne'er
   so full of gentlemen.

SIR BOUNTEOUS: But, passion of me, where be these knaves?   40
   Will they not come away? Methinks they stay very long.

PENITENT: Oh, you must bear a little, sir, they have many shifts
   to run into.

     25. *Term*: law term, period during which court is in session.
     42. *shifts*: (i) costume changes, (ii) stratagems.

SIR BOUNTEOUS: Shifts call you 'em? They're horrible long things.

(FOLLYWIT *returns in a fury.*)

FOLLYWIT [*aside*]: A pox of such fortune! The plot's betray'd! All come out. Yonder they come, taken upon suspicion and brought back by a constable. I was accurs'd to hold society with such coxcombs! What's to be done? I shall be sham'd
50   for ever, my wife here and all. Ah, pox! By light, happily thought upon – the chain! Invention stick to me this once, and fail me ever hereafter. So, so. –

SIR BOUNTEOUS: Life, I say, where be these players? Oh, are you come? Troth it's time, I was e'en sending for you.

HAREBRAIN: How moodily he walks! What plays he, troth?

SIR BOUNTEOUS: A justice, upon my credit; I know by the chain there.

FOLLYWIT: *Unfortunate justice!*

SIR BOUNTEOUS: Ah-a-a –.

60 FOLLYWIT: *In thy kin unfortunate,*
  Here comes thy nephew now upon suspicion,
  Brought by a constable before thee, his vild associates with him,
  But so disguis'd none knows him but myself.
  Twice have I set him free from officers' fangs,
  And, for his sake, his fellows; let him look to't:
  My conscience will permit but one wink more.

SIR BOUNTEOUS: Yea, shall we take justice winking!

FOLLYWIT: *For this time I have bethought a means to work thy freedom, tho' hazarding myself; should the law seize him,*
70   *Being kin to me, 'twould blemish much my name.*
  No, I'd rather lean to danger, than to shame.

(*Enter* CONSTABLE *with them* [MAWWORM, HOBOY *and company*].)

SIR BOUNTEOUS: A very explete justice.

CONSTABLE: Thank you, good neighbours, let me alone with 'em now.

MAWWORM: 'Sfoot, who's yonder?

HOBOY: Dare he sit there?

---

72. *explete*: complete.

SECOND [COMPANION]: Follywit!

THIRD [COMPANION]: Captain! Puh!

FOLLYWIT: How now, constable, what news with thee?

CONSTABLE [*to* SIR BOUNTEOUS]: May it please your worship,   80
sir, here are a company of auspicious fellows.

SIR BOUNTEOUS: To me? Puh, turn to th' justice, you whoreson
hobby horse! This is some new player now; they put all their
fools to the constable's part still.

FOLLYWIT: What's the matter, constable, what's the matter?

CONSTABLE: I have nothing to say to your worship. [*To* SIR
BOUNTEOUS] They were all riding a-horseback, an't please
your worship.

SIR BOUNTEOUS: Yet again! A pox of all asses still, they could
not ride afoot unless 'twere in a bawdy house.   90

CONSTABLE: The ostler told me they were all unstable fellows,
sir.

FOLLYWIT: *Why, sure, the fellow's drunk!*

MAWWORM: *We spied that weakness in him long ago, sir. Your
worship must bear with him, the man's much o'erseen; only in
respect of his office we obey'd him, both to appear conformable
to law and clear of all offence. For I protest, sir, he found us but
a-horseback.*

FOLLYWIT: *What, he did?*

MAWWORM: *As I have a soul, that's all, and all he can lay to us.*   100

CONSTABLE: I' faith, you were not all riding away, then?

MAWWORM: *S'foot, being a-horseback, sir, that must needs
follow.*

FOLLYWIT: *Why, true, sir.*

SIR BOUNTEOUS: Well said, justice; he helps his kinsman
well.

FOLLYWIT: *Why, sirrah, do you use to bring gentlemen before us
for riding away? What, will you have 'em stand still when they're
up, like Smug upo' th' white horse yonder? Are your wits steep'd?
I'll make you an example for all dizzy constables, how they abuse*   110
justice. Here, bind him to this chair.

CONSTABLE: Ha, bind him, ho?

---

95. *o'erseen*: (i) deceived, (ii) drunk.
108. *steep'd*: soaked, drunk.

FOLLYWIT: *If you want cords, use garters.*

CONSTABLE: Help, help, gentlemen!

MAWWORM: *As fast as we can, sir.*

CONSTABLE: Thieves, thieves!

FOLLYWIT: *A gag will help all this. Keep less noise, you knave!*

CONSTABLE: Oh help, rescue the constable! Oh, oh!
　　[*They gag him.*]

SIR BOUNTEOUS: Ho, ho, ho, ho!

120 FOLLYWIT: *Why la you, who lets you now? You may ride quietly, I'll see you to take horse myself. I have nothing else to do.*
　　(*Exit* [*with* MAWWORM, HOBOY *and others*].)

CONSTABLE: Oh, oh, oh!

SIR BOUNTEOUS: Ha, ha, ha! By my troth, the maddest piece of justice, gentlemen, that ever was committed!

HAREBRAIN: I'll be sworn for the madness on't, sir.

SIR BOUNTEOUS: I am deceiv'd if this prove not a merry comedy and a witty.

PENITENT: Alas, poor constable, his mouth's open, and ne'er a wise word.

130 SIR BOUNTEOUS: Faith, he speaks now e'en as many as he has done; he seems wisest when he gapes and says nothing. Ha, ha, he turns and tells his tale to me like an ass. What have I to do with their riding away? They may ride for me, thou whoreson coxcomb thou; nay, thou art well enough serv'd, i' faith.

PENITENT: But what follows all this while, sir? Methinks some should pass by before this time and pity the constable.

SIR BOUNTEOUS: By th' mass, and you say true, sir. Go sirrah,
140　step in; I think they have forgot themselves. Call the knaves away; they're in a wood, I believe.

CONSTABLE: Ay, ay, ay!

SIR BOUNTEOUS: Hark, the constable says ay, they're in a wood, ha, ha!

112. *want*: lack.
120. *lets*: hinders.
141. *in a wood*: mad, confused.

GUNWATER: He thinks long of the time, Sir Bounteous.
    [*Enter* SERVANT.]

SIR BOUNTEOUS: How now, when come they?

SERVANT: Alas, an't please your worship, there's not one of them to be found, sir.

SIR BOUNTEOUS: How?

HAREBRAIN: What says the fellow?   150

SERVANT: Neither horse nor man, sir.

SIR BOUNTEOUS: Body of me, thou liest!

SERVANT: Not a hair of either, sir.

HAREBRAIN: How now, Sir Bounteous?

SIR BOUNTEOUS: Cheated and defeated! Ungag that rascal! I'll hang him for's fellows, I'll make him bring 'em out.

CONSTABLE: Did not I tell your worship this before, brought 'em before you for suspected persons? Stay'd 'em at towns and upon warning given? Made signs that my very jaw bone aches? Your worship would not hear me, call'd me ass, saving 160 your worship's presence, laugh'd at me.

SIR BOUNTEOUS: Ha?

HAREBRAIN: I begin to taste it.

SIR BOUNTEOUS: Give me leave, give me leave. Why, art not thou the constable i' th' comedy?

CONSTABLE: I' th' comedy? Why, I am the constable i' th' commonwealth, sir.

SIR BOUNTEOUS: I am gull'd, i' faith, I am gull'd! When wast thou chose?

CONSTABLE: On Thursday last, sir.   170

SIR BOUNTEOUS: A pox go with't, there't goes!

PENITENT: I seldom heard jest match it.

HAREBRAIN: Nor I, i' faith.

SIR BOUNTEOUS: Gentlemen, shall I entreat a courtesy?

HAREBRAIN: What is't, sir?

SIR BOUNTEOUS: Do not laugh at me seven year hence.

PENITENT: We should betray and laugh at our own folly then, for of my troth none here but was deceiv'd in't.

SIR BOUNTEOUS: Faith, that's some comfort yet. Ha, ha, it was featly carried! Troth, I commend their wits. Before our faces 180

180. *featly*: deftly.

make us asses, while we sit still and only laugh at ourselves!

PENITENT: Faith, they were some counterfeit rogues, sir.

SIR BOUNTEOUS: Why, they confess so much themselves; they said they'd play *The Slip*; they should be men of their words. I hope the justice will have more conscience, i' faith, than to carry away a chain of a hundred mark of that fashion.

HAREBRAIN: What, sir?

SIR BOUNTEOUS: Ay, by my troth, sir, besides a jewel, and a jewel's fellow, a good fair watch that hung about my neck, 190 sir.

HAREBRAIN: 'Sfoot, what did you mean, sir?

SIR BOUNTEOUS: Methinks my Lord Owemuch's players should not scorn me so, i' faith; they will come and bring all again, I know. Push, they will, i' faith; but a jest, certainly.

(*Enter* FOLLYWIT *in his own shape, and all the rest* [MAW-WORM, HOBOY, *etc.*].)

FOLLYWIT: Pray, grandsire, give me your blessing.

SIR BOUNTEOUS: Who? Son Follywit?

FOLLYWIT: This shows like kneeling after the play, I praying for my Lord Owemuch and his good countess, our honourable lady and mistress.

200 SIR BOUNTEOUS: Rise richer by a blessing; thou art welcome.

FOLLYWIT: Thanks good grandsire. I was bold to bring those gentlemen my friends.

SIR BOUNTEOUS: They're all welcome. Salute you that side and I'll welcome this side. – Sir, to begin with you.

HAREBRAIN: Master Follywit.

FOLLYWIT: I am glad 'tis our fortune so happily to meet, sir.

SIR BOUNTEOUS: Nay, then you know me not, sir.

FOLLYWIT: Sweet Mistress Harebrain.

SIR BOUNTEOUS: You cannot be too bold, sir.

210 FOLLYWIT [*aside*]: Our marriage known?

COURTESAN [*aside*]: Not a word yet.

FOLLYWIT [*aside*]: The better.

SIR BOUNTEOUS: Faith, son, would you had come sooner with these gentlemen.

FOLLYWIT: Why, grandsire?

SIR BOUNTEOUS: We had a play here.

FOLLYWIT: A play, sir? No.

SIR BOUNTEOUS: Yes, faith, a pox o' th' author!

FOLLYWIT: Bless us all! Why, were they such vild ones, sir?

SIR BOUNTEOUS: I am sure villainous ones, sir.   220

FOLLYWIT: Some raw, simple fools?

SIR BOUNTEOUS: Nay by th' mass, these were enough for
thievish knaves.

FOLLYWIT: What, sir?

SIR BOUNTEOUS: Which way came you, gentlemen? You could
not choose but meet 'em.

FOLLYWIT: We met a company with hampers after 'em.

SIR BOUNTEOUS: Oh these were they, those were they, a pox
hamper 'em!

FOLLYWIT [aside]: Bless us all again!   230

SIR BOUNTEOUS: They have hamper'd me finely, sirrah.

FOLLYWIT: How, sir?

SIR BOUNTEOUS: How, sir? I lent the rascals properties to furnish out their play, a chain, a jewel and a watch, and they
watch'd their time, and rid quite away with 'em.

FOLLYWIT: Are they such creatures?

[Watch rings in FOLLYWIT's pocket.]

SIR BOUNTEOUS: Hark, hark, gentlemen! By this light, the
watch rings alarum in his pocket! There's my watch come
again, or the very cousin german to't! Whose is't, whose is't?
By th' mass, 'tis he. Hast thou one, son? Prithee bestow it   240
upon thy grandsire. I now look for mine again, i' faith.
[Reaches into Follywit's pocket.] Nay, come with a good will
or not at all; I'll give thee a better thing. A prize, a prize,
gentlemen!

HAREBRAIN: Great or small?

SIR BOUNTEOUS [drawing out stolen goods]: At once I have
drawn chain, jewel, watch and all!

PENITENT: By my faith, you have a fortunate hand, sir.

HAREBRAIN: Nay, all to come at once!

MAWWORM: A vengeance of this foolery!   250

FOLLYWIT: Have I 'scap't the constable to be brought in by
the watch?

COURTESAN: Oh destiny! Have I married a thief, mother?

MOTHER: Comfort thyself; thou art beforehand with him, daughter.

SIR BOUNTEOUS: Why son, why gentlemen, how long have you been my Lord Owemuch's servants, i' faith?

FOLLYWIT: Faith, grandsire, shall I be true to you?

SIR BOUNTEOUS: I think 'tis time, thou'st been a thief already.

260 FOLLYWIT: I, knowing the day of your feast, and the natural inclination you have to pleasure and pastime, presum'd upon your patience for a jest as well to prolong your days as –

SIR BOUNTEOUS: Whoop! Why then, you took my chain along with you to prolong my days, did you?

FOLLYWIT: Not so neither, sir; and that you may be seriously assured of my hereafter stableness of life, I have took another course.

SIR BOUNTEOUS: What?

FOLLYWIT: Took a wife.

270 SIR BOUNTEOUS: A wife? 'Sfoot, what is she for a fool would marry thee, a madman? When was the wedding kept in Bedlam?

FOLLYWIT: She's both a gentlewoman and a virgin.

SIR BOUNTEOUS: Stop there, stop there; would I might see her!

FOLLYWIT: You have your wish, she's here.

SIR BOUNTEOUS: Ah? – Ha, ha, ha! This makes amends for all.

FOLLYWIT: How now?

MAWWORM: Captain, do you hear? Is she your wife in earnest?

280 FOLLYWIT: How then?

MAWWORM: Nothing but pity you, sir.

SIR BOUNTEOUS: Speak, son, is't true?
Can you gull us, and let a quean gull you?

FOLLYWIT: Ha?

COURTESAN: What I have been is past, be that forgiven,
And have a soul true both to thee and heaven.

FOLLYWIT: Is't come about? Tricks are repaid, I see.

SIR BOUNTEOUS: The best is, sirrah, you pledge none but me;
And since I drink the top, take her, and hark,
290 I spice the bottom with a thousand mark.

272. *Bedlam*: Bethlehem Hospital, a lunatic asylum.

FOLLYWIT: By my troth, she is as good a cup of nectar as any
   bachelor needs to sip at.
   Tut, give me gold, it makes amends for vice.
   Maids without coin are caudles without spice.
SIR BOUNTEOUS: Come, gentlemen, to th' feast, let not time
   waste;
   We have pleas'd our ear, now let us please our taste.
   Who lives by cunning, mark it, his fate's cast;
   When he has gull'd all, then is himself the last.
   [*Exeunt.*]

                      FINIS

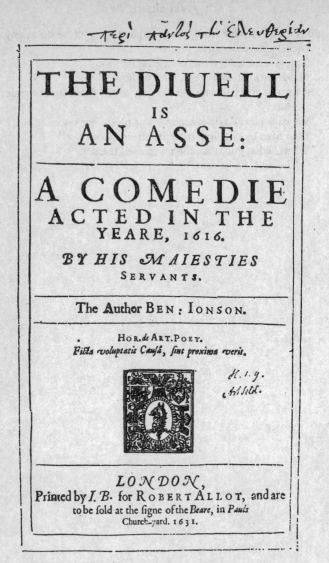

THE DIUELL
IS
AN ASSE:

A COMEDIE
ACTED IN THE
YEARE, 1616.

BY HIS MAIESTIES
SERVANTS.

The Author BEN: IONSON.

HOR. *de* ART. POET.

Ficta voluptatis Cauſâ, ſint proxima veris.

H. 1. y.
Aſhld.

LONDON,
Printed by *I. B.* for ROBERT ALLOT, and are
to be ſold at the ſigne of the *Beare,* in *Pauls*
Church-yard. 1631.

Facsimile of the title-page of the first edition, the quarto of 1631.

THE DEVIL IS AN ASS

by

Ben Jonson

THE PERSONS OF THE PLAY

SATAN, the great devil
PUG, the less devil
INIQUITY, the Vice
FITZDOTTREL, a Squire of Norfolk
MISTRESS FRANCES, his wife
MEERCRAFT, the Projector
EVERILL, his champion
WITTIPOL, a young Gallant
MANLY, his Friend
ENGINE, a Broker
TRAINS, the Projector's man
GILTHEAD, a Goldsmith
PLUTARCHUS, his son
SIR PAUL EITHERSIDE, a Lawyer and Justice
LADY EITHERSIDE, his wife
LADY TAILBUSH, the Lady Projectress
PITFALL, her Woman
AMBLER, her Gentleman usher
SLEDGE, a Smith, the Constable
SHACKLES, Keeper of Newgate
SERJEANTS [and other Officers of the law and Servants]

The Scene, LONDON

Pug: imp.
Iniquity: the Vice, comical figure who accompanied the Devil in the old interludes.
Gilthead: a name for the gold-spotted pike, with a possible allusion to usurers.

THE PROLOGUE

The Devil is an ass. That is, today,
The name of what you are met for, a new play.
Yet, grandees, would you were not come to grace
Our matter, with allowing us no place.
Though you presume Satan a subtle thing,
And may have heard he's worn in a thumb-ring,
Do not on these presumptions force us act,
In compass of a cheese-trencher. This tract
Will ne'er admit our Vice, because of yours.
Anon, who, worse than you, the fault endures   10
That yourselves make? When you will thrust and spurn,
And knock us o' the elbows, and bid turn;
As if, when we had spoke, we must be gone,
Or, till we speak, must all run in to one,
Like the young adders at the old one's mouth!
Would we could stand due north, or had no south,
If that offend: or were Muscovy glass,
That you might look our scenes through as they pass.
We know not how to affect you. If you'll come
To see new plays, pray you afford us room,   20
And show this, but the same face you have done
Your dear delight, the Devil of Edmonton.

4. *no place*: a reference to spectators sitting on the stage.
6. *thumb-ring*: signet-ring. Spirits were supposed to be carried in them.
8. *tract*: space (the stage).
15. *young adders*: these were supposed to live in their mothers' mouths.
16. *no south*: no backs.
17. *Muscovy glass:* mica.
22. *The Devil of Edmonton*: a popular anonymous play *The Merry Devil of Edmonton.*

Or, if, for want of room it must miscarry,
'Twill be but justice, that your censure tarry
Till you give some. And when six times you ha' seen't,
If this play do not like, the Devil is in't.

ACT ONE

SCENE ONE

([*Enter*] DEVIL, PUG.)

SATAN: Hoh, hoh, hoh, hoh, hoh, hoh, hoh, hoh!
  To earth? And why to earth, thou foolish spirit?
  What would'st thou do on earth?

PUG: For that, great chief,
  As time shall work. I do but ask my month,
  Which every petty puisne devil has;
  Within that term, the court of Hell will hear
  Something may gain a longer grant, perhaps.

SATAN: For what? The laming a poor cow or two?
  Ent'ring a sow, to make her cast her farrow?
  Or crossing of a market-woman's mare,   10
  'Twixt this and Tottenham? These were wont to be
  Your main achievements, Pug; you have some plot now,
  Upon a tunning of ale, to stale the yeast,
  Or keep the churn so, that the butter come not,
  Spite o' the housewife's cord, or her hot spit?
  Or some good ribibe, about Kentish Town
  Or Hogsden, you would hang now, for a witch,
  Because she will not let you play round robin.
  And you'll go sour the citizens' cream 'gainst Sunday,
  That she may be accus'd for't, and condemn'd   20
  By a Middlesex jury, to the satisfaction
  Of their offended friends, the Londoners' wives
  Whose teeth were set on edge with it? Foolish fiend,

1. *Hoh, hoh*: traditional roar of Devil in medieval plays.
5. *puisne*: junior, inferior.
10. *crossing . . . mare*: i.e. diverting it from the road to market.
13. *tunning*: storing in casks.
15. *housewife's cord or spit*: popular remedies for de-witching butter.
16. *ribibe*: old hag.
18. *play round robin*: act madly, like Robin Goodfellow (Puck).

Stay i' your place, know your own strengths, and put not
Beyond the sphere of your activity.
You are too dull a devil to be trusted
Forth in those parts, Pug, upon any affair
That may concern our name on earth. It is not
Every one's work. The state of Hell must care
30   Whom it employs, in point of reputation,
Here about London. You would make, I think,
An agent to be sent for Lancashire,
Proper enough; or some parts of Northumberland,
So you had good instructions, Pug.

PUG: O chief,
You do not know, dear chief, what there is in me.
Prove me but for a fortnight, for a week,
And lend me but a Vice, to carry with me,
To practise there with any play-fellow,
And you will see, there will come more upon't,
Than you'll imagine, precious chief.

40 SATAN: What Vice?
What kind wouldst th' have it of?

PUG: Why any; Fraud,
Or Covetousness, or Lady Vanity,
Or old Iniquity: I'll call him hither.
    [*Enter* INIQUITY.]

INIQUITY: What is he calls upon me, and would seem to lack a
    Vice?
Ere his words be half spoken, I am with him in a trice,
Here, there, and everywhere, as the cat is with the mice,
True *vetus Iniquitas*. Lack'st thou cards, friend, or dice?
I will teach thee cheat, child, to cog, lie and swagger,
And ever and anon, to be drawing forth thy dagger:
50   To swear by Gogs-nowns, like a lusty Juventus,

    41-2. *Fraud; Covetousness*: names of characters in interludes.
    48. *cog*: swindle.
    49. *dagger*: the stage Vice carried a wooden dagger (cf. *Twelfth Night*, IV,
ii, 120-26).
    50. *Gogs-nowns*: God's wounds.
    50. *lusty Juventus*: popular interlude by Robert Weever (printed 1565).

In a cloak to thy heel, and a hat like a pent-house.
Thy breeches of three fingers and thy doublet all belly,
With a wench that shall feed thee with cock-stones and jelly.
PUG: Is it not excellent, chief? How nimble he is!
INIQUITY: Child of hell, this is nothing! I will fetch thee a leap
From the top of Paul's steeple to the Standard in Cheap
And lead thee a dance through the streets without fail,
Like a needle of Spain, with a thread at my tail.
We will survey the suburbs, and make forth our sallies
Down Petticoat Lane, and up the Smock-alleys,   60
To Shoreditch, Whitechapel, and so to Saint Kather'n's,
To drink with the Dutch there, and take forth their patterns.
From thence we will put in at Custom-house quay there,
And see how the factors and prentices play there,
False with their masters; and geld many a full pack,
To spend it in pies, at the Dagger, and the Woolsack.
PUG: Brave, brave, Iniquity! Will not this do, chief?
INIQUITY: Nay, boy, I will bring thee to the bawds, and the
    roysters
At Billingsgate, feasting with claret-wine and oysters;
From thence shoot the Bridge, child, to the Cranes i' the
    Vintry,   70
And see there the gimblets, how they make their entry!
Or, if thou hadst rather, to the Strand down to fall,
'Gainst the lawyers come dabbled from Westminster hall,
And mark how they cling, with their clients together,
Like ivy to oak, so velvet to leather.
Ha, boy, I would show thee.
PUG: Rare, rare!
SATAN: Peace, dotard,
And thou more ignorant thing, that so admir'it.

52. *three fingers*: i.e. thickness of padding.
53. *cock-stones*: aphrodisiac.
56. *Standard*: a conduit set up in 1430.
61. *Shoreditch, Whitechapel*: areas of ill repute.
66. *Dagger, Woolsack*: taverns.
70. *Cranes i' the Vintry*: a well-known tavern.
71. *gimblets*: ? fops.
73. *dabbled*: bespattered.

Art thou the spirit thou seem'st? So poor, to choose
This for a Vice, t'advance the cause of hell,
80 Now, as Vice stands this present year? Remember
What number it is. Six hundred and sixteen.
Had it but been five hundred, though some sixty
Above; that's fifty years agone, and six,
(When every great man had his Vice stand by him,
In his long coat, shaking his wooden dagger)
I could consent that then this your grave choice
Might have done that, with his lord chief, the which
Most of his chamber can do now. But Pug,
As the times are, who is it will receive you?
90 What company will you go to, or whom mix with?
Where canst thou carry him, except to taverns,
To mount upon a joint-stool, with a Jew's trump,
To put down Cokely, and that must be to citizens?
He ne'er will be admitted, there, where Vennor comes.
He may perchance, in tail of a sheriff's dinner,
Skip with a rime o' the table, from New-nothing,
And take his Almain leap into a custard,
Shall make my lady Mayoress and her sisters
Laugh all their hoods over their shoulders. But
100 This is not that will do, they are other things
That are receiv'd now upon earth for Vices,
Stranger, and newer, and chang'd every hour.
They ride 'em like their horses off their legs,
And here they come to hell, whole legions of 'em,
Every week tir'd. We still strive to breed
And rear 'em up new ones; but they do not stand;
When they come there, they turn 'em on our hands.
And it is fear'd they have a stud o' their own
Will put down ours. Both our breed, and trade
110 Will suddenly decay, if we prevent not.
Unless it be a Vice of quality,

93. *Cokely*: a jester known for improvisations.
96. *New-nothing*: new-fangled bauble.
97. *Almain leap*: dance step. The Lord Mayor's fool jumped into a huge custard at City dinners.

Or fashion, now, they take none from us. Carmen
Are got into the yellow starch, and chimney-sweepers
To their tobacco and strong-waters, Hum,
Meath, and Obarni. We must therefore aim
At extraordinary subtle ones now,
When we do send to keep us up in credit,
Not old Iniquities. Get you e'en back, sir,
To making of your rope of sand again.
You are not for the manners, nor the times: 120
They have their vices there, most like to virtues;
You cannot know 'em apart by any difference.
They wear the same clothes, eat the same meat,
Sleep i' the selfsame beds, ride i' those coaches,
Or very like, four horses in a coach,
As the best men and women. Tissue gowns,
Garters and roses, fourscore pound a pair,
Embroider'd stockings, cut-work smocks and shirts,
More certain marks of lechery now, and pride,
Than ere they were of true nobility!   130
But Pug, since you do burn with such desire
To do the commonwealth of hell some service,
I am content, assuming of a body,
You go to earth, and visit men a day.
But you must take a body ready made, Pug,
I can create you none: nor shall you form
Yourself an airy one, but become subject
To all impression of the flesh you take,
So far as human frailty. So, this morning,
There is a handsome cutpurse hang'd at Tyburn   140
Whose spirit departed; you may enter his body.
For clothes, employ your credit with the hangman,

---

113. *yellow starch*: yellow-starched linen was introduced by Mrs Turner, a murderess, who was ordered to wear it at her execution.

114. *Hum*: strong ale.

115. *Meath, and Obarni*: mead and scalded mead.

127. *roses*: shoe-ties.

142. *clothes . . . hangman*: an executed man's clothes were the hangman's perquisite.

Or let our tribe of brokers furnish you.
And look how far your subtlety can work
Thorough those organs; with that body spy
Amongst mankind (you cannot there want vices,
And therefore the less need to carry 'em wi' you)
But as you make your soon-at-night's relation,
And we shall find it merits from the state,
150   You shall have both trust from us, and employment.

PUG: Most gracious chief!

SATAN: Only, thus more I bind you,
To serve the first man that you meet; and him
I'll show you now: observe him. Yon' is he;
    (*He shows* FITZDOTTREL *to him, coming forth.*)
You shall see first after your clothing. Follow him,
But once engag'd, there you must stay and fix,
Not shift, until the midnight's cock do crow.

PUG: Any conditions, to be gone.

SATAN: Away, then.
    [*Exeunt.*]

[SCENE TWO]

    ([*Enter*] FITZDOTTREL.)

FITZDOTTREL: Ay, they do now name Bretnor as before,
They talk'd of Gresham and of Doctor Foreman,
Franklin, and Fiske, and Savory (he was in too).
But there's not one of these that ever could
Yet show a man the devil in true sort.
They have their crystals, I do know, and rings,
And virgin parchment, and their dead men's skulls,
Their ravens' wings, their lights, and pentacles,

143. *brokers*: pawn-broker, pedlar.
7. *virgin parchment*: unused parchment, used for love-letters, by lovers who dabbled in magic.
8. *ravens' wings*: standard equipment of necromancers.
8. *pentacles*: three intersecting triangles making up five lines, sometimes associated with five wounds of Christ.

With characters; I ha' seen all these. But —
Would I might see the devil! I would give   10
A hundred o' these pictures, to see him
Once out of picture. May I prove a cuckold
(And that's the one main mortal thing I fear)
If I begin not now to think, the painters
Have only made him. 'Slight, he would be seen,
One time or other else. He would not let
An ancient gentleman, of a good house,
As most are now in England, the Fitzdottrels,
Run wild, and call upon him thus in vain,
As I ha' done this twelvemonth. If he be not   20
At all, why are there conjurers? If they be not,
Why are there laws against 'em? The best artists
Of Cambridge, Oxford, Middlesex and London,
Essex and Kent, I have had in pay to raise him,
These fifty weeks, and yet h'appears not. 'Sdeath,
I shall suspect they can make circles only
Shortly, and know but his hard names. They do say,
H'will meet a man (of himself) that has a mind to him.
If he would so, I have a mind and a half for him:
He should not be long absent. Pray thee, come, 30
I long for thee! An I were with child by him,
And my wife too, I could not more. Come yet,
Good Beelzebub! Were he a kind devil,
And had humanity in him, he would come, but
To save one's longing. I should use him well,
I swear, and with respect (would he would try me),
Not, as the conjurers do, when they ha' rais'd him,
Get him in bonds, and send him post, on errands,
A thousand miles; it is preposterous, that,
And I believe, is the true cause he comes not.   40
And he has reason. Who would be engag'd,
That might live freely, as he may do? I swear,
They are wrong all. The burnt child dreads the fire.
They do not know to entertain the devil.

9. *characters*: magical symbols.
22. *artists*: learned men.

199

I would so welcome him, observe his diet,
Get him his chamber hung with arras, two of 'em,
I' my own house; lend him my wife's wrought pillows –
And as I am an honest man, I think
If he had a mind to her, too, I should grant him,
50   To make our friendship perfect. So I would not
To every man. If he but hear me, now,
And should come to me in a brave young shape,
And take me at my word? Ha! Who is this?
   [*Enter* PUG.]
  PUG: Sir, your good pardon, that I thus presume
Upon your privacy. I am born a gentleman,
A younger brother; but in some disgrace
Now, with my friends, and want some little means
To keep me upright, while things be reconcil'd.
Please you to let my service be of use to you, sir.
FITZDOTTREL (*He looks and surveys his feet over and over*):
60   Service? 'Fore hell, my heart was at my mouth,
Till I had view'd his shoes well; for those roses
Were big enough to hide a cloven foot.
No friend, my number's full. I have one servant
Who is my all, indeed, and, from the broom
Unto the brush, for just so far I trust him.
He is my wardrobe man, my cater, cook,
Butler and steward; looks unto my horse,
And helps to watch my wife. H'has all the places
That I can think on, from the garret downward,
70   E'en to the manger and the curry-comb.
  PUG: Sir, I shall put your worship to no charge,
More than my meat, and that but very little;
I'll serve you for your love.
FITZDOTTREL: Ha? Without wages?
I'll hearken o' that ear, were I at leisure,
But now I'm busy. Prithee, friend, forbear me.
An thou hadst been a devil, I should say

47. *wrought*: embroidered.
58. *while*: until.
66. *cater*: purveyor.

Somewhat more to thee. Thou dost hinder now
My meditations.

PUG: Sir, I am a devil.

FITZDOTTREL: How!

PUG: A true devil, sir.

FITZDOTTREL: Nay, now you lie.
Under your favour, friend, for I'll not quarrel;   80
I look'd o' your feet afore, you cannot cozen me,
Your shoe's not cloven. Sir, you are whole-hoof'd.

PUG: Sir, that's a popular error deceives many.
But I am that I tell you.

FITZDOTTREL: What's your name?

PUG: My name is Devil, sir.

FITZDOTTREL (*He views his feet again*): Say'st thou true?

PUG: Indeed, sir.

FITZDOTTREL: 'Slid! There's some omen i' this! What country-
man?

PUG: Of Derbyshire, sir, about the Peak.   90

FITZDOTTREL: That hole belong'd to your ancestors?

PUG: Yes, Devil's arse, sir.

FITZDOTTREL [*aside*]: I'll entertain him for the namesake. Ha,
And turn away my tother man and save
Four pound a year by that! There's luck, and thrift too!
The very devil may come hereafter, as well. –
Friend, I receive you. But withal, I acquaint you
Aforehand, if yo' offend me, I must beat you.
It is a kind of exercise I use
And cannot be without.

PUG: Yes, if I do not   100
Offend, you can, sure.

FITZDOTTRELL: Faith, Devil, very hardly.
I'll call you by your surname, 'cause I love it.

([*Enter*] ENGINE, WITTIPOL, MANLY.)

ENGINE: Yonder he walks, sir, I'll go lift him for you.

WITTIPOL: To him, good Engine, raise him up by degrees,
Gently, and hold him there too; you can do it.
Show yourself now a mathematical broker.

106. *mathematical*: exact.

ENGINE: I'll warrant you for half a piece.

WITTIPOL: 'Tis done, sir.

MANLY: Is't possible there should be such a man?

WITTIPOL: You shall be your own witness; I'll not labour
  To tempt you past your faith.

110 MANLY: And is his wife
  So very handsome, say you?

WITTIPOL: I ha' not seen her
  Since I came home from travel, and they say
  She is not alter'd. Then, before I went,
  I saw her once; but so, as she hath stuck
  Still i' my view, no object hath remov'd her.

MANLY: 'Tis a fair guest, friend, beauty; and once lodg'd
  Deep in the eyes, she hardly leaves the inn.
  How does he keep her?

WITTIPOL: Very brave. However,
  Himself be sordid, he is sensual that way.

120   In every dressing he does study her.

MANLY: And furnish forth himself so from the brokers?

WITTIPOL: Yes, that's a hir'd suit, he now has on,
  To see *The Devil is an Ass*, today, in.
  (This Engine gets three or four pound a week by him.)
  He dares not miss a new play, or a feast,
  What rate soever clothes be at, and thinks
  Himself still new in other men's old.

MANLY: But stay,
  Does he love meat so?

WITTIPOL: Faith, he does not hate it,
  But that's not it. His belly and his palate

130   Would be compounded with for reason. Marry,
  A wit he has, of that strange credit with him,
  'Gainst all mankind; as it doth make him do
  Just what it list: it ravishes him forth
  Whither it please, to any assembly or place,
  And would conclude him ruin'd, should he 'scape
  One public meeting, out of the belief

107. *piece*: double sovereign, worth one pound ten pence.
118. *brave*: splendidly attired.

He has of his own great and catholic strengths
In arguing and discourse.
    (*Engine hath won* FITZDOTTREL *to* [*try*] *on the cloak.*)
                      It takes, I see:
H'has got the cloak upon him.

FITZDOTTREL: A fair garment,
  By my faith, Engine!

ENGINE: It was never made, sir,   140
  For three score pound, I assure you; 'twill yield thirty.
  The plush, sir, cost three pound, ten shillings a yard!
  And then the lace, and velvet.

FITZDOTTREL: I shall, Engine,
  Be look'd at prettily in it! Art thou sure
  The play is play'd today?

ENGINE: O, here's the bill, sir.
    (*He gives him the play-bill.*)
  I had forgot to gi't you.

FITZDOTTREL: Ha, *The Devil*!
  I will not lose you, sirrah. But, Engine, think you,
  The gallant is so furious in his folly,
  So mad upon the matter that he'll part
  With's cloak upo' these terms?

ENGINE: Trust not your Engine,   150
  Break me to pieces else, as you would do
  A rotten crane, or an old rusty jack,
  That has not one true wheel in him. Do but talk with him.

FITZDOTTREL: I shall do that, to satisfy you, Engine,
  And myself too. (*He turns to Wittipol.*) With your leave,
    gentlemen,
  Which of you is it, is so mere idolater
  To my wife's beauty, and so very prodigal
  Unto my patience, that for the short parley
  Of one swift hour's quarter with my wife,
  He will depart with (let me see) this cloak here,   160
  The price of folly? Sir, are you the man?

WITTIPOL: I am that vent'rer, sir.

           137. *catholic*: wide-ranging.

FITZDOTTREL: Good time! Your name
 Is Wittipol?

WITTIPOL: The same, sir.

FITZDOTTREL: And 'tis told me,
 Yo' have travell'd lately?

WITTIPOL: That I have, sir.

FITZDOTTREL: Truly,
 Your travels may have alter'd your complexion,
 But sure, your wit stood still.

WITTIPOL: It may well be, sir.
 All heads ha' not like growth.

FITZDOTTREL: The good man's gravity
 That left you land, your father, never taught you
 These pleasant matches?

WITTIPOL: No, nor can his mirth,
 With whom I make 'em, put me off.

170 FITZDOTTREL: You are
 Resolv'd then?

WITTIPOL: Yes, sir.

FITZDOTTREL: Beauty is the saint,
 You'll sacrifice yourself into the shirt to?

WITTIPOL: So I may still clothe and keep warm your wisdom.

FITZDOTTREL: You lade me, sir!

WITTIPOL: I know what you will bear, sir.

FITZDOTTREL: Well, to the point. 'Tis only, sir, you say,
 To speak unto my wife?

WITTIPOL: Only to speak to her.

FITZDOTTREL: And in my presence?

WITTIPOL: In your very presence

FITZDOTTREL: And in my hearing?

WITTIPOL: In your hearing, so
 You interrupt us not.

FITZDOTTREL: For the short space
180 You do demand, the fourth part of an hour,
 I think I shall, with some convenient study,
 And this good help to boot, bring myself to't.
  (*He shrugs himself up in the cloak.*)

174. *lade*: load heavily.

WITTIPOL: I ask no more.

FITZDOTTREL: Please you, walk to'ard my house;
    Speak what you list, that time is yours; my right
    I have departed with. But not beyond
    A minute, or a second, look for. Length,
    And drawing out ma' advance much to these matches.
    And I except all kissing. Kisses are
    Silent petitions still with willing lovers.

WITTIPOL: Lovers? How falls that o' your fant'sie?

FITZDOTTREL: Sir,   190
    I do know somewhat; I forbid all lip-work.

WITTIPOL: I am not eager at forbidden dainties.
    Who covets unfit things, denies himself.

FITZDOTTREL: You say well, sir, 'twas prettily said, that same;
    He does indeed. I'll have no touches therefore,
    Nor takings by the arms, nor tender circles
    Cast 'bout the waist, but all be done at distance.
    Love is brought up with those soft migniard handlings;
    His pulse lies in his palm: and I defend
    All melting joints and fingers, that's my bargain,   200
    I do defend 'em any thing like action.
    But talk, sir, what you will. Use all the tropes
    And schemes that prince Quintilian can afford you:
    And much good do your rhetoric's heart. You are welcome,
        sir.

ENGINE: God b' w' you.

WITTIPOL: Sir, I must condition
    To have this gentleman by, a witness.

FITZDOTTREL: Well,
    I am content, so he be silent.

MANLY: Yes, sir.

FITZDOTTREL: Come Devil, I'll make you room straight. But
        I'll show you

190. *fant'sie*: imagination.
198. *migniard*: wanton, dainty.
199. *defend*: forbid.
202–3. *tropes and schemes*: figures of rhetoric.
203. *Quintilian*: an acknowledged classical authority on rhetoric.

First to your mistress, who's no common one,
210 You must conceive, that brings this gain to see her.
I hope thou'st brought me good luck.
PUG: I shall do't, sir.
  [*Exeunt.*]

[SCENE THREE]

([*Enter*] WITTIPOL, MANLY, [*and* ENGINE].)
WITTIPOL: Engine, you hope o' your half piece? 'Tis there, sir.
Be gone.
  [*Exit Engine.*]
          Friend Manly, who's within here? Fixed!
  (WITTIPOL *knocks his friend* [MANLY] *o' the breast.*)
MANLY: I am directly in a fit of wonder
What'll be the issue of this conference!
WITTIPOL: For that, ne'er vex yourself, till the event.
How like yo' him?
MANLY: I would fain see more of him.
WITTIPOL: What think you of this?
MANLY: I am past degrees of thinking.
Old Afric and the new America,
With all their fruit of monsters, cannot show
So just a prodigy.
10 WITTIPOL: Could you have believ'd,
Without your sight, a mind so sordid inward,
Should be so specious, and laid forth abroad,
To all the show that ever shop or ware was?
MANLY: I believe anything now, though I confess
His vices are the most extremities
I ever knew in nature. But why loves he
The devil so?
WITTIPOL: O sir, for hidden treasure
He hopes to find; and has propos'd himself
So infinite a mass, as to recover,
20 He cares not what he parts with, of the present,
To his men of art, who are the race may coin him.
Promise gold mountains and the covetous

Are still most prodigal.

MANLY: But ha' you faith
That he will hold his bargain?

WITTIPOL: O dear sir!
He will not off on't. Fear him not. I know him.
One baseness still accompanies another.
See, he is here already, and his wife too.

MANLY: A wondrous handsome creature, as I live!

[*Enter* FITZDOTTREL *with* FRANCES, *his wife.*]

FITZDOTTREL: Come, wife, this is the gentleman. Nay, blush
not.

MISTRESS FITZDOTTREL: Why, what do you mean, sir? Ha' you
your reason?

FITZDOTTREL: Wife,   30
I do not know that I have lent it forth
To any one; at least, without a pawn, wife;
Or that I have eat or drunk the thing of late,
That should corrupt it. Wherefore, gentle wife,
Obey, it is thy virtue. Hold no acts
Of disputation.

MISTRESS FITZDOTTREL: Are you not enough
The talk of feasts and meetings, but you'll still
Make argument for fresh?

FITZDOTTREL: Why, careful wedlock,
If I have a longing to have one tale more
Go of me, what is that to thee, dear heart?   40
Why shouldst thou envy my delight, or cross it
By being solicitous, when it not concerns thee?

MISTRESS FITZDOTTREL: Yes, I have share in this. The
scorn will fall
As bitterly on me, where both are laugh'd at.

FITZDOTTREL: Laugh'd at, sweet bird? Is that the scruple?
Come, come,
Thou art a niaise. Which of your great houses
(I will not mean at home here, but abroad),

38. *wedlock*: wife.
46. *niaise*: 'a young hawk, ta'en crying out of the nest' (original side
note).

Your families in France, wife, send not forth
Something within the seven year, may be laugh'd at?
50 I do not say seven months, nor seven weeks,
Nor seven days, nor hours: but seven year, wife,
I give 'em time. Once within seven year,
I think they may do something may be laugh'd at
In France, I keep me there still. Wherefore, wife,
Let them that list, laugh still, rather than weep
For me. Here is a cloak cost fifty pound, wife,
Which I can sell for thirty, when I ha' seen
All London in't, and London has seen me.
Today I go to the Blackfriars playhouse,
60 Sit i' the view, salute all my acquaintance,
Rise up between the acts, let fall my cloak,
Publish a handsome man, and a rich suit
(As that's a special end, why we go thither,
All that pretend to stand for't o' the stage).
The ladies ask who's that? (For they do come
To see us, love, as we do to see them.)
Now shall I lose all this, for the false fear
Of being laugh'd at? Yes, wusse. Let 'em laugh, wife,
Let me have such another cloak tomorrow,
70 And let 'em laugh again, wife, and again,
And then grow fat with laughing, and then fatter,
All my young gallants, let 'em bring their friends too;
Shall I forbid 'em? No, let heaven forbid 'em,
Or wit, if't have any charge on 'em. Come, thy ear, wife,
Is all I'll borrow of thee. Set your watch, sir,
Thou only art to hear, not speak a word, dove,
To aught he says. That I do gi' you in precept,
No less than counsel, on your wife-hood, wife,
Not though he flatter you, or make court, or love
80 (As you must look for these), or say he rail;
What e'er his arts be, wife, I will have thee
Delude 'em with a trick, thy obstinate silence.
I know advantages, and I love to hit

62 *Publish*: declare (myself).
68. *wusse*: certainly.

These pragmatic young men at their own weapons.
Is your watch ready? Here my sail bears, for you:
Tack toward him, sweet pinnace.
    (*He disposes his wife to his place, and sets his watch.*)
                        Where's your watch?

WITTIPOL: I'll set it, sir, with yours.
MISTRESS FITZDOTTREL: I must obey.
MANLY: Her modesty seems to suffer with her beauty,
  And so, as if his folly were away,
  It were worth pity.
FITZDOTTREL: Now, they're right, begin, sir.   90
  But first, let me repeat the contract, briefly.
  I am, sir, to enjoy this cloak I stand in
  Freely and as your gift, upon condition
  You may as freely speak here to my spouse,
  Your quarter of an hour, always keeping
  The measur'd distance of your yard, or more,
  From my said spouse, and in my sight and hearing.
  This is your covenant?
WITTIPOL: Yes, but you'll allow
  For this time spent, now?
FITZDOTTREL: Set 'em so much back.
WITTIPOL: I think I shall not need it.
FITZDOTTREL: Well, begin, sir,   100
  There is your bound, sir. Not beyond that rush.
WITTIPOL: If you interrupt me, sir, I shall discloak you. –
  The time I have purchas'd, lady, is but short,
  And therefore, if I employ it thriftily,
  I hope I stand the nearer to my pardon.
  I am not here to tell you you are fair,
  Or lovely, or how well you dress you, lady;
  I'll save myself that eloquence of your glass,
  Which can speak these things better to you than I.
  And 'tis a knowledge wherein fools may be   110
  As wise as a court-parliament. Nor come I

        84. *pragmatic*: intrusive, self-important.
        86. *pinnace*: lit. sailing vessel.
        101. *rush*: floors were strewn with rushes.

With any prejudice or doubt, that you
Should, to the notice of your own worth, need
Least revelation. She's a simple woman
Knows not her good (whoever knows her ill)
And at all caracts. That you are the wife
To so much blasted flesh as scarce hath soul,
Instead of salt, to keep it sweet, I think
Will ask no witnesses to prove. The cold

120   Sheets that you lie in, with the watching candle,
That sees how dull to any thaw of beauty,
Pieces and quarters, half, and whole nights sometimes,
The devil-given elfin-squire, your husband,
Doth leave you, quitting here his proper circle,
For a much worse i' the walks of Lincoln's Inn,
Under the elms, t'expect the fiend in vain there,
Will confess for you.

FITZDOTTREL: I did look for this gear.

WITTIPOL: And what a daughter of darkness he does make
      you,
Lock'd up from all society, or object,

130   Your eye not let to look upon a face
Under a conjurer's (or some mould for one,
Hollow and lean like his) but by great means,
As I now make; your own too sensible sufferings,
Without the extraordinary aids
Of spells or spirits, may assure you, lady.
For my part, I protest 'gainst all such practice,
I work by no false arts, medicines, or charms
To be said forward and backward.

FITZDOTTREL: No, I except –

WITTIPOL: Sir, I shall ease you.
    (*He offers to discloak him.*)

FITZDOTTREL: Mum.

WITTIPOL: Nor have I ends, lady,

140   Upon you, more than this: to tell you how love,

116. *at all caracts*: to the greatest value.
124. *proper*: own, distinctive.
131. *Under*: except.

Beauty's good angel, he that waits upon her
At all occasions, and no less than Fortune
Helps th'adventurous, in me makes that proffer,
Which never fair one was so fond to lose,
Who could but reach a hand forth to her freedom.
On the first sight, I lov'd you: since which time,
Though I have travell'd, I have been in travail
More for this second blessing of your eyes
Which now I have purchas'd, than for all aims else.
Think of it, lady, be your mind as active   150
As is your beauty; view your object well.
Examine both my fashion and my years.
Things that are like are soon familiar,
And nature joys still in equality.
Let not the sign o' the husband fright you, lady,
But ere your spring be gone, enjoy it. Flowers,
Though fair, are oft but of one morning. Think,
All beauty doth not last until the autumn.
You grow old, while I tell you this. And such
As cannot use the present are not wise.   160
If Love and Fortune will take care of us,
Why should our will be wanting? This is all.
What do you answer, lady?
   (She stands mute.)

FITZDOTTREL: Now the sport comes.
  Let him still wait, wait, wait: while the watch goes,
And the time runs. Wife!

WITTIPOL: How! Not any word?
  Nay, then, I taste a trick in't. Worthy lady,
I cannot be so false to mine own thoughts
Of your presumed goodness to conceive
This as your rudeness, which I see's impos'd.
Yet, since your cautelous jailor here stands by you.   170
And yo' are deni'd the liberty o' the house,
Let me take warrant, lady, from your silence
(Which ever is interpreted consent),

        144. *fond*: foolish.
        170. *cautelous*: devious, over-cautious.

      To make your answer for you, which shall be
      To as good purpose as I can imagine,
      And what I think you'ld speak.
FITZDOTTREL: No, no, no, no.
WITTIPOL: I shall resume, sir.
MANLY: Sir, what do you mean?
WITTIPOL: One interruption more, sir, and you go
      Into your hose and doublet, nothing saves you.
180   And therefore hearken. This is for your wife.
MANLY: You must play fair, sir.
WITTIPOL: Stand for me, good friend.
      (*He sets* MASTER MANLY, *his friend, in her place and speaks
      for her.*)
      Troth, sir, 'tis more than true that you have utter'd
      Of my unequal and so sordid match here,
      With all the circumstances of my bondage.
      I have a husband and a two-legg'd one,
      But such a moonling as no wit of man
      Or roses can redeem from being an ass.
      He's grown too much the story of men's mouths,
      To 'scape his lading, should I make't my study,
190   And lay all ways, yea, call mankind to help,
      To take his burden off; why, this one act
      Of his, to let his wife out to be courted,
      And at a price, proclaims his asinine nature
      So loud, as I am weary of my title to him.
      But sir, you seem a gentleman of virtue
      No less than blood, and one that every way
      Looks as he were of too good quality
      To entrap a credulous woman, or betray her.
      Since you have paid thus dear, sir, for a visit,
200   And made such venture on your wit and charge
      Merely to see me, or at most to speak to me,
      I were too stupid, or, what's worse, ingrate
      Not to return your venture. Think but how

           186. *moonling*: lunatic, dolt.
           189. *lading*: burden.
           196. *blood*: spirit and good birth.

I may with safety do it. I shall trust
My love and honour to you, and presume
You'll ever husband both, against this husband,
Who, if we chance to change his liberal ears
To other ensigns, and with labour make
A new beast of him, as he shall deserve,
Cannot complain he is unkindly dealt with.   210
This day he is to go to a new play, sir,
From whence no fear, no, nor authority,
Scarcely the king's command, sir, will restrain him,
Now you have fitted him with a stage garment,
For the mere name's sake, were there nothing else;
And many more such journeys he will make,
Which, if they now, or any time hereafter,
Offer us opportunity, you hear, sir,
Who'll be as glad, and forward to embrace,
Meet, and enjoy it cheerfully as you. —   220
I humbly thank you, lady.

FITZDOTTREL: Keep your ground, sir.

WITTIPOL: Will you be lighten'd?

FITZDOTTREL: Mum.

WITTIPOL: And but I am,
By the sad contract, thus to take my leave of you
At this so envious distance, I had taught
Our lips, ere this, to seal the happy mixture
Made of our souls. But we must both now yield
To the necessity. Do not think yet, lady,
But I can kiss, and touch, and laugh, and whisper,
And do those crowning courtships too, for which
Day and the public have allow'd no name;   230
But now my bargain binds me. 'Twere rude injury,
T'importune more, or urge a noble nature
To what of its own bounty it is prone to,
Else, I should speak — But, lady, I love so well,
As I will hope, you'll do so too! I have done, sir.

207–8. *liberal ... ensigns*: An allusion to changing the ass's ears into
cuckold's horns.
222. *lighten'd*: i.e. relieved of the cloak.

FITZDOTTREL: Well, then, I ha' won?

WITTIPOL: Sir, and I may win, too.

FITZDOTTREL: O yes, no doubt on't! I'll take careful order,
That she shall hang forth ensigns at the window,
To tell you when I am absent. Or I'll keep
240   Three or four footmen ready still of purpose
To run and fetch you at her longings, sir.
I'll go bespeak me straight a gilt caroch,
For her and you to take the air in: yes,
Into Hyde Park, and thence into Blackfriars,
Visit the painters, where you may see pictures,
And note the properest limbs, and how to make 'em.
Or what do you say unto a middling gossip
To bring you aye together at her lodging
Under pretext of teaching o' my wife
250   Some rare receipt of drawing almond milk, ha?
It shall be a part of my care. Good sir, God b' w' you.
I ha' kept the contract, and the cloak is mine own.

WITTIPOL: Why, much good do't you, sir; it may fall out
That you ha' bought it dear, though I ha' not sold it.

FITZDOTTREL: A pretty riddle! Fare you well, good sir.
   (*He turns his wife about.*)
Wife, your face this way, look on me, and think
Yo' have had a wicked dream, wife, and forget it.

MANLY: This is the strangest motion I e'er saw.

FITZDOTTREL: Now wife, sits this fair cloak the worse upon me,
260   For my great sufferings, or your little patience, ha?
They laugh, you think?

MISTRESS FITZDOTTREL: Why, sir, an you might see't
What thought they have of you may be soon collected
By the young gentleman's speech.

FITZDOTTREL: Young gentleman?

242. *caroch*: coach.
244. *Hyde Park*: just beginning to be fashionable city resort.
244. *Blackfriars*: residential quarter of painters.
247. *middling gossip*: go-between.
250. *receipt*: recipe.
258. *motion*: show, performance.

Death! You are in love with him, are you? Could he not
Be nam'd the gentleman, without the young?
Up to your cabin again!

MISTRESS FITZDOTTREL: My cage, yo' were best
To call it.

FITZDOTTREL: Yes, sing there. You'ld fain be making
Blanc-manger with him at your mother's! I know you.
Go get you up.

    [*Exit* MISTRESS FITZDOTTREL. *Enter* PUG.]
        How now! What say you, Devil?

PUG: Here is one Engine, sir, desires to speak with you.   270

FITZDOTTREL: I thought he brought some news of a broker!
    Well,
Let him come in, good Devil: fetch him else.
    [*Exit* PUG. *Enter* ENGINE.]
O, my fine Engine! What's th' affair? More cheats?

ENGINE: No, sir; the wit, the brain, the great projector
I told you of, is newly come to town.

FITZDOTTREL: Where, Engine?

ENGINE: I ha' brought him – he's without –
Ere he pull'd off his boots, sir, but so follow'd,
For businesses!

FITZDOTTREL: But what is a projector?
I would conceive.

ENGINE: Why, one, sir, that projects
Ways to enrich men, or to make 'em great,   280
By suits, by marriages, by undertakings:
According as he sees they humour it.

FITZDOTTREL: Can he not conjure at all?

ENGINE: I think he can, sir,
To tell you true. But you do know, of late,
The state hath ta'en such note of 'em and compell'd em
To enter such great bonds, they dare not practise.

FITZDOTTREL: 'Tis true, and I lie fallow for't the while!

ENGINE: O, sir, you'll grow the richer for the rest.

FITZDOTTREL: I hope I shall; but Engine, you do talk
Somewhat too much o' my courses. My cloak-customer   290

266. *cabin*: room.

Could tell me strange particulars.

ENGINE: By my means?

FITZDOTTREL: How should he have 'em else?

ENGINE: You do not know, sir,
What he has, and by what arts! A money'd man, sir,
And is as great with your almanac-men, as you are.

FITZDOTTREL: That gallant?

ENGINE: You make the other wait too long here,
And he is extreme punctual.

FITZDOTTREL: Is he a gallant?

ENGINE: Sir, you shall see: he is in his riding suit,
As he comes now from court. But hear him speak,
Minister matter to him, and then tell me.

    [*Exeunt*].

ACT TWO

SCENE ONE

([*Enter*] MEERCRAFT, FITZDOTTREL, ENGINE, TRAINS, SERVANTS.)

MEERCRAFT: Sir, money's a whore, a bawd, a drudge
Fit to run out on errands; let her go.
Via, pecunia! when she's run and gone,
And fled and dead, then will I fetch her again,
With aqua vitae, out of an old hogshead!
While there are lees of wine, or dregs of beer,
I'll never want her. Coin her out of cobwebs,
Dust, but I'll have her! Raise wool upon egg-shells,
Sir, and make grass grow out o' marrow-bones
To make her come. [*To* 1 SERVANT] Commend me to your   10
    mistress,
Say, let the thousand pound but be had ready,
And it is done.
    [*Exit* 1 SERVANT.]
                 I would but see the creature
Of flesh, and blood, the man, the prince indeed,
That could employ so many millions
As I would help him to.
FITZDOTTREL: How talks he, millions?
MEERCRAFT [*to* 2 SERVANT]: I'll give you an account of this
    tomorrow.
    [*Exit* 2 SERVANT.]
Yes, I will talk no less, and do it too,
If they were myriads: and without the devil,
By direct means, it shall be good in law.
ENGINE: Sir –

---

    3. *Via, pecunia!*: Away, lucre!
    6. *lees of wine, or dregs of beer*: for adulterating aqua vitae.

MEERCRAFT [*to* 3 SERVANT]: Tell Master Woodcock I'll
20   not fail to meet him
    Upon th'Exchange at night. Pray him to have
    The writings there, and we'll dispatch it.
    [*Exit* 3 SERVANT.]

                          [*To* FITZDOTTREL] Sir,
    You are a gentleman of a good presence,
    A handsome man. I have considered you
    As a fit stock to graft honours upon.
    I have a project to make you a duke, now.
    That you must be one, within so many months
    As I set down, out of true reason of state,
    You sha' not avoid it. But you must hearken, then.
30 ENGINE: Hearken? Why sir, do you doubt his ears? Alas,
    You do not know Master Fitzdottrel.
  FITZDOTTREL: He does not know me indeed. I thank you,
    Engine,
    For rectifying him.
  MEERCRAFT: Good! Why, Engine, then
    I'll tell it you. (I see you ha' credit here,
    And that you can keep counsel, I'll not question.)
    He shall but be an undertaker with me,
    In a most feasible bus'ness. It shall cost him
    Nothing.
  ENGINE: Good, sir –
  MEERCRAFT: Except he please, but's count'nance
    (That I will have) t'appear in't, to great men,
40   For which I'll make him one. He shall not draw
    A string of's purse. I'll drive his patent for him.
    We'll take in citizens, commoners and aldermen
    To bear the charge, and blow 'em off again,
    Like so many dead flies, when 'tis carried.
    The thing is for recovery of drown'd land,
    Whereof the crown's to have a moiety,
    If it be owner; else the crown and owners
    To share that moiety, and the recoverers
    T'enjoy the t'other moiety for their charge.

              46. *moiety*: part.

ENGINE: Throughout England?

MEERCRAFT: Yes, which will arise   50
  To eighteen millions, seven the first year.
  I have computed all, and made my survey
  Unto an acre. I'll begin at the pan,
  Not at the skirts, as some ha' done, and lost
  All that they wrought, their timber-work, their trench,
  Their banks all borne away, or else fill'd up
  By the next winter. Tut, they never went
  The way; I'll have it all.

ENGINE: A gallant tract
  Of land it is!

MEERCRAFT: 'Twill yield a pound an acre.
  We must let cheap ever, at first. But sir,   60
  This looks too large for you, I see. Come hither,
  We'll have a less. [*Indicates* TRAINS] Here's a plain fellow,
      you see him,
  Has his black bag of papers there, in buckram,
  Wi' not be sold for th'earldom of Pancridge. Draw,
  Gi' me out one, by chance.
      [TRAINS *hands him a paper.*]
                          Project Four: Dogs' skins –
  Twelve thousand pound ! The very worst at first.

FITZDOTTREL: Pray you let's see't, sir.

MEERCRAFT: 'Tis a toy, a trifle!

FITZDOTTREL: Trifle! Twelve thousand pound for dogs'
  skins?

MEERCRAFT: Yes,
  But, by my way of dressing, you must know, sir,   70
  And medicining the leather, to a height
  Of improv'd ware, like your borachio
  Of Spain, sir. I can fetch nine thousand for't –

ENGINE: Of the King's glover?

MEERCRAFT: Yes, how heard you that?

ENGINE: Sir, I do know you can.

MEERCRAFT: Within this hour,

53. *pan*: bottom, lowest ground.
72. *borachio*: goat- or pig-skin wine-bottle.

And reserve half my secret. Pluck another;
  [TRAINS *does so.*]
See if thou hast a happier hand: I thought so.
The very next worse to it! *Bottle-ale.*
Yet this is two and twenty thousand. Prithee
Pull out another, two or three.

80 FITZDOTTREL: Good, stay, friend –
  By bottle-ale, two and twenty thousand pound?
  MEERCRAFT: Yes, sir, it's cast to penny-halfpenny-farthing,
    O' the back side, there you may see it, read,
    I will not bate a Harrington o' the sum.
    I'll win it i' my water, and my malt,
    My furnaces and hanging o' my coppers,
    The tunning and the subtlety o' my yeast;
    And then the earth of my bottles, which I dig,
    Turn up and steep, and work, and neal myself,
90 To a degree of porcelain. You will wonder
    At my proportions, what I will put up
    In seven years (for so long time, I ask
    For my invention). I will save in cork,
    In my mere stop'ling, 'bove three thousand pound,
    Within that term: by gouging of 'em out
    Just to the size of my bottles, and not slicing.
    There's infinite loss i' that.
      [TRAINS *draws out another.*]
                                What hast thou there?
  O, *Making wine of raisins:* this is in hand, now.
100 ENGINE: Is not that strange, sir, to make wine of raisins?
  MEERCRAFT: Yes, and as true a wine as th' wines of France,
    Or Spain or Italy. Look of what grape
    My raisin is, that wine I'll render perfect,
    As of the muscatel grape I'll render muscatel,
    Of the Canary, his, the claret, his;
    So of all kinds, and bate you of the prices,
    Of wine, throughout the kingdom, half in half.

89. *neal:* temper, anneal.
94. *stop'ling:* corking.
106. *bate:* abate, save.

ENGINE: But, how sir, if you raise the other commodity,
Raisins?
MEERCRAFT: Why, then I'll make it out of blackberries:
And it shall do the same. 'Tis but more art,   110
And the charge less. Take out another.
FITZDOTTREL: No, good sir.
Save you the trouble, I'll not look, nor hear
Of any, but your first, there, the drown'd land:
If 'twill do, as you say.
MEERCRAFT: Sir, there's not place,
To gi' you demonstration of these things,
They are a little too subtle. But I could show you
Such a necessity in't, as you must be
But what you please, against the receiv'd heresy
That England bears no dukes. Keep you the land,
sir,   120
The greatness of th'estate shall throw't upon you.
If you like better turning it to money,
What may not you, sir, purchase with that wealth?
Say you should part with two o' your millions,
To be the thing you would, who would not do't?
As I protest I will, out of my dividend,
Lay for some pretty principality
In Italy, from the Church. Now you, perhaps,
Fancy the smoke of England rather? But –
Ha' you no private room, sir, to draw to,   130
T'enlarge ourselves more upon?
FITZDOTTREL: O yes. – Devil!
MEERCRAFT: These, sir, are bus'nesses ask to be carried
With caution, and in cloud.
FITZDOTTREL: I apprehend
They do so, sir.
    [*Enter* PUG.]
                    Devil, which way is your mistress?
PUG: Above, sir, in her chamber.
FITZDOTTREL: O that's well.

127. *Lay for*: bid for.
128. *from*: outside jurisdiction of.

221

Then this way, good sir.

MEERCRAFT: I shall follow you.
Trains, gi' me the bag, and go you presently,
Commend my service to my Lady Tailbush.
Tell her I am come from court this morning; say
I have got our bus'ness mov'd, and well. Entreat her
That she give you the fourscore angels, and see 'em
Dispos'd of to my counsel, Sir Paul Eitherside.
Sometime today, I'll wait upon her ladyship
With the relation.

    [*Exit* TRAINS.]

ENGINE: Sir, of what dispatch
He is! Do you mark?

MEERCRAFT: Engine, when did you see
My cousin Everill? Keeps he still your quarter
I' the Bermudas?

ENGINE: Yes, sir, he was writing
This morning, very hard.

MEERCRAFT: Be not you known to him,
That I am come to town; I have effected
A business for him, but I would have it take him
Before he thinks for't.

ENGINE: Is it past?

MEERCRAFT: Not yet.
'Tis well o' the way.

ENGINE: O sir, your worship takes
Infinite pains.

MEERCRAFT: I love friends to be active:
A sluggish nature puts off man, and kind.

ENGINE: And such a blessing follows it.

MEERCRAFT: I thank
My fate. Pray you, let's be private, sir.

FITZDOTTREL: In here.

MEERCRAFT: Where none may interrupt us.

    [*Exeunt* MEERCRAFT *and* ENGINE.]

> 141. *angels*: coins worth about fifty pence.
> 154. *kind*: woman.

FITZDOTTREL: You hear, Devil,
Lock the street doors fast, and let no one in
(Except they be this gentleman's followers)
To trouble me. Do you mark? Yo' have heard and seen   160
Something today, and by it you may gather
Your mistress is a fruit that's worth the stealing
And therefore worth the watching. Be you sure now,
Yo' have all your eyes about you; and let in
No lace-woman, nor bawd, that brings French masques
And cut-works. See you? Nor old crones with wafers,
To convey letters. Nor no youths disguis'd
Like country-wives, with cream and marrow-puddings.
Much knavery may be vented in a pudding,
Much bawdy intelligence; they are shrewd ciphers.   170
Nor turn the key to any neighbour's need,
Be't but to kindle fire, or beg a little,
Put it out, rather, all out to an ash,
That they may see no smoke. Or water, spill it:
Knock o' the empty tubs, that by the sound,
They may be forbid entry. Say we are robb'd,
If any come to borrow a spoon or so.
I wi' not have Good Fortune, or God's Blessing
Let in while I am busy.
PUG: I'll take care, sir:
They sha' not trouble you, if they would.
FITZDOTTREL: Well, do so.   180
    [*Exit* FITZDOTTREL.]
PUG: I have no singular service of this now,
Nor no superlative master! I shall wish
To be in hell again, at leisure, bring
A Vice from thence! That had been such a subtlety
As to bring broad-cloths hither, or transport
Fresh oranges into Spain. I find it now,
My chief was i' the right. Can any fiend
Boast of a better Vice than here by nature
And art they're owners of? Hell ne'er own me,

170. *ciphers*: 'figures' (i.e. 'smart numbers').

190 But I am taken! The fine tract of it
    Pulls me along! To hear men such professors
    Grown in our subtlest sciences! My first act now
    Shall be to make this master of mine cuckold:
    The primitive work of darkness I will practise.
    I will deserve so well of my fair mistress,
    By my discoveries, first, my counsels after,
    And keeping counsel after that: as who—
    Soever is one, I'll be another, sure,
    I'll ha' my share. Most delicate damn'd flesh!
200 She will be! O, that I could stay time now!
    Midnight will come too fast upon me, I fear,
    To cut my pleasure –

    [*Enter* MISTRESS FITZDOTTREL.]

MISTRESS FITZDOTTREL [*to* PUG]: Look at the back door,
    One knocks, see who it is.

PUG: [*aside*]:   Dainty she-devil! [*Exit.*]

MISTRESS FITZDOTTREL: I cannot get this venture of the cloak
    Out of my fancy, nor the gentleman's way
    He took, which though 'twere strange, yet 'twas handsome,
    And had a grace withal, beyond the newness.
    Sure he will think me that dull stupid creature
    He said, and may conclude it, if I find not
210 Some thought to thank th'attempt. He did presume,
    By all the carriage of it, on my brain,
    For answer; and will swear 'tis very barren,
    If it can yield him no return.

    [*Re-enter* PUG.]

                  Who is it?

PUG: Mistress, it is – but first, let me assure
    The excellence of mistresses, I am,
    Although my master's man, my mistress' slave,
    The servant of her secrets and sweet turns,
    And know what fitly will conduce to either.

MISTRESS FITZDOTTREL: What's this? I pray you come to
    yourself and think
220 What your part is: to make an answer. Tell,

190. *tract*: attraction.

Who is at the door?

PUG: The gentleman, mistress,
Who was at the cloak-charge to speak with you
This morning, who expects only to take
Some small commandments from you, what you please,
Worthy your form, he says, and gentlest manners.

MISTRESS FITZDOTTREL: O! You'll anon prove his hir'd
    man, I fear;
What has he giv'n you for this message? Sir,
Bid him put off his hopes of straw, and leave
To spread his nets in view thus. Though they take
Master Fitzdottrel, I am no such foul,   230
Nor fair one, tell him, will be had with stalking.
And wish him to forbear his acting to me
At the gentleman's chamber-window in Lincoln's Inn there,
That opens to my gallery: else I swear
T'acquaint my husband with his folly, and leave him
To the just rage of his offended jealousy.
Or if your master's sense be not so quick
To right me, tell him I shall find a friend
That will repair me. Say, I will be quiet
In mine own house. Pray you, in those words give it
    him.   240

PUG: This is some fool turn'd! [*Exit* PUG.]

MISTRESS FITZDOTTREL: If he be the master,
Now, of that state and wit which I allow him,
Sure, he will understand me: I durst not
Be more direct. For this officious fellow,
My husband's new groom, is a spy upon me,
I find already. Yet, if he but tell him
This in my words, he cannot but conceive
Himself both apprehended and requited.
I would not have him think he met a statue,
Or spoke to one not there, though I were silent.   250
    [*Re-enter* PUG.]
How now? Ha' you told him?

228. *leave*: i.e. leave off.
248. *apprehended*: understood.

PUG: Yes.

MISTRESS FITZDOTTREL: And what says he?

PUG: Says he? That which myself would say to you, if I durst.
  That you are proud, sweet mistress, and withal
  A little ignorant, to entertain
  The good that's proffer'd; and (by your beauty's leave)
  Not all so wise as some true politic wife
  Would be, who having match'd with such a nupson
  (I speak it with my master's peace) whose face
  Hath left t'accuse him, now for't doth confess him,

260   What you can make him, will yet (out of scruple,
  And a spic'd conscience) defraud the poor gentleman,
  At least delay him in the thing he longs for,
  And makes it his whole study how to compass,
  Only a title. Could but he write cuckold,
  He had his ends. For look you –

MISTRESS FITZDOTTREL [*aside*]: This can be
  None but my husband's wit.

PUG: My precious mistress –

MISTRESS FITZDOTTREL [*aside*]: It creaks his engine: the
  groom never durst
  Be else so saucy.

PUG: If it were not clearly
  His worshipful ambition, and the top of it,

270   The very forked top too, why should he
  Keep you thus mur'd up in a back room, mistress,
  Allow you ne'er a casement to the street,
  Fear of engendering by the eyes with gallants?
  Forbid you paper, pen and ink, like ratsbane,
  Search your half pint of muscatel, lest a letter
  Be sunk i' the pot: and hold your new-laid egg
  Against the fire, lest any charm be writ there?
  Will you make benefit of truth, dear mistress,

---

256. *politic*: shrewd, cunning.
257. *nupson*: simpleton.
261. *spic'd*: finicky.
270. *forked top*: the cuckold joke rearing its horned head again.
271. *mur'd*: walled, i.e. imprisoned.

If I do tell it you? I do't not often.
I am set over you, employ'd indeed,   280
To watch your steps, your looks, your very breathings,
And to report them to him. Now, if you
Will be a true, right, delicate sweet mistress,
Why, we will make a Cokes of this wise master,
We will, my mistress, an absolute fine Cokes,
And mock to air all the deep diligences
Of such a solemn and effectual ass,
An ass to so good purpose, as we'll use him.
I will contrive it so that you shall go
To plays, to masques, to meetings and to feasts.   290
For why is all this rigging, and fine tackle, mistress,
If you neat handsome vessels of good sail
Put not forth ever and anon, with your nets
Abroad into the world? It is your fishing.
There you shall choose your friends, your servants, lady,
Your squires of honour; I'll convey your letters,
Fetch answers, do you all the offices
That can belong to your blood and beauty. And,
For the variety, at my times, although
I am not in due symmetry, the man   300
Of that proportion; or in rule
Of physic, of the just complexion;
Or of that truth of Picardil, in clothes,
To boast a sovereignty o'er ladies; yet
I know to do my turns, sweet mistress. Come, kiss –
MISTRESS FITZDOTTREL: How now!
PUG: Dear delicate mistress, I
    am your slave,
  Your little worm, that loves you: your fine monkey,
  Your dog, your jack, your Pug, that longs to be
  Styl'd o' your pleasures.
MISTRESS FITZDOTTREL (*She thinks her husband watches*):
                          Hear you all this? Sir, pray you,

284. *Cokes*: ass, dolt.
287. *effectual*: complete, out-and-out.
303. *Picardil*: Fr. peccadelle, frame of stiffened linen to hold broad collar
erect.

310   Come from your standing, do, a little, spare
        Yourself, sir, from your watch, t'applaud your squire,
        That so well follows your instructions!
        [*Enter* FITZDOTTREL.]
  FITZDOTTREL: How now, sweetheart, what's the matter?
  MISTRESS FITZDOTTREL: Good!
        You are a stranger to the plot! You set not
        Your fancy devil here to tempt your wife,
        With all the insolent uncivil language
        Or action he could vent?
  FITZDOTTREL: Did you so, Devil?
  MISTRESS FITZDOTTREL: Not you? You were not planted i'
        your hole to hear him
        Upo' the stairs, or here, behind the hangings?
320   I do not know your qualities? He durst do it,
        And you not give directions!
  FITZDOTTREL: You shall see, wife,
        Whether he durst, or no: and what it was,
        I did direct.
        (*Her husband goes out, and enters presently with a cudgel upon*
        him.)
  PUG: Sweet mistress, are you mad?
  FITZDOTTREL: You most mere rogue! You open manifest
        villain!
        You fiend apparent, you! You declar'd hell-hound!
  PUG: Good sir!
  FITZDOTTREL: Good knave, good rascal, and good traitor!
        Now I do find you parcel devil indeed.
        Upo' the point of trust! I' your first charge,
        The very day o' your probation,
        To tempt your mistress!
        [*Beats* PUG.]
330   You do see, good wedlock,
        How I directed him.
  MISTRESS FITZDOTTREL: Why, where, sir, were you?
  FITZDOTTREL: Nay, there is one blow more, for exercise!
        [*Beats him again.*]

327. *parcel*: part.

I told you I should do it.

PUG: Would you had done, sir.

FITZDOTTREL: O wife, the rarest man!

(*After a pause he strikes him again and again.*)

Yet there's another
To put you in mind o' the last. Such a brave man, wife!
Within, he has his projects, and does vent 'em
The gallantest! [*to Pug*] Were you tentiginous, ha?
Would you be acting of the incubus?
Did her silks rustling move you?

PUG: Gentle sir!

FITZDOTTREL: Out of my sight! If thy name were not Devil, 340
Thou should'st not stay a minute with me. In,
Go – yet stay – yet go too. I am resolv'd
What I will do, and you shall know't aforehand,
Soon as the gentleman is gone, do you hear?
I'll help your lisping.

[*Exit* PUG.]

Wife, such a man, wife!
He has such plots! He will make me a duke,
No less by heaven! Six mares to your coach, wife,
That's your proportion! And your coach-man bald!
Because he shall be bare enough. Do not you laugh;
We are looking for a place, and all, i' the map 350
What to be of. Have faith, be not an infidel.
You know I am not easy to be gull'd.
I swear, when I have my millions, else, I'll make
Another duchess, if you ha' not faith.

MISTRESS FITZDOTTREL: You'll ha' too much, I fear, in these
false spirits.

FITZDOTTREL: Spirits? O, no such thing, wife! Wit, mere
wit!
This man defies the devil and all his works!
He does't by Engine, and devices, he!
He has his wingéd ploughs that go with sails,

337. *tentiginous*: sexually excited.
338. *incubus*: devil who cohabits with human females.
348. *bald*: bare, as was customary for a fine lady's coachman.

360 Will plough you forty acres at once! And mills,
Will spout you water ten miles off! All Crowland
Is ours, wife; and the fens, from us in Norfolk
To the utmost bound of Lincolnshire! We have view'd it,
And measur'd it within all, by the scale;
The richest tract of land, love, i' the kingdom!
There will be made seventeen or eighteen millions
Or more, as't may be handled! Wherefore think,
Sweetheart, if th'hast a fancy to one place
More than another, to be duchess of,
370 Now, name it: I will ha't, whate'er it cost
(If't will be had for money), either here,
Or'n France, or Italy.

MISTRESS FITZDOTTREL: You ha' strange fantasies!
    [*Enter* MEERCRAFT *and* ENGINE.]

MEERCRAFT: Where are you, sir?

FITZDOTTREL: I see thou hast no talent
This way, wife. Up to thy gallery, do, chuck,
Leave us to talk of it who understand it.
    [*Exit* MISTRESS FITZDOTTREL.]

MEERCRAFT: I think we ha' found a place to fit you now, sir.
    Gloucester.

FITZDOTTREL: O, no, I'll none!

MEERCRAFT: Why, sir?

FITZDOTTREL: 'Tis fatal.

MEERCRAFT: That you say right in. Spenser, I think the
    younger,
Had his last honour thence. But he was but Earl.

380 FITZDOTTREL: I know not that, sir. But Thomas of Woodstock
I'm sure was duke, and he was made away
At Calice, as Duke Humphrey was at Bury:
And Richard the Third – you know what end he came to.

MEERCRAFT: By m' faith, you are cunning i' the chronicle,
    sir.

FITZDOTTREL: No, I confess I ha't from the play-books,
And think they are more authentic!

        382. *Calice*: Calais.

ENGINE: That's sure, sir.

MEERCRAFT: What say you to this then?
(*He whispers him of a place.*)

FITZDOTTREL: No, a noble house
Pretends to that. I will do no man wrong.

MEERCRAFT: Then take one proposition more, and hear it
As past exception.

FITZDOTTREL: What's that?

MEERCRAFT: To be   390
Duke of those lands you shall recover: take
Your title thence, sir, Duke of the Drown'd Lands,
Or Drown'd-land.

FITZDOTTREL: Ha! That last has a good sound;
I like it well. The Duke of Drown'd-land!

ENGINE: Yes,
It goes like Groen-land, sir, if you mark it.

MEERCRAFT: Ay,
And drawing thus your honour from the work,
You make the reputation of that greater
And stay't the longer i' your name.

FITZDOTTREL: 'Tis true.
Drown'd-lands will live in Drown'd-land!

MEERCRAFT: Yes, when you
Ha' no foot left, as that must be, sir, one day,   400
And, though it tarry in your heirs, some forty,
Fifty descents, the longer liver at last, yet,
Must thrust 'em out on't, if no quirk in law,
Or odd vice o' their own not do it first.
We see those changes daily: the fair lands
That were the clients', are the lawyers' now;
And those rich manors there, of goodman tailor's,
Had once more wood upon 'em than the yard
By which th' were measur'd out for the last purchase.
Nature hath these vicissitudes. She makes   410
No man a state of perpetuity, sir.

395. *Groen-land*: Dutch form, common in seventeenth-century English,
of Greenland.

FITZDOTTREL: Y'are i' the right. Let's in then, and conclude.
   [*Re-enter* PUG.]
  I' my sight again? I'll talk with you, anon.
   [*Exeunt* FITZDOTTREL, MEERCRAFT, ENGINE.]
PUG: Sure he will geld me if I stay, or worse,
  Pluck out my tongue, one o' the two. This fool,
  There is no trusting of him; and to quit him,
  Were a contempt against my chief past pardon.
  It was a shrewd disheart'ning this, at first!
  Who would ha' thought a woman so well harness'd,
420 Or rather well-caparison'd, indeed,
  That wears such petticoats, and lace to her smocks,
  Broad-seaming laces (as I see 'em hang there)
  And garters which are lost, if she can show 'em,
  Could ha' done this? Hell! Why is she so brave?
  It cannot be to please Duke Dottrel, sure,
  Nor the dull pictures in her gallery,
  Nor her own dear reflection in her glass;
  Yet that may be: I have known many of 'em
  Begin their pleasure, but none end it, there:
430 (That I consider, as I go along with it)
  They may, for want of better company,
  Or that they think the better, spend an hour,
  Two, three, or four, discoursing with their shadow:
  But sure they have a farther speculation.
  No woman drest with so much care and study
  Doth dress herself in vain. I'll vex this problem
  A little more before I leave it, sure.
   [*Exit.*]

[SCENE TWO]

[*Enter* WITTIPOL *and* MANLY.]
WITTIPOL: This was a fortune happy above thought,
  That this should prove thy chamber which I fear'd

423. *garters ... show 'em*: gallants begged their mistresses' garters as
keepsakes.

Would be my greatest trouble! This must be
The very window and that the room.
MANLY: It is.
  I now remember, I have often seen there
  A woman, but I never mark'd her much.
WITTIPOL: Where was your soul, friend?
MANLY: Faith, but now and then
  Awake unto those objects.
WITTIPOL: You pretend so.
  Let me not live if I am not in love
  More with her wit for this direction now   10
  Than with her form, though I ha' prais'd that prettily,
  Since I saw her, and you, today.
    (*He gives him a paper, wherein is the copy of a song.*)
                                Read those;
  They'll go unto the air you love so well.
  Try 'em unto the note; may be the music
  Will call her sooner. Light, she's here! Sing quickly!
    [MISTRESS FITZDOTTREL *appears at a chamber window.*]
MISTRESS FITZDOTTREL: Either he understood him not, or
    else
  The fellow was not faithful in delivery
  Of what I bade. And I am justly paid,
  That might have made my profit of his service,
  But by mistaking have drawn on his envy,   20
  And done the worse defeat upon myself.
    (MANLY *sings,* PUG *enters, perceives it.*)
  How! Music? Then he may be there, and is sure.
PUG [*aside*]: O! Is it so? Is there the interview?
  Have I drawn to you at last, my cunning lady?
  The devil is an ass! Fool'd oft and beaten,
  Nay, made an instrument, and could not scent it!
  Well, since yo' have shown the malice of a woman,
  No less than her true wit and learning, mistress,
  I'll try if little Pug have the malignity
  To recompense it and so save his danger.   30
  'Tis not the pain but the discredit of it –
  The devil should not keep a body entire. [*Exit* PUG.]

WITTIPOL: Away, fall back, she comes.

MANLY: I'll leave you, sir,
  The master of my chamber; I have business. [*Exit* MANLY.]
    (*This scene is acted at two windows, as out of two contiguous
    buildings.*)

WITTIPOL: Mistress!

MISTRESS FITZDOTTREL: You make me paint, sir.

WITTIPOL: They're fair colours,
  Lady, and natural. I did receive
  Some commands from you lately, gentle lady,
  But so perplex'd and wrapp'd in the delivery,
  As I may fear t'have misinterpreted,
40 But must make suit still, to be near your grace.

MISTRESS FITZDOTTREL: Who is there with you, sir?

WITTIPOL: None but myself.
  It falls out, lady, to be a dear friend's lodging.
  Wherein there's some conspiracy of fortune
  With your poor servant's blest affections.

MISTRESS FITZDOTTREL: Who was it sung?

WITTIPOL: He, lady, but he's gone,
  Upon my entreaty of him, seeing you
  Approach the window. Neither need you doubt him,
  If he were here. He is too much a gentleman.

MISTRESS FITZDOTTREL: Sir, if you judge me by this simple
    action,
50 And by the outward habit and complexion
  Of easiness it hath to your design,
  You may with justice say I am a woman,
  And a strange woman. But when you shall please
  To bring but that concurrence of my fortune
  To memory, which today yourself did urge,
  It may beget some favour like excuse,
  Though none like reason.

WITTIPOL: No, my tuneful mistress?
  Then surely love hath none, nor beauty any,
  Nor nature violenced in both these,

---

35. *paint*: blush.
38. *perplex'd*: involved.

234

With all whose gentle tongues you speak at once.   60
I thought I had enough remov'd, already,
That scruple from your breast, and left yo' all reason,
When through my morning's perspective I show'd you
A man so above excuse, as he is the cause
Why anything is to be done upon him,
And nothing call'd an injury, misplac'd.
I rather now had hope to show you how love
By his accesses grows more natural:
And, what was done, this morning, with such force
Was but devis'd to serve the present, then –   70
   (*He grows more familiar in his courtship, plays with her paps,*
   kisses her hands, etc.)
That since love hath the honour to approach
These sister-swelling breasts, and touch this soft
And rosy hand; he hath the skill to draw
Their nectar forth with kissing, and could make
More wanton saults from this brave promontory
Down to this valley than the nimble roe;
Could play the hopping sparrow 'bout these nets,
And sporting squirrel in these crispéd groves;
Bury himself in every silkworm's kell
Is here unravell'd; run into the snare,   80
Which every hair is, cast into a curl
To catch a Cupid flying; bath himself
In milk and roses here, and dry him, there;
Warm his cold hands to play with this smooth, round
And well-turn'd chin, as with the billiard ball;
Roll on these lips, the banks of love, and there
At once both plant and gather kisses. Lady,
Shall I, with what I have made to-day here, call
All sense to wonder, and all faith to sign
The mysteries revealéd in your form?   90
And will love pardon me the blasphemy
I utter'd, when I said a glass could speak

      75. *saults*: leaps.
      78. *crisped*: tightly curled.
      79. *silkworm's kell*: cocoon.

This beauty, or that fools had power to judge it?

> Do but look on her eyes! They do light
>   All that love's world compriseth.
> Do but look on her hair! It is bright
>   As love's star when it riseth.
> Do but mark, her forehead's smoother
>   Than words that soothe her.

100 And from her arched brows, such a grace
>   Sheds itself through the face
> As alone, there triumphs to the life,
>   All the gain, all the good, of the element's strife!

> Have you seen but a bright lily grow,
>   Before rude hands have touch'd it?
> Have you mark'd but the fall of the snow,
>   Before the soil hath smutch'd it?
> Have you felt the wool o' the beaver,
>   Or swan's down ever?

110 Or have smelt o' the bud o' the briar,
>   Or the nard i' the fire?
> Or have tasted the bag o' the bee?
>   O so white, O so soft, O so sweet is she!

(*Her husband appears at her back.*)

FITZDOTTREL: Is she so, sir? And I will keep her so,
If I know how, or can; that wit of man
Will do't, I'll go no farther. At this windo'
She shall no more be buzz'd at. Take your leave on't.
If you be sweetmeats, wedlock or sweet flesh,
All's one: I do not love this hum about you.

120 A fly-blown wife is not so proper. [*To his wife*] In! –
(*He speaks out of his wife's window.*)
For you, sir, look to hear from me.

WITTIPOL: So I do, sir.

FITZDOTTREL: No, but in other terms. There's no man offers
This to my wife, but pays for't.

WITTIPOL: That have I, sir.

111. *nard*: aromatic balsam.

FITZDOTTREL: Nay then, I tell you, you are –

WITTIPOL: What am I, sir?

FITZDOTTREL: Why, that I'll think on, when I ha' cut your
throat.

WITTIPOL: Go, you are an ass.

FITZDOTTREL: I am resolv'd on't, sir.

WITTIPOL: I think you are.

FITZDOTTREL: To call you to a reckoning.

WITTIPOL: Away, you broker's block, you property!

FITZDOTTREL: S'light, if you strike me, I'll strike your
mistress.

(*He strikes his wife.*)

WITTIPOL: O! I could shoot mine eyes at him for that
now,   130
Or leave my teeth in him, were they cuckold's bane,
Enough to kill him. What prodigious,
Blind and most wicked change of fortune's this?
I ha' no air of patience; all my veins
Swell, and my sinews start at iniquity of it.
I shall break, break. [*Exit.*]

[SCENE THREE]

(*The devil* [PUG] *speaks below.*)

PUG: This for the malice of it,
And my revenge may pass! But now my conscience
Tells me I have profited the cause of hell
But little, in the breaking-off their loves.
Which, if some other act of mine repair not,
I shall hear ill of in my accompt.

(FITZDOTTREL *enters with his wife as* [*if*] *come down* [*from
the window*].)

FITZDOTTREL: O bird,
Could you do this? 'gainst me? And at this time, now?
When I was so employ'd, wholly for you,
Drown'd i' my care (more than the land, I swear,
I have hope to win) to make you peerless? Studying   10

237

For footmen for you, fine-paced ushers, pages,
To serve you o' the knee; with what knight's wife
To bear your train, and sit with your four women
In council, and receive intelligences
From foreign parts, to dress you at all pieces!
Y'have a'most turn'd my good affection to you,
Sour'd my sweet thoughts, all my pure purposes.
I could now find i' my very heart to make
Another lady duchess and depose you.
Well, go your ways in.
    [*Exit* MISTRESS FITZDOTTREL.]
20   Devil, you have redeem'd all.
I do forgive you, and I'll do you good. [*Exit* PUG.]
    [*Enter* MEERCRAFT *and* ENGINE.]
MEERCRAFT: Why ha' you these excursions? Where ha' you
    been, sir?
FITZDOTTREL: Where I ha' been vex'd a little with a toy.
MEERCRAFT: O sir, no toys must trouble your grave head,
    Now it is growing to be great. You must
    Be above all those things.
FITZDOTTREL: Nay, nay, so I will.
MEERCRAFT: Now you are to'ard the lord, you must put off
    The man, sir.
ENGINE: He says true.
MEERCRAFT: You must do nothing
    As you ha' done it heretofore; not know
    Or salute any man.
30 ENGINE: That was your bed-fellow
    The other month.
MEERCRAFT: The other month? the week.
    Thou dost not know the privileges, Engine,
    Follow that title, nor how swift; today,
    When he has put on his lord's face once, then –
FITZDOTTREL: Sir, for these things I shall do well enough,
    There is no fear of me. But then, my wife is
    Such an untoward thing, she'll never learn

15. *at all pieces*: at all points.
23. *toy*: trifle.

238

How to comport with it! I am out of all
Conceit, on her behalf.

MEERCRAFT: Best have her taught, sir.

FITZDOTTREL: Where? Are there any schools for ladies?   40
Is there an academy for women? I do know,
For men, there was: I learn'd in it myself,
To make my legs and do my postures.

ENGINE (*whispers* MEERCRAFT):   Sir,
Do you remember the conceit you had –
O' the Spanish gown at home?

MEERCRAFT: Ha! I do thank thee
With all my heart, dear Engine. (*Turns to* FITZDOTTREL)
   Sir, there is
A certain lady here about the town,
An English widow, who hath lately travell'd,
But she's call'd the Spaniard, 'cause she came
Latest from thence, and keeps the Spanish habit.   50
Such a rare woman! All our women here
That are of spirit and fashion flock unto her,
As to their president, their law, their canon,
More than they ever did to oracle Foreman.
Such rare receipts she has, sir, for the face,
Such oils, such tinctures, such pomatums,
Such perfumes, med'cines, quintessences, et cetera;
And such a mistress of behaviour,
She knows from the duke's daughter to the doxy,
What is their due just, and no more!

FITZDOTTREL: O sir,   60
You please me i' this, more than mine own greatness.
Where is she? Let us have her.

MEERCRAFT: By your patience,
We must use means, cast how to be acquainted –

FITZDOTTREL: Good sir, about it.

MEERCRAFT: We must think how, first.

FITZDOTTREL: O,
I do not love to tarry for a thing

54. *oracle Foreman*: see additional note to I, ii, 1–2.
59. *doxy*: vagrant's woman.

When I have a mind to't. You do not know me,
If you do offer it.

MEERCRAFT:　　　　Your wife must send
Some pretty token to her, with a compliment,
And pray to be receiv'd in her good graces;
All the great ladies do't.

70 FITZDOTTREL:　　　　She shall, she shall.
What were it best to be?

MEERCRAFT:　　　　　Some little toy;
I would not have it any great matter, sir:
A diamond ring of forty or fifty pound
Would do it handsomely, and be a gift
Fit for your wife to send, and her to take.

FITZDOTTREL: I'll go and tell my wife on't straight.
　　(FITZDOTTREL goes out.)

MEERCRAFT:　　　　　　　　　Why this
Is well! The clothes we have now, but where's this lady?
If we could get a witty boy now, Engine;
That were an excellent crack. I could instruct him
80 To the true height, for anything takes this dottrel.

ENGINE: Why, sir your best will be one o' the players!

MEERCRAFT: No, there's no trusting them. They'll talk on't,
And tell their poets.

ENGINE:　　　　　What if they do? The jest
Will brook the stage. But there be some of 'em
Are very honest lads. There's Dick Robinson,
A very pretty fellow, and comes often
To a gentleman's chamber, a friend's of mine. We had
The merriest supper of it there one night;
The gentleman's landlady invited him
90 To a gossips' feast. Now he, sir, brought Dick Robinson,
Drest like a lawyer's wife, amongst 'em all;
(I lent him clothes) but, to see him behave it,
And lay the law, and carve, and drink unto 'em;
And then talk bawdy, and send frolics! O,

94. *frolics*: couplets, often amorous or satiric, wrapped round a sweetmeat
and passed round at supper.

It would have burst your buttons, or not left you
A seam.

MEERCRAFT: They say he's an ingenious youth.

ENGINE: O sir! and dresses himself the best! Beyond
Forty o'your very ladies! Did you ne'er see him?

MEERCRAFT: No, I do seldom see those toys. But think you,
That we may have him?

ENGINE: Sir, the young gentleman   100
I tell you of, can command him. Shall I attempt it?

MEERCRAFT: Yes, do it.

    [*Re-enter* FITZDOTTREL.]

FITZDOTTREL: S'light, I cannot get my wife
To part with a ring on any terms, and yet
The sullen monkey has two.

MEERCRAFT: It were 'gainst reason
That you should urge it. Sir, send to a goldsmith,
Let not her lose by't.

FITZDOTTREL: How does she lose by't?
Is't not for her?

MEERCRAFT: Make it your own bounty,
It will ha' the better success. What is a matter
Of fifty pound to you, sir?

FITZDOTTREL: I have but a hundred
Pieces to show here, that I would not break –   110

MEERCRAFT: You shall ha' credit, sir. I'll send a ticket
Unto my goldsmith.

    (TRAINS *enters.*)

                Here my man comes too,
To carry it fitly. How now, Trains? What birds?

TRAINS: Your Cousin Everill met me, and has beat me,
Because I would not tell him where you were:
I think he has dogg'd me to the house too.

[MEERCRAFT:]   Well –
You shall go out at the back door then, Trains.
You must get Gilthead hither by some means.

TRAINS: 'Tis impossible!

FITZDOTTREL: Tell him we have venison,

241

120   I'll gi' him a piece, and send his wife a pheasant.
TRAINS: A forest moves not, till that forty pound
   Yo' had of him last be paid. He keeps more stir
   For that same petty sum than for your bond
   Of six, and statute of eight hundred.
MEERCRAFT: Tell him
   We'll hedge in that. Cry up Fitzdottrel to him,
   Double his price; make him a man of metal.
TRAINS: That will not need, his bond is current enough.
      [*Exeunt.*]

121. *forest*: i.e. of deer.
124. *statute*: creditor's authorization to hold debtor's land in case of
default.
125. *hedge in*: secure a lesser debt by including it in a larger one with
better security.

ACT THREE

SCENE ONE

[*Enter* GILTHEAD *and* PLUTARCHUS.]

GILTHEAD: All this is to make you a gentleman
    I'll have you learn, son. Wherefore have I plac'd you
    With Sir Paul Eitherside, but to have so much law
    To keep your own? Besides, he is a justice
    Here i' the town; and dwelling, son, with him,
    You shall learn that in a year, shall be worth twenty
    Of having stay'd you at Oxford or at Cambridge,
    Or sending you to the Inns of Court, or France.
    I am call'd for now in haste by Master Meercraft
    To trust Master Fitzdottrel, a good man,   10
    (I have inquir'd him, eighteen hundred a year,
    His name is current) for a diamond ring
    Of forty, shall not be worth thirty that's gain'd;
    And this is to make you a gentleman!
PLUTARCHUS: O, but good father, you trust too much!
GILTHEAD: Boy, boy,
    We live by finding fools out to be trusted.
    Our shop-books are our pastures, our corn-grounds;
    We lay 'em op'n, for them to come into;
    And when we have 'em there, we drive 'em up
    Int' one of our two pounds, the compters, straight,   20
    And this is to make you a gentleman!
    We citizens never trust, but we do cozen:
    For if our debtors pay, we cozen them,
    And if they do not, then we cozen ourselves.
    But that's a hazard every one must run
    That hopes to make his son a gentleman!
PLUTARCHUS: I do not wish to be one, truly, father.

    10. *good*: financially sound.
    20. *two pounds, the compters*: the two city prisons or compters.

In a descent or two we come to be
Just i' their state, fit to be cozen'd, like 'em.
30   And I had rather ha' tarried i' your trade;
For, since the gentry scorn the city so much,
Methinks we should in time, holding together,
And matching in our own tribes, as they say,
Have got an act of common council for it,
That we might cozen them out of *rerum natura*.

GILTHEAD: Ay, if we had an act first to forbid
The marrying of our wealthy heirs unto 'em,
And daughters with such lavish portions:
That confounds all.

PLUTARCHUS: And makes a mongrel breed, father.
40   And when they have your money, then they laugh at you,
Or kick you down the stairs. I cannot abide 'em;
I would fain have 'em cozen'd, but not trusted.
      [*Enter* MEERCRAFT.]

MEERCRAFT: O, is he come? I knew he would not fail me.
Welcome, good Gilthead, I must ha' you do
A noble gentleman a courtesy here,
In a mere toy, some pretty ring or jewel
Of fifty, or threescore pound. Make it a hundred,
And hedge in the last forty that I owe you,
And your own price for the ring. He's a good man, sir,
50   And you may hap see him a great one. He
Is likely to bestow hundreds and thousands
Wi' you if you can humour him. A great prince
He will be shortly. What do you say?

GILTHEAD: In truth, sir
I cannot; 't has been a long vacation with us.

FITZDOTTREL: Of what, I pray thee? of wit? or honesty?
Those are your citizens' long vacations.

PLUTARCHUS: Good father, do not trust 'em.

MEERCRAFT: Nay, Tom Gilthead,
He will not buy a courtesy and beg it;
He'll rather pay than pray. If you do for him,

33. *matching*: marrying.
35. *rerum natura*: 'of the scheme of things', i.e. of everything.

You must do cheerfully. His credit, sir,   60
Is not yet prostitute. Who's this? Thy son?
A pretty youth, what's his name?

PLUTARCHUS: Plutarchus, sir.

MEERCRAFT: Plutarchus! How came that about?

GILTHEAD: That year, sir,
That I begot him, I bought Plutarch's *Lives*,
And fell so in love with the book, as I call'd my son
By his name, in hope he should be like him
And write the lives of our great men.

MEERCRAFT   I' the city?
And you do breed him there?

GILTHEAD: His mind, sir, lies
Much to that way.

MEERCRAFT: Why then, he is i' the right way.

GILTHEAD: But now, I had rather get him a good wife,   70
And plant him i' the country, there to use
The blessing I shall leave him.

MEERCRAFT: Out upon't!
And lose the laudable means thou hast at home here,
T'advance and make him a young alderman?
Buy him a captain's place, for shame, and let him
Into the world early, and with his plume
And scarfs march through Cheapside, or along Cornhill,
And by the virtue of those draw down a wife
There from a windo', worth ten thousand pound!
Get him the posture book and's leaden men   80
To set upon a table, 'gainst his mistress
Chance to come by, that he may draw her in,
And show her Finsbury battles.

GILTHEAD: I have plac'd him
With Justice Eitherside, to get so much law –

MEERCRAFT: As thou hast conscience. Come come, thou
    dost wrong
Pretty Plutarchus, who had not his name

---

76. *plume*: A scarlet ostrich feather was worn by Gentlemen of the Artillery,
a London train-band.

For nothing, but was born to train the youth
Of London in the military truth –
   [*Enter* EVERILL.]
That way his genius lies. My cousin Everill!
90 EVERILL: O, are you here, sir? Pray you, let us whisper.
   [*They talk apart.*]
  PLUTARCHUS: Father, dear father, trust him if you love me.
  GILTHEAD: Why, I do mean it, boy; but, what I do
Must not come easily from me. We must deal
With courtiers, boy, as courtiers deal with us.
If I have a business there, with any of them,
Why, I must wait, I am sure on't, son; and though
My lord dispatch me, yet his worshipful man
Will keep me for his sport a month or two,
To show me with my fellow citizens.
100 I must make his train long and full, one quarter,
And help the spectacle of his greatness. There
Nothing is done at once but injuries, boy:
And they come headlong! All their good turns move not,
Or very slowly.
  PLUTARCHUS: Yet, sweet father, trust him.
  GILTHEAD: Well, I will think.
  EVERILL: Come, you must do't, sir.
I am undone else, and your Lady Tailbush
Has sent for me to dinner, and my clothes
Are all at pawn. I had sent out this morning,
Before I heard you were come to town, some twenty
110 Of my epistles, and no one return –
  MEERCRAFT: Why, I ha' told you o' this. This comes of
      wearing
Scarlet, gold lace, and cut-works, your fine gart'ring,
With your blown roses, cousin, and your eating
Pheasant and godwit, here in London, haunting
The Globes and Mermaids! Wedging in with lords,
Still at the table, and affecting lechery,

87–8. *train ... truth*: a quotation from some verses on the city train-
bands.
115. *Globes and Mermaids*: i.e. theatres and taverns.

In velvet! Where could you ha' contented yourself
With cheese, saltbutter and a pickled herring,
I' the Low Countries, there worn cloth, and fustian,
Been satisfied with a leap o' your host's daughter,   120
In garrison, a wench of a stoter, or
Your sutler's wife i' the leaguer, of two blanks!
You never then had run upon this flat,
To write your letters missive, and send out
Your privy seals, that thus have frighted off
All your acquaintance, that they shun you at distance,
Worse than you do the bailies!

EVERILL: Pox upon you.
I come not to you for counsel, I lack money.

MEERCRAFT: You do not think what you owe me already?

EVERILL: I?
They owe you that mean to pay you. I'll be sworn   130
I never meant it. Come, you will project,
I shall undo your practice for this month else;
You know me.

MEERCRAFT: Ay, yo'are a right sweet nature!

EVERILL: Well, that's all one!

MEERCRAFT: You'll leave this empire one day;
You will not ever have this tribute paid,
Your sceptre o' the sword.

EVERILL: Tie up your wit,
Do, and provoke me not!

MEERCRAFT: Will you, sir, help
To what I shall provoke another for you?

EVERILL: I cannot tell; try me: I think I am not
So utterly of an ore un-to-be-melted   140
But I can do myself good on occasions.
   [*Enter* FITZDOTTREL.]

MEERCRAFT: Strike in then, for your part, Master Fitzdottrel,
If I transgress in point of manners, afford me
Your best construction; I must beg my freedom
From your affairs, this day. (MEERCRAFT *pretends business*.)

        121. *stoter*: Dutch coin.
        122. *blanks*: small French coins.

FITZDOTTREL: How, sir?

MEERCRAFT: It is
In succour of this gentleman's occasions,
My kinsman –

FITZDOTTREL: You'll not do me that affront, sir.

MEERCRAFT: I am sorry you should so interpret it,
But, sir, it stands upon his being invested
150   In a new office, he has stood for long:
Master of the Dependences. A place
Of my projection too, sir, and hath met
Much opposition; but the state now sees
That great necessity of it, as after all
Their writing and their speaking against duels,
They have erected it. His book is drawn –
For, since there will be differences, daily,
'Twixt gentlemen, and that the roaring manner
Is grown offensive, that those few, we call
160   The civil men o' the sword, abhor the vapours;
They shall refer now, hither, for their process,
And such as trespass 'gainst the rule of court,
Are to be fin'd.

FITZDOTTREL: In troth, a pretty place!

MEERCRAFT: A kind of arbitrary court 'twill be, sir.

FITZDOTTREL: I shall have matter for it, I believe,
Ere it be long: I had a distaste.

MEERCRAFT: But now, sir,
My learned counsel, they must have a feeling,
They'll part, sir, with no books, without the hand-gout
Be oil'd, and I must furnish. If't be money
170   To me straight. I am mine, mint and exchequer,
To supply all. What is't? A hundred pound?

EVERILL: No, th'harpy now stands on a hundred pieces.

MEERCRAFT: Why, he must have 'em, if he will. Tomorrow,
   sir,
Will equally serve your occasions,

160. *vapours*: boasts.
166. *distaste*: quarrel.
172. *harpy*: rapacious person.

And therefore let me obtain that you will yield
To timing a poor gentleman's distresses,
In terms of hazard.

FITZDOTTREL: By no means.

MEERCRAFT: I must
Get him this money, and will.

FITZDOTTREL: Sir, I protest,
I'd rather stand engag'd for it myself
Than you should leave me.

MEERCRAFT: O good sir, do you think   180
So coarsely of our manners that we would,
For any need of ours, be prest to take it,
Though you be pleas'd to offer it?

FITZDOTTREL: Why, by heaven,
I mean it!

MEERCRAFT: I can never believe less.
But we, sir, must preserve our dignity,
As you do publish yours. By your fair leave, sir.
    (*He offers to be gone.*)

FITZDOTTREL: As I am a gentleman, if you do offer
To leave me now, or if you do refuse me,
I will not think you love me.

MEERCRAFT: Sir, I honour you.
And with just reason, for these noble notes,   190
Of the nobility you pretend to. But, sir,
I would know why; a motive (he a stranger)
You should do this?

EVERILL [*aside to* MEERCRAFT]: You'll mar all with your
    fineness!

FITZDOTTREL: Why, that's all one, if 'twere, sir, but my
    fancy.
But I have a business that perhaps I'd have
Brought to his office.

MEERCRAFT: O sir, I have done, then,
If he can be made profitable to you.

FITZDOTTREL: Yes, and it shall be one of my ambitions

---

193. *fineness*: over-subtlety.
195. *business*: (technical term) occasion for quarrel.

To have it the first business; may I not?

200 EVERILL: So you do mean to make't a perfect business?

FITZDOTTREL: Nay, I'll do that, assure you: show me once.

MEERCRAFT: Sir, it concerns the first be a perfect business,
For his own honour.

EVERILL: Aye, and th' reputation,
Too, of my place.

FITZDOTTREL: Why, why do I take this course else?
I am not altogether an ass, good gentlemen.
Wherefore should I consult you, do you think?
To make a song on't? How's your manner? Tell us.

MEERCRAFT: Do, satisfy him; give him the whole course.

EVERILL: First, by request or otherwise, you offer
210   Your business to the court: wherein you crave
The judgement of the master and the assistants.

FITZDOTTREL: Well, that's done now; what do you upon it?

EVERILL: We straight, sir, have recourse to the spring-head;
Visit the ground, and so disclose the nature,
If it will carry, or no. If we do find
By our proportions it is like to prove
A sullen and black bus'ness, that it be
Incorrigible and out of treaty, then
We file it, a dependence!

220 FITZDOTTREL: So, 'tis fil'd,
What follows? I do love the order of these things.

EVERILL: We then advise the party, if he be
A man of means and havings, that forthwith
He settle his estate: if not, at least
That he pretend it. For by that the world
Takes notice that it now is a dependence.
And this we call, sir, publication.

FITZDOTTREL: Very sufficient! After publication, now?

EVERILL: Then we grant out our process, which is diverse;
230   Either by chartel, sir, or *ore-tenus*,
Wherein the challenger and challengee
Or (with your Spaniard) your provocador

---

230. *chartel*: written challenge.
230. *ore-tenus*: by word of mouth.

And provocado, have their several courses –

FITZDOTTREL: I have enough on't. For an hundred pieces?
Yes, for two hundred, underwrite me, do!
Your man will take my bond?

MEERCRAFT: That he will, sure,
But, these same citizens, they are such sharks!
(*He whispers* FITZDOTTREL *aside.*)
There's an old debt of forty, I ga' my word
For one is run away to the Bermudas,
And he will hook in that, or he wi' not do.   240

FITZDOTTREL: Why, let him. That and the ring and a
hundred pieces,
Will all but make two hundred.

MEERCRAFT: No more, sir.
What ready arithmetic you have! [*Aside to* GILTHEAD] Do
you hear?
A pretty morning's work for you, this! Do it,
You shall ha' twenty pound on't.

GILTHEAD: Twenty pieces?

PLUTARCHUS: Good father, do't.

MEERCRAFT: You will hook still? Well,
Show us your ring. You could not ha' done this, now,
With gentleness at first – we might ha' thank'd you –
But groan, and ha' your courtesies come from you
Like a hard stool, and stink? A man may draw   250
Your teeth out easier than your money. Come,
Were little Gilthead here no better a nature,
I should ne'er love him, that could pull his lips off, now!
(*He pulls* PLUTARCHUS *by the lips.*)
Was not thy mother a gentlewoman?

PLUTARCHUS: Yes, sir.

MEERCRAFT: And went to the court at Christmas, and St
George's-tide,
And lent the lords' men chains?

PLUTARCHUS: Of gold and pearl, sir.

MEERCRAFT: I knew thou must take after somebody,
Thou could'st not be else. This was no shop-look.
I'll ha' thee Captain Gilthead, and march up,

255–6. *St George's-tide . . . chains*: see Jonson's *Underwoods*, lxiv, 10–17.

260　And take in Pimlico, and kill the bush
　　　At every tavern! Thou shalt have a wife,
　　　If smocks will mount, boy. (*He turns to old Gilthead.*) How
　　　　　now? You ha' there now
　　　Some Bristol stone or Cornish counterfeit
　　　You'd put upon us.
GILTHEAD:　　　　　　No, sir, I assure you:
　　　Look on his lustre, he will speak himself!
　　　I'll gi' you leave to put him i' the mill,
　　　He's no great, large stone, but a true paragon,
　　　H'has all his corners, view him well.
MEERCRAFT:　　　　　　　　　　　He's yellow.
GILTHEAD: Upo' my faith, sir, o' the right blackwater,
270　And very deep! He's set without a foil too.
　　　Here's one o' the yellow water I'll sell cheap.
MEERCRAFT: And what do you value this at? Thirty pound?
GILTHEAD: No, sir, he cost me forty ere he was set.
MEERCRAFT: Turnings, you mean? I know your equivoques;
　　　You are grown the better fathers of 'em o' late.
　　　Well, where't must go 'twill be judg'd, and, therefore,
　　　Look you't be right. You shall have fifty pound for't.
　　　Not a denier more! (*Now to* FITZDOTTREL.) And because
　　　　　you would
　　　Have things dispatch'd, sir, I'll go presently,
280　Inquire out this lady. If you think good, sir,
　　　Having an hundred pieces ready, you may
　　　Part with those, now, to serve my kinsman's turns,
　　　That he may wait upon you anon the freer,
　　　And take 'em when you ha' seal'd, again, of Gilthead –
FITZDOTTREL: I care not if I do.
MEERCRAFT:　　　　　　　　And dispatch all
　　　Together.

260. *kill the bush*: drink heavily (bush = tavern, from ivy branch hung outside).
263. *Bristol stone*: transparent rock-crystal.
263. *Cornish counterfeit*: stone resembling diamond found in Cornwall.
267. *paragon*: perfect diamond.
274. *Turnings*: equivocations.
278. *denier*: copper coin of very small value.

FITZDOTTREL: There, th'are just a hundred pieces;
  I ha' told 'em over twice a day these two months.
    (*He turns 'em out together. And* EVERILL *and he fall to*
    share.)

MEERCRAFT: Well, go and seal then, sir; make your return
  As speedy as you can.

    [*Exeunt* FITZDOTTREL, GILTHEAD *and* PLUTARCHUS.]

EVERILL: Come, gi' me.

MEERCRAFT: Soft, sir.

EVERILL: Marry, and fair too then. I'll no delaying, sir.   290

MEERCRAFT: But you will hear?

EVERILL: Yes, when I have my dividend.

MEERCRAFT: There's forty pieces for you.

EVERILL: What is this for?

MEERCRAFT: Your half; you know that Gilthead must ha'
  twenty.

EVERILL: And what's your ring there? Shall I ha' none o'
  that?

MEERCRAFT: O, that's to be given to a lady.

EVERILL: Is't so?

MEERCRAFT: By that good light, it is.

EVERILL: Come, gi' me
  Ten pieces more, then.

MEERCRAFT: Why?

EVERILL: For Gilthead, sir;
  Do you think I'll 'low him any such share?

MEERCRAFT: You must.

EVERILL: Must I? Do you your musts, sir, I'll do mine.
  You wi' not part with the whole, sir, will you? Go to,   300
  Gi' me ten pieces!

MEERCRAFT: By what law do you this?

EVERILL: E'n lion-law, sir, I must roar else.

MEERCRAFT: Good!

EVERILL: Yo' have heard how th'ass made his divisions wisely?

MEERCRAFT: And I am he: I thank you.

EVERILL: Much good do you, sir!

287. *told*: counted.
303. *ass . . . wisely*: see Aesop's fable of the Lion, the Ass and the Fox.

MEERCRAFT: I shall be rid o' this tyranny one day.

EVERILL: Not
 While you do eat; and lie about the town here,
 And cozen i' your bullions, and I stand
 Your name of credit, and compound your business;
 Adjourn your beatings every term, and make
310 New parties for your projects. I have now
 A pretty task of it, to hold you in
 Wi' your Lady Tailbush: but the toy will be,
 How we shall both come off?

MEERCRAFT: Leave you your doubting
 And do your portion, what's assign'd you. I
 Never fail'd yet.

EVERILL: With reference to your aids!
 You'll still be unthankful. Where shall I meet you anon?
 You ha' some feat to do alone now, I see
 You wish me gone; well, I will find you out,
 And bring you after to the audit. [*Exit* EVERILL.]

MEERCRAFT: S'light,
320 There's Engine's share too, I had forgot! This reign
 Is too-too-unsupportable! I must
 Quit myself of this vassalage.

  [*Enter* ENGINE *and* WITTIPOL.]
        Engine! Welcome.

 How goes the cry?

ENGINE: Excellent well.

MEERCRAFT: Will't do?
 Where's Robinson?

ENGINE: Here is the gentleman, sir,
 Will undertake't himself. I have acquainted him.

MEERCRAFT: Why did you so?

ENGINE: Why, Robinson would ha' told him,
 You know. And he's a pleasant wit, will hurt
 Nothing you purpose. Then, he is of opinion,

---

307. *bullions*: bullion – hose, trunk hose with upper part puffed out.
309. *Adjourn . . . term*: get your punishments delayed from one (law) term to next.
315. *reference to*: relying on.
319. *audit*: reckoning.

That Robinson might want audacity,
She being such a gallant. Now, he has been   330
In Spain, and knows the fashions there; and can
Discourse; and being but mirth, he says, leave much
To his care.
MEERCRAFT: But he is too tall!
ENGINE: For that,
    He has the bravest device (you'll love him for't!)
    To say, he wears cioppinos: and they do so
    In Spain. And Robinson's as tall as he.
MEERCRAFT: Is he so?
ENGINE: Every jot.
MEERCRAFT: Nay, I had rather
    To trust a gentleman with it, o' the two.
ENGINE: Pray you go to him then, sir, and salute him.
MEERCRAFT [to WITTIPOL]: Sir, my friend Engine has   340
    acquainted you
    With a strange business here.
WITTIPOL: A merry one, sir.
    The Duke of Drown'd-land, and his duchess?
MEERCRAFT: Yes, sir.
    Now that the conjurers ha' laid him by,
    I ha' made bold to borrow him awhile.
WITTIPOL: With purpose yet to put him out, I hope,
    To his best use?
MEERCRAFT: Yes, sir.
WITTIPOL: For that small part
    That I am trusted with, put off your care.
    I would not lose to do it for the mirth
    Will follow of it; and, well, I have a fancy.
MEERCRAFT: Sir, that will make it well.
WITTIPOL: You will report it so.   350
    Where must I have my dressing?
ENGINE: At my house, sir.
MEERCRAFT: You shall have caution, sir, for what he yields,
    To sixpence.

> 335. *cioppinos*: chopines, high-heeled shoes.
> 352. *caution*: security.

WITTIPOL: You shall pardon me, I will share, sir,
        I' your sports only, nothing i' your purchase.
        But you must furnish me with complements,
        To th' manner of Spain – my coach, my guarda-
            duennas.

MEERCRAFT: Engine's your provedor. But sir, I must,
        Now I have enter'd trust wi' you thus far,
        Secure still i' your quality, acquaint you
360   With somewhat beyond this. The place design'd
        To be the scene for this our merry matter,
        Because it must have countenance of women,
        To draw discourse and offer it, is hereby,
        At the lady Tailbush's.

WITTIPOL: I know her, sir,
        And her gentleman usher.

MEERCRAFT: Master Ambler?

WITTIPOL: Yes, sir.

MEERCRAFT: Sir, it shall be no shame to me to confess
        To you, that we poor gentlemen that want acres
        Must for our needs turn fools up, and plough ladies
        Sometimes, to try what glebe they are: and this
370   Is no unfruitful piece. She and I now
        Are on a project for the fact and venting
        Of a new kind of fucus (paint for ladies)
        To serve the kingdom; wherein she herself
        Hath travail'd specially, by way of service
        Unto her sex, and hopes to get the monopoly
        As the reward of her invention.

WITTIPOL: What is her end in this?

EVERILL: Merely ambition,
        Sir, to grow great, and court it with the secret,
        Though she pretend some other. For she's dealing
380   Already upon caution for the shares,
        And Master Ambler is he nam'd examiner
        For the ingredients, and the register

357. *provedor*: purveyor.
371. *fact*: making.
371. *venting*: selling.

Of what is vented, and shall keep the office.
Now, if she break with you of this (as I
Must make the leading thread to your acquaintance
That, how experience gotten i' your being
Abroad, will help our business) think of some
Pretty additions, but to keep her floating:
It may be, she will offer you a part;
Any strange names of –

WITTIPOL: Sir, I have my instructions.   390
Is it not high time to be making ready?

MEERCRAFT: Yes, sir.

ENGINE: The fool's in sight, Dottrel.

MEERCRAFT: Away, then.
    [*Exeunt* WITTIPOL *and* ENGINE. *Re-enter* FITZDOTTREL.]

MEERCRAFT: Return'd so soon?

FITZDOTTREL: Yes, here's the ring; I ha' seal'd.
But there's not so much gold in all the Row, he says,
Till't come fro' the mint. 'Tis ta'en up for the gamesters.

MEERCRAFT: There's a shop-shift! Plague on 'em!

FITZDOTTREL: He does swear it.

MEERCRAFT: He'll swear and forswear too, it is his trade;
You should not have left him.

FITZDOTTREL: 'Slid, I can go back
And beat him yet.

MEERCRAFT: No, now let him alone.

FITZDOTTREL: I was so earnest, after the main business,   400
To have this ring gone.

MEERCRAFT: True, and 'tis time.
I have learn'd, sir, sin' you went, her ladyship eats
With the lady Tailbush here, hard by.

FITZDOTTREL: I' the lane here?

MEERCRAFT: Yes, if you had a servant now, of presence,
Well cloth'd, and of an airy voluble tongue,
Neither too big or little for his mouth,
That could deliver your wife's compliment,
To send along withal.

FITZDOTTREL: I have one, sir,

394. *the Row*: Goldsmith's Row, a prosperous London street, built in 1491.

A very handsome, gentleman-like-fellow,
410   That I do mean to make my duchess' usher.
I entertain'd him but this morning too.
I'll call him to you. The worst of him is his name.
MEERCRAFT: She'll take no note of that, but of his message.
FITZDOTTREL: Devil!
   [*Enter* PUG.]
               How like you him, sir?
  (*He shows him his* PUG.)
                            Pace, go a little.
Let's see you move.
MEERCRAFT: He'll serve, sir; give it him,
And let him go along with me. I'll help
To present him and it.
FITZDOTTREL: Look you do, sirrah,
Discharge this well, as you expect your place.
Do your hear? Go on, come off with all your honours.
I would fain see him do it.
420 MEERCRAFT: Trust him with it.
FITZDOTTREL: Remember kissing of your hand, and
    answering
With the French time, in flexure of your body.
I could now so instruct him – and for his words –
MEERCRAFT: I'll put them in his mouth.
FITZDOTTREL: O, but I have 'em
O' the very academies.
MEERCRAFT: Sir, you'll have use for 'em
Anon yourself, I warrant you; after dinner,
When you are call'd.
FITZDOTTREL: 'Slight, that'll be just play-time.
It cannot be, I must not lose the play!
MEERCRAFT: Sir, but you must, if she appoint to sit.
And she's president.
430 FITZDOTTREL: 'Slid, it is *The Devil*!
MEERCRAFT: An 'twere his dam too, you must now apply
    Yourself, sir, to this wholly, or lose all.
FITZDOTTREL: If I could but see a piece –

      422. *the French time*: the *conge*, a low bow.

MEERCRAFT: Sir, never think on't.

FITZDOTTREL: Come but to one act, and I did not care,
But to be seen to rise and go away,
To vex the players and to punish their poet –
Keep him in awe!

MEERCRAFT: But say that he be one
Wi' not be aw'd, but laugh at you. How then?

FITZDOTTREL: Then he shall pay for his dinner himself.

MEERCRAFT: Perhaps,
He would do that twice rather than thank you.   440
Come, get *The Devil* out of your head, my lord,
(I'll call you so in private still) and take
Your lordship i' your mind. You were, sweet lord,
In talk to bring a business to the office.

FITZDOTTREL: Yes.

MEERCRAFT: Why should not you, sir, carry it o' yourself,
Before the office be up, and show the world
You had no need of any man's direction
In point, sir, of sufficiency? I speak
Against a kinsman, but as one that tenders
Your grace's good.

FITZDOTTREL: I thank you; to proceed –   450

MEERCRAFT: To publications: ha' your deed drawn presently.
And leave a blank to put in your feoffees,
One, two or more, as you see cause –

FITZDOTTREL: I thank you
Heartily, I do thank you. Not a word more
I pray you, as you love me. Let me alone.
[*Aside*] That I could not think o' this as well as he!
O, I could beat my infinite blockhead.

MEERCRAFT: Come, we must this way.

PUG: How far is't?

MEERCRAFT: Hard by here
Over the way. Now, to achieve this ring
From this same fellow, that is to assure it   460
Before he give it. Though my Spanish lady
Be a young gentleman of means, and scorn

452. *feoffees*: trustees invested with freehold in land.

To share, as he doth say, I do not know
How such a toy may tempt his ladyship,
And therefore I think best it be assur'd.

PUG: Sir, be the ladies brave we go unto?

MEERCRAFT: O yes.

PUG: And shall I see 'em and speak to 'em?

MEERCRAFT: What else?

    [*Enter* TRAINS.]

                  Ha' you your false beard about you, Trains?

TRAINS: Yes.

MEERCRAFT: And is this one of your double cloaks?

TRAINS: The best of 'em.

470 MEERCRAFT: Be ready then.

    [*Exeunt*.]

[SCENE TWO]

    [*Enter* MEERCRAFT *and* PUG, *met by* PITFALL.]

MEERCRAFT: Sweet Pitfall! Come, I must buss –

    (*Offers to kiss.*)

PITFALL: Away!

MEERCRAFT: I'll set thee up again,
Never fear that. Canst thou get ne'er a bird?
No thrushes hungry? Stay till cold weather come,
I'll help thee to an ousel or a fieldfare.
Who's within with Madam?

PITFALL: I'll tell you straight.

    (*She runs in in haste: he follows.*)

MEERCRAFT: Please you stay here awhile sir, I'll go in. [*Exit*.]

PUG: I do so long to have a little venery
While I am in this body! I would taste

10 Of every sin a little, if it might be
After the manner of man. –

    (PUG *leaps at* PITFALL's *coming in.*)

                Sweetheart!

PITFALL: What would you, sir?

        469. *double cloaks*: reversible cloaks.
        8. *venery*: sexual indulgence.

PUG: Nothing but fall in to you, be your blackbird,
  My pretty Pit, as the gentleman said, your throstle:
  Lie tame, and taken with you; here is gold,
  To buy you so much new stuffs from the shop,
  As I may take the old up –
    [*Enter* TRAINS *in disguise.*]
TRAINS: You must send, sir,
  The gentleman the ring. [*Exit* TRAINS.]
PUG: There 'tis – Nay look,
  Will you be foolish, Pit?
PITFALL: This is strange rudeness!
PUG: Dear Pit!
PITFALL: I'll call, I swear.
    [*Enter* MEERCRAFT.]
MEERCRAFT: Where are you, sir?
  Is your ring ready? Go with me.
PUG: I sent it you.   20
MEERCRAFT: Me? When? By whom?
PUG: A fellow here, e'en now,
  Came for it i' your name.
MEERCRAFT: I sent none, sure.
  My meaning ever was you should deliver it
  Yourself; so was your master's charge, you know.
  What fellow was it? Do you know him?
PUG: Here
  But now, he had it.
    [*Enter* TRAINS *undisguised.*]
MEERCRAFT: Saw you any, Trains?
TRAINS: Not I.
PUG: The [gentlewoman] saw him.
MEERCRAFT: Enquire.
PUG [*aside*]: I was so earnest upon her I mark'd not.
  My devilish chief has put me here in flesh
  To shame me! This dull body I am in,   30
  I perceive nothing with! I offer at nothing
  That will succeed!
TRAINS: Sir, she saw none, she says.

16. *take . . . up*: lift, with pun on 'buy'.

PUG: Satan himself has ta'en a shape t'abuse me.
It could not be else!

MEERCRAFT: This is above strange,
That you should be so reckless. What'll you do, sir?
How will you answer this when you are question'd?

PUG: Run from my flesh if I could; put off mankind!
[*Aside*] This's such a scorn, and will be a new exercise
For my archduke. Woe to the several cudgels
40   Must suffer on this back! – Can you no succours, sir?

MEERCRAFT: Alas! the use of it is so present.

PUG: I ask, sir, credit for another, but till tomorrow.

MEERCRAFT: There is not so much time, sir. But however,
The lady is a noble lady, and will
(To save a gentleman from check) be entreated
To say she has receiv'd it.

PUG: Do you think so?
Will she be won?

MEERCRAFT: No doubt, to such an office,
It will be a lady's bravery and her pride.

PUG: And not be known on't after, unto him?

50 MEERCRAFT: That were a treachery. Upon my word,
Be confident. Return unto your master,
My lady president sits this afternoon,
Has ta'en the ring, commends her services
Unto your lady duchess. You may say
She's a civil lady, and does give her
All her respects already; bade you tell her
She lives but to receive her wish'd commandments,
And have the honour here to kiss her hands,
For which she'll stay this hour yet. Hasten you
Your prince, away.

60 PUG: And sir, you will take care
Th'excuse be perfect?

MEERCRAFT: You confess your fears
Too much.

PUG: The shame is more.

MEERCRAFT: I'll quit you of either.
[*Exeunt.*]

ACT FOUR

SCENE ONE

[*Enter* LADY TAILBUSH *and* MEERCRAFT.]

LADY TAILBUSH: Pox upo' referring to commissioners!
    I had rather hear that it were past the seals.
    Your courtiers move so snail-like i' your business.
    Would I had not begun wi' you!

MEERCRAFT: We must move,
    Madam, in order, by degrees, not jump.

LADY TAILBUSH: Why, there was Sir John Moneyman could
    jump
    A business quickly.

MEERCRAFT: True, he had great friends;
    But because some, sweet madam, can leap ditches,
    We must not all shun to go over bridges.
    The harder parts I make account are done: 10
    Now 'tis referr'd. You are infinitely bound
    Unto the ladies, they ha' so cri'd it up!

LADY TAILBUSH: Do they like it then?

MEERCRAFT: They ha' sent the Spanish lady,
    To gratulate with you.

LADY TAILBUSH: I must send 'em thanks
    And some remembrances.

MEERCRAFT: That you must, and visit 'em.
    Where's Ambler?

LADY TAILBUSH: Lost today, we cannot hear of him.

MEERCRAFT: Not, madam?

LADY TAILBUSH: No, in good faith. They say he lay not
    At home tonight. And here has fall'n a business

---

2. *past the seals*: officially confirmed.
14. *gratulate*: greet, enjoy company of.
18. *tonight*: last night.

Between your cousin and Master Manly, has
Unquieted us all.

20 MEERCRAFT: So I hear, madam.
Pray you how was it?

LADY TAILBUSH: Troth, it but appears
Ill o' your kinsman's part. You may have heard
That Manly is a suitor to me, I doubt not?

MEERCRAFT: I guess'd it, madam.

LADY TAILBUSH: And it seems he trusted
Your cousin to let fall some fair reports
Of him unto me.

MEERCRAFT: Which he did?

LADY TAILBUSH: So far
From it, as he came in and took him railing
Against him.

MEERCRAFT: How! And what said Manly to him?

LADY TAILBUSH: Enough, I do assure you: and with that
    scorn
30 Of him, and the injury, as I do wonder
How Everill bore it! But that guilt undoes
Many men's valours.
    [*Enter* MANLY.]

MEERCRAFT: Here comes Manly.

MANLY: Madam,
I'll take my leave –

LADY TAILBUSH: You sha' not go, i' faith.
I'll ha' you stay and see this Spanish miracle,
Of our English lady.

MANLY: Let me pray your ladyship,
Lay your commands on me some other time.

LADY TAILBUSH: Now, I protest, and I will have all piec'd,
And friends again.

MANLY: It will be but ill solder'd.

LADY TAILBUSH: You are too much affected with it.

MANLY: I cannot,
Madam, but think on't for th'injustice.

40 LADY TAILBUSH: Sir,
His kinsman here is sorry.

MEERCRAFT: Not I, madam,
  I am no kin to him, we but call cousins,
  And if we were, sir, I have no relation
  Unto his crimes.
MANLY: You are not urged with 'em.
  I can accuse, sir, none but mine own judgement,
  For though it were his crime, so to betray me,
  I am sure, 'twas more mine own at all to trust him.
  But he, therein, did use but his old manners,
  And savour strongly what he was before.
LADY TAILBUSH: Come, he will change.
MANLY: Faith, I must never think it,   50
  Nor were it reason in me to expect
  That for my sake he should put off a nature
  He suck'd in with his milk. It may be, madam,
  Deceiving trust is all he has to trust to:
  If so, I shall be loath that any hope
  Of mine should bate him of his means.
LADY TAILBUSH: Yo' are sharp, sir.
  This act may make him honest.
MANLY: If he were
  To be made honest by an act of Parliament,
  I should not alter i' my faith of him.
    [*Enter* LADY EITHERSIDE.]
LADY TAILBUSH: Eitherside!   60
  Welcome, dear Eitherside! How has thou done, good wench?
  Thou hast been a stranger; I ha' not seen thee this week.
LADY EITHERSIDE: Ever your servant, madam.
LADY TAILBUSH: Where hast 'hou been?
  I did so long to see thee.
LADY EITHERSIDE: Visiting, and so tir'd!
  I protest, madam, 'tis a monstrous trouble.
LADY TAILBUSH: And so it is. I swear I must tomorrow
  Begin my visits (would they were over) at court;
  It tortures me to think on 'em.
LADY EITHERSIDE: I do hear
  You ha' cause, madam, your suit goes on.
LADY TAILBUSH: Who told thee?

LADY EITHERSIDE: One that can tell, Master Eitherside.
70 LADY TAILBUSH: O, thy husband!
    Yes faith, there's life in't, now: it is referr'd.
    If we once see it under the seals, wench, then
    Have with 'em for the great caroche, six horses,
    And the two coachmen, with my Ambler, bare,
    And my three women. We will live, i' faith,
    The examples o' the town, and govern it.
    I'll lead the fashion still.
LADY EITHERSIDE: You do that now,
    Sweet madam.
LADY TAILBUSH: O, but then I'll every day
    Bring up some new device. Thou and I, Eitherside,
80   Will first be in it, I will give it thee,
    And they shall follow us. Thou shalt, I swear,
    Wear every month a new gown out of it.
LADY EITHERSIDE: Thank you, good madam.
LADY TAILBUSH: Pray thee call me Tailbush
    As I thee, Eitherside; I not love this madam.
LADY EITHERSIDE: Then I protest to you, Tailbush, I am
    glad
    Your business so succeeds.
LADY TAILBUSH: Thank thee, good Eitherside.
LADY EITHERSIDE: But Master Eitherside tells me that he
    likes
    Your other business better.
LADY TAILBUSH: Which?
LADY EITHERSIDE: O' the tooth-picks.
LADY TAILBUSH: I never heard on't.
LADY EITHERSIDE: Ask Master Meercraft.
    (MEERCRAFT *hath whisper'd with* [MANLY] *the while.*)
MEERCRAFT: Madam? [*Aside to* MANLY] He is one, in a word,
90   I'll trust his malice,
    With any man's credit, I would have abus'd.
MANLY: Sir, if you think you do please me in this,
    You are deceiv'd!
MEERCRAFT: No, but because my lady

        73. *Have with 'em*: go with them.

Nam'd him my kinsman, I would satisfy you,
What I think of him: and pray you, upon it
To judge me!
MANLY: So I do, that ill men's friendship
Is as unfaithful as themselves.
LADY TAILBUSH [*to* MEERCRAFT]: Do you hear?
Ha' you a business about tooth-picks?
MEERCRAFT: Yes, madam.
Did I ne'er tell't you? I meant to have offer'd it
Your ladyship, on the perfecting the patent.   100
LADY TAILBUSH: How is't?
MEERCRAFT: For serving the whole state with tooth-picks;
Somewhat an intricate business to discourse, but
I show how much the subject is abus'd,
First, in that one commodity; then what diseases
And putrefactions in the gums are bred,
By those are made of adult'rate and false wood.
My plot for reformation of these follows:
To have all toothpicks, brought unto an office,
There seal'd; and such as counterfeit 'em mulcted.
And last, for venting 'em to have a book   110
Printed, to teach their use, which every child
Shall have throughout the kingdom, that can read,
And learn to pick his teeth by. Which beginning
Early to practise, with some other rules,
Of never sleeping with the mouth open, chewing
Some grains of mastic, will preserve the breath
Pure, and so free from taint –
     (TRAINS *his man* [*enters and*] *whispers him.*)
                              Ha! What is't, say'st thou?
LADY TAILBUSH: Good faith, it sounds a very pretty bus'ness!
LADY EITHERSIDE: So Master Eitherside says, madam.
MEERCRAFT: The lady is come.
LADY TAILBUSH: Is she? Good, wait upon her in.
     [*Exit* MEERCRAFT.]
                              My Ambler   120
Was never so ill absent. Eitherside,

116. *mastic*: aromatic herb.

How do I look today? (*She looks in her glass.*) Am I not
  drest
Spruntly?

LADY EITHERSIDE: Yes, verily, madam.

LADY TAILBUSH: Pox o' madam,
  Will you not leave that?

LADY EITHERSIDE: Yes, good Tailbush.

LADY TAILBUSH: So.
  Sounds not that better? What vile fucus is this
  Thou hast got on?

LADY EITHERSIDE: 'Tis pearl.

LADY TAILBUSH: Pearl? Oyster-shells
  As I breathe, Eitherside, I know't. Here comes
  They say, a wonder, sirrah, has been in Spain!
  Will teach us all! She's sent to me, from court
130 To gratulate with me! Prithee, let's observe her,
  What faults she has, that we may laugh at 'em
  When she is gone.

LADY EITHERSIDE: That we will heartily, Tailbush.

    [MEERCRAFT *leads in* WITTIPOL *dressed as a Spanish*
    lady.]

LADY TAILBUSH: O, me, the very infanta of the giants!

MEERCRAFT: Here is a noble lady, madam, come
  From your great friends at court to see your ladyship
  And have the honour of your acquaintance.

LADY TAILBUSH: Sir,
  She does us honour.

WITTIPOL (*excuses himself for not kissing*): Pray you, say to
    her ladyship,
  It is the manner of Spain to embrace only,
140 Never to kiss. She will excuse the custom.

LADY TAILBUSH: Your use of it is law. Please you, sweet
  madam,
  To take a seat.

WITTIPOL: Yes, madam; I have had
  The favour, through a world of fair report,

---

123. *Spruntly*: trimly.

To know your virtues, madam; and in that
Name, have desir'd the happiness of presenting
My service to your ladyship.

LADY TAILBUSH:　　　　　　Your love, madam,
I must not own it else.

WITTIPOL:　　　　　Both are due, madam,
To your great undertakings.

LADY TAILBUSH:　　　　　Great? In troth, madam,
They are my friends, that think 'em anything:
If I can do my sex by 'em any service,　　　　　　　　150
I have my ends, madam.

WITTIPOL:　　　　　　And they are noble ones,
That make a multitude beholden, madam:
The commonwealth of ladies must acknowledge from you.

LADY EITHERSIDE: Except some envious, madam.

WITTIPOL:　　　　　　　　Yo' are right in that, madam,
Of which race I encounter'd some but lately,
Who't seems have studied reasons to discredit
Your business.

LADY TAILBUSH:　　How, sweet madam?

WITTIPOL:　　　　　　　　　Nay, the parties
Wi' not be worth your pause – Most ruinous things, madam,　160
That have put off all hope of being recover'd
To a degree of handsomeness.

LADY TAILBUSH:　　　　　　But their reasons, madam,
I would fain hear.

WITTIPOL:　　　Some, madam, I remember.
They say that painting quite destroys the face –

LADY EITHERSIDE: O, that's an old one, madam.

WITTIPOL:　　　　　　　　　There are new ones too:
Corrupts the breath; hath left so little sweetness
In kissing as 'tis now us'd but for fashion,
And shortly will be taken for a punishment;
Decays the fore-teeth, that should guard the tongue,
And suffers that run riot everlasting.　　　　　　　170
And, which is worse, some ladies when they meet
Cannot be merry and laugh, but they do spit
In one another's faces!

MANLY [*aside*]: I should know
This voice, and face too.

WITTIPOL: Then they say, 'tis dangerous
To all the fall'n, yet well dispos'd mad dames
That are industrious, and desire to earn
Their living with their sweat! For any distemper
Of heat and motion may displace the colours;
And if the paint once run about their faces,
180 Twenty to one, they will appear so ill-favour'd,
Their servants run away too, and leave the pleasure
Imperfect, and the reckoning als' unpaid.

LADY EITHERSIDE: Pox, these are poets' reasons!

LADY TAILBUSH: Some old lady
That keeps a poet has devis'd these scandals.

LADY EITHERSIDE: Faith, we must have the poets banish'd, madam,
As Master Eitherside says.

MEERCRAFT: Master Fitzdottrel
And his wife!

WITTIPOL: Where?
[*Enter* MASTER *and* MISTRESS FITZDOTTREL *and* PUG.]

MEERCRAFT: Madam, the Duke of Drown'd-land,
That will be shortly.

WITTIPOL: Is this my lord?

MEERCRAFT: The same.

FITZDOTTREL: Your servant, madam!

WITTIPOL [*aside to* MANLY]: How now, friend? Offended,
That I have found your haunt here?

190 MANLY: No, but wond'ring
At your strange-fashion'd venture hither.

WITTIPOL: It is
To show you what they are you so pursue.

MANLY: I think 'twill prove a med'cine against marriage
To know their manners.

WITTIPOL: Stay and profit then.

MEERCRAFT: The lady, madam, whose prince has brought her here
To be instructed.

(He presents MISTRESS FITZDOTTREL.)

WITTIPOL: Please you sit with us, lady.

MEERCRAFT: That's lady-president.

FITZDOTTREL: A goodly woman!
  I cannot see the ring, though.

MEERCRAFT: Sir, she has it.

LADY TAILBUSH: But, madam, these are very feeble reasons!

WITTIPOL: So I urg'd, madam, that the new complexion   200
  Now to come forth, in name o' your ladyship's fucus,
  Had no ingredient –

LADY TAILBUSH: But I durst eat, I assure you.

WITTIPOL: So do they in Spain.

LADY TAILBUSH: Sweet madam, be so liberal
  To give us some o' your Spanish fucuses!

WITTIPOL: They are infinite, madam.

LADY TAILBUSH: So I hear.

WITTIPOL: They have
  Water of gourds, of radish, the white beans,
  Flowers of glass, of thistles, rose-marine,
  Raw honey, mustard-seed, and bread dough-bak'd,
  The crumbs o' bread, goat's milk, and whites of eggs,
  Camphire, and lily roots, the fat of swans,   210
  Marrow of veal, white pigeons, and pine-kernels,
  The seeds of nettles, purseline, and hare's gall,
  Lemons, thin-skinn'd –

LADY EITHERSIDE: How her ladyship has studied
  All excellent things!

WITTIPOL: But ordinary, madam.
  No, the true rarities are th'*alvagada*
  And *argentata* of queen Isabella.

LADY TAILBUSH: Ay, what are their ingredients, gentle
    madam?

WITTIPOL: Your *alum scagliola,* or *pol di pedra,*
  And *zuccarino,* turpentine of Abezzo,
  Wash'd in nine waters; *soda di levante,*   220
  Or your fern ashes, *benjamin di gotta,*

207. *Flowers*: ashes.
215. *alvagada, etc.*: see Additional Notes.

Grasso di serpe, porcelletto marino,
Oils of *lentisco, zucche mugia,* make
The admirable varnish for the face,
Gives the right lustre; but two drops rub'd on
With a piece of scarlet makes a lady of sixty
Look as sixteen. But above all, the water
Of the white hen, of the Lady Estifanias!

LADY TAILBUSH: O, ay, that same, good madam, I have
    heard of;
How is it done?

230 WITTIPOL: Madam, you take your hen,
Plume it and skin it, cleanse it o' the inwards:
Then chop it, bones and all: add to four ounces
Of *carravicins, pipitas,* soap of Cyprus,
Make the decoction, strain it. Then distil it,
And keep it in your gallipot well glidder'd.
Three drops preserves from wrinkles, warts, spots, moles,
Blemish, or sun-burnings, and keeps the skin
In decimo sexto ever bright, and smooth
As any looking-glass; and indeed, is call'd

240 The virgin's milk for the face, *oglio reale;*
A ceruse neither cold or heat will hurt;
And mix'd with oil of myrrh and the red gilliflower
Call'd *cataputia,* and flowers of *rovistico,*
Makes the best *muta* or dye of the whole world.

LADY TAILBUSH: Dear madam, will you let us be familiar?
WITTIPOL: Your ladyship's servant.
MEERCRAFT: How do you like her?
FITZDOTTREL: Admirable!
But, yet, I cannot see the ring.
PUG: Sir?
MEERCRAFT [*aside*]:   I must
Deliver it, or mar all. This fool's so jealous.

233. *pipitas:* tender top of herbs.
235. *gallipot:* small earthen pot.
235. *glidder'd:* glazed over.
238. *In decimo sexto:* i.e. as at sixteen (cf. line 227).
240. *oglio reale:* lit. 'royal oil'.
243. *rovistico:* hops.

Madam – [*to* WITTIPOL] Sir, wear this ring, and pray you
    take knowledge,
'Twas sent you by his wife. And give her thanks. –   250
[*To* PUG] Do not you dwindle, sir, bear up.
PUG: I thank you, sir.
LADY TAILBUSH: But for the manner of Spain! Sweet
    madam, let us
Be bold, now we are in; are all the ladies
There i' the fashion?
WITTIPOL: None but grandees, madam,
O' the clasp'd train, which may be worn at length, too,
Or thus, upon my arm.
LADY TAILBUSH: And do they wear
 Cioppinos all?
WITTIPOL: If they be drest *in punto*, madam.
LADY EITHERSIDE: Gilt as those are, madam?
WITTIPOL: Of goldsmith's work, madam,
And set with diamonds; and their Spanish pumps
Of perfum'd leather.
LADY TAILBUSH: I should think it hard   260
To go in 'em, madam.
WITTIPOL: At the first it is, madam.
LADY TAILBUSH: Do you never fall in 'em?
WITTIPOL: Never.
LADY EITHERSIDE: I swear I should,
Six times an hour.
LADY TAILBUSH: But you have men at hand, still,
To help you if you fall?
WITTIPOL: Only one, madam,
The guarda-duennas, such a little old man,
As this. [*Indicates* TRAINS.]
LADY EITHERSIDE: Alas, he can do nothing, this!
WITTIPOL: I'll tell you, madam, I saw i' the court of Spain
    once,
A lady fall i' the king's sight, along.
And there she lay, flat spread as an umbrella,

251. *dwindle*: shrink (from).
257. *in punto*: exactly in fashion.

270   Her hoop here crack'd; no man durst reach a hand
     To help her, till the guarda-duennas came,
     Who is the person onl' allow'd to touch
     A lady there: and he but by this finger.

LADY EITHERSIDE: Ha' they no servants, madam, there, nor
     friends?

WITTIPOL: An escudero or so, madam, that waits
     Upon 'em in another coach, at distance,
     And when they walk, or dance, holds by a handkercher,
     Never presumes to touch 'em.

LADY EITHERSIDE: This's scurvy,
     And a forc'd gravity! I do not like it.
     I like our own much better.

280 LADY TAILBUSH: 'Tis more French,
     And courtly, ours.

LADY EITHERSIDE: And tastes more liberty.
     We may have our dozen of visitors at once
     Make love t'us.

LADY TAILBUSH: And before our husbands!

LADY EITHERSIDE: Husband?
     As I am honest, Tailbush, I do think
     If nobody should love me but my poor husband,
     I should e'en hang myself.

LADY TAILBUSH: Fortune forbid, wench,
     So fair a neck should have so foul a necklace.

LADY EITHERSIDE: 'Tis true, as I am handsome!

WITTIPOL: I receiv'd, lady,
     A token from you, which I would not be
290   Rude to refuse, being your first remembrance.

FITZDOTTREL [aside to MEERCRAFT]: O, I am satisfied now!

MEERCRAFT: Do you see it, sir?

WITTIPOL: But since you come to know me nearer, lady,
     I'll beg the honour you will wear it for me,
     It must be so.
        [Gives ring to MISTRESS FITZDOTTREL.]

MISTRESS FITZDOTTREL [aside]: Sure I have heard this
     tongue.

275. escudero: lady's serving man.

MEERCRAFT [*aside to* WITTIPOL]: What do you mean, sir?

WITTIPOL: Would you ha'me mercenary?
  We'll recompense it anon, in somewhat else.
  [*Exeunt* MEERCRAFT *and* TRAINS.]

FITZDOTTREL: I do not love to be gull'd, though in a toy.
  Wife, do you hear? Yo'are come into the school, wife,
  Where you may learn, I do perceive it, anything!   300
  How to be fine, or fair, or great, or proud,
  Or what you will indeed, wife; here 'tis taught.
  And I am glad on't, that you may not say,
  Another day, when honours come upon you,
  You wanted means. I ha'done my parts: been,
  Today, at fifty pound charge:
    (*He upbraids her with his bill of costs.*)
                              first, for a ring,
  To get you enter'd; then left my new play,
  To wait upon you here, to see't confirm'd,
  That I may say, both to mine own eyes and ears,
  Senses, you are my witness, she hath enjoy'd   310
  All helps that could be had for love or money –

MISTRESS FITZDOTTREL: To make a fool of her.

FITZDOTTREL: Wife, that's your malice,
  The wickedness o' your nature, to interpret
  Your husband's kindness thus. But I'll not leave
  Still to do good, for your deprav'd affections:
  Intend it; bend this stubborn will; be great.

LADY TAILBUSH: Good madam, whom do they use in
    messages?

WITTIPOL: They commonly use their slaves, madam.

LADY TAILBUSH: And does your ladyship
  Think that so good, madam?

WITTIPOL: No indeed, madam; I   320
  Therein prefer the fashion of England far,
  Of your young delicate page, or discreet usher.

FITZDOTTREL: And I go with your ladyship in opinion,
  Directly for your gentleman usher,
  There's not a finer officer goes on ground.

WITTIPOL: If he be made and broken to his place once.

FITZDOTTREL: Nay, so I presuppose him.

WITTIPOL: And they are fitter
Managers too, sir; but I would have'em call'd
Our escuderos.

FITZDOTTREL: Good.

[WITTIPOL]:   Say I should send
330 To your ladyship, who, I presume, has gather'd
All the dear secrets, to know how to make
Pastillos of the Duchess of Braganza,
Coquettas, almoiavanas, mantecadas,
Alcoreas, mustaccioli; or say it were
The *peladore* of Isabella, or balls
Against the itch, or *aqua nanfa,* or oil
Of jessamine for gloves, of the Marquess Muja;
Or for the head, and hair: why, these are offices –

FITZDOTTREL: Fit for a gentleman, not a slave.

WITTIPOL: They only
340 Might ask for your *piveti,* Spanish coal,
To burn, and sweeten a room: but the arcana
Of ladies' cabinets –

FITZDOTTREL: Should be elsewhere trusted.
Yo'are much about the truth.
    (*He enters himself with the ladies.*)
                              Sweet honoured ladies,
Let me fall in wi' you. I ha' my female wit,
As well as my male. And I do know what suits
A lady of spirit or a woman of fashion.

WITTIPOL: And you would have your wife such?

FITZDOTTREL: Yes, madam, airy,
Light; not to plain dishonesty I mean,
But somewhat o' this side.

WITTIPOL: I take you, sir.
350 H'has reason, ladies. I'll not give this rush
For any lady that cannot be honest
Within a thread.

LADY TAILBUSH: Yes, madam, and yet venture
As far for th'other in her fame –

---

332. *Pastillos, etc.*: see Additional Notes.

WITTIPOL: As can be;
  Coach it to Pimlico; dance the saraband,
  Hear and talk bawdy, laugh as loud as a 'larum,
  Squeak, spring, do anything.

LADY EITHERSIDE: In young company, madam.

LADY TAILBUSH: Or afore gallants. If they be brave, or lords,
  A woman is engag'd.

FITZDOTTREL: I say so, ladies,
  It is civility to deny us nothing.

PUG [aside]: You talk of a University! Why, hell is   360
  A grammar school to this!

LADY EITHERSIDE: But then
  She must not lose a look on stuffs, or cloth, madam.

LADY TAILBUSH: Nor no coarse fellow.

WITTIPOL: She must be guided, madam,
  By the clothes he wears, and company he is in;
  Whom to salute, how far –

FITZDOTTREL: I ha' told her this.
  And how that bawdry too, upo' the point,
  Is in itself as civil a discourse –

WITTIPOL: As any other affair of flesh whatever.

FITZDOTTREL: But she will ne'er be capable, she is not
  So much as coming, madam; I know not how   370
  She loses all her opportunities
  With hoping to be forc'd. I have entertain'd
  A gentleman, a younger brother, here,
  Whom I would fain breed up her escudero
  Against some expectations that I have,
  And she'll not countenance him.

WITTIPOL: What's his name?

FITZDOTTREL: Devil O' Darbishire. (*He shows his* PUG.)

LADY EITHERSIDE: Bless us from him!

LADY TAILBUSH: Devil?
  Call him De-vile, sweet madam.

MISTRESS FITZDOTTREL: What you please, ladies.

LADY TAILBUSH: De-vile's a prettier name.

LADY EITHERSIDE: And sounds, methinks,
  As it came in with the conqueror –

380 MANLY [*aside*]:   Over smocks!
　　What things they are! That nature should be at leisure
　　Ever to make 'em! My wooing is at an end! (MANLY *goes*
　　　out with indignation.)
WITTIPOL: What can he do?
LADY EITHERSIDE: Let's hear him.
LADY TAILBUSH: Can he manage?
FITZDOTTREL: Please you to try him, ladies. Stand forth,
　　Devil.
PUG [*aside*]: Was all this but the preface to my torment?
FITZDOTTREL: Come, let their ladyships see your honours.
LADY EITHERSIDE: O,
　　He makes a wicked leg!
LADY TAILBUSH: As ever I saw.
WITTIPOL: Fit for a devil.
LADY TAILBUSH: Good madam, call him De-vile.
WITTIPOL: De-vile, what property is there most required
390 I' your conceit now, in the escudero?
FITZDOTTREL: Why do you not speak?
PUG: A settled discreet pace, madam.
WITTIPOL: I think a barren head, sir, mountain-like,
　　To be expos'd to the cruelty of weathers –
FITZDOTTREL: Ay, for his valley is beneath the waste,
　　madam,
　　And to be fruitful there, it is sufficient –
　　Dulness upon you! Could not you hit this?
　　(*He strikes him.*)
PUG: Good sir –
WITTIPOL: He then had had no barren head.
　　You daw him too much, in troth, sir.
FITZDOTTREL: I must walk
　　With the French stick, like an old verger for you.
400 PUG [*aside*]: O, chief, call me to hell again, and free me.
　　(*The devil prays.*)
FITZDOTTREL: Do you murmur now?
PUG: Not I, sir.
WITTIPOL: What do you take,
　　Master De-vile, the height of your employment

278

In the true perfect escudero?

FITZDOTTREL: When?
What do you answer?

PUG: To be able, madam,
First to enquire, then report the working,
Of any ladies' physic in sweet phrase.

WITTIPOL: Yes, that's an act of elegance and importance.
But what above?

FITZDOTTREL: O, that I had a goad for him!

PUG: To find out a good corn-cutter.

LADY TAILBUSH: Out on him!

LADY EITHERSIDE: Most barbarous!

FITZDOTTREL: Why did you do this now?   410
Of purpose to discredit me? You damn'd devil!

PUG [aside]: Sure, if I be not yet, I shall be. All
My days in hell were holidays to this!

LADY TAILBUSH: 'Tis labour lost, madam.

LADY EITHERSIDE: He's a dull fellow
Of no capacity.

LADY TAILBUSH: Of no discourse.
O, if my Ambler had been here!

LADY EITHERSIDE: Ay, madam,
You talk of a man; where is there such another?

WITTIPOL: Master De-vile, put case one of my ladies here,
Had a fine brach and would employ you forth
To treat 'bout a convenient match for her;   420
What would you observe?

PUG: The colour and the size, madam.

WITTIPOL: And nothing else?

FITZDOTTREL: The moon, you calf, the moon!

WITTIPOL: Ay, and the sign.

LADY TAILBUSH: Yes, and receipts for proneness.

WITTIPOL: Then when the puppies came, what would you
do?

PUG: Get their nativities cast.

WITTIPOL: This's well. What more?

419. *brach*: bitch.

PUG: Consult the Almanac-man which would be least,
Which cleanliest.

WITTIPOL: And which silentest. This's well, madam.
And while she were with puppy?

PUG: Walk her out
And air her every morning.

WITTIPOL: Very good!

430 And be industrious to kill her fleas?

PUG: Yes.

WITTIPOL: He will make a pretty proficient.

PUG [*aside*]: Who,
Coming from hell, could look for such catechising?
The devil is an ass, I do acknowledge it.

(FITZDOTTREL *admires* WITTIPOL.)

FITZDOTTREL: The top of woman! All her sex in abstract!
I love her to each syllable falls from her.

LADY TAILBUSH: Good madam, give me leave to go aside
with him.
And try him a little.

WITTIPOL: Do, and I'll withdraw, madam,
With this fair lady: read to her, the while.

LADY TAILBUSH: Come, sir.

(*The devil prays again.*)

PUG: Dear chief, relieve me, or I perish!

440 WITTIPOL: Lady, we'll follow – You are not jealous, sir?

FITZDOTTREL: O madam! You shall see. Stay wife, behold,
I give her up here absolutely to you,
She is your own.

(*He gives his wife to him, taking him to be a lady.*)

Do with her what you will!
Melt, cast, and form her as you shall think good,
Set any stamp on. I'll receive her from you
As a new thing, by your own standard. [*Exit.*]

WITTIPOL: Well, sir!

[*Exeunt.*]

[SCENE TWO]

[*Enter* MEERCRAFT *and* FITZDOTTREL.]

MEERCRAFT: But what ha' you done i' your dependence since?

FITZDOTTREL: O, it goes on. I met your cousin the master –

MEERCRAFT: You did not acquaint him, sir?

FITZDOTTREL: Faith, but I did, sir,
  And upon better thought, not without reason.
  He being chief officer might ha' ta'en it ill else,
  As a contempt against his place, and that
  In time, sir, ha' drawn on another dependence.
  No, I did find him in good terms, and ready
  To do me any service.

MEERCRAFT: So he said to you,
  But, sir, you do not know him.

FITZDOTTREL: Why, I presum'd   10
  Because this business of my wife's requir'd me,
  I could not ha' done better: and he told
  Me that he would go presently to your counsel,
  A knight here i' the lane –

MEERCRAFT: Yes, justice Eitherside.

FITZDOTTREL: And get the feoffment drawn, with a letter of attorney,
  For livery and seisin.

MEERCRAFT: That I know's the course.
  But sir, you mean not to make him feoffee?

FITZDOTTREL: Nay, that I'll pause on.

   [*Enter* PITFALL.]

MEERCRAFT: How now, little Pitfall!

PITFALL: Your cousin, Master Everill, would come in –
  But he would know if Master Manly were here.   20

MEERCRAFT: No, tell him, if he were, I ha' made his peace!
  He's one, sir, has no state, and a man knows not
  How such a trust may tempt him.

FITZDOTTREL: I conceive you.

   [*Enter* EVERILL *and* PLUTARCHUS.]

     16. *livery and seisin*: legal delivery of freehold property.

EVERILL: Sir, this same deed is done here.

MEERCRAFT: Pretty Plutarchus!
Art thou come with it? and has Sir Paul view'd it?

PLUTARCHUS: His hand is to the draft.

MEERCRAFT: Will you step in, sir,
And read it?

FITZDOTTREL: Yes.

EVERILL [aside to FITZDOTTREL]: I pray you, a word wi' you.
Sir Paul Eitherside will'd me gi' you caution,
30   Whom you did make feoffee: for 'tis the trust
O' your whole state: and though my cousin here
Be a worthy gentleman, yet his valour has
At the tall board been question'd; and we hold
Any man so impeach'd of doubtful honesty.
I will not justify this, but give it you
To make your profit of it: if you utter it,
I can forswear it.

FITZDOTTREL: I believe you and thank you, sir.
    [Exeunt.]

[SCENE THREE]

[Enter WITTIPOL and MISTRESS FITZDOTTREL.]

WITTIPOL: Be not afraid, sweet lady: yo' are trusted
To love, not violence here. I am no ravisher,
But one whom you, by your fair trust again,
May of a servant make a most true friend.
    [Enter MANLY unseen.]

MISTRESS FITZDOTTREL: And such a one I need, but not
    this way.
Sir, I confess me to you, the mere manner
Of your attempting me this morning took me,
And I did hold m'invention and my manners
Were both engag'd to give it a requital;

---

31. state: wealth, estate.
32. valour: credit-worthiness.
33. tall board: gaming table.

But not unto your ends. My hope was then   10
(Though interrupted ere it could be utter'd)
That whom I found the master of such language,
That brain and spirit, for such an enterprise,
Could not, but if those succours were demanded
To a right use, employ them virtuously,
And make that profit of his noble parts,
Which they would yield. Sir, you have now the ground
To exercise them in: I am a woman
That cannot speak more wretchedness of myself
Than you can read; match'd to a mass of folly   20
That every day makes haste to his own ruin,
The wealthy portion that I brought him spent,
And, through my friends' neglect, no jointure made me.
My fortunes standing in this precipice,
'Tis counsel that I want, and honest aids,
And in this name, I need you, for a friend;
Never in any other; for his ill
Must not make me, sir, worse.

    (MANLY, *conceal'd this while, shows himself.*)

MANLY: O friend, forsake not
The brave occasion virtue offers you,
To keep you innocent. I have fear'd for both,   30
And watch'd you to prevent the ill I fear'd.
But since the weaker side hath so assur'd me,
Let not the stronger fall by his own vice,
Or be the less a friend, 'cause virtue needs him.

WITTIPOL: Virtue shall never ask my succours twice;
Most friend, most man; your counsels are commands. —
Lady, I can love goodness in you more
Than I did beauty; and do here entitle
Your virtue to the power upon a life
You shall engage in any fruitful service,   40
Even to forfeit.

    [*Enter* MEERCRAFT.]

MEERCRAFT [*aside to* WITTIPOL]: Madam — Do you hear,
    sir,

    23. *jointure*: estate limited to wife, effective on husband's death.

We have another leg strain'd for this Dottrel.
He has a quarrel to carry, and has caus'd
A deed of feoffment of his whole estate
To be drawn yonder; h'has't within: and you,
Only, he means to make feoffee. He's fall'n
So desperately enamour'd on you, and talks
Most like a madman: you did never hear
A frantic so in love with his own favour!
50 Now, you do know, 'tis of no validity
In your name, as you stand; therefore advise him
To put in me.

    [*Enter* FITZDOTTREL, EVERILL *and* PLUTARCHUS.]
        He's come here. You shall share, sir.

FITZDOTTREL: Madam, I have a suit to you, and aforehand,
  I do bespeak you; you must not deny me,
  I will be granted.

WITTIPOL: Sir, I must know it, though.

FITZDOTTREL: No, lady; you must not know it: yet, you
    must too,
  For the trust of it, and the fame indeed,
  Which else were lost me. I would use your name
  But in a feoffment: make my whole estate
60 Over unto you: a trifle, a thing of nothing,
  Some eighteen hundred.

WITTIPOL: Alas! I understand not
  Those things, sir. I am a woman, and most loath
  To embark myself –

FITZDOTTREL: You will not slight me, madam?

WITTIPOL: Nor you'll not quarrel me?

FITZDOTTREL: No, sweet madam, I have
  Already a dependence, for which cause
  I do this: let me put you in, dear madam,
  I may be fairly kill'd.

WITTIPOL: You have your friends, sir,
  About you here, for choice.

EVERILL: She tells you right, sir. (*He hopes to be the man.*)

---

42. *leg . . . Dottrel*: scheme for stalking this bird.
49. *favour*: countenance, attributes.

FITZDOTTREL: Death, if she do, what do I care for that?
　　Say, I would have her tell me wrong.
WITTIPOL:　　　　　　　　　　　　Why, sir,　　　　　　70
　　If for the trust, you'll let me have the honour
　　To name you one.
FITZDOTTREL:　　　Nay, you do me the honour, madam:
　　Who is't?
WITTIPOL: This gentleman. [*Indicates* MANLY.]
FITZDOTTREL:　　　　　　　　O no, sweet madam,
　　He's friend to him with whom I ha' the dependence.
WITTIPOL: Who might he be?
FITZDOTTREL:　　　　　　　One Wittipol: do you know him?
WITTIPOL: Alas sir, he! a toy: this gentleman
　　A friend to him? No more than I am, sir!
FITZDOTTREL: But will your ladyship undertake that, madam?
WITTIPOL: Yes, and what else, for him, you will engage me.
FITZDOTTREL: What is his name?
WITTIPOL:　　　　　　　　His name is Eustace Manly.　　80
FITZDOTTREL: Whence does he write himself?
WITTIPOL:　　　　　　　　　　　　Of Middlesex,
　　Esquire.
FITZDOTTREL: Say nothing, madam. [*To* PLUTARCHUS]
　　　Clerk, come hither;
　　Write Eustace Manly, Squire o' Middlesex.
MEERCRAFT [*aside to* WITTIPOL]: What ha' you done, sir?
WITTIPOL:　　　　　　　　　　　Nam'd a gentleman
　　That I'll be answerable for to you, sir.
　　Had I nam'd you, it might ha' been suspected:
　　This way 'tis safe.
FITZDOTTREL:　　Come, gentlemen, your hands,
　　For witness.
MANLY:　　What is this?
EVERILL:　　　　　　　You ha' made election
　　Of a most worthy gentleman.
MANLY:　　　　　　　　　Would one of worth
　　Had spoke it: whence it comes, it is　　　　　90
　　Rather a shame to me than a praise.
EVERILL: Sir, I will give you any satisfaction.

MANLY: Be silent then: falsehood commends not truth.

PLUTARCHUS: You do deliver this, sir, as your deed,
To th'use of Master Manly?

FITZDOTTREL: Yes, [*to* MANLY] and sir,
When did you see young Wittipol? I am ready
For process now; sir, this is publication.
He shall hear from me; he would needs be courting
My wife, sir.

MANLY: Yes: so witnesseth his cloak there.

100 FITZDOTTREL: Nay, good sir, – Madam, you did undertake –

WITTIPOL: What?

FITZDOTTREL: That he was not Wittipol's friend.

WITTIPOL: I hear,
Sir, no confession of it.

FITZDOTTREL: O she knows not;
Now I remember. – madam, this young Wittipol
Would ha' debauch'd my wife and made me cuckold
Through a casement; he did fly her home
To mine own window: but I think I [sous'd] him,
And ravish'd her away out of his pounces.
I ha' sworn to ha' him by the ears: I fear
The toy wi' not do me right.

WITTIPOL: No? That were pity!

110 What right do you ask, sir? Here he is will do't you.
     (WITTIPOL *discovers himself.*)

FITZDOTTREL: Ha? Wittipol?

WITTIPOL: Ay, sir, no more lady now,
Nor Spaniard!

MANLY: No indeed, 'tis Wittipol.

FITZDOTTREL: Am I the thing I fear'd?

WITTIPOL: A cuckold? No, sir,
But you were late in possibility,
I'll tell you so much.

MANLY: But your wife's too virtuous.

WITTIPOL: We'll see her sir, at home, and leave you here,
To be made Duke o' Shoreditch with a project.

---

106. *sous'd*: ? pounced upon (original 'sou't').
109. *toy*: worthless person.

FITZDOTTREL: Thieves, ravishers!

WITTIPOL: Cry but another note, sir,
  I'll mar the tune o' your pipe!

FITZDOTTREL: Gi' me my deed, then.

WITTIPOL: Neither: that shall be kept for your wife's good,   120
  Who will know better how to use it.

FITZDOTTREL: Ha,
  To feast you with my land?

WITTIPOL: Sir, be you quiet,
  Or I shall gag you ere I go; consult
  Your master of dependences how to make this
  A second business; you have time, sir.

    (WITTIPOL *bafflles him, and goes out.*)

FITZDOTTREL: Oh!
  What will the ghost of my wise grandfather,
  My learned father, with my worshipful mother,
  Think of me now, that left me in this world
  In state to be their heir? that am become
  A cuckold and an ass, and my wife's ward;   130
  Likely to lose my land, ha' my throat cut,
  All by her practice!

MEERCRAFT: Sir, we are all abus'd!

FITZDOTTREL: And be so still! Who hinders you? I pray you,
  Let me alone, I would enjoy myself,
  And be the Duke o' Drown'd-land you ha' made me.

MEERCRAFT: Sir, we must play an after-game o' this.

FITZDOTTREL: But I am not in case to be a gamester,
  I tell you once again –

MEERCRAFT: You must be rul'd
  And take some counsel.

FITZDOTTREL: Sir, I do hate counsel
  As I do hate my wife, my wicked wife!   140

MEERCRAFT: But we may think how to recover all,
  If you will act.

FITZDOTTREL: I will not think nor act,
  Nor yet recover; do not talk to me.

       Stage direction. *baffles*: publicly disgraces.
       132. *practice*: trickery.

I'll run out o' my wits rather than hear.
I will be what I am, Fabian Fitzdottrel,
Though all the world say nay to't. [*Exit*.]

MEERCRAFT: Let's follow him.
    [*Exeunt*.]

ACT FIVE

SCENE ONE

[*Enter* AMBLER *and* PITFALL.]

AMBLER: But has my lady miss'd me?

PITFALL: Beyond telling.
Here has been that infinity of strangers!
And then she would ha' had you, to ha' sampled you
With one within, that they are now a-teaching;
And does pretend to your rank.

AMBLER: Good fellow,
Tell Master Meercraft I entreat a word with him.
    [*Exit* PITFALL.]
This most unlucky accident will go near
To be the loss o' my place, I am in doubt.
    [*Enter* MEERCRAFT.]

MEERCRAFT: With me? – What say you, Master Ambler?

AMBLER: Sir,
I would beseech your worship stand between   10
Me and my lady's displeasure for my absence.

MEERCRAFT: O, is that all? I warrant you.

AMBLER: I would tell you, sir,
But how it happened.

MEERCRAFT: Brief, good Master Ambler,
Put yourself to your rack: for I have task
Of more importance. (*Meercraft seems full of business.*)

AMBLER: Sir, you'll laugh at me:
But (so is truth) a very friend of mine,
Finding by conference with me, that I liv'd
Too chaste for my complexion, and indeed,
Too honest for my place, sir, did advise me
If I did love myself (as that I do,   20
I must confess) –

MEERCRAFT: Spare your parenthesis.

289

AMBLER: To gi' my body a little evacuation –

MEERCRAFT: Well, and you went to a whore?

AMBLER: No, sir, I durst not
  (For fear it might arrive at somebody's ear
  It should not) trust myself to a common house
    (AMBLER *tells this with extraordinary speed.*)
  But got the gentlewoman to go with me,
  And carry her bedding to a conduit-head,
  Hard by the place toward Tyburn, which they call
  My Lord Mayor's banqueting house. Now, sir, this morning
30 Was execution; and I ne'er dream't on't,
  Till I heard the noise o' the people, and the horses,
  And neither I nor the poor gentlewoman
  Durst stir till all was done and past: so that
  I' the interim, we fell asleep again. (*He flags.*)

MEERCRAFT: Nay, if you fall from your gallop I am gone, sir.

AMBLER: But when I wak'd, to put on my clothes, a suit
  I made new for the action, it was gone,
  And all my money, with my purse, my seals,
  My hard-wax, and my table-books, my studies,
40 And a fine new device I had to carry
  My pen and ink, my civet, and my tooth-picks,
  All under one. But, that which griev'd me was
  The gentlewoman's shoes (with a pair of roses
  And garters I had given her for the business)
  So as that made us stay till it was dark.
  For I was fain to lend her mine, and walk
  In a rug by her, barefoot, to Saint Giles' –

MEERCRAFT: A kind of Irish penance! Is this all, sir?

AMBLER: To satisfy my lady.

MEERCRAFT: I will promise you, sir.

AMBLER: I ha' told the true disaster.

50 MEERCRAFT: I cannot stay wi' you,

---

22. *evacuation*: cleaning out.
41. *civet*: perfume.
42. *All under one*: all at once.
47. *St Giles'*: Cripplegate.
48. *Irish penance*: allusion to rough rugs worn by Irish.

Sir, to condole, but gratulate your return. [*Exit.*]
AMBLER: An honest gentleman, but he's never at leisure
　　To be himself, he has such tides of business.　[*Exit.*]

[SCENE TWO]

　[*Enter* PUG.]
PUG: O call me home again, dear chief, and put me
　　To yoking foxes, milking of he-goats,
　　Pounding of water in a mortar, laving
　　The sea dry with a nut-shell, gathering all
　　The leaves are fall'n this autumn, drawing farts
　　Out of dead bodies, making ropes of sand,
　　Catching the winds together in a net,
　　Must'ring of ants, and numb'ring atoms – all
　　That hell and you thought exquisite torments, rather
　　Than stay me here a thought more: I would sooner　　　10
　　Keep fleas within a circle, and be accomptant
　　A thousand year which of 'em and how far
　　Out-leap'd the other, than endure a minute
　　Such as I have within. There is no hell
　　To a lady of fashion. All your tortures there
　　Are pastimes to it. 'Twould be a refreshing
　　For me, to be i' the fire again, from hence –
　　　(AMBLER *comes in and surveys him.*)
AMBLER: This is my suit, and those the shoes and roses!
PUG: Th'have such impertinent vexations,
　　A general council o' devils could not hit –　　　20
　　　(PUG *perceives it, and starts.*)
　　Ha! This is he I took asleep with his wench,
　　And borrow'd his clothes. What might I do to balk him?
AMBLER: Do you hear, sir?
PUG [*aside*]:　　　　　　Answer him, but not to th' purpose.
AMBLER: What is your name, I pray you, sir?
PUG: Is't so late, sir?
AMBLER:　　　　I ask not o' the time, but of your name, sir.
PUG: I thank you, sir. Yes it does hold, sir, certain.

AMBLER: Hold, sir? What holds? I must both hold, and talk
   to you
  About these clothes.

PUG: A very pretty lace!
  But the tailor cozen'd me.

AMBLER: No, I am cozen'd
  By you! Robb'd.

30 PUG: Why, when you please sir, I am
  For three-penny gleek, your man.

AMBLER: Pox o' your gleek,
  And three-pence! Give me an answer.

PUG: Sir,
  My master is the best at it.

AMBLER: Your master!
  Who is your master?

PUG: Let it be Friday night.

AMBLER: What should be then?

PUG: Your best songs, Tom o' Bedlam.

AMBLER: I think you are he. [*Aside*] Does he mock me trow,
   from purpose?
  Or do not I speak to him what I mean?
  Good sir, your name.

PUG: Only a couple o' cocks, sir,
  If we can get a widgeon, 'tis in season. [*Exit.*]

40 AMBLER: He hopes to make one o' these sceptics o' me
  (I think I name 'em right) and does not fly me;
  I wonder at that! 'Tis a strange confidence!
  I'll prove another way to draw his answer. [*Exit.*]

[SCENE THREE]

[*Enter* MEERCRAFT, FITZDOTTREL *and* EVERILL.]

MEERCRAFT: It is the easiest thing, sir, to be done.
  As plain as fizzling: roll but wi' your eyes,

31. *gleek*: card-game.

40. *sceptics*: sceptics, historically, philosophers who doubted possibility of
objective knowledge.

2. *fizzling*: farting silently.

And foam at th' mouth. A little castle-soap
Will do't, to rub your lips: and then a nutshell,
With tow and touch-wood in it to spit fire.
Did you ne'er read, sir, little Darrel's tricks,
With the boy o' Burton, and the seven in Lancashire,
Somers at Nottingham? All these do teach it.
And we'll give out, sir, that your wife has bewitch'd you.

EVERILL: And practised with those two as sorcerers.   10

MEERCRAFT: And ga' you potions, by which means you were
Not *compos mentis*, when you made your feoffment.
There's no recovery o' your state but this;
This, sir, will sting.

EVERILL: And move in a court of equity.

MEERCRAFT: For it is more than manifest that this was
A plot o' your wife's to get your land.

FITZDOTTREL: I think it.

EVERILL: Sir, it appears.

MEERCRAFT: Nay, and my cousin has known
These gallants in these shapes –

EVERILL: T'have done strange things, sir.
One as the lady, the other as the squire.

MEERCRAFT: How a man's honesty may be fool'd! I thought him   20
A very lady.

FITZDOTTREL: So did I: renounce me else.

MEERCRAFT: But this way, sir, you'll be reveng'd at height.

EVERILL: Upon 'em all.

MEERCRAFT: Yes, faith, and since your wife
Has run the way of woman thus, e'en give her –

FITZDOTTREL: Lost by this hand, to me; dead to all joys
Of her dear Dottrel! I shall never pity her
That could pity [not] herself.

MEERCRAFT: Princely resolv'd, sir,
And like yourself still, *in potentia*.

    (*Enter* GILTHEAD, PLUTARCHUS, SLEDGE *and*
    SERJEANTS.)

    3. *castle-soap*: Castile soap, with olive oil and soda.
    12. *compos mentis*: of sound mind.
    28. *in potentia*: in possibility.

MEERCRAFT: Gilthead, what news?

FITZDOTTREL: O sir, my hundred pieces:
Let me ha' them yet.

30 GILTHEAD: Yes, sir. – Officers,
Arrest him.

FITZDOTTREL: Me?

SERJEANT: I arrest you.

SLEDGE: Keep the peace,
I charge you, gentlemen.

FITZDOTTREL: Arrest me! Why?

GILTHEAD: For better security, sir. My son Plutarchus
Assures me y'are not worth a groat.

PLUTARCHUS: Pardon me, father,
I said his worship had no foot of land left:
And that I'll justify, for I writ the deed.

FITZDOTTREL: Ha' you these tricks i' the city?

GILTHEAD: Yes, and more.
Arrest this gallant too, here, at my suit.
    (*Meaning* MEERCRAFT.)

SLEDGE: Ay, and at mine. He owes me for his lodging
Two year and a quarter.

40 MEERCRAFT: Why, Master Gilthead, – landlord,
Thou art not mad, though th'art constable
Puff'd up with th' pride of the place? Do you hear, sirs,
Have I deserv'd this from you two for all
My pains at court, to get you each a patent?

GILTHEAD: For what?

MEERCRAFT: Upo' my project o' the forks.

SLEDGE: Forks? What be they?

MEERCRAFT: The laudable use of forks,
Brought into custom here, as they are in Italy,
To th' sparing o' napkins. That, that should have made
Your bellows go at the forge, as his at the furnace.

50 I ha' procur'd it, ha' the signet for it,
Dealt with the linen drapers on my private,
By cause I fear'd they were the likeliest ever

44. *patent*: monopoly.
50. *signet*: small official seal.

To stir against, to cross it: for 'twill be
A mighty saver of linen through the kingdom
(As that is one o' my grounds, and to spare washing).
Now, on you two had I laid all the profits:
Gilthead to have the making of all those
Of gold and silver, for the better personages,
And you of those of steel for the common sort,
And both by patent, I had brought you your seals in.   60
But now you have prevented me, and I thank you.
   (SLEDGE *is brought about, and* GILTHEAD *comes.*)
SLEDGE: Sir, I will bail you, at mine own apperil.
MEERCRAFT: Nay, choose.
PLUTARCHUS: Do you so too, good father.
GILTHEAD: I like the fashion o' the project well,
  The forks! It may be a lucky one! and is not
  Intricate, as one would say, but fit for
  Plain heads, as ours, to deal in. Do you hear,
  Officers, we discharge you.
   [*Exeunt* SERJEANTS.]
MEERCRAFT: Why, this shows
  A little good nature in you, I confess;
  But do not tempt your friends thus. Little Gilthead,   70
  Advise your sire, great Gilthead, from these courses.
  And here, to trouble a great man in reversion,
  For a matter o' fifty on a false alarm!
  Away, it shows not well. Let him get the pieces
  And bring 'em. Yo'll hear more else.
PLUTARCHUS: Father.
  [*Exeunt* GILTHEAD *and* PLUTARCHUS.]
  [*Enter* AMBLER *with* PUG.]
AMBLER: O Master Sledge, are you here? I ha' been to seek
  you.
  You are the constable, they say. Here's one
  That I do charge with felony, for the suit
  He wears, sir.

62. *apperil*: risk.
72. *reversion*: right of succession; power to redeem an estate held as
security for debt.

MEERCRAFT: Who? Master Fitzdottrel's man?
'Ware what you do, Master Ambler.

80 AMBLER: Sir, these clothes,
I'll swear, are mine, and the shoes the gentlewoman's
I told you of: and ha' him afore a justice, I will.

PUG: My master, sir, will pass his word for me.

AMBLER: O, can you speak to purpose now?

FITZDOTTREL: Not I.
If you be such a one, sir, I will leave you
To your godfathers-in-law; let twelve men work.

PUG: Do you hear sir? Pray, in private.

     [*Draws* FITZDOTTREL *aside.*]

FITZDOTTREL: Well, what say you?
Brief, for I have no time to lose.

PUG: Truth is, sir,
I am the very devil, and had leave
90 To take this body I am in, to serve you;
Which was a cutpurse's, and hang'd this morning.
And it is likewise true, I stole this suit
To clothe me with. But, sir, let me not go
To prison for it. I have hitherto
Lost time, done nothing; shown, indeed, no part
O' my devil's nature. Now, I will so help
Your malice 'gainst these parties, so advance
The business that you have in hand of witchcraft,
And your possession, as myself were in you;
100 Teach you such tricks, to make your belly swell,
And your eyes turn, to foam, to stare, to gnash
Your teeth together, and to beat yourself,
Laugh loud, and feign six voices –

FITZDOTTREL: Out, you rogue!
You most infernal counterfeit wretch, avaunt!
Do you think to gull me with your Aesop's fables?
Here, take him to you, I ha' no part in him.

PUG: Sir! –

---

86. *godfathers-in-law*: humorous term for jury (Gifford quotes *The Merchant of Venice*, IV, i, 393–5).

FITZDOTTREL: Away! I do disclaim, I will not hear you.
  [*Exit* SLEDGE *with* PUG.]
MEERCRAFT: What said he to you, sir?
FITZDOTTREL: Like a lying rascal
  Told me he was the devil.
MEERCRAFT: How! a good jest!   110
FITZDOTTREL: And that he would teach me such fine devil's
  tricks
  For our new resolution.
EVERILL: O, pox on him,
  'Twas excellent wisely done, sir, not to trust him.
MEERCRAFT: Why, if he were the devil, we sha' not need him,
  If you'll be rul'd. Go throw yourself on a bed, sir,
  And feign you ill. We'll not be seen wi' you,
  Till after that you have a fit, and all
  Confirm'd within. [*To* EVERILL] Keep you with the two
    ladies
  And persuade them. I'll to justice Eitherside,
  And possess him with all. Trains shall seek out Engine,   120
  And they two fill the town with't; every cable
  Is to be veer'd. We must employ out all
  Our emissaries now; sir, I will send you
  Bladders and bellows. Sir, be confident;
  'Tis no hard thing t'outdo the devil in:
  A boy o' thirteen year old made him an ass
  But t'other day.
FITZDOTTREL: Well, I'll begin to practise,
  And 'scape the imputation of being cuckold,
  By mine own act.
MEERCRAFT: You're right.
EVERILL: Come, you ha' put
  Yourself to a simple coil here, and your friends,   130
  By dealing with new agents, in new plots.
MEERCRAFT: No more o' that, sweet cousin.
EVERILL: What had you
  To do with this same Wittipol, for a lady?

        122. *veer'd*: let out.
        130. *coil*: trouble, complication.

MEERCRAFT: Question not that: 'tis done.

EVERILL: You had some strain
'Bove E, la?

MEERCRAFT: I had indeed.

EVERILL: And, now, you crack for't.

MEERCRAFT: Do not upbraid me.

EVERILL: Come, you must be told on't;
You are so covetous, still, to embrace
More than you can, that you lose all.

MEERCRAFT: 'Tis right.
What would you more, than guilty? Now, your succours.
    [*Exeunt.*]

[SCENE FOUR]

    (PUG *is brought to Newgate.*)
    [*Enter* SHACKLES *with* PUG.]

SHACKLES: Here you are lodg'd, sir; you must send your
    garnish,
If you'll be private.

PUG: There it is, sir; leave me.
    [*Exit* SHACKLES.]
To Newgate brought! How is the name of devil
Discredited in me! What a lost fiend
Shall I be on return? My chief will roar
In triumph, now that I have been on earth
A day, and done no noted thing, but brought
That body back here, was hang'd out this morning.
Well! Would it once were midnight, that I knew
10 My utmost. I think Time be drunk, and sleeps,
He is so still and moves not! I do glory
Now i' my torment. Neither can I expect it,
I have it with my fact.
    (*Enter* INIQUITY *the Vice.*)

    135. *'Bove E la*: above the highest note.
    1. *garnish*: exaction of money or clothes from new prisoners.
    12. *expect*: await.
    13. *fact*: crime.

INIQUITY: Child of hell, be thou merry:
  Put a look on as round, boy, and red as a cherry.
  Cast care at thy posterns and firk i' thy fetters,
  They are ornaments, baby, have gracéd thy betters:
  Look upon me and hearken: our chief doth salute thee,
  And lest the cold iron should chance to confute thee,
  H'hath sent thee grant-parole by me to stay longer
  A month here on earth against cold, child, or hunger.   20

PUG: How? Longer here a month!

INIQUITY: Yes, boy, till the session,
  That so thou mayest have a triumphal egression.

PUG: In a cart, to be hang'd?

INIQUITY: No, child, in a car,
  The chariot of triumph, which most of them are.
  And in the meantime, to be greasy, and boozy,
  And nasty, and filthy, and ragged and lousy,
  With 'Damn me!' Renounce me! and all the fine phrases
  That bring unto Tyburn the plentiful gazes.

PUG: He is a devil, and may be our chief,
  The great superior devil for his malice!   30
  Arch-devil I acknowledge him! He knew
  What I would suffer when he tied me up thus
  In a rogue's body; and he has, I thank him,
  His tyrannous pleasure on me, to confine me
  To the unlucky carcass of a cutpurse,
  Wherein I could do nothing.

    ([SATAN] *the great Devil enters, and upbraids him with all
    his day's work.*)

SATAN: Impudent fiend,
  Stop thy lewd mouth. Dost thou not shame and tremble
  To lay thine own dull damn'd defects upon
  An innocent case there? Why, thou heavy slave!
  The spirit that did possess that flesh before   40
  Put more true life in a finger and a thumb

15. *posterns*: back ways.
15. *firk*: move briskly.
18. *confute*: pun on Lat. confuto, to allay by mixing cold water and hot.
37. *lewd*: vulgar, ignorant.

Than thou in the whole mass. Yet thou rebell'st
And murmur'st! What one proffer hast thou made,
Wicked enough, this day, that might be call'd
Worthy thine own, much less the name that sent thee?
First, thou didst help thyself into a beating
Promptly, and with't endangered'st too thy tongue:
A devil, and could not keep a body entire
One day! That, for our credit! And to vindicate it,
50 Hinder'dst, for aught thou know'st, a deed of darkness:
Which was an act of that egregious folly,
As no one to'ard the devil could ha' thought on.
This for your acting! But for suffering! Why,
Thou hast been cheated on with a false beard,
And a turn'd cloak. Faith, would your predecessor
The cutpurse, think you, ha' been so? Out upon thee!
The hurt th'hast done, to let men know their strength,
And that they're able to out-do a devil
Put in a body, will for ever be
60 A scar upon our name! Whom hast thou dealt with,
Woman or man, this day, but have out-gone thee
Some way, and most have prov'd the better fiends?
Yet, you would be employ'd? Yes, hell shall make you
Provincial o' the cheaters, or bawd-ledger
For this side o' the town! No doubt you'll render
A rare accompt of things. Bane o' your itch
And scratching for employment! I'll ha' brimstone
To allay it sure, and fire to singe your nails off.
But that I would not such a damn'd dishonour
70 Stick on our state, as that the devil were hang'd,
And could not save a body that he took
From Tyburn, but it must come thither again,
You should e'en ride. But up, away with him –
  (INIQUITY *takes him on his back.*)
 INIQUITY: Mount, dearling of darkness, my shoulders are
     broad:

64. *Provincial*: spiritual head of province.
64. *bawd-ledger*: resident bawd (cf. lieger ambassador).
Stage direction. *Iniquity ... back*: in mystery plays the Devil carried the
Vice on his back.

He that carries the fiend is sure of his load.
The devil was wont to carry away the Evil;
But now the Evil outcarries the devil.
   [*Exeunt.*]
   (*A great noise is heard in Newgate, and the keepers come out affrighted.*)
   [*Enter* SHACKLES *and* KEEPERS.]

SHACKLES: O me!

I KEEPER: What's this?

2 KEEPER: A piece of Justice Hall
Is broken down.

3 KEEPER: Fough! What a steam of brimstone
Is here!

4 KEEPER: The prisoner's dead, came in but now.   80

SHACKLES: Ha! Where?

4 KEEPER: Look here.

I KEEPER: 'Slid, I should know his countenance:
It is Gill Cutpurse, was hang'd out this morning!

SHACKLES: 'Tis he!

2 KEEPER: The devil, sure, has a hand in this!

3 KEEPER: What shall we do?

SHACKLES: Carry the news of it
Unto the sheriffs.

I KEEPER: And to the justices.

4 KEEPER: This [is] strange!

3 KEEPER: And savours of the devil strongly!

2 KEEPER: I ha' the sulphur of hell-coal i' my nose.

I KEEPER: Fough!

SHACKLES: Carry him in.

I KEEPER: Away!

2 KEEPER: How rank it is!
   [*Exeunt with body.*]

        82. *Gill*: short for William.

[SCENE FIVE]

[FITZDOTTREL *in bed;* LADY TAILBUSH, LADY EITHER-
SIDE, AMBLER, TRAINS *and* PITFALL *by him. Enter* SIR
PAUL EITHERSIDE, MEERCRAFT *and* EVERILL.]

SIR PAUL: This was the notablest conspiracy,
That e'er I heard of.

MEERCRAFT: Sir, they had giv'n him potions,
That did enamour him on the counterfeit lady –

EVERILL: Just to the time o' delivery o' the deed –

MEERCRAFT: And then the witchcraft 'gan t'appear, for
      straight
He fell into his fit.

EVERILL: Of rage at first, sir,
Which since has so increased –

LADY TAILBUSH: Good Sir Paul, see him,
And punish the imposters.

SIR PAUL: Therefore I come, madam.

LADY EITHERSIDE: Let Master Eitherside alone, madam.

SIR PAUL: Do you hear?
10   Call in the constable, I will have him by,
He's the king's officer: and some citizens
Of credit. I'll discharge my conscience clearly.

MEERCRAFT: Yes, sir, and send for his wife.

EVERILL: And the two sorcerers,
By any means.
      [*Exit* AMBLER.]

LADY TAILBUSH: I thought one a true lady,
I should be sworn; so did you, Eitherside.

LADY EITHERSIDE: Yes, by that light, would I might ne'er
      stir else, Tailbush.

LADY TAILBUSH: And the other a civil gentleman.

EVERILL: But, madam,
You know what I told your ladyship.

LADY TAILBUSH: I now see it:
I was providing of a banquet for 'em

9. *Let . . . alone*: rely on.

After I had done instructing o' the fellow　　　　　　20
De-vile, the gentleman's man.

MEERCRAFT: 　　　　　　　Who's found a thief, madam.
And to have robb'd your usher, Master Ambler
This morning.

LADY TAILBUSH: How?

MEERCRAFT: 　　　　　I'll tell you more anon.

FITZDOTTREL: Gi' me some garlic, garlic, garlic, garlic!
　　(*He begins his fit.*)

MEERCRAFT: Hark the poor gentleman, how he is tormented!

FITZDOTTREL: *My wife is a whore, I'll kiss her no more: and*
　　why?
　　May'st not thou be a cuckold as well as I?
　　Ha, ha, ha, ha, ha, ha, ha, ha! etc.

SIR PAUL: That is the devil speaks and laughs in him.

MEERCRAFT: Do you think so, sir?

SIR PAUL: 　　　　　　　I discharge my conscience.　30

FITZDOTTREL: *And is not the devil good company? Yes, wis.*

EVERILL: How he changes, sir, his voice!

FITZDOTTREL: 　　　　　　　*And a cuckold is*
　　Where e'er he put his head, with a wanion,
　　If his horns be forth, the devil's companion!
　　Look, look, look, else!

MEERCRAFT: 　　　　How he foams!

EVERILL: 　　　　　　　　And swells!

LADY TAILBUSH: O me! What's that there, rises in his belly?

LADY EITHERSIDE: A strange thing! Hold it down.

TRAINS and PITFALL: 　　　　　We cannot, madam.

SIR PAUL: 'Tis too apparent, this!

FITZDOTTREL: 　　　　　　Wittipol, Wittipol!
　　(WITTIPOL, MANLY *and* MISTRESS FITZDOTTREL *enter.*)

WITTIPOL: How now, what play ha' we here?

MANLY: 　　　　　　　What fine new matters?

WITTIPOL: *The Cockscomb and the Coverlet.*

MEERCRAFT: 　　　　　　　O strange impudence,　40

31. *wis*: certainly.
33. *with a wanion*: with a vengeance.
40. *coverlet*: Somers apparently brought off many of his effects under one.

That these should come to face their sin!

EVERILL: And outface
Justice! They are the parties, sir.

SIR PAUL: Say nothing.

MEERCRAFT: Did you mark, sir, upon their coming in,
How he call'd Wittipol?

EVERILL: And never saw 'em.

SIR PAUL: I warrant you did I; let 'em play awhile.

FITZDOTTREL: *Buz, buz, buz, buz.*

LADY TAILBUSH: 'Las, poor gentleman,
How he is tortur'd!

MISTRESS FITZDOTTREL: Fie, Master Fitzdottrel!
What do you mean to counterfeit thus?
    (*His wife goes to him.*)

FITZDOTTREL: *O, O!*
She comes with a needle, and thrusts it in,
50 *She pulls out that and she puts in a pin,*
And now, and now, I do not know how, nor where,
But she pricks me here, and she pricks me there: oh, oh!

SIR PAUL: Woman, forbear.

WITTIPOL: What, sir?

SIR PAUL: A practice foul
For one so fair.

WITTIPOL: Hath this, then, credit with you?

MANLY: Do you believe in't?

SIR PAUL: Gentlemen, I'll discharge
My conscience. 'Tis a clear conspiracy,
A dark and devilish practice! I detest it.

WITTIPOL: The justice sure will prove the merrier man.

MANLY: This is most strange, sir!

SIR PAUL: Come not to confront
60 Authority with impudence; I tell you,
I do detest it.
    [*Re-enter* AMBLER, *with* SLEDGE *and* GILTHEAD.]
        Here comes the king's constable,
And with him a right worshipful commoner;
My good friend, Master Gilthead! I am glad
I can before such witnesses profess

My conscience, and my detestation of it.
Horrible! Most unnatural! Abominable!

EVERILL: You do not tumble enough.

MEERCRAFT: Wallow, gnash:
  (*They whisper him* [FITZDOTTREL], *and give him soap to act
  with.*)

LADY TAILBUSH: O, how he is vexed!

SIR PAUL: 'Tis too manifest.

EVERILL [*to* MEERCRAFT]: Give him more soap to foam with;
  [*to* FITZDOTTREL] now lie still.

MEERCRAFT: And act a little.

LADY TAILBUSH: What does he now, sir?

SIR PAUL: Show   70
  The taking of tobacco, with which the devil
  Is so delighted.

FITZDOTTREL: *Hum!*

SIR PAUL: And calls for hum.
  You takers of strong waters, and tobacco,
  Mark this.

FITZDOTTREL: *Yellow, yellow, yellow, yellow!* etc.

SIR PAUL: That's starch! the devil's idol of that colour.
  He ratifies it with clapping of his hands.
  The proofs are pregnant.

GILTHEAD: How the devil can act!

SIR PAUL: He is the master of players, Master Gilthead,
  And poets too; you heard him talk in rhyme;
  I had forgot to observe it to you, erewhile.   80

LADY TAILBUSH: See, he spits fire.

SIR PAUL: O no, he plays at figgum;
  The devil is the author of wicked figgum –

MANLY: Why speak you not unto him?

WITTIPOL: If I had
  All innocence of man to be endanger'd,
  And he could save or ruin it, I'd not breathe
  A syllable in request, to such a fool
  He makes himself.

FITZDOTTREL: *O they whisper, whisper, whisper.*

81. *figgum*: ? figging = pocket-picking.

We shall have more of devils a score
To come to dinner in me the sinner.

LADY EITHERSIDE: Alas, poor gentleman!

90 SIR PAUL: Put 'em asunder.
Keep 'em one from the other.

MANLY: Are you frantic, sir,
Or what grave dotage moves you to take part
With so much villainy? We are not afraid
Either of law or trial; let us be
Examin'd what our ends were, what the means
To work by, and possibility of those means;
Do not conclude against us ere you hear us.

SIR PAUL: I will not hear you, yet I will conclude
Out of the circumstances.

MANLY: Will you so, sir?

SIR PAUL: Yes, they are palpable.

100 MANLY: Not as your folly.

SIR PAUL: I will discharge my conscience, and do all
To the meridian of justice.

GILTHEAD: You do well, sir.

FITZDOTTREL: *Provide me to eat, three or four dishes o' good*
meat,
I'll feast them, and their trains, a justice' head and brains
Shall be the first.

SIR PAUL: The devil loves not justice,
There you may see.

FITZDOTTREL: *A spare rib o' my wife,*
And a whore's purt'nance; a Gilthead whole.

SIR PAUL: Be not you troubled, sir, the devil speaks it.

FITZDOTTREL: *Yes, wis, knight, shite, Paul, joul, owl, foul,*
troul, boul.

110 SIR PAUL: Crambo, another of the devil's games!

MEERCRAFT: Speak, sir, some Greek if you can. Is not the
justice
A solemn gamester?

EVERILL: Peace!

110. *Crambo*: game in which rhymes had to be found for a given word.

FITZDOTTREL: *Oi, moi, kakodaimon, kai triskakodaimon, kai*
   tetrakis, kai pentakis,
Kai dodekakis, kai muriakis.

SIR PAUL: He curses
   In Greek, I think.

EVERILL [*aside to* FITZDOTTREL]: Your Spanish, that I
   taught you.

FITZDOTTREL: *Quebremos el ojo de burlas.*

EVERILL: How! Your rest –
   Let's break his neck in jest, the devil says.

FITZDOTTREL: *Di gratia, signor mio, se havete denari*
   fatamene parte.

MEERCRAFT: What, would the devil borrow money?

FITZDOTTREL: *Oui,*
   Oui, Monsieur, un pauvre diable, diabletin.   120

SIR PAUL: It is the devil, by his several languages.

   [*Enter* SHACKLES, *with the dead Cutpurse's belongings.*]

SHACKLES: Where's Sir Paul Eitherside?

SIR PAUL: Here, what's the matter?

SHACKLES: O! Such an accident fall'n out at Newgate, sir:
   A great piece of the prison is rent down!
   The devil has been there, sir, in the body
   Of the young cutpurse was hang'd out this morning,
   But, in new clothes, sir; every one of us know him.
   These things were found in his pocket.

AMBLER: Those are mine, sir.

SHACKLES: I think he was committed on your charge, sir,
   For a new felony.

AMBLER: Yes.

SHACKLES: He's gone sir, now,   130
   And left us the dead body. But withal, sir,
   Such an infernal stink and steam behind,
   You cannot see St Pulchre's steeple yet.
   They smell't as far as Ware, as the wind lies,
   By this time, sure.

116. *Quebremos . . . burlas*: dog-Spanish, 'let us burst his eye'.
118. *Di gratia . . . parte*: 'Please sir, if you have money, give me some'.
119–20. *Oui . . . diabletin*: 'Yes, yes sir, a poor devil, an imp'.
133. *St Pulchre's*: St Sepulchre's, near Newgate.

FITZDOTTREL: Is this upon your credit, friend?

SHACKLES: Sir, you may see and satisfy yourself.

FITZDOTTREL (*leaves counterfeiting*): Nay, then, 'tis time to
    leave off counterfeiting.
    Sir, I am not bewitch'd, nor have a devil,
    No more than you. I do defy him, I,

140   And did abuse you. These two gentlemen
    [*Indicating* MEERCRAFT *and* EVERILL]
    Put me upon it (I have faith against him).
    They taught me all my tricks. I will tell truth,
    And shame the fiend. See here, sir, are my bellows,
    And my false belly, and my mouse, and all
    That should ha' come forth!

MANLY: Sir, are not you asham'd
    Now of your solemn, serious vanity?

SIR PAUL: I will make honourable amends to truth.

FITZDOTTREL: And so will I. But these are cozeners still,
    And ha' my land, as plotters, with my wife:

150   Who, though she be not a witch, is worse, a whore.

MANLY: Sir, you belie her. She is chaste and virtuous,
    And we are honest. I do know no glory
    A man should hope by venting his own follies,
    But you'll still be an ass, in spite of providence –
    Please you go in, sir, and hear truths, then judge 'em
    And make amends for your late rashness; when
    You shall but hear the pains and care was taken,
    To save this fool from ruin, his Grace of Drown'd-land.

FITZDOTTREL: My land is drown'd indeed –

SIR PAUL: Peace!

MANLY: And how much

160   His modest and too worthy wife hath suffer'd
    By misconstruction from him; you will blush,
    First, for your own belief, more for his actions!
    His land is his: and never, by my friend,
    Or by myself, meant to another use,
    But for her succours, who hath equal right.

144. *false belly*: standard equipment of several self-proclaimed exorcists.
153. *venting*: proclaiming.

If any other had worse counsels in't
(I know I speak to those can apprehend me),
Let 'em repent 'em, and be not detected.
It is not manly to take joy or pride
In human errors; we do all ill things;
They do 'em worst that love 'em, and dwell there   170
Till the plague comes. The few that have the seeds
Of goodness left, will sooner make their way
To a true life by shame than punishment.
   [*Exeunt.*]

THE END

THE EPILOGUE

Thus, the Projector here is overthrown;
    But I have now a project of mine own,
If it may pass: that no man would invite
    The poet from us, to sup forth tonight,
If the play please. If it displeasant be,
    We do presume that no man will, nor we.

A NEW WAY TO PAY

OLD DEBTS
A COMOEDIE

As it hath beene often acted at the Phœnix in Drury-Lane, by the Queenes Maiesties seruants.

The Author.

PHILIP MASSINGER.

LONDON,
Printed by *E. P.* for *Henry Seyle*, dwelling in S. *Pauls* Church-yard, at the signe of the Tygers head. Anno. M. DC.
XXXIII.

Facsimile of the title-page of the first edition, the quarto of 1633.

A NEW WAY
TO PAY OLD DEBTS

by

Philip Massinger

To the Ingenious
Author Master
PHILIP MASSINGER
on his comedy
Called, A New Way to Pay
Old Debts

'Tis a rare charity, and thou couldst not
So proper to the time have found a plot:
Yet whilst you teach to pay, you lend; the age
We wretches live in, that to come, the stage,
The throngéd audience that was thither brought
Invited by your fame, and to be taught
This lesson. All are grown indebted more,
And when they look for freedom run in score.
It was a cruel courtesy to call
In hope of liberty, and then enthrall.   10
The nobles are your bondmen, gentry, and
All besides those that did not understand.
They were no men of credit, bankrupts born
Fit to be trusted with no stock but scorn.
You have more wisely credited to such,
That though they cannot pay, can value much.
I am your debtor too, but to my shame
Repay you nothing back but your own fame.
                              Henry Moody, *miles.*

To his friend the Author

You may remember how you chid me when
I rank'd you equal with those glorious men,
Beaumont and Fletcher; if you love not praise
You must forbear the publishing of plays.
The crafty mazes of the cunning plot;
The polish'd phrase, the sweet expressions got
Neither by theft, nor violence; the conceit
Fresh and unsullied; all is of weight,
Able to make the captive reader know
I did but justice when I plac'd you so.   10
A shamefast blushing would become the brow
Of some weak virgin writer; we allow
To you a kind of pride; and there, where most
Should blush at commendations, you should boast.
If any think I flatter, let him look
Off from my idle trifles on thy book.

> Thomas Jay, *miles.*

DRAMATIS PERSONAE

LOVELL, an English Lord

SIR GILES OVERREACH, a cruel extortioner

WELBORNE, a prodigal

ALWORTH, a young gentleman, page to Lord Lovell

GREEDY, a hungry Justice of [the] Peace

MARRALL, a term-driver. A creature of Sir Giles Overreach

ORDER
AMBLE } Servants to the Lady Alworth
FURNACE
WATCHALL

WILL-DO, a parson

TAPWELL, an alehouse keeper

THREE CREDITORS

THE LADY ALWORTH, a rich widow

MARGARET, Overreach's daughter

WAITING WOMAN

CHAMBERMAID

FROTH, Tapwell's wife

[*The action takes place in* NOTTINGHAMSHIRE]

ACT ONE

SCENE ONE

([*Enter*] WELBORNE, TAPWELL, FROTH.)

WELBORNE: No booze? nor no tobacco?

TAPWELL: Not a suck, sir,
  Nor the remainder of a single cane
  Left by a drunken porter, all night pall'd too.

FROTH: Not the dropping of the tap for your morning's
      draught, sir,
  'Tis verity I assure you.

WELBORNE: Verity, you brach!
  The devil turn'd precisian? Rogue, what am I?

TAPWELL: Troth, durst I trust you with a looking glass,
  To let you see your trim shape, you would quit me,
  And take the name yourself.

WELBORNE: How, dog?

TAPWELL: Even so, sir.
  And I must tell you, if you but advance   10
  Your Plimworth cloak, you shall be soon instructed;
  There dwells, and within call, if it please your worship,
  A potent monarch, call'd the constable,
  That does command a citadel, call'd the stocks,
  Whose guards are certain files of rusty billmen,
  Such as with great dexterity will hale
  Your tatter'd, lousy –

WELBORNE: Rascal, slave!

FROTH: No rage, sir.

TAPWELL: At his own peril; do not put yourself

---

3. *pall'd*: flat.
5. *brach*: bitch.
6. *precisian*: Puritan.
15. *rusty billmen*: officers with rusty bills (halberds).

In too much heat, there being no water near
20 To quench your thirst, and sure, for other liquor,
As mighty ale, or beer, they are things, I take it,
You must no more remember, not in a dream, sir.
WELBORNE: Why, thou unthankful villain, dar'st thou talk
thus?
Is not thy house and all thou hast my gift?
TAPWELL: I find it not in chalk, and Timothy Tapwell
Does keep no other register.
WELBORNE: Am not I he
Whose riots fed and cloth'd thee? Wert thou not
Born on my father's land, and proud to be
A drudge in his house?
TAPWELL: What I was, sir, it skills not;
30 What you are is apparent. Now for a farewell,
Since you talk of father, in my hope it will torment you,
I'll briefly tell your story. Your dead father,
My quondam master, was a man of worship,
Old Sir John Welborne, Justice of Peace, and *quorum*,
And stood fair to be *Custos rotulorum*;
Bare the whole sway of the shire, kept a great house,
Reliev'd the poor, and so forth; but he dying,
And the twelve hundred a year coming to you,
Late Master Francis, but now forlorn Welborne.
WELBORNE: Slave, stop, or I shall lose myself!
40 FROTH: Very hardly;
You cannot out of your way.
TAPWELL: But to my story.
You were then a lord of acres, the prime gallant,
And I your under-butler; note the change now.
You had a merry time of't. Hawks and hounds,
With choice of running horses; mistresses
Of all sorts and all sizes, yet so hot

25. *not in chalk*: not recorded.

29. *skills*: matters.

34. *quorum*: one of the important judges whose presence was needed to constitute a bench.

35. *Custos rotulorum*: custodian of rolls and records of session.

As their embraces made your lordships melt;
Which your uncle Sir Giles Overreach observing,
Resolving not to lose a drop of 'em,
On foolish mortgages, statutes, and bonds,   50
For a while supplied your looseness, and then left you.

WELBORNE: Some curate hath penn'd this invective,
    mongrel,
And you have studied it.

TAPWELL: I have not done yet:
Your land gone, and your credit not worth a token,
You grew the common borrower, no man 'scap'd
Your paper pellets, from the gentleman
To the beggars on highways, that sold you switches
In your gallantry.

WELBORNE: I shall switch your brains out.

TAPWELL: Where poor Tim Tapwell with a little stock,
Some forty pounds or so, bought a small cottage,   60
Humbled myself to marriage with my Froth here;
Gave entertainment.

WELBORNE: Yes, to whores, and canters,
Clubbers by night.

TAPWELL: True, but they brought in profit,
And had a gift to pay for what they call'd for,
And stuck not like your mastership. The poor income
I glean'd from them hath made me in my parish
Thought worthy to be scavenger, and in time
May rise to be overseer of the poor;
Which if I do, on your petition, Welborne,
I may allow you thirteen pence a quarter,   70
And you shall thank my worship.

47. *lordships*: estates.
50. *statutes*: bonds involving forfeiture of land for default.
54. *token*: small coin issued by tradesmen and tavern-keepers.
56. *paper pellets*: I.O.U.s.
59. *Where*: while.
62. *canters . . . night*: vagrants, riff-raff.
65. *stuck not*: were not reluctant.
68. *overseer of the poor*: an office instituted in Elizabeth's reign.
70. *thirteen pence a quarter*: i.e. a penny a week dole.

WELBORNE: Thus, you dogbolt,
  And thus!
    (*Beats and kicks him.*)
TAPWELL: Cry out for help!
WELBORNE: Stir, and thou diest!
  Your potent prince the constable shall not save you.
  Hear me, ungrateful hell-hound! Did not I
  Make purses for you? Then you lick'd my boots,
  And thought your holiday cloak too coarse to clean 'em.
  'Twas I, that when I heard thee swear, if ever
  Thou could'st arrive at forty pounds, thou would'st
80 Live like an emperor, 'twas I that gave it,
  In ready gold. Deny this, wretch!
TAPWELL: I must, sir,
  For from the tavern to the taphouse, all
  On forfeiture of their licences stand bound
  Never to remember who their best guests were,
  If they grew poor like you.
WELBORNE: They are well rewarded
  That beggar themselves to make such cuckolds rich.
  Thou viper, thankless viper, impudent bawd!
  But since you are grown forgetful, I will help
  Your memory, and tread thee into mortar,
  Not leave one bone unbroken.
TAPWELL: Oh!
90 FROTH: Ask mercy.
    (*Enter* ALWORTH.)
WELBORNE: 'Twill not be granted.
ALWORTH: Hold, for my sake hold.
  Deny me, Frank? They are not worth your anger.
WELBORNE: For once thou hast redeem'd them from this
    sceptre;
  But let 'em vanish, creeping on their knees,
  And if they grumble, I revoke my pardon.
FROTH: This comes of your prating, husband; you presum'd
  On your ambling wit, and must use your glib tongue
  Though you are beaten lame for't.

       71. *dogbolt*: blunt arrow, i.e. worthless object.

TAPWELL: Patience, Froth,
  There's law to cure our bruises.
      (*They go off on their hands and knees.*)
WELBORNE: Sent to your mother?
ALWORTH: My lady, Frank, my patroness, my all!   100
  She's such a mourner for my father's death,
  And in her love to him, so favours me,
  That I cannot pay too much observance to her.
  There are few such stepdames.
WELBORNE: 'Tis a noble widow,
  And keeps her reputation pure and clear
  From the least taint of infamy; her life,
  With the splendour of her actions, leaves no tongue
  To envy or detraction. Prithee tell me,
  Has she no suitors?
ALWORTH: Even the best of the shire, Frank,
  My lord excepted. Such as sue, and send,   110
  And send, and sue again, but to no purpose.
  Their frequent visits have not gain'd her presence;
  Yet she's so far from sullenness and pride,
  That I dare undertake you shall meet from her
  A liberal entertainment. I can give you
  A catalogue of her suitors' names.
WELBORNE: Forbear it,
  While I give you good counsel. I am bound to it;
  Thy father was my friend, and that affection
  I bore to him, in right descends to thee;
  Thou art a handsome and a hopeful youth,   120
  Nor will I have the least affront stick on thee,
  If I with any danger can prevent it.
ALWORTH: I thank your noble care, but pray you in what
  Do I run the hazard?
WELBORNE: Art thou not in love?
  Put it not off with wonder.
ALWORTH: In love at my years?

  99. *Sent*: i.e. by Lord Lovell.
  120. *hopeful*: promising.
  125. *Put . . . wonder*: don't evade by pretending surprise.

WELBORNE: You think you walk in clouds, but are transparent;
    I have heard all, and the choice that you have made,
    And with my finger can point out the north star
    By which the loadstone of your folly's guided.
130   And to confirm this true, what think you of
    Fair Margaret, the only child and heir
    Of cormorant Overreach? Does it blush and start
    To hear her only nam'd? Blush at your want
    Of wit and reason.
ALWORTH: You are too bitter, sir.
WELBORNE: Wounds of this nature are not to be cur'd
    With balms, but corrosives. I must be plain:
    Art thou scarce manumiz'd from the porter's lodge,
    And yet sworn servant to the pantofle,
    And dar'st thou dream of marriage? I fear
140   'Twill be concluded for impossible,
    That there is now, nor e'er shall be hereafter,
    A handsome page, or players' boy of fourteen,
    But either loves a wench, or drabs love him;
    Court-waiters not exempted.
ALWORTH: This is madness.
    How e'er you have discover'd my intents,
    You know my aims are lawful; and if ever
    The queen of flowers, the glory of the spring,
    The sweetest comfort to our smell, the rose
    Sprang from an envious briar, I may infer
150   There's such disparity in their conditions,
    Between the goddess of my soul, the daughter,
    And the base churl her father.
WELBORNE: Grant this true
    As I believe it; canst thou ever hope
    To enjoy a quiet bed with her, whose father
    Ruin'd thy state?

129. *loadstone*: lit. magnet; here, compass-needle.
137. *manumiz'd*: manumitted; freed.
137. *porter's lodge*: where servants were punished (Gifford).
138. *sworn . . . pantofle*: i.e. in the service of a lady (pantofle = slipper).
149. *envious*: wicked.
155. *state*: fortune.

ALWORTH: And yours too.

WELBORNE: I confess it.
  True I must tell you as a friend, and freely,
  That where impossibilities are apparent
  'Tis indiscretion to nourish hopes.
  Canst thou imagine – let not self-love blind thee –   160
  That Sir Giles Overreach, that to make her great
  In swelling titles, without touch of conscience
  Will cut his neighbour's throat, and I hope his own too,
  Will e'er consent to make her thine? Give o'er
  And think of some course suitable to thy rank,
  And prosper in it.

ALWORTH: You have well advis'd me.
  But in the meantime, you, that are so studious
  Of my affairs, wholly neglect your own.
  Remember yourself, and in what plight you are.

WELBORNE: No matter, no matter.

ALWORTH: Yes, 'tis much material;   170
  You know my fortune, and my means, yet something,
  I can spare from myself, to help your wants.

WELBORNE: How's this?

ALWORTH: Nay, be not angry. There's eight pieces
  To put you in better fashion.

WELBORNE: Money from thee?
  From a boy, a stipend[i]ary? one that lives
  At the devotion of a stepmother,
  And the uncertain favour of a lord?
  I'll eat my arms first. Howsoe'er blind fortune
  Hath spent the utmost of her malice on me,
  Though I am vomited out of an alehouse,   180
  And thus accoutred, know not where to eat,
  Or drink, or sleep, but underneath this canopy,
  Although I thank thee, I despise thy offer.
  And as I in my madness broke my state
  Without th'assistance of another's brain,

173. *piece(s)*: double sovereign (worth about one pound ten pence).
182. *canopy*: sky (also roofed part of stage).
184. *broke . . . state*: lost my wealth.

In my right wits I'll piece it; at the worst
Die thus, and be forgotten.

ALWORTH: A strange humour.
   (*Exeunt.*)

[SCENE TWO]

   ([*Enter*] ORDER, AMBLE, FURNACE, WATCHALL.)

ORDER: Set all things right, or as my name is Order,
   And by this staff of office that commands you,
   This chain and double ruff, symbols of power,
   Who ever misses in his function
   For one whole week makes forfeiture of his breakfast,
   And privilege in the wine-cellar.

AMBLE: You are merry,
   Good master steward.

FURNACE: Let him; I'll be angry.

AMBLE: Why, fellow Furnace, 'tis not twelve o' clock yet,
   Nor dinner taking up; then 'tis allow'd
10   Cooks by their places may be choleric.

FURNACE: You think you have spoke wisely, goodman Amble,
   My lady's go-before.

ORDER: Nay, nay, no wrangling.

FURNACE: Twit me with the authority of the kitchen?
   At all hours and all places I'll be angry;
   And thus provok'd, when I am at my prayers,
   I will be angry.

AMBLE: There was no hurt meant.

FURNACE: I am friends with thee, and yet I will be angry.

ORDER: With whom?

FURNACE: No matter whom; yet now I think on't,
   I am angry with my lady.

WATCHALL: Heaven forbid, man.

20 ORDER: What cause has she given thee?

FURNACE: Cause enough, master steward.
   I was entertain'd by her to please her palate,

187. *humour*: whim.
12. *go-before*: i.e. usher.

And till she forswore eating I perform'd it.
Now, since our master, noble Alworth, died,
Though I crack my brains to find out tempting sauces,
And raise fortifications in the pastry
Such as might serve for models in the Low Countries,
Which if they had been practis'd at Breda
Spinola might have thrown his cap at it, and ne'er took it –

AMBLE: But you had wanted matter there to work on.   30

FURNACE: Matter? With six eggs, and a strike of rye-meal,
  I had kept the town till doomsday, perhaps longer.

ORDER: But what's this to your pet against my lady?

FURNACE: What's this? Marry, this; when I am three parts
  roasted,
  And the fourth part parboil'd, to prepare her viands,
  She keeps her chamber, dines with a panada,
  Or water-gruel; my sweat never thought on.

ORDER: But your art is seen in the dining-room.

FURNACE: By whom?
  By such as pretend love to her, but come
  To feed upon her. Yet of all the harpies   40
  That do devour her, I am out of charity
  With none so much as the thin-gutted squire
  That's stol'n into commission.

ORDER: Justice Greedy?

FURNACE: The same, the same. Meat's cast away upon him,
  It never thrives. He holds this paradox,
  Who eats not well, can ne'er do justice well.
  His stomach's as insatiate as the grave,
  Or strumpets' ravenous appetites.

    (ALWORTH *knocks. and enters.*)

WATCHALL: One knocks.

ORDER: Our late young master.

AMBLE: Welcome, sir.

FURNACE: Your hand;

30. *wanted matter*: lacked provisions (due to scarcity during siege).
31. *strike*: bushel.
35. *parboil'd*: boiled through.
36. *panada*: boiled and flavoured bread.
43. *stol'n into commission*: become J.P. by fraud or corruption.

50   If you have a stomach, a cold bake-meat's ready.

ORDER [*aside*]: His father's picture in little.

FURNACE: We are all your servants.

AMBLE: In you he lives.

ALWORTH: At once, my thanks to all.

(*Enter the* LADY ALWORTH, WAITING WOMAN, CHAM-
BERMAID.)

This is yet some comfort. Is my lady stirring?

ORDER: Her presence answer for us.

LADY ALWORTH: Sort those silks well.

I'll take the air alone.

(*Exeunt* WAITING WOMAN *and* CHAMBERMAID.)

FURNACE: You air and air,

But will you never taste but spoon-meat more?

To what use serve I?

LADY ALWORTH: Prithee be not angry,

I shall ere long; i' the meantime, there is gold

To buy thee aprons and a summer suit.

60 FURNACE: I am appeas'd, and Furnace now grows coo[l].

LADY ALWORTH: And as I gave directions, if this morning

I am visited by any, entertain 'em

As heretofore; but say in my excuse

I am indispos'd.

ORDER: I shall, madam.

LADY ALWORTH: Do, and leave me.

Nay, stay you, Alworth.

(*Exeunt* ORDER, AMBLE, FURNACE, WATCHALL.)

ALWORTH: I shall gladly grow here,

To wait on your commands.

LADY ALWORTH: So soon turn'd courtier?

ALWORTH: Style not that courtship, madam, which is duty,

Purchas'd on your part.

LADY ALWORTH: Well, you shall o'ercome,

I'll not contend in words. How is it with

Your noble master?

56. *spoon-meat*: soft diet, invalid food.
60. *cool*: Q – 'cooke'.
67. *courtship*: courtiers' flattery.

ALWORTH: Ever like himself;   70
  No scruple lessen'd in the full weight of honour,
  He did command me – pardon my presumption –
  As his unworthy deputy, to kiss
  Your ladyship's fair hands.

LADY ALWORTH: I am honour'd in
  His favour to me. Does he hold his purpose
  For the Low Countries?

ALWORTH: Constantly, good madam,
  But he will in person first present his service.

LADY ALWORTH: And how approve you of his course? You
    are yet
  Like virgin parchment, capable of any
  Inscription, vicious or honourable.   80
  I will not force your will, but leave you free
  To your own election.

ALWORTH: Any form you please,
  I will put on; but might I make my choice
  With humble emulation I would follow
  The path my lord marks to me.

LADY ALWORTH: 'Tis well answer'd,
  And I commend your spirit. You had a father
  (Bless'd be his memory) that some few hours
  Before the will of heaven took him from me,
  Who did commend you, by the dearest ties
  Of perfect love between us, to my charge: 90
  And therefore what I speak, you are bound to hear
  With such respect as if he liv'd in me;
  He was my husband, and howe'er you are not
  Son of my womb, you may be of my love,
  Provided you deserve it.

ALWORTH: I have found you,
  Most honour'd madam, the best mother to me,
  And with my utmost strengths of care and service,
  Will labour that you never may repent
  Your bounties shower'd upon me.

LADY ALWORTH: I much hope it.
  These were your father's words. If e'er my son   100

Follow the war, tell him it is a school
Where all the principles tending to honour
Are taught, if truly followed. But for such
As repair thither as a place in which
They do presume they may with licence practise
Their lusts and riots, they shall never merit
The noble name of soldiers. To dare boldly
In a fair cause, and for the country's safety
To run upon the cannon's mouth undaunted;
110   To obey their leaders, and shun mutinies;
To bear with patience the winter's cold,
And summer's scorching heat, and not to faint,
When plenty of provision fails, with hunger,
Are the essential parts make up a soldier,
Not swearing, dice, or drinking.

ALWORTH: There's no syllable
You speak but is to me an oracle,
Which but to doubt were impious.

LADY ALWORTH: To conclude:
Beware ill company, for often men
Are like to those with whom they do converse,
120   And from one man I warn'd you, and that's Welborne:
Not cause he's poor – that rather claims your pity –
But that he's in his manners so debauch'd,
And hath to vicious courses sold himself.
'Tis true your father lov'd him, while he was
Worthy the loving, but if he had liv'd
To have seen him as he is, he had cast him off
As you must do.

ALWORTH: I shall obey in all things.

LADY ALWORTH: Yet follow me to my chamber, you shall
    have gold
To furnish you like my son, and still supplied,
As I hear from you.

130 ALWORTH: I am still your creature.
    (*Exeunt.*)

130. *still*: always.

[SCENE THREE]

([*Enter*] OVERREACH, GREEDY, ORDER, AMBLE, FURNACE, WATCHALL, MARRALL.)

GREEDY: Not to be seen?

OVERREACH: Still cloistered up? Her reason
I hope assures her, though she make herself
Close prisoner ever for her husband's loss,
'Twill not recover him.

ORDER: Sir, it is her will,
Which we that are her servants ought to serve it,
And not dispute. Howe'er, you are nobly welcome,
And if you please to stay, that you may think so,
There came not six days since from Hull, a pipe
Of rich canary, which shall spend itself
For my lady's honour.

GREEDY: Is it of the right race?   10

ORDER: Yes, Master Greedy.

AMBLE [*aside*]:   How his mouth runs o'er!

FURNACE [*aside*]: I'll make it run, and run. – Save your good
  worship!

GREEDY: Honest master cook, thy hand again. How I love
  thee!
Are the good dishes still in being? Speak, boy.

FURNACE: If you have a mind to feed, there is a chine
Of beef well seasoned.

GREEDY: Good!

FURNACE: A pheasant larded.

GREEDY: That I might now give thanks for't!

FURNACE: Other kickshaws.
Besides there came last night from the forest of Sherwood
The fattest stag I ever cook'd.

GREEDY: A stag, man?

FURNACE: A stag sir, part of it prepar'd for dinner,   20

8. *pipe*: cask.
10. *race*: variety and flavour.
17. *kickshaws*: fancy dishes.

331

And bak'd in puffpaste.

GREEDY: Puffpaste too, Sir Giles!
  A ponderous chine of beef! A pheasant larded!
  And red deer too, Sir Giles, and bak'd in puffpaste!
  All business set aside; let us give thanks here!

FURNACE [aside]: How the lean skeleton's rapt!

OVERREACH: You know we cannot.

MARRALL: Your worships are to sit on a commission,
  And if you fail to come you lose the cause.

GREEDY: Cause me no causes. I'll prove't, for such a dinner
  We may put off a commission: you shall find it
  Henrici decimo quarto.

30 OVERREACH: Fie, Master Greedy,
  Will you lose me a thousand pounds for a dinner?
  No more, for shame. We must forget the belly
  When we think of profit.

GREEDY: Well, you shall o'errule me.
  I could ev'n cry now. Do you hear, master cook,
  Send but a corner of that immortal pasty,
  And I, in thankfulness, will by your boy
  Send you a brace of threepences.

FURNACE: Will you be so prodigal?
    (*Enter* WELBORNE.)

OVERREACH: Remember me to your lady. Who have we here?

WELBORNE: You know me.

OVERREACH: I did once, but now I will not.
40   Thou art no blood of mine. Avaunt, thou beggar!
  If ever thou presume to own me more,
  I'll have thee cag'd and whipp'd.

GREEDY: I'll grant the warrant,
  Think of Pie Corner, Furnace.
    (*Exeunt* OVERREACH, GREEDY, MARRALL.)

WATCHALL: Will you out, sir?
  I wonder how you durst creep in.

ORDER: This is rudeness,
  And saucy impudence.

---

43. *Pie Corner*: with an allusion to a district in Smithfield noted for cooks' shops.

AMBLE: Cannot you stay
To be serv'd among your fellows from the basket,
But you must press in to the hall?

FURNACE: Prithee vanish
Into some outhouse, though it be the pig-sty,
My scullion shall come to thee.
(*Enter* ALWORTH.)

WELBORNE: This is rare:
Oh here's Tom Alworth. Tom –

ALWORTH: We must be strangers, 50
Nor would I have you seen here for a million.
(*Exit* ALWORTH.)

WELBORNE: Better, and better. He contemns me too?
(*Enter* WOMAN *and* CHAMBERMAID.)

WOMAN: Foh, what a smell's here! What thing's this?

CHAMBERMAID: A creature
Made out of the privy. Let us hence, for love's sake,
Or I shall swoon.

WOMAN: I begin to faint already.
(*Exeunt* WOMAN *and* CHAMBERMAID.)

WATCHALL: Will' know your way?

AMBLE: Or shall we teach it you,
By the head and shoulders?

WELBORNE: No; I will not stir.
Do you mark, I will not. Let me see the wretch
That dares attempt to force me. Why, you slaves,
Created only to make legs, and cringe; 60
To carry in a dish, and shift a trencher;
That have not souls only to hope a blessing
Beyond blackjacks or flagons; you that were born
Only to consume meat and drink, and batten
Upon reversions: who advances? Who
Shows me the way?

ORDER: My lady.

46. *basket*: alms-basket of leftovers.
60. *make legs*: bow low.
63. *blackjacks*: leathern beer-jugs.
65. *reversions*: i.e. leftovers.

(*Enter* LADY ALWORTH, WOMAN [*and*] CHAMBERMAID.)

CHAMBERMAID: Here's the monster.

WOMAN: Sweet madam, keep your glove to your nose.

CHAMBERMAID: Or let me
 Fetch some perfumes may be predominant;
 You wrong yourself else.

WELBORNE: Madam, my designs
70 Bear me to you.

LADY ALWORTH: To me?

WELBORNE: And though I have met with
 But ragged entertainment from your grooms here,
 I hope from you to receive that noble usage
 As may become the true friend of your husband,
 And then I shall forget these.

LADY ALWORTH: I am amaz'd
 To see and hear this rudeness. Dar'st thou think,
 Though sworn, that it can ever find belief
 That I, who to the best men of this country
 Deni'd my presence since my husband's death,
80 Can fall so low as to change words with thee?
 Thou son of infamy, forbear my house,
 And know and keep the distance that's between us,
 Or, though it be against my gentler temper,
 I shall take order you no more shall be
 An eye-sore to me.

WELBORNE: Scorn me not, good lady,
 But, as in form you are angelical,
 Imitate the heavenly natures, and vouchsafe
 At the least awhile to hear me. You will grant
 The blood that runs in this arm is as noble
90 As that which fills your veins; those costly jewels,
 And those rich clothes you wear, your men's observance,
 And women's flattery, are in you no virtues,
 Nor these rags, with my poverty, in me vices.
 You have a fair fame, and I know deserve it,
 Yet, lady, I must say in nothing more

   67. *glove . . . nose*: gloves were frequently perfumed.
   84. *take order*: arrange.

Than in the pious sorrow you have shown
For your late noble husband.

ORDER [*aside*]:   How she starts!

FURNACE [*aside*]: And hardly can keep finger from the eye
To hear him nam'd.

LADY ALWORTH: Have you aught else to say?

WELBORNE: That husband, madam, was once in his fortune   100
Almost as low as I. Want, debts, and quarrels
Lay heavy on him; let it not be thought
A boast in me, though I say, I reliev'd him.
'Twas I that gave him fashion; mine the sword
That did on all occasions second his;
I brought him on and off with honour, lady.
And when in all men's judgements he was sunk,
And in his own hopes not to be bung'd up,
I step'd unto him, took him by the hand,
And set him upright.

FURNACE: Are not we base rogues   110
That could forget this?

WELBORNE: I confess you made him
Master of your estate, nor could your friends,
Though he brought no wealth with him, blame you for't.
For he had a shape, and to that shape a mind
Made up of all parts, either great, or noble,
So winning a behaviour, not to be
Resisted, madam.

LADY ALWORTH: 'Tis most true, he had.

WELBORNE: For his sake then, in that I was his friend,
Do not contemn me.

LADY ALWORTH: For what's past, excuse me.   120
I will redeem it. Order, give the gentleman
A hundred pounds.

WELBORNE: No, madam, on no terms.
I will nor beg, nor borrow sixpence of you,
But be suppli'd elsewhere, or want thus ever.
Only one suit I make, which you deny not

104. *fashion*: i.e. elegant clothes.
108. *bung'd*: frequently and needlessly amended to 'buoy'd'.

To strangers; and 'tis this. (*Whispers to her.*)
LADY ALWORTH: Fie, nothing else?
WELBORNE: Nothing. Unless you please to charge your
    servants,
To throw away a little respect upon me.
LADY ALWORTH: What you demand is yours.
WELBORNE: I thank you, lady.
130   Now what can be wrought out of such a suit,
Is yet in supposition; I have said all,
When you please you may retire.
    [*Exit* LADY ALWORTH.]
                        Nay, all's forgotten,
And for a lucky omen to my project,
Shake hands, and end all quarrels in the cellar.
ORDER: Agreed, agreed.
FURNACE: Still merry, Master Welborne.
    (*Exeunt.*)

ACT TWO

SCENE ONE

([*Enter*] OVERREACH, MARRALL.)

OVERREACH: He's gone, I warrant thee; this commission
    crush'd him.

MARRALL: Your worship have the way out, and ne'er miss
    To squeeze these unthrifts into air; and yet
    The chap-fall'n Justice did his part, returning
    For your advantage the certificate
    Against his conscience, and his knowledge too
    (With your good favour), to the utter ruin
    Of the poor farmer.

OVERREACH: 'Twas for these good ends
    I made him a Justice. He that bribes his belly
    Is certain to command his soul.

MARRALL: I wonder   10
    (Still with your licence) why your worship, having
    The power to put this thin-gut in commission,
    You are not in't yourself?

OVERREACH: Thou art a fool;
    In being out of office I am out of danger,
    Where if I were a Justice, besides the trouble,
    I might, or out of wilfulness, or error,
    Run myself finely into a *praemunire*,
    And so become a prey to the informer.
    No, I'll have none of't; 'tis enough I keep
    Greedy at my devotion; so he serve   20
    My purposes, let him hang, or damn, I care not.
    Friendship is but a word.

---

4. *chap-fall'n*: open-jawed.

15. *Where*: whereas.

17. *praemunire*: writ ordering sheriff to produce person charged with
certain offences (here 'predicament').

MARRALL: You are all wisdom.

OVERREACH: I would be worldly wise, for the other wisdom
That does prescribe us a well-govern'd life,
And to do right to others, as ourselves,
I value not an atom.

MARRALL: What course take you
(With your good patience) to hedge in the manor
Of your neighbour Master Frugal? As 'tis said,
He will nor sell, nor borrow, nor exchange,
30 And his land, lying in the midst of your many lordships,
Is a foul blemish.

OVERREACH: I have thought on't, Marrall,
And it shall take. I must have all men sellers,
And I the only purchaser.

MARRALL: 'Tis most fit, sir.

OVERREACH: I'll therefore buy some cottage near his manor,
Which done, I'll make my men break ope his fences,
Ride o'er his standing corn, and in the night
Set fire on his barns, or break his cattle's legs.
These trespasses draw on suits, and suits expenses,
Which I can spare, but will soon beggar him.
40 When I have harried him thus two or three year,
Though he sue *in forma pauperis*, in spite
Of all his thrift and care he'll grow behind-hand.

MARRALL: The best I ever heard; I could adore you!

OVERREACH: Then, with the favour of my man of law,
I will pretend some title. Want will force him
To put it to arbitrement; then if he sell
For half the value, he shall have ready money,
And I possess his land.

MARRALL: 'Tis above wonder!
Welborne was apt to sell, and needed not
These fine arts, sir, to hook him in.

50 OVERREACH: Well thought on.
This varlet, Marrall, lives too long to upbraid me

---

27. *hedge in*: acquire.
41. *in forma pauperis*: as a pauper (without paying legal costs).

With my close cheat put upon him. Will nor cold
Nor hunger kill him?

MARRALL: I know not what to think on 't.
I have us'd all means, and the last night I caus'd
His host the tapster to turn him out of doors;
And have been since with all your friends and tenants,
And on the forfeit of your favour charg'd 'em,
Though a crust of mouldy bread would keep him from
  starving
Yet they should not relieve him. This is done, sir.

OVERREACH: That was something, Marrall, but thou must
  go further,   60
And suddenly, Marrall.

MARRALL: Where and when you please, sir.

OVERREACH: I would have thee seek him out, and if thou
  canst
Persuade him that 'tis better steal than beg.
Then if I prove he has but robb'd a hen-roost,
Not all the world shall save him from the gallows.
Do any thing to work him to despair,
And 'tis thy masterpiece.

MARRALL: I will do my best, sir.

OVERREACH: I am now on my main work with the Lord
  Lovell,
The gallant minded, popular Lord Lovell,
The minion of the people's love; I hear   70
He's come into the country, and my aims are
To insinuate myself into his knowledge,
And then invite him to my house.

MARRALL: I have you.
This points at my young mistress.

OVERREACH: She must part with
That humble title, and write honourable,
Right honourable, Marrall, my right honourable daughter,
If all I have, or e'er shall get will do it.
I will have her well attended; there are ladies

52. *close cheat*: private fraud.
73. *have*: 'get'.

Of errant knights decay'd, and brought so low,
80 That for cast clothes, and meat, will gladly serve her.
And 'tis my glory, though I come from the city,
To have their issue, whom I have undone,
To kneel to mine, as bond-slaves.

MARRALL: 'Tis fit state, sir.

OVERREACH: And therefore, I'll not have a chambermaid
That ties her shoes, or any meaner office,
But such whose fathers were right worshipful.
'Tis a rich man's pride, there having ever been
More than a feud, a strange antipathy
Between us and true gentry.

(*Enter* WELBORNE.)

MARRALL: See, who's here, sir.

OVERREACH: Hence monster, prodigy!

90 WELBORNE: Sir, your wife's nephew;
She and my father tumbled in one belly.

OVERREACH: Avoid my sight, thy breath's infectious, rogue!
I shun thee as a leprosy, or the plague.
[*Aside*] Come hither, Marrall, this is the time to work him.

MARRALL: I warrant you, sir.

(*Exit* OVERREACH.)

WELBORNE: By this light, I think he's mad.

MARRALL: Mad? Had you took compassion on yourself,
You long since had been mad.

WELBORNE: You have took a course
Between you and my venerable uncle
To make me so.

MARRALL: The more pale-spirited you,
100   That would not be instructed. I swear deeply –

WELBORNE: By what?

MARRALL: By my religion.

WELBORNE: Thy religion!
The devil's creed! But what would you have done?

MARRALL: Had there been but one tree in all the shire,
Nor any hope to compass a penny halter,
Before, like you, I had outliv'd my fortunes,

104. *compass*: come by.

A withe had serv'd my turn to hang myself.
I am zealous in your cause; pray you hang yourself
And presently, as you love your credit.

WELBORNE: I thank you.

MARRALL: Will you stay till you die in a ditch? Or lice
    devour you?
Or if you dare not do the feat yourself,   110
But that you'll put the state to charge and trouble,
Is there no purse to be cut? House to be broken?
Or market women with eggs that you may murder,
And so dispatch the business?

WELBORNE: Here's variety,
I must confess; but I'll accept of none
Of all your gentle offers, I assure you.

MARRALL: Why, have you hope ever to eat again,
Or drink? Or be the master of three farthings?
If you like not hanging, drown yourself; take some course
For your reputation.

WELBORNE: 'Twill not do, dear tempter,   120
With all the rhetoric the fiend hath taught you.
I am as far as thou art from despair,
Nay, I have confidence, which is more than hope,
To live, and suddenly better than ever.

MARRALL: Ha, ha! These castles you build in the air
Will not persuade me or to give, or lend
A token to you.

WELBORNE: I'll be more kind to thee;
Come, thou shalt dine with me.

MARRALL: With you?

WELBORNE: Nay more, dine gratis.

MARRALL: Under what hedge, I pray you? Or at whose cost?
Are they padders, or Abram-men, that are your consorts?   130

WELBORNE: Thou art incredulous, but thou shalt dine
Not alone at her house, but with a gallant lady,
With me, and with a lady.

108. *presently*: at once.
108. *credit*: reputation.
130. *padders*: footpads.

MARRALL: Lady! What lady?
   With the Lady of the Lake, or Queen of Fairies?
   For I know, it must be an enchanted dinner.
WELBORNE: With the Lady Alworth, knave.
MARRALL: Nay, now there's hope
   Thy brain is crack'd.
WELBORNE: Mark there, with what respect
   I am entertain'd.
MARRALL: With choice no doubt of dog-whips.
   Why, dost thou ever hope to pass her porter?
140 WELBORNE: 'Tis not far off, go with me; trust thine own eyes.
MARRALL: Troth, in my hope, or my assurance rather,
   To see thee curvet and mount like a dog in a blanket
   If ever thou presume to pass her threshold,
   I will endure thy company.
WELBORNE: Come along, then.
   (*Exeunt.*)

[SCENE TWO]

([*Enter*] ALWORTH, WAITING-WOMAN, CHAMBERMAID,
ORDER, AMBLE, FURNACE, WATCHALL.)

WAITING-WOMAN: Could you not command your leisure one
   hour longer?
CHAMBERMAID: Or half an hour?
ALWORTH: I have told you what my haste is;
   Besides being now another's, not mine own,
   Howe'er I much desire to enjoy you longer,
   My duty suffers if to please myself
   I should neglect my lord.
WAITING-WOMAN: Pray you do me the favour
   To put these few quince-cakes into your pocket –
   They are of mine own preserving.
CHAMBERMAID: And this marmalade;
   'Tis comfortable for your stomach.
WAITING-WOMAN: And at parting
10   Excuse me if I beg a farewell from you.

142. *curvet*: leap about (i.e. when thrown out).

CHAMBERMAID: You are still before me. I move the same
    suit, sir.
    (*Kisses 'em severally.*)
FURNACE: How greedy these chamberers are of a beardless
    chin!
  I think the tits will ravish him.
ALWORTH: My service
  To both.
WAITING-WOMAN: Ours waits on you.
CHAMBERMAID: And shall do ever.
ORDER: You bear my lady's charge, be therefore careful
  That you sustain your parts.
WAITING-WOMAN: We can bear, I warrant you.
    (*Exeunt* WOMAN *and* CHAMBERMAID.)
FURNACE: Here, drink it off, the ingredients are cordial,
  And this the true elixir; it hath boil'd
  Since midnight for you. 'Tis the quintessence   20
  Of five cocks of the game, ten dozen of sparrows,
  Knuckles of veal, potato roots and marrow,
  Coral and ambergris; were you two years elder,
  And I had a wife, or gamesome mistress,
  I durst trust you with neither. You need not bait
  After this, I warrant you; though your journey's long,
  You may ride on the strength of this till tomorrow morning.
ALWORTH: Your courtesies overwhelm me; I much grieve
  To part from such true friends, and yet find comfort;
  My attendance on my honourable lord   30
  (Whose resolution holds to visit my lady)
  Will speedily bring me back.
    (*Knocking at the gate;* MARRALL *and* WELBORNE *within.*)
MARRALL: Dar'st thou venture further?
WELBORNE: Yes, yes, and knock again.
ORDER: 'Tis he; disperse.
AMBLE: Perform it bravely.
FURNACE: I know my cue, ne'er doubt me.
    (*They go off several ways.*)

        13. *tits*: women.
        25. *bait*: break journey for refreshment.

WATCHALL: Beast that I was to make you stay; most welcome,
  You were long since expected.

WELBORNE: Say so much
  To my friend, I pray you.

WATCHALL: For your sake I will, sir.

MARRALL: For his sake!

WELBORNE: Mum, this is nothing.

MARRALL: More than ever
  I would have believ'd though I had found it in my primer.

ALWORTH: When I have giv'n you reasons for my late
40   harshness,
  You'll pardon and excuse me; for, believe me,
  Though now I part abruptly, in my service
  I will deserve it.

MARRALL: Service! With a vengeance!

WELBORNE: I am satisfied; farewell, Tom.

ALWORTH: All joy stay with you. (*Exit* ALWORTH.)
    (*Enter* AMBLE.)

AMBLE: You are happily encounter'd: I yet never
  Presented one so welcome, as I know
  You will be to my lady.

MARRALL: This is some vision,
  Or sure these men are mad, to worship a dunghill;
  It cannot be a truth.

WELBORNE: Be still a pagan,
50 An unbelieving infidel, be so miscreant,
  And meditate on blankets, and on dog-whips.
    (*Enter* FURNACE.)

FURNACE: I am glad you are come; until I know your
    pleasure
  I knew not how to serve up my lady's dinner.

MARRALL: His pleasure! Is it possible?

WELBORNE: What's thy will?

FURNACE: Marry, sir, I have some grouse and turkey chicken,
  Some rails, and quails, and my lady will'd me ask you
  What kind of sauces best affect your palate,

---

3. . *primer*: originally, children's prayer book.
56. *rails*: variety of game bird.

That I may use my utmost skill to please it.

MARRALL [*aside*]: The devil's enter'd this cook! Sauce for his
    palate!

That on my knowledge, for almost this twelve-month,   60

Durst wish but cheeseparings, and brown bread on Sundays!

WELBORNE: That way I like 'em best.

FURNACE: It shall be done, sir. (*Exit* FURNACE.)

WELBORNE: What think you of the hedge we shall dine under?
    Shall we feed gratis?

MARRALL: I know not what to think;

Pray you, make me not mad.

    (*Enter* ORDER.)

ORDER: This place becomes you not;

Pray you walk, sir, to the dining room.

WELBORNE: I am well here

Till her ladyship quits her chamber.

MARRALL: Well here, say you?

'Tis a rare change! But yesterday you thought

Yourself well in a barn, wrapp'd up in pease-straw.

    (*Enter* WOMAN, *and* CHAMBERMAID.)

WAITING-WOMAN: O sir, you are wish'd for.

CHAMBERMAID: My lady dreamt, sir, of you.   70

WAITING-WOMAN: And the first command she gave after
    she rose

Was (her devotions done) to give her notice

When you approach'd here.

CHAMBERMAID: Which is done, on my virtue.

MARRALL: I shall be converted, I begin to grow

Into a new belief, which saints, nor angels

Could have won me to have faith in.

WAITING-WOMAN: Sir, my lady.

    (*Enter* LADY ALWORTH.)

LADY ALWORTH: I come to meet you, and languish'd till I
    saw you

This first kiss is for form; I allow a second

To such a friend.

MARRALL: To such a friend! Heav'n bless me!

WELBORNE: I am wholly yours; yet madam, if you please   80

To grace this gentleman with a salute –

MARRALL: Salute me at his bidding!

WELBORNE: I shall receive it
As a most high favour.

LADY ALWORTH: Sir, you may command me.

   [LADY ALWORTH *offers to kiss* MARRALL, *who retreats.*]

WELBORNE: Run backward from a lady? And such a lady?

MARRALL: To kiss her foot is to poor me a favour
I am unworthy of. (*Offers to kiss her foot.*)

LADY ALWORTH: Nay, pray you rise,
And since you are so humble, I'll exalt you;
You shall dine with me today, at mine own table.

MARRALL: Your ladyship's table? I am not good enough
To sit at your steward's board.

90 LADY ALWORTH: You are too modest:
I will not be denied.

   (*Enter* FURNACE.)

FURNACE: Will you still be babbling
Till your meat freeze on the table? The old trick still.
My art ne'er thought on.

LADY ALWORTH: Your arm, Master Welborne;
[*to* MARRALL] Nay, keep us company.

MARRALL: I was never so grac'd.

   (*Exeunt* WELBORNE, LADY ALWORTH, AMBLE, MARRALL,
   WAITING-WOMAN *and* CHAMBERMAID.)

ORDER: So we have play'd our parts, and are come off well.
But if I know the mystery why my lady
Consented to it, or why Master Welborne
Desir'd it, may I perish.

FURNACE: Would I had
The roasting of his heart, that cheated him,
100 And forces the poor gentleman to these shifts.
By fire (for cooks are Persians, and swear by it)
Of all the griping and extorting tyrants
I ever heard, or read of, I ne'er met
A match to Sir Giles Overreach.

Stage direction. *offers*: tries.
101. *Persians*: i.e. fire-worshippers.

WATCHALL: What will you take
  To tell him so, fellow Furnace?
FURNACE: Just as much
  As my throat is worth, for that would be the price on't.
  To have a usurer that starves himself,
  And wears a cloak of one and twenty years
  On a suit of fourteen groats bought of the hangman,
  To grow rich, and then purchase, is too common;   110
  But this Sir Giles feeds high, keeps many servants,
  Who must at his command do any outrage;
  Rich in his habit, vast in his expenses;
  Yet he to admiration still increases
  In wealth and lordships.
ORDER: He frights men out of their estates,
  And breaks through all law-nets, made to curb ill men,
  As they were cobwebs. No man dares reprove him.
  Such a spirit to dare, and power to do, were never
  Lodg'd so unluckily.
      (Enter AMBLE.)
AMBLE: Ha, ha, I shall burst!
ORDER: Contain thyself, man.
FURNACE: Or make us partakers   120
  Of your sudden mirth.
AMBLE: Ha, ha! My lady has got
  Such a guest at her table, this term-driver Marrall,
  This snip of an attorney –
FURNACE: What of him, man?
AMBLE: The knave thinks still he's at the cook's shop in
      Ram-Alley,
  Where the clerks divide, and the elder is to choose;
  And feeds so slovenly.
FURNACE: Is this all?
AMBLE: My lady
  Drank to him for fashion sake, or to please Master Welborne.
  As I live he rises, and takes up a dish,
  In which there were some remnants of a boil'd capon,

  109. *suit . . . hangman*: a hanged man's clothes went to the hangman.
  124. *Ram-Alley*: off Fleet Street; famous for cooks' shops.

And pledges her in white broth.

130 FURNACE: Nay, 'tis like
   The rest of his tribe.

AMBLE: And when I brought him wine,
   He leaves his stool, and after a leg or two
   Most humbly thanks my worship.

ORDER: Rose already!

AMBLE: I shall be chid.

   (*Enter* LADY ALWORTH, WELBORNE, MARRALL.)

FURNACE: My lady frowns.

LADY ALWORTH: You wait well.
   Let me have no more of this; I observ'd your jeering,
   Sirrah, I'll have you know, whom I think worthy
   To sit at my table, be he ne'er so mean,
   When I am present, is not your companion.

ORDER [*to* AMBLE]: Nay, she'll preserve what's due to her.

FURNACE [*to* AMBLE]:   This refreshing
   Follows your flux of laughter.

140 LADY ALWORTH [*to* WELBORNE]: You are master
   Of your own will. I know so much of manners
   As not to enquire your purposes; in a word
   To me you are ever welcome, as to a house
   That is your own.

WELBORNE [*to* MARRALL]: Mark that.

MARRALL: With reverence, sir,
   An it like your worship.

WELBORNE: Trouble yourself no farther,
   Dear madam; my heart's full of zeal and service,
   How ever in my language I am sparing.
   Come, Master Marrall.

MARRALL: I attend your worship.

   (*Exeunt* WELBORNE, MARRALL.)

LADY ALWORTH: I see in your looks you are sorry, and you
      know me

150   An easy mistress; be merry, I have forgot all.

                    130. *white broth*: white sauce.
                    132. *leg*: bow.
                    138. *companion*: equal.

348

Order and Furnace, come with me, I must give you
Further directions.

ORDER: What you please.

FURNACE: We are ready.

    [Exeunt.]

[SCENE THREE]

    (*[Enter]* WELBORNE, MARRALL.)

WELBORNE: I think I am in a good way.

MARRALL: Good, sir? The best way.
The certain best way.

WELBORNE: There are casualties
That men are subject to.

MARRALL: You are above 'em
And as you are already worshipful,
I hope ere long you will increase in worship
And be right worshipful.

WELBORNE: Prithee do not flout me.
What I shall be, I shall be. Is't for your ease,
You keep your hat off?

MARRALL: Ease, an it like your worship?
I hope Jack Marrall shall not live so long,
To prove himself such an unmannerly beast,   10
Though it hail hazel nuts, as to be cover'd
When your worship's present.

WELBORNE [*aside*]:   Is not this a true rogue
That out of mere hope of a future coz'nage
Can turn thus suddenly? 'Tis rank already.

MARRALL: I know your worship's wise and needs no counsel,
Yet if in my desire to do you service
I humbly offer my advice (but still
Under correction), I hope I shall not
Incur your high displeasure.

WELBORNE: No; speak freely.

MARRALL: Then in my judgement, sir, my simple judgement   20

---

13. *coz'nage*: usually 'cheating', but here possibly 'claiming kindred for advantage'.

(Still with your worship's favour), I could wish you
A better habit, for this cannot be
But much distasteful to the noble lady
(I say no more) that loves you, for this morning
To me (and I am but a swine to her)
Before the' assurance of her wealth perfum'd you
You savour'd not of amber.

WELBORNE: I do now then?
    (*Kisses the end of his cudgel.*)

MARRALL: This your baton hath got a touch of it.
    Yet if you please for change, I have twenty pounds here
30 Which, out of my true love, I presently
    Lay down at your worship's feet: 'twill serve to buy you
    A riding suit.

WELBORNE: But where's the horse?

MARRALL: My gelding
    Is at your service: nay, you shall ride me
    Before your worship shall be put to the trouble
    To walk a foot. Alas, when you are lord
    Of this lady's manor (as I know you will be)
    You may with the lease of glebe land, call'd Knave's Acre,
    A place I would manure, requite your vassall.

WELBORNE: I thank thy love, but must make no use of it.
    What's twenty pounds?

40 MARRALL: 'Tis all that I can make, sir.

WELBORNE: Dost thou think though I want clothes I could
        not have 'em,
    For one word to my lady?

MARRALL: As [if] I know not that!

WELBORNE: Come, I'll tell thee a secret, and so leave thee.
    I'll not give her the advantage, though she be
    A gallant-minded lady, after we are married
    (There being no woman, but is sometimes froward)

---

22. *habit*: clothes.
29. *change*: i.e. of clothes.
38. *manure*: (i) cultivate, (ii) be tenant of.
40. *make*: get together.
46. *froward*: self-willed.

To hit me in the teeth, and say she was forc'd
To buy my wedding clothes, and took me on
With a plain riding-suit and an ambling nag.
No, I'll be furnish'd something like myself   50
And so farewell; for thy suit touching Knave's Acre,
When it is mine, 'tis thine.

MARRALL: I thank your worship.

   (*Exit* WELBORNE.)

How was I cozen'd in the calculation
Of this man's fortune! My master cozen'd too
Whose pupil I am in the art of undoing men,
For that is our profession; well, well, Master Welborne,
You are of a sweet nature, and fit again to be cheated,
Which, if the fates please, when you are possess'd
Of the land, and lady, you sans question shall be.
I'll presently think of the means. (*Walk by, musing.*)

   (*Enter* OVERREACH.)

OVERREACH: Sirrah, take my horse.   60
I'll walk to get me an appetite; 'tis but a mile
And exercise will keep me from being pursy.
Ha, Marrall! Is he conjuring? Perhaps
The knave has wrought the prodigal to do
Some outrage on himself, and now he feels
Compunction in his conscience for't; no matter
So it be done. Marrall –

MARRALL: Sir?

OVERREACH: How succeed we
In our plot on Welborne?

MARRALL: Never better, sir.

OVERREACH: Has he hang'd or drown'd himself?

MARRALL: No sir, he lives.
Lives once more to be made a prey to you,   70
A greater prey then ever.

OVERREACH: Art thou in thy wits?
If thou art, reveal this miracle, and briefly.

MARRALL: A lady, sir, is fall'n in love with him.

OVERREACH: With him? What lady?

     62. *pursy*: short-winded.

351

MARRALL: The rich Lady Alworth.

OVERREACH: Thou dolt; how dar'st thou speak this?

MARRALL: I speak truth,
And I do so but once a year, unless
It be to you, sir. We din'd with her ladyship,
I thank his worship.

OVERREACH: His worship!

MARRALL: As I live, sir;
I din'd with him at the great lady's table,
80   Simple as I stand here, and saw when she kiss'd him,
And would at his request, have kiss'd me too,
But I was not so audacious, as some youths are,
That dare do anything, be it ne'er so absurd,
And sad after performance.

OVERREACH: Why, thou rascal,
To tell me these impossibilities!
Dine at her table? And kiss him, or thee?
Impudent varlet! Have not I myself
To whom great countesses' doors have oft flew open,
Ten times attempted, since her husband's death,
90   In vain to see her, though I came a suitor?
And yet your good solicitorship, and rogue Welborne,
Were brought into her presence, feasted with her!
But that I know thee a dog that cannot blush
This most incredible lie would call up one
On thy buttermilk cheeks.

MARRALL: Shall I not trust my eyes, sir?
Or taste? I feel her good cheer in my belly.

OVERREACH: You shall feel me if you give not over, sirrah;
Recover your brains again, and be no more gull'd
With a beggar's plot assisted by the aids
100   Of serving men and chambermaids; for beyond these
Thou never saw'st a woman, or I'll quit you
From my employments.

MARRALL: Will you credit this yet?
On my confidence of their marriage I offer'd Welborne

80. *Simple*: as true.
84. *sad*: unfortunate, serious.

(I would give a crown now, I durst say his worship)
My nag and twenty pounds.

OVERREACH: Did you so, idiot?
    (*Strikes him down.*)
Was this the way to work him to despair
Or rather to cross me?

MARRALL: Will your worship kill me?

OVERREACH: No, no, but drive the lying spirit out of you.

MARRALL: He's gone.

OVERREACH: I have done then; now forgetting
Your late imaginary feast and lady,   110
Know my Lord Lovell dines with me tomorrow.
Be careful naught be wanting to receive him,
And bid my daughter's women trim her up,
Though they paint her, so she catch the lord, I'll thank
    'em.
There's a piece for my late blows.
    [*Gives him money.*]

MARRALL [*aside*]:   I must yet suffer:
But there may be a time.

OVERREACH: Do you grumble?

MARRALL: No, sir.
    [*Exeunt.*]

ACT THREE

SCENE ONE

([*Enter*] LOVELL, ALWORTH, SERVANTS.)

LOVELL: Walk the horses down the hill; something in private
  I must impart to Alworth.
    (*Exit* SERVANTS.)

ALWORTH: O my lord,
  What sacrifice of reverence, duty, watching,
  Although I could put off the use of sleep,
  And ever wait on your commands [to] serve 'em,
  What dangers, though in ne'er so horrid shapes,
  Nay, death itself, though I should run to meet it,
  Can I, and with a thankful willingness, suffer;
  But still the retribution will fall short
  Of your bounties shower'd upon me.

10 LOVELL: Loving youth,
  Till what I purpose be put into act,
  Do not o'er-prize it; since you have trusted me
  With your soul's nearest, nay, her dearest secret,
  Rest confident 'tis in a cabinet lock'd,
  Treachery shall never open. I have found you
  (For so much to your face I must profess,
  How e'er you guard your modesty with a blush for't)
  More zealous in your love and service to me
  Than I have been in my rewards.

ALWORTH: Still great ones
  Above my merit.

20 LOVELL: Such your gratitude calls 'em:
  Nor am I of that harsh and rugged temper
  As some great men are tax'd with, who imagine
  They part from the respect due to their honours
  If they use not all such as follow 'em

17. *guard*: adorn.

354

Without distinction of their births, like slaves.
I am not so condition'd: I can make
A fitting difference between my foot-boy
And a gentleman, by want compell'd to serve me.
ALWORTH: 'Tis thankfully acknowledg'd; you have been
    More like a father to me than a master.   30
    Pray you pardon the comparison.
LOVELL: I allow it;
    And to give you assurance I am pleas'd in't,
    My carriage and demeanour to your mistress,
    Fair Margaret, shall truly witness for me
    I can command my passions.
ALWORTH: 'Tis a conquest
    Few lords can boast of when they are tempted. Oh!
LOVELL: Why do you sigh? Can you be doubtful of me?
    By that fair name I in the wars have purchas'd,
    And all my actions hitherto untainted,
    I will not be more true to mine own honour   40
    Than to my Alworth.
ALWORTH: As you are the brave Lord Lovell,
    Your bare word only given is an assurance
    Of more validity and weight to me
    Than all the oaths, bound up with imprecations,
    Which, when they would deceive, most courtiers practise.
    Yet being a man (for sure to style you more
    Would relish of gross flattery) I am forc'd,
    Against my confidence of your worth and virtues,
    To doubt, nay more, to fear.
LOVELL: So young, and jealous?
ALWORTH: Were you to encounter with a single foe,   50
    The victory were certain; but to stand
    The charge of two such potent enemies,
    At once assaulting you, as wealth and beauty,
    And those too seconded with power, is odds
    Too great for Hercules.
LOVELL: Speak your doubts and fears,
    Since you will nourish 'em, in plainer language,

26. *not so condition'd*: not of that temperament.

355

That I may understand 'em.

ALWORTH: What's your will,
Though I lend arms against my self (provided
They may advantage you), must be obeyed.

60 My much lov'd lord, were Margaret only fair,
The cannon of her more than earthly form,
Though mounted high, commanding all beneath it,
And ramn'd with bullets of her sparkling eyes,
Of all the bulwarks that defend your senses
Could batter [none], but that which guards your sight.
But when the well-tun'd accents of her tongue
Make music to you, and with numerous sounds
Assault your hearing (such as if Ulysses
Now liv'd again, how e'er he stood the Sirens,
70 Could not resist) the combat must grow doubtful,
Between your reason and rebellious passions.
Add this too; when you feel her touch and breath,
Like a soft western wind, when it glides o'er
Arabia, creating gums and spices,
And in the van the nectar of her lips
Which you must taste, bring the battalia on
Well arm'd, and strongly lin'd with her discourse,
And knowing manners, to give entertainment.
Hippolytus himself would leave Diana
To follow such a Venus.

80 LOVELL: Love hath made you
Poetical, Alworth.

ALWORTH: Grant all these beat off,
Which if it be in man to do, you'll do it,
Mammon in Sir Giles Overreach steps in
With heaps of ill-got gold, and so much land,
To make her more remarkable, as would tire
A falcon's wings in one day to fly over.
O my good lord, these powerful aids, which would
Make a misshapen negro beautiful

---

65. *none*: Q – 'more'.
67. *numerous*: in 'numbers', i.e. rhythmical.
77. *lin'd*: strengthened.

(Yet are but ornaments to give her lustre
That in herself is all perfection) must   90
Prevail for her. I here release your trust.
'Tis happiness enough for me to serve you,
And sometimes with chaste eyes to look upon her.

LOVELL: Why, shall I swear?

ALWORTH: O by no means, my lord;
And wrong not so your judgement to the world
As from your fond indulgence to a boy,
Your page, your servant, to refuse a blessing
Divers great men are rivals for.

LOVELL: Suspend
Your judgement till the trial. How far is it
T'Overreach'[s] house?

ALWORTH: At the most some half hour's riding;   100
You'll soon be there.

LOVELL: And you the sooner freed
From your jealous fears.

ALWORTH: O, that I durst but hope it!
    (*Exeunt.*)

[SCENE TWO]

([*Enter*] OVERREACH, GREEDY, MARRALL.)

OVERREACH: Spare for no cost, let my dressers crack with
    the weight
Of curious viands.

GREEDY: Store indeed's no sore, sir.

OVERREACH: That proverb fits your stomach, Master Greedy.
And let no plate be seen, but what's pure gold,
Or such whose workmanship exceeds the matter
That it is made of; let my choicest linen
Perfume the room, and when we wash, the water,
With precious powders mix'd, so please my lord
That he may with envy wish to bath so ever.

MARRALL: 'Twill be very chargeable.

OVERREACH: Avaunt, you drudge!   10

10. *chargeable*: expensive.

Now all my labour'd ends are at the stake,
Is't a time to think of thrift? Call in my daughter.
   (*Exit* MARRALL.)
And master Justice, since you love choice dishes,
And plenty of 'em –

GREEDY: As I do indeed, sir,
Almost as much as to give thanks for 'em.

OVERREACH: I do confer that providence, with my power
Of absolute command to have abundance,
To your best care.

GREEDY: I'll punctually discharge it
And give the best directions. Now am I

20   In mine own conceit a monarch, at the least
Arch-president of the boil'd, the roast, the bak'd,
For which I will eat often, and give thanks,
When my belly's brac'd up like a drum, and that's pure
    justice. (*Exit* GREEDY.)

OVERREACH: I[t] must be so: should the foolish girl prove
    modest,
She may spoil all; she had it not from me,
But from her mother; I was ever forward,
As she must be, and therefore I'll prepare her.
   (*Enter* MARGARET.)
Alone, and let your women wait without.

MARGARET: Your pleasure, sir?

OVERREACH: Ha, this is a neat dressing!

30   These orient pearls, and diamonds well-plac'd too!
The gown affects me not, it should have been
Embroider'd o'er and o'er with flowers of gold,
But these rich jewels and quaint fashion help it.
And how below? Since oft the wanton eye,
The face observ'd, descends unto the foot,
Which, being well proportion'd, as yours is,

> 16. *providence*: task of providing.
> 20. *conceit*: imagination.
> 31. *affects me not*: I don't care for.
> 33. *quaint*: finely wrought.

Invites as much as perfect white and red,
Though without art. How like you your new woman
The Lady Downfal'n?

MARGARET: Well for a companion,
Not as a servant.

OVERREACH: Is she humble, Meg?   40
And careful too? Her ladyship forgotten?

MARGARET: I pity her fortune.

OVERREACH: Pity her? Trample on her.
I took her up in an old tamin gown
(Even starv'd for want of two penny chops) to serve thee:
And if I understand she but repines
To do thee any duty, though ne'er so servile,
I'll pack her to her knight where I have lodg'd him,
Into the Counter, and there let 'em howl together.

MARGARET: You know your own ways, but for me I blush
When I command her, that was once attended   50
With persons not inferior to myself
In birth.

OVERREACH: In birth? Why, art thou not my daughter?
The blest child of my industry and wealth?
Why, foolish girl, was't not to make thee great
That I have run, and still pursue those ways
That hale down curses on me, which I mind not?
Part with these humble thoughts, and apt thyself
To the noble state I labour to advance thee,
Or by my hopes to see thee honourable,   60
I will adopt a stranger to my heir,
And throw thee from my care; do not provoke me.

MARGARET: I will not, sir; mould me which way you please.
    (*Enter* GREEDY.)

OVERREACH: How, interrupted?

GREEDY: 'Tis matter of importance.
The cook, sir, is self-will'd and will not learn

---

43. *tamin*: thin coarse woollen.
48. *Counter*: one of the two city prisons.
61. *to*: as.

From my experience. There's a fawn brought in, sir,
And for my life I cannot make him roast it
With a Norfolk dumpling in the belly of it.
And, sir, we wise men know, without the dumpling
'Tis not worth threepence.

70 OVERREACH: Would it were whole in thy belly
To stuff it out! Cook it any way, prithee leave me.

GREEDY: Without order for the dumpling?

OVERREACH: Let it be dumpl'd
Which way thou wilt, or tell him I will scald him
In his own cauldron.

GREEDY: I had lost my stomach,
Had I lost my mistress dumpling; I'll give thanks for'[t].
    (*Exit* GREEDY.)

OVERREACH: But to our business, Meg; you have heard who
dines here?

MARGARET: I have, sir.

OVERREACH: 'Tis an honourable man,
A lord, Meg, and commands a regiment
Of soldiers, and, what's rare, is one himself,
80 A bold and understanding one; and to be
A lord, and a good leader, in one volume
Is granted unto few, but such as rise up
The kingdom's glory.
    (*Enter* GREEDY.)

GREEDY: I'll resign my office,
If I be not better obey'd.

OVERREACH: 'Slight, art thou frantic?

GREEDY: Frantic? 'Twould make me a frantic, and stark mad,
Were I not a justice of peace, and *coram* too,
Which this rebellious cook cares not a straw for.
There are a dozen of woodcocks.

OVERREACH: Make thyself
Thirteen, the baker's dozen.

GREEDY: I am contented
90 So they may be dress'd to my mind. He has found out

86. *coram*: coram populo = in public.
88. *woodcocks*: the word also signified a simpleton.

A new device for sauce, and will not dish 'em
With toasts and butter. My father was a tailor,
And my name though a justice, Greedy Woodcock,
And ere I'll see my lineage so abus'd,
I'll give up my commission.

OVERREACH [*shouting off*]:   Cook, rogue, obey him.
I have given the word; pray you now remove yourself
To a collar of brawn and trouble me no farther.

GREEDY: I will, and meditate what to eat at dinner.
  (*Exit* GREEDY.)

OVERREACH: And as I said, Meg, when this gull disturb'd us,
This honourable lord, this colonel   100
I would have thy husband.

MARGARET: There's too much disparity
Between his quality and mine to hope it.

OVERREACH: I more than hope't, and doubt not to effect it.
Be thou no enemy to thyself; my wealth
Shall weigh his titles down and make you equals.
Now for the means to assure him thine, observe me;
Remember he's a courtier, and a soldier,
And not to be trifl'd with, and therefore when
He comes to woo you, see you do not coy it.
This mincing modesty hath spoil'd many a match   110
By a first refusal, in vain after hop'd for.

MARGARET: You'll have me, sir, preserve the distance that
Confines a virgin?

OVERREACH: Virgin me no virgins!
I must have you lose that name, or you lose me.
I will have you private. Start not, I say private;
If thou art my true daughter, not a bastard,
Thou wilt venture alone with one man, though he came
Like Jupiter to Semele, and come off too.
And therefore when he kisses you, kiss close.

92. *tailor*: these were credited with hearty appetites.
102. *quality*: rank.
104. *Be . . . thyself*: i.e. provided you are not.
115. *private*: intimate.
118. *come off*: bring things to a head.

120 MARGARET: I have heard this is the strumpet's fashion, sir,
    Which I must never learn.

OVERREACH: Learn any thing,
    And from any creature that may make thee great;
    From the devil himself.

MARGARET: This is but devilish doctrine.

OVERREACH: Or if his blood grow hot, suppose he offer
    Beyond this, do not you stay till it cool,
    But meet his ardour; if a couch be near,
    Sit down on't, and invite him.

MARGARET: In your house?
    Your own house, sir? For heav'n's sake, what are you then?
    Or what shall I be, sir?

OVERREACH: Stand not on form;
    Words are no substances.

130 MARGARET: Though you could dispense
    With your own honour, cast aside religion,
    The hopes of heaven, or fear of hell, excuse me
    In worldly policy, this is not the way
    To make me his wife; his whore I grant it may do.
    My maiden honour so soon yielded up,
    Nay, prostituted, cannot but assure him
    I that am light to him will not hold weight
    When he is tempted by others; so in judgement
    When to his lust I have given up my honour
    He must, and will, forsake me.

140 OVERREACH: How? Forsake thee?
    Do I wear a sword for fashion? Or is this arm
    Shrunk up, or wither'd? Does there live a man,
    Of that large list I have encounter'd with,
    Can truly say I e'er gave inch of ground
    Not purchas'd with his blood that did oppose me?
    Forsake thee when the thing is done? He dares not.
    Give me but proof he has enjoy'd thy person,
    Though all his captains, echoes to his will,
    Stood arm'd by his side to justify the wrong,

137-8. *I . . . others*: i.e. her laxity would encourage his infidelity. Often amended to 'when I am tempted by others'.

And he himself in the head of his bold troop,   150
Spite of his lordship, and his colonelship,
Or the judge's favour, I will make him render
A bloody and a strict accompt, and force him,
By marrying thee, to cure thy wounded honour;
I have said it.
    (*Enter* MARRALL.)

MARRALL: Sir, the man of honour's come,
Newly alighted.

OVERREACH: In without reply,
And do as I command, or thou art lost.
    (*Exit* MARGARET.)
Is the loud music I gave order for
Ready to receive him?

MARRALL: 'Tis, sir.

OVERREACH: Let 'em sound
A princely welcome.
    [*Exit* MARRALL.]
                Roughness, awhile leave me,   160
For fawning now, a stranger to my nature,
Must make way for me.
    (*Loud music. Enter* LOVELL, GREEDY, ALWORTH, MAR-
    RALL.)

LOVELL: Sir, you meet your trouble.

OVERREACH: What you are pleas'd to style so is an honour
Above my worth and fortunes.

ALWORTH [*aside*]:   Strange, so humble.

OVERREACH: A justice of peace, my lord.
    (*Presents* GREEDY *to him.*)

LOVELL: Your hand, good sir.

GREEDY [*aside*]: This is a lord and some think this a favour,
But I had rather have my hand in my dumpling.

OVERREACH: Room for my lord.

LOVELL: I miss, sir, your fair daughter
To crown my welcome.

OVERREACH: May it please my lord

---

155. *man of honour*: nobleman.

170 To taste a glass of Greek wine first, and suddenly
　　She shall attend my lord.
LOVELL: 　　　　　　　　You'll be obey'd, sir.
　　(*Exeunt all but* OVERREACH.)
OVERREACH: 'Tis to my wish; as soon as come, ask for her!
　　[*Enter* MARGARET.]
　　Why, Meg? Meg Overreach! How? Tears in your eyes?
　　Ha! Dry 'em quickly, or I'll dig 'em out.
　　Is this a time to whimper? Meet that greatness
　　That flies into thy bosom: think what 'tis
　　For me to say, *My honourable daughter*.
　　And thou, when I stand bare, to say Put on,
　　Or, Father, you forget yourself. No more,
180 But be instructed, or expect – he comes.
　　(*Enter* LOVELL, GREEDY, ALWORTH, MARRALL. *They salute*.)
　　A black-brow'd girl, my lord.
LOVELL: 　　　　　　　As I live, a rare one.
ALWORTH [*aside*]: He's took already: I am lost.
OVERREACH: 　　　　　　　　　That kiss
　　Came twanging off; I like it. Quit the room:
　　(*The rest off*.)
　　A little bashful, my good lord, but you,
　　I hope, will teach her boldness.
LOVELL: 　　　　　　　I am happy
　　In such a scholar; but –
OVERREACH: 　　　　I am past learning,
　　And therefore leave you to yourselves: (*to his daughter*)
　　remember. (*Exit* OVERREACH.)
LOVELL: You see, fair lady, your father is solicitous
　　To have you change the barren name of virgin
　　Into a hopeful wife.
190 MARGARET: 　　　　His haste, my lord
　　Holds no power o'er my will.
LOVELL: 　　　　　　　But o'er your duty.
MARGARET: Which forc'd too much may break.

170. *suddenly*: promptly.
181. *black-brow'd*: gentlemen preferred blondes.

LOVELL: Bend rather, sweetest;
  Think of your years.

MARGARET: Too few to match with yours:
  And choicest fruits, too soon plucked, rot and wither.

LOVELL: Do you think I am old?

MARGARET: I am sure I am too young.

LOVELL: I can advance you.

MARGARET: To a hill of sorrow,
  Where every hour I may expect to fall,
  But never hope firm footing. You are noble,
  I of a low descent, however rich;
  And tissues match'd with scarlet suit but ill.   200
  O my good lord, I could say more, but that
  I dare not trust these walls.

LOVELL: Pray you trust my ear, then.
    (*Enter* OVERREACH, *listening*.)

OVERREACH: Close at it! Whispering! This is excellent!
  And by their postures, a consent on both parts.
    (*Enter* GREEDY.)

GREEDY: Sir Giles, Sir Giles!

OVERREACH: The great fiend stop that clapper!

GREEDY: It must ring out, sir, when my belly rings noon;
  The bak'd meats are run out, the roast turn'd powder.

OVERREACH: I shall powder you.

GREEDY: Beat me to dust, I care not,
  In such a cause as this, I'll die a martyr.

OVERREACH: Marry, and shall, you Barathrum of the
    shambles.   210
    (*Strikes him*.)

GREEDY: How! Strike a justice of peace? 'Tis petty treason,
  Edwardi quinto; but that you are my friend
  I could commit you without bail or main-prize.

OVERREACH: Leave your bawling, sir; or I shall commit you
  Where you shall not dine today; disturb my lord,
  When he is in discourse?

      207. *run out*: i.e. of the crust.
      210. *Barathrum*: devouring gulf. cf. Horace, *Epistles*, I, xv, 31.
      213. *main-prize*: 'taking in hand', hence acting as surety.

GREEDY: Is't a time to talk
When we should be munching?

LOVELL: Ha! I heard some noise.

OVERREACH [*to* GREEDY]: Mum, villain, vanish! Shall we
   break a bargain
Almost made up?
   (*Thrust* GREEDY *off.*)

LOVELL: Lady, I understand you
220 And rest most happy in your choice, believe it;
I'll be a careful pilot to direct
Your yet uncertain bark to a port of safety.

MARGARET: So shall your honour save two lives, and bind us
Your slaves for ever.

LOVELL: I am in the act rewarded,
Since it is good. Howe'er you must put on
An amorous carriage towards me, to delude
Your subtle father.

MARGARET: I am prone to that.

LOVELL: Now break we off our conference – Sir Giles!
Where is Sir Giles?
   (*Enter* OVERREACH, *and the rest.*)

OVERREACH: My noble lord; and how
Does your lordship find her?

230 LOVELL: Apt, Sir Giles, and coming,
And I like her the better.

OVERREACH: So do I too.

LOVELL: Yet, should we take forts at the first assault
'Twere poor in the defendant. I must confirm her
With a love letter or two, which I must have
Deliver'd by my page, an you give way to't.

OVERREACH: With all my soul, a towardly gentleman.
Your hand, good Master Alworth; know my house
Is ever open to you.

ALWORTH [*aside*]: 'Twas shut 'till now.

OVERREACH [*aside*]: Well done, well done, my honourable
   daughter:
240 Th'art so **already**: know this gentle youth,

236. *towardly*: promising.

And cherish him, my honourable daughter.

MARGARET: I shall with my best care.

    (*Noise within as of a coach.*)

OVERREACH: A coach.

GREEDY: More stops

Before we go to dinner! O my guts!

    (*Enter* LADY ALWORTH *and* WELBORNE.)

LADY ALWORTH: If I find welcome

You share in it; if not I'll back again,

Now I know your ends, for I come arm'd for all

Can be objected.

LOVELL: How! The Lady Alworth!

OVERREACH: And thus attended!

MARRALL: No, I am a dolt;

    (LOVELL *salutes the* LADY ALWORTH, *the* LADY ALWORTH
    salutes MARGARET.)

The spirit of lies had enter'd me.

OVERREACH: Peace, patch;

'Tis more than wonder! An astonishment

That does possess me wholly!

LOVELL: Noble lady,   250

This is a favour to prevent my visit,

The service of my life can never equal.

LADY ALWORTH: My lord, I laid wait for you, and much
    hop'd

You would have made my poor house your first inn:

And therefore, doubting that you might forget me,

Or too long dwell here, having such ample cause

In this unequall'd beauty for your stay,

And fearing to trust any but myself

With the relation of my service to you,

I borrow'd so much from my long restraint,   260

And took the air in person to invite you.

LOVELL: Your bounties are so great they rob me, madam,

247. *And thus attended*: Welborne is still poorly dressed, contrasting even
more strongly with Lady Alworth, now that she is probably out of mourning
(see III, ii, 260).

    248. *patch*: fool.

    256. *doubting*: fearing.

Of words to give you thanks.

LADY ALWORTH: Good Sir Giles Overreach.
    (*Salutes him.*)
    How dost thou, Marrall? Lik'd you my meat so ill,
    You'll dine no more with me?

GREEDY: I will when you please,
    An it like your ladyship.

LADY ALWORTH: When you please, Master Greedy.
    If meat can do it, you shall be satisfied.
    And now, my lord, pray take into your knowledge
    This gentleman; how e'er his outside's coarse,
      (*Presents* WELBORNE.)
270 His inward linings are as fine and fair
    As any man's; wonder not I speak at large;
    And how soe'er his humour carries him
    To be thus accoutred, or what taint soever
    For his wild life hath stuck upon his fame,
    He may ere long with boldness rank himself
    With some that have contemn'd him. Sir Giles Overreach,
    If I am welcome, bid him so.

OVERREACH: My nephew! –
    He has been too long a stranger: faith, you have;
    Pray let it be mended.
      (LOVELL *conferring with* WELBORNE.)

MARRALL: Why sir, what do you mean?
280 This is rogue Welborne, monster, prodigy,
    That should hang, or drown himself, no man of worship,
    Much less your nephew.

OVERREACH: Well, sirrah, we shall reckon
    For this hereafter.

MARRALL: I'll not lose my jeer
    Though I be beaten dead for't.

WELBORNE: Let my silence plead
    In my excuse, my lord, till better leisure
    Offer itself to hear a full relation
    Of my poor fortunes.

LOVELL: I would hear, and help 'em.

           271. *at large*: expansively.

OVERREACH: Your dinner waits you.

LOVELL: Pray you lead, we follow.

LADY ALWORTH: Nay, you are my guest, come, dear Master
    Welborne.

    (*Exeunt:* GREEDY *remains.*)

GREEDY: 'Dear Master Welborne'! So she said; heav'n, heav'n! 290
    If my belly would give me leave I could ruminate
    All day on this: I have granted twenty warrants
    To have him committed, from all prisons in the shire,
    To Nottingham jail; and now 'dear Master Welborne'
    And 'my good nephew'! But I play the fool
    To stand here prating, and forget my dinner.

    (*Enter* MARRALL.)

    Are they set, Marrall?

MARRALL: Long since; pray you, a word, sir.

GREEDY: No wording now.

MARRALL: In troth I must; my master,
    Knowing you are his good friend, makes bold with you,
    And does entreat you, more guests being come in   300
    Than he expected, especially his nephew,
    The table being full too, you would excuse him
    And sup with him on the cold meat.

GREEDY: How! No dinner
    After all my care?

MARRALL: 'Tis but a penance for
    A meal; besides, you broke your fast.

GREEDY: That was
    But a bit to stay my stomach; a man in commission
    Give place to a tatterdemalion?

MARRALL: No bug words, sir.
    Should his worship hear you –

GREEDY: Lose my dumpling too,
    And butter'd toasts, and woodcocks?

MARRALL: Come, have patience.
    If you will dispense a little with your worship,   310

---

307. *tatterdemalion*: beggarly wretch.
307. *bug*: pompous.
308–9. *dumpling, woodcock, etc.*: see Additional Notes.

And sit with the waiting women, you have dumpling,
Woodcock and butter'd toasts too.

GREEDY: This revives me.
I will gorge there sufficiently.

MARGARET: This is the way, sir.
    (*Exeunt.*)

[SCENE THREE]

([*Enter*] OVERREACH *as from dinner.*)

OVERREACH: She's caught! O women! She neglects my lord,
And all her compliments appli'd to Welborne!
The garments of her widowhood laid by,
She now appears as glorious as the spring,
Her eyes fix'd on him; in the wine she drinks,
He being her pledge, she sends him burning kisses,
And sits on thorns till she be private with him.
She leaves my meat to feed upon his looks;
And if in our discourse he be but nam'd
10   From her a deep sigh follows. But why grieve I
At this? It makes for me, if she prove his,
All that is hers is mine, as I will work him.
    (*Enter* MARRALL.)

MARRALL: Sir, the whole board is troubled at your rising.

OVERREACH: No matter, I'll excuse it. Prithee, Marrall,
Watch an occasion to invite my nephew
To speak with me in private.

MARRALL: Who, the rogue
The lady scorn'd to look on?

OVERREACH: You are a wag.
    (*Enter* LADY ALWORTH *and* WELBORNE.)

MARRALL: See sir, she's come, and cannot be without him.

LADY ALWORTH: With your favour, sir, after a plenteous
    dinner,
20   I shall make bold to walk a turn or two
In your rare garden.

OVERREACH: There's an arbour too
If your ladyship please to use it.

LADY ALWORTH: Come, Master Welborne.
　　(*Exeunt* LADY ALWORTH *and* WELBORNE.)

OVERREACH: Grosser and grosser! Now I believe the poet
　Feign'd not but was historical when he wrote
　Pasiphae was enamour'd of a bull;
　This lady's lust's more monstrous. My good lord,
　Excuse my manners.
　　(*Enter* LOVELL, MARGARET *and the rest.*)

LOVELL: There needs none, Sir Giles –
　I may e'er long say father – when it pleases
　My dearest mistress to give warrant to it.

OVERREACH: She shall seal to it my lord, and make me happy.   30

MARGARET: My lady is return'd.
　　(*Enter* WELBORNE *and the* LADY ALWORTH.)

LADY ALWORTH: Provide my coach,
　I'll instantly away. My thanks, Sir Giles,
　For my entertainment.

OVERREACH: 'Tis your nobleness
　To think it such.

LADY ALWORTH: I must do you a further wrong
　In taking away your honourable guest.

LOVELL: I wait on you, madam; farewell, good Sir Giles.

LADY ALWORTH: Good mistress Margaret: nay come, Master
　　Welborne,
　I must not leave you behind, in sooth I must not.

OVERREACH: Rob me not, madam, of all joys at once;
　Let my nephew stay behind; he shall have my coach,   40
　And (after some small conference between us)
　Soon overtake your ladyship.

LADY ALWORTH [*to* WELBORNE]: Stay not long, sir.

LOVELL [*to* MARGARET]: This parting kiss; you shall every day
　　hear from me
　By my faithful page.

ALWORTH: 'Tis a service I am proud of.
　　(*Exeunt* LOVELL, LADY ALWORTH, ALWORTH, MAR-
　　GARET, MARRALL.)

　　　　23. *the poet*: Ovid (*Metamorphoses*, XV, 500 ff.).
　　　　27. *Excuse my manners*: i.e. in rising from table first.

OVERREACH: Daughter, to your chamber.
   [*Exit* MARGARET.]
  You may wonder, nephew,
  After so long an enmity between us
  I should desire your friendship.
WELBORNE: So I do, sir.
  'Tis strange to me.
OVERREACH: But I'll make it no wonder,
50 And what is more, unfold my nature to you.
  We worldly men, when we see friends and kinsmen
  Past hope sunk in their fortunes, lend no hand
  To lift 'em up, but rather set our feet
  Upon their heads, to press 'em to the bottom,
  As, I must yield, with you I practis'd it.
  But now I see you in a way to rise,
  I can and will assist you; this rich lady
  (And I am glad of't) is enamour'd of you;
  'Tis too apparent, nephew.
WELBORNE: No such thing;
  Compassion rather, sir.
60 OVERREACH: Well, in a word,
  Because your stay is short, I'll have you seen
  No more in this base shape, nor shall she say
  She married you like a beggar, or in debt.
WELBORNE [*aside*]: He'll run into the noose and save my
    labour.
OVERREACH: You have a trunk of rich clothes, not far hence
  In pawn; I will redeem 'em, and that no clamour
  May taint your credit for your petty debts,
  You shall have a thousand pounds to cut 'em off,
  And go a free man to the wealthy lady.
70 WELBORNE: This done, sir, out of love, and no ends else –
OVERREACH: As it is, nephew.
WELBORNE: Binds me still your servant.
OVERREACH: No compliments; you are stay'd for; ere y'ave
    supp'd

55. *yield*: admit.
62. *shape*: garment.

You shall hear from me. – My coach, knaves, for my
   nephew;
Tomorrow I will visit you.
WELBORNE [*aside*]:   Here's an uncle
In a man's extremes! – How much they do belie you
That say you are hard-hearted.
OVERREACH: My deeds, nephew,
   Shall speak my love; what men report, I weigh not.
   (*Exeunt.*)

75. *extremes*: extremity.

ACT FOUR

SCENE ONE

([*Enter*] LOVELL, ALWORTH.)

LOVELL: 'Tis well; give me my cloak: I now discharge you
  From further service. Mind your own affairs,
  I hope they will prove successful.

ALWORTH: What is blest
  With your good wish, my lord, cannot but prosper.
  Let after-times report, and to your honour,
  How much I stand engag'd, for I want language
  To speak my debt: yet if a tear or two
  Of joy for your much goodness can supply
  My tongue's defects, I could.

LOVELL: Nay, do not melt;
10 This ceremonial thanks to me's superfluous.

OVERREACH (*within*): Is my lord stirring?

LOVELL: 'Tis he; oh, here's your letter; let him in.
    (*Enter* OVERREACH, GREEDY [*and*] MARRALL.)

OVERREACH: A good day to my lord.

LOVELL: You are an early riser,
  Sir Giles.

OVERREACH: And reason, to attend your lordship.

LOVELL: And you too, Master Greedy; up so soon?

GREEDY: In troth, my lord, after the sun is up.
  I cannot sleep, for I have a foolish stomach
  That croaks for breakfast. With your lordship's favour;
  I have a serious question to demand
  Of my worthy friend Sir Giles.

20 LOVELL: Pray you use your pleasure.

GREEDY: How far, Sir Giles, and pray you answer me,
  Upon your credit, hold you it to be
  From your manor house to this of my Lady Alworth's?

OVERREACH: Why, some four mile.

GREEDY: How! four mile? Good Sir Giles,
Upon your reputation think better;
For if you do abate but one half quarter
Of five, you do yourself the greatest wrong
That can be in the world: for four miles, riding
Could not have rais'd so huge an appetite
As I feel gnawing on me.

MARRALL: Whether you ride   30
Or go afoot, you are that way still provided,
An it please your worship.

OVERREACH: How now, sirrah? Prating
Before my lord? No difference? Go to my nephew;
See all his debts discharg'd, and help his worship
To fit on his rich suit.

MARRALL [aside]: I may fit you too;
Toss'd like a dog still.

     (Exit MARRALL.)

LOVELL: I have writ this morning
A few lines to my mistress your fair daughter.

OVERREACH: 'Twill fire her, for she's wholly yours already:
Sweet Master Alworth, take my ring, 'twill carry you
To her presence I dare warrant you, and there plead
For my good lord, if you shall find occasion.   40
That done, pray ride to Nottingham, get a licence,
Still by this token, I'll have it dispatch'd,
And suddenly, my lord, that I may say
My honourable, nay, right honourable daughter.

GREEDY: Take my advice, young gentleman; get your
breakfast.
'Tis unwholesome to ride fasting. I'll eat with you
And eat to purpose.

OVERREACH: Some fury's in that gut:
Hungry again! Did you not devour this morning
A shield of brawn, and a barrel of Colchester oysters?   50

GREEDY: Why, that was, sir, only to scour my stomach,
A kind of a preparative. Come, gentlemen,

---

33. *difference*: distinction of persons, deference due to rank.
50. *shield of brawn*: roll of brawn cooked in boar's skin.

    I will not have you feed like the hangman of Flushing
    Alone, while I am here.

LOVELL: Haste your return.

ALWORTH: I will not fail, my lord.

GREEDY: Nor I to line
    My Christmas coffer.

      (*Exeunt* GREEDY *and* ALWORTH.)

OVERREACH: To my wish, we are private.
    I come not to make offer with my daughter
    A certain portion, that were poor, and trivial;
    In one word, I pronounce all that is mine,
60   In lands or leases, ready coin, or goods,
    With her, my lord, comes to you, nor shall you have
    One motive to induce you to believe
    I live too long, since every year I'll add
    Something unto the heap, which shall be yours too.

LOVELL: You are a right kind father.

OVERREACH: You shall have reason
    To think me such. How do you like this seat?
    It is well wooded and well water'd, the acres
    Fertile and rich; would it not serve for change
    To entertain your friends in a summer progress?
    What thinks my noble lord?

70 LOVELL: 'Tis a wholesome air,
    And well-built pile, and she that's mistress of it
    Worthy the large revenue.

OVERREACH: She the mistress?
    It may be so for a time; but let my lord
    Say only that he likes it, and would have it,
    I say, ere long 'tis his.

LOVELL: Impossible.

OVERREACH: You do conclude too fast, not knowing me,
    Nor the engines that I work by; 'tis not alone
    The Lady Alworth's lands, for those once Welborne's

---

53. *hangman of Flushing*: ?
56. *Christmas coffer*: i.e. stomach.
69. *progress*: tour.
77. *engines*: devices, means.

(As by her dotage on him, I know they will be)
Shall soon be mine, but point out any man's   80
In all the shire, and say they lie convenient,
And useful for your lordship, and once more
I say aloud, they are yours.

LOVELL: I dare not own
What's by unjust and cruel means extorted;
My fame and credit are more dear to me
Than so to expose 'em to be censur'd by
The public voice.

OVERREACH: You run, my lord, no hazard.
Your reputation shall stand as fair
In all good men's opinions as now.
Nor can my actions, though condemn'd for ill,   90
Cast any foul aspersion upon yours;
For though I do contemn report myself
As a mere sound, I still will be so tender
Of what concerns you in all points of honour,
That the immaculate whiteness of your fame,
Nor your unquestion'd integrity
Shall e'er be sullied with one taint or spot
That may take from your innocence and candour.
All my ambition is to have my daughter
Right honourable, which my lord can make her.   100
And might I live to dance upon my knee
A young Lord Lovell, born by her unto you,
I write *nil ultra* to my proudest hopes.
As for possessions, and annual rents
Equivalent to maintain you in the port
Your noble birth and present state requires,
I do remove that burden from your shoulders,
And take it on mine own; for though I ruin
The country to supply your riotous waste,
The scourge of prodigals, want, shall never find you.   110

LOVELL: Are you not frighted with the imprecations

98. *candour*: spotless name.
103. *nil ultra*: nothing beyond this.
105. *port*: style.

And curses of whole families made wretched
By your sinister practices?
OVERREACH: Yes, as rocks are,
When foamy billows split themselves against
Their flinty ribs; or as the moon is mov'd,
When wolves, with hunger pin'd, howl at her brightness.
I am of a solid temper, and like these
Steer on a constant course: with mine own sword,
If call'd into the field, I can make that right,
120 Which fearful enemies murmur'd at as wrong.
Now, for these other piddling complaints
Breath'd out in bitterness, as when they call me
Extortioner, tyrant, cormorant, or intruder
On my poor neighbour's right, or grand encloser
Of what was common to my private use –
Nay, when my ears are pierc'd with widows' cries,
And undone orphans wash with tears my threshold,
I only think what 'tis to have my daughter
Right honourable; and 'tis a powerful charm
130 Makes me insensible of remorse or pity,
Or the least sting of conscience.
LOVELL: I admire
The toughness of your nature.
OVERREACH: 'Tis for you,
My lord, and for my daughter, I am marble.
Nay more, more; if you will have my character
In little, I enjoy more true delight
In my arrival to my wealth these dark
And crooked ways, than you shall e'er take pleasure
In spending what my industry hath compass'd.
My haste commands me hence. In one word, therefore,
Is it a match?
140 LOVELL: I hope that is past doubt now.
OVERREACH: Then rest secure; not the hate of all mankind
here,
Nor fear of what can fall on me hereafter,

---

113. *sinister*: corrupt (lit. 'left-handed').
131. *admire*: marvel at.

Shall make me study aught but your advancement
One storey higher. An earl! if gold can do it.
Dispute not my religion, nor my faith.
Though I am borne thus headlong by my will,
You may make choice of what belief you please;
To me they are equal. So my lord, good morrow. (*Exit.*)

LOVELL: He's gone; I wonder how the earth can bear
   Such a portent. I, that have liv'd a soldier,   150
   And stood the enemy's violent charge undaunted,
   To hear this blasphemous beast, am bath'd all over
   In a cold sweat; yet like a mountain he,
   Confirm'd in atheistical assertions,
   Is no more shaken than Olympus is
   When angry Boreas loads his double head
   With sudden drifts of snow.

     (*Enter* AMBLE, LADY ALWORTH, WOMAN.)

LADY ALWORTH: Save you, my lord.
   Disturb I not your privacy?

LOVELL: No, good madam;
   For your own sake I am glad you came no sooner,
   Since this bold, bad man, Sir Giles Overreach,   160
   Made such a plain discovery of himself,
   And read this morning such a devilish matins,
   That I should think it a sin next to his
   But to repeat it.

LADY ALWORTH: I ne'er press'd, my lord,
   On others' privacies, yet against my will,
   Walking, for health sake, in the gallery
   Adjoining to your lodgings, I was made
   (So vehement and loud he was) partaker
   Of his tempting offers.

LOVELL: Please you to command
   Your servants hence, and I shall gladly hear   170
   Your wiser counsel.

LADY ALWORTH: 'Tis my lord, a woman's,
   But true, and hearty; [*to servants*] wait in the next room,
   But be within call; yet not so near to force me
   To whisper my intents.

AMBLE: We are taught better
By you, good madam.
WOMAN: And well know our distance.
LADY ALWORTH: Do so, and talk not, 'twill become your
    breeding.
    (*Exeunt* AMBLE *and* WOMAN.)
Now my good lord; if I may use my freedom
As to an honour'd friend?
LOVELL: You lessen else
Your favour to me.
LADY ALWORTH: I dare then say thus:
180   As you are noble (howe'er common men
Make sordid wealth the object and sole end
Of their industrious aims) 'twill not agree
With those of eminent blood (who are engag'd
More to prefer their honours than to increase
The state left to 'em by their ancestors)
To study large additions to their fortunes
And quite neglect their births; though I must grant
Riches well got to be a useful servant
But a bad master.
LOVELL: Madam, 'tis confessed;
But what infer you from it?
190 LADY ALWORTH: This, my lord;
That as all wrongs, though thrust into one scale,
Slide of themselves off when right fills the other
And cannot bide the trial, so all wealth
(I mean if ill acquir'd) cemented to honour
By virtuous ways achiev'd, and bravely purchas'd,
Is but as rubbage pour'd into a river
(Howe'er intended to make good the bank)
Rend'ring the water that was pure before
Polluted and unwholesome. I allow
200   The heir of Sir Giles Overreach, Margaret,

> 185. *state*: estate.
> 195. *purchas'd*: obtained.
> 196. *rubbage*: rubbish.
> 199. *allow*: grant.

A maid well qualified, and the richest match
Our north part can make boast of; yet she cannot
With all that she brings with her, fill their mouths
That never will forget who was her father;
Or that my husband Alworth's lands, and Welborne's
(How wrung from both needs now no repetition)
Were real motive, that more work'd your lordship
To join your families than her form and virtues.
You may conceive the rest.

LOVELL: I do, sweet madam,
And long since have consider'd it. I know   210
The sum of all that makes a just man happy
Consists in the well choosing of his wife,
And there well to discharge it, does require
Equality of years, of birth, of fortune.
For beauty being poor, and not cried up
By birth or wealth, can truly mix with neither.
And wealth, where there's such difference in years
And fair descent, must make the yoke uneasy;
But I come nearer.

LADY ALWORTH: Pray you do, my lord.

LOVELL: Were Overreach's 'states thrice centupl'd, his
     daughter   220
Millions of degrees much fairer than she is,
(Howe'er I might urge precedents to excuse me)
I would not so adulterate my blood
By marrying Margaret, and so leave my issue
Made up of several pieces, one part scarlet
And the other London blue. In my own tomb
I will inter my name first.

LADY ALWORTH (aside):   I am glad to hear this –
Why then, my lord, pretend you marriage to her?
Dissimulation but ties false knots

203. *fill their mouths*: silence them.
209. *conceive*: imagine.
215. *cried up*: (i) praised. (ii) enhanced.
219. *come nearer*: touch on more particular matters.
225–6. *scarlet ... blue*: cf. III, ii, 199. London blue = servant's livery.

230   On that strait line by which you hitherto
Have measur'd all your actions.
LOVELL: I make answer,
And aptly, with a question. Wherefore have you,
That since your husband's death have liv'd a strict
And chaste nun's life, on the sudden giv'n yourself
To visits and entertainments? Think you, madam,
'Tis not grown public conference? Or the favours
Which you too prodigally have thrown on Welborne,
Being too reserv'd before, incur not censure?
LADY ALWORTH: I am innocent here, and on my life I swear
My ends are good.
240 LOVELL: On my soul, so are mine
To Margaret; but leave both to the event,
And since this friendly privacy does serve
But as an offer'd means unto ourselves
To search each other farther, you having shown
Your care of me, I, my respect to you,
Deny me not, but still in chaste words, madam,
An afternoon's discourse.
LADY ALWORTH: So I shall hear you.
    (*Exeunt.*)

[SCENE TWO]

    ([*Enter*] TAPWELL, FROTH.)
TAPWELL: Undone, undone! This was your counsel, Froth.
FROTH: Mine! I defy thee! Did not Master Marrall
(He has marr'd all, I am sure) strictly command us
(On pain of Sir Giles Overreach' displeasure)
To turn the gentleman out of doors?
TAPWELL: 'Tis true,
But now he's his uncle's darling, and has got
Master Justice Greedy (since he fill'd his belly)
At his commandment to do anything.
Woe, woe to us!

                236. *public conference*: common gossip.
                247. *So*: as long as.

FROTH: He may prove merciful.

TAPWELL: Troth, we do not deserve it at his hands.   10
  Though he knew all the passages of our house,
  As the receiving of stol'n goods, and bawdry,
  When he was rogue Welborne, no man would believe him,
  And then his information could not hurt us.
  But now he is right worshipful again,
  Who dares but doubt his testimony? Methinks
  I see thee, Froth, already in a cart
  For a close bawd, thine eyes ev'n pelted out
  With dirt and rotten eggs, and my hand hissing
  (If I scape the halter) with the letter R   20
  Printed upon it.

FROTH: Would that were the worst!
  That were but nine days' wonder. As for credit,
  We have none to lose; but we shall lose the money
  He owes us and his custom; there's the hell on't.

TAPWELL: He has summon'd all his creditors by the drum,
  And they swarm about him like so many soldiers
  On the pay day, and has found out such a new way
  To pay his old debts, as 'tis very likely
  He shall be chronicl'd for it.

FROTH: He deserves it
  More than ten pageants. But are you sure his worship   30
  Comes this way to my ladies?

    (*A cry within*, '*Brave Master Welborne!*')

TAPWELL: Yes, I hear him.

FROTH: Be ready with your petition and present it
  To his good grace.

    (*Enter* WELBORNE, *in a rich habit*, GREEDY, [MARRALL],
    ORDER, FURNACE, *three creditors:* TAPWELL *kneeling
    delivers his bill of debt.*)

11. *passages*: goings-on.
17. *cart*: bawds were carted through the streets.
18. *close*: secret.
19. *hissing*: i.e. from being branded.
20. *R*: for 'Rogue' or 'Receiver' (of stolen goods).
22. *credit*: reputation.
30. *pageants*: triumphal processions, described in detail in chronicles.

WELBORNE: How's this! Petition'd too?
But note what miracles the payment of
A little trash, and a rich suit of clothes,
Can work upon these rascals. I shall be,
I think, Prince Welborne.

MARRALL: When your worship's married
You may be; I know what I hope to see you.

WELBORNE: Then look thou for advancement.

MARRALL: To be known
40 Your worship's bailiff is the mark I shoot at.

WELBORNE: And thou shalt hit it.

MARRALL: Pray you sir, dispatch
These needy followers, and for my admittance,
Provided you'll defend me from Sir Giles,
Whose service I am weary of, I'll say something
You shall give thanks for.

WELBORNE: Fear me not Sir Giles.
(*This interim*, TAPWELL *and* FROTH *flattering and bribing*
JUSTICE GREEDY.)

GREEDY: Who? Tapwell? I remember thy wife brought me,
Last new year's tide, a couple of fat turkeys.

TAPWELL: And shall do every Christmas, let your worship
But stand my friend now.

GREEDY: How? With Master Welborne?
50 I can do anything with him, on such terms;
[*To* WELBORNE] See you this honest couple? They are good
souls
As ever drew out fosset; have they not
A pair of honest faces?

WELBORNE: I o'erheard you,
And the bribe he promis'd; you are cozen'd in 'em,
For of all the scum that grew rich by my riots
This for a most unthankful knave, and this
For a base bawd and whore, have worst deserv'd me,
And therefore speak not for 'em; by your place

42. *admittance*: i.e. to office of Welborne's bailiff.
45. *Fear me not*: fear not; 'ethical' dative.
52. *fosset*: barrel-tap.
57. *deserv'd me*: deserved from me.

You are rather to do me justice; lend me your ear,
Forget his turkeys and call in his licence,   60
And at the next fair I'll give you a yoke of oxen
Worth all his poultry.

GREEDY: I am chang'd on the sudden
In my opinion! Come near; nearer, rascal!
And now I view him better, did you e'er see
One look so like an arch-knave? His very countenance,
Should an understanding judge but look upon him,
Would hang him, though he were innocent.

TAPWELL *and* FROTH: Worshipful sir!

GREEDY: No, though the great Turk came, instead of turkeys,
To beg my favour, I am inexorable.
Thou hast an ill name; besides thy musty ale   70
That hath destroy'd many of the king's liege people,
Thou never hadst in thy house to stay men's stomachs
A piece of Suffolk cheese, or gammon of bacon,
Or any esculent, as the learned call it,
For their emolument, but sheer drink only.
For which gross fault I here do damn thy licence,
Forbidding thee ever to tap or draw.
For instantly, I will in mine own person
Command the constable to pull down thy sign,
And do it before I eat.

FROTH: No mercy?

GREEDY: Vanish!   80
If I show any, may my promis'd oxen gore me.

TAPWELL: Unthankful knaves are ever so rewarded.
      (*Exeunt* GREEDY, TAPWELL, FROTH.)

WELBORNE: Speak; what are you?

1 CREDITOR: A decay'd vintner, sir,
That might have thrived but that your worship broke me
With trusting you with muscadine and eggs,
And five-pound suppers with your after-drinkings,

74. *esculent*: eatables.
75. *emolument*: benefit.
84. *broke*: bankrupted.
85. *muscadine*: Muscatel; with eggs, an aphrodisiac.
86. *after-drinkings*: drinks between meals.

When you lodg'd upon the Bankside.

WELBORNE: [I] remember.

1 CREDITOR: I have not been hasty, nor e'er laid to arrest you.
And therefore, sir –

WELBORNE: Thou art an honest fellow:
90   I'll set thee up again; see his bill paid.
What are you?

2 CREDITOR: A tailor once, but now mere botcher.
I gave you credit for a suit of clothes,
Which was all my stock, but you failing in payment,
I was remov'd from the shop-board and confin'd
Under a stall.

WELBORNE: See him paid – and botch no more.

2 CREDITOR: I ask no interest, sir.

WELBORNE: Such tailors need not;
If their bills are paid in one and twenty year
They are seldom losers. [To 3 Creditor] O, I know thy face:
Thou wert my surgeon; you must tell no tales.
100   Those days are done. I will pay you in private.

ORDER: A royal gentleman.

FURNACE: Royal as an emperor!
He'll prove a brave master. My good lady knew
To choose a man.

WELBORNE: See all men else discharg'd
And since *Old debts are clear'd by a new way*
A little bounty will not misbecome me;
There's something, honest cook, for thy good breakfasts,
And this for your respect; take't, 'tis good gold
And I able to spare it.

ORDER: You are too munificent.

FURNACE: He was ever so.

WELBORNE: Pray you on before.

3 CREDITOR: Heaven bless you!
110 MARRALL: At four o' clock the rest know where to meet me.
          (*Exeunt* ORDER, FURNACE, CREDITORS.)

88. *laid*: engaged an officer.
91. *botcher*: mender.
99. *surgeon*: presumably when Welborne had the pox.

WELBORNE: Now, Master Marrall, what's the weighty secret
  You promis'd to impart?

MARRALL: Sir, time nor place
  Allow me to relate each circumstance;
  This only in a word; I know Sir Giles
  Will come upon you for security
  For his thousand pounds, which you must not consent to;
  As he grows in heat, as I am sure he will,
  Be you but rough, and say he's in your debt
  Ten times the sum, upon sale of your land;
  I had a hand in't (I speak it to my shame)   120
  When you were defeated of it.

WELBORNE: That's forgiven.

MARRALL: I shall deserve't; then urge him to produce
  The deed in which you pass'd it over to him,
  Which I know he'll have about him to deliver
  To the Lord Lovell, with many other writings,
  And present moneys. I'll instruct you further,
  As I wait on your worship; if I play not my prize
  To your full content, and your uncle's much vexation,
  Hang up Jack Marrall.

WELBORNE: I rely upon thee.
  (*Exeunt.*)

[SCENE THREE]

  ([*Enter*] ALWORTH, MARGARET.)

ALWORTH: Whether to yield the first praise to my lord's
  Unequall'd temperance, or your constant sweetness,
  That I yet live, my weak hands fasten'd on
  Hope's anchor, spite of all storms of despair,
  I yet rest doubtful.

MARGARET: Give it to Lord Lovell.
  For what in him was bounty, in me's duty.
  I make but payment of a debt, to which

121. *defeated*: deprived.

127. *play . . . prize*: play my part well (lit. 'engage in a contest', especially fencing).

My vows in that high office register'd
Are faithful witnesses.

ALWORTH: 'Tis true, my dearest,
10   Yet when I call to mind how many fair ones
Make wilful shipwreck of their faiths and oaths
To God and man to fill the arms of greatness,
And you rise up [no] less than a glorious star
To the amazement of the world, that hold out
Against the stern authority of a father,
And spurn at honour when it comes to court you,
I am so tender of your good, that faintly
With your wrong I can wish myself that right
You yet are pleas'd to do me.

MARGARET: Yet, and ever.
20   To me what's title, when content is wanting?
Or wealth rak'd up together with much care,
And to be kept with more, when the heart pines
In being disposses'd of what it longs for
Beyond the Indian mines; or the smooth brow
Of a pleas'd sire that slaves me to his will?
And so his ravenous humour may be feasted
By my obedience, and he see me great,
Leaves to my soul nor faculties nor power
To make her own election.

ALWORTH: But the dangers
That follow the repulse?

30 MARGARET: To me they are nothing:
Let Alworth love, I cannot be unhappy.
Suppose the worst, that in his rage he kill me,
A tear or two, by you dropp'd on my hearse
In sorrow for my fate, will call back life
So far as but to say that I die yours;
I then shall rest in peace. Or should he prove
So cruel, as one death would not suffice
His thirst of vengeance, but with ling'ring torments
In mind and body I must waste to air,

---

8. *high office*: i.e. in the sky.

In poverty join'd with banishment; so you share   40
In my afflictions (which I dare not wish you),
So high I prize you, I could undergo 'em
With such a patience as should look down
With scorn on his worst malice.

ALWORTH: Heaven avert
Such trials of your true affection to me!
Nor will it, unto you that are all mercy,
Show so much rigour. But since we must run
Such desperate hazards, let us do our best
To steer between 'em.

MARGARET: Your lord's ours, and sure;
And though but a young actor second me   50
In doing to the life what he has plotted,
The end may yet prove happy: now my Alworth –
   (*Enter* OVERREACH.)

ALWORTH: To your letter, and put on a seeming anger.

MARGARET: I'll pay my lord all debts due to his title,
And when with terms, not taking from his honour,
He does solicit me, I shall gladly hear him.
But in this peremptory, nay, commanding way,
T'appoint a meeting, and without my knowledge,
A priest to tie the knot can ne'er be undone
'Till death unloose it, is a confidence   60
In his lordship, will deceive him.

ALWORTH: I hope better,
Good lady.

MARGARET: Hope, sir, what you please; for me,
I must take a safe and secure course. I have
A father, and without his full consent,
Though all lords of the land kneel'd for my favour,
I can grant nothing.

OVERREACH [*aside*]: I like this obedience.
But whatsoever my lord writes must and shall be
Accepted, and embrac'd. – Sweet Master Alworth,

40. *so*: as long as.
49. *ours*: on our side.
51. *plotted*: with an allusion to theatrical sense.

    You show yourself a true and faithful servant
70   To your good lord, he has a jewel of you.
    How? Frowning, Meg? Are these looks to receive
    A messenger from my lord? What's this? Give me it.
MARGARET: A piece of arrogant paper, like th'inscriptions.
OVERREACH [*reads the letter*]: 'Fair mistress, from your
      servant learn, all joys
    That we can hope for, if deferr'd, prove toys;
    Therefore this instant, and in private meet
    A husband that will gladly at your feet
    Lay down his honours, tend'ring them to you,
    With all content, the church being paid her due.'
80   Is this the arrogant piece of paper? Fool,
    Will you still be one? In the name of madness, what
    Could his good honour write more to content you?
    Is there aught else to be wish'd after these two,
    That are already offer'd? Marriage first,
    And lawful pleasure after; what would you more?
MARGARET: Why, sir, I would be married like your daughter;
    Not hurried away i' th' night I know not whither,
    Without all ceremony, no friends invited
    To honour the solemnity.
ALWORTH: An't please your honour –
90   For so before tomorrow I must style you –
    My lord desires this privacy in respect
    His honourable kinsmen are far off,
    And his desires to have it done brook not
    So long delay as to expect their coming;
    And yet he stands resolv'd, with all due pomp,
    As running at the ring, plays, masques, and tilting,
    To have his marriage at court celebrated
    When he has brought your honour up to London.
OVERREACH: He tells you true; 'tis the fashion, on my
      knowledge,

75. *toys*: trifles.

94. *expect*: wait for.

96. *running at the ring*: thrusting a lance through a suspended ring while riding at speed.

Yet the good lord to please your peevishness   100
Must put it off forsooth, and lose a night
In which perhaps he might get two boys on thee.
Tempt me no farther; if you do, this goad
Shall prick you to him.

MARGARET: I could be contented,
Were you but by to do a father's part,
And give me in the church.

OVERREACH: So my lord have you
What do I care who gives you? Since my lord
Does purpose to be private, I'll not cross him.
I know not, Master Alworth, how my lord
May be provided, and therefore there's a purse   110
Of gold; 'twill serve this night's expense; tomorrow
I'll furnish him with any sums: in the meantime
Use my ring to my chaplain, he is benefic'd
At my manor of Gotham, and call'd Parson Will-do.
'Tis no matter for a licence, I'll bear him out in't.

MARGARET: With your favour, sir, what warrant is your ring?
He may suppose I got that twenty ways
Without your knowledge; and then to be refus'd
Were such a stain upon me. If you please, sir,
Your presence would do better.

OVERREACH: Still perverse?   120
I say again, I will not cross my lord,
Yet I'll prevent you too. Paper and ink there!

ALWORTH: I can furnish you.

OVERREACH: I thank you, I can write then.
   (*Writes on his book.*)

ALWORTH: You may, if you please, put out the name of my
   lord
In respect he comes disguis'd, and only write
'Marry her to this gentleman'.

OVERREACH: Well advis'd –
   (MARGARET *kneels.*)
'Tis done, away. My blessing, girl? Thou hast it,

---

103. *goad*: his sword (Q – 'good').
122. *prevent you*: anticipate your objections.

Nay, no reply, begone; good Master Alworth,
This shall be the best night's work you ever made.
ALWORTH: I hope so, sir.
    (*Exeunt* ALWORTH *and* MARGARET.)
130 OVERREACH: Farewell. Now all's cock-sure:
Methinks I hear already knights and ladies
Say, 'Sir Giles Overreach, how is it with
Your honourable daughter? Has her honour
Slept well tonight? Or will her honour please
To accept this monkey, dog, or parakeet?'
(This is state in ladies.) 'Or my eldest son
To be her page, and wait upon her trencher?'
My ends, my ends are compass'd! Then for Welborne
And the lands; were he once married to the widow,
140 I have him here. I can scarce contain myself,
I am so full of joy; nay, joy all over. (*Exit.*)

> 130. *cock-sure*: quite secure.
> 134. *tonight*: last night.
> 136. *state*: dignity.

ACT FIVE

SCENE ONE

([*Enter*] LOVELL, LADY ALWORTH, AMBLE.)

LADY ALWORTH: By this you know how strong the motives
    were
  That did, my lord, induce me to dispense
  A little with my gravity, to advance
  (In personating some few favours to him)
  The plots and projects of the down-trod Welborne.
  Nor shall I e'er repent (although I suffer
  In some few men's opinions for't) the action.
  For he that ventur'd all for my dear husband
  Might justly claim an obligation from me
  To pay him such a courtesy, which had I   10
  Coyly or over-curiously denied
  It might have argu'd me of little love
  To the deceas'd.

LOVELL: What you intended, madam,
  For the poor gentleman, hath found good success;
  For, as I understand, his debts are paid,
  And he once more furnish'd for fair employment.
  But all the arts that I have us'd to raise
  The fortunes of your joy, and mine, young Alworth,
  Stand yet in supposition, though I hope well,
  For the young lovers are in wit more pregnant   20
  Than their years can promise; and for their desires
  On my knowledge they are equal.

LADY ALWORTH: As my wishes
  Are with yours, my lord, yet give me leave to fear
  The building, though well grounded: to deceive
  Sir Giles, that's both a lion and a fox

> 4. *personating*: feigning.
> 11. *over-curiously*: too scrupulously.

In his proceedings, were a work beyond
The strongest undertakers, not the trial
Of two weak innocents.

LOVELL: Despair not, madam:
Hard things are compass'd oft by easy means,
30 And judgement, being a gift deriv'd from heaven,
Though sometimes lodg'd i' th' hearts of worldly men
(That ne'er consider from whom they receive it),
Forsakes such as abuse the giver of it;
Which is the reason that the politic
And cunning statesman, that believes he fathoms
The counsels of all kingdoms on the earth,
Is by simplicity oft overreach'd.

LADY ALWORTH: May he be so, yet in his name to express it
Is a good omen.

LOVELL: May it to myself
40 Prove so good, lady, in my suit to you;
What think you of the motion?

LADY ALWORTH: Troth, my lord,
My own unworthiness may answer for me;
For had you, when that I was in my prime,
My virgin-flower uncropp'd, presented me
With this great favour, looking on my lowness
Not in a glass of self-love but of truth,
I could not but have thought it as a blessing
Far, far beyond my merit.

LOVELL: You are too modest,
And undervalue that which is above
50 My title, or whatever I call mine.
I grant, were I a Spaniard, to marry
A widow might disparage me, but being
A true-born Englishman, I cannot find
How it can taint my honour; nay, what's more,
That which you think a blemish is to me
The fairest lustre. You already, madam,

34. *politic*: devious.
38. *in his name*: see previous line.
41. *motion*: suggestion.

Have given sure proofs how dearly you can cherish
A husband that deserves you: which confirms me,
That if I am not wanting in my care
To do you service, you'll be still the same   60
That you were to your Alworth; in a word,
Our years, our states, our births are not unequal,
You being descended nobly and alli'd so;
If then you may be won to make me happy,
But join your lips to mine, and that shall be
A solemn contract.

LADY ALWORTH: I were blind to my own good
Should I refuse it. Yet, my lord, receive me
As such a one the study of whose whole life
Shall know no other object but to please you.

LOVELL: If I return not with all tenderness   70
Equal respect to you, may I die wretched.

LADY ALWORTH: There needs no protestation, my lord,
To her that cannot doubt.

[*Enter* WELBORNE.]

                                You are welcome, sir.
Now you look like yourself.

WELBORNE: And will continue
Such in my free acknowledgement that I am
Your creature, madam, and will never hold
My life mine own when you please to command it.

LOVELL: It is a thankfulness that well becomes you;
You could not make choice of a better shape
To dress your mind in.

LADY ALWORTH: For me I am happy   80
That my endeavours prosper'd. Saw you of late
Sir Giles, your uncle?

WELBORNE: I heard of him, madam,
By his minister Marrall; he's grown into strange passions
About his daughter. This last night he look'd for
Your lordship at his house, but missing you,
And she not yet appearing, his wise head
Is much perplex'd and troubl'd.

74. *Now . . . yourself*: Welborne is now elegantly dressed.

LOVELL: It may be,
Sweetheart, my project took.

LADY ALWORTH: I strongly hope.
(*Enter* OVERREACH *with distracted looks, driving in* MAR-
RALL *before him.*)

OVERREACH: Ha! Find her, booby, thou huge lump of
nothing,
I'll bore thine eyes out else.

90 WELBORNE: May it please your lordship
For some ends of mine own but to withdraw
A little out of sight, though not of hearing;
You may perhaps have sport.

LOVELL: You shall direct me. (*Steps aside.*)

OVERREACH: I shall sol fa you, rogue.

MARRALL: Sir, for what cause
Do you use me thus?

OVERREACH: Cause, slave? Why, I am angry,
And thou a subject only fit for beating,
And so, to cool my choler, look to the writing.
Let but the seal be broke upon the box,
That has slept in my cabinet these three years,
I'll rack thy soul for't.

100 MARRALL [*aside*]: I may yet cry quittance,
Though now I suffer, and dare not resist.

OVERREACH: Lady, by your leave, did you see my daughter,
lady?
And the lord her husband? Are they in your house?
If they are, discover, that I may bid 'em joy;
And as an entrance to her place of honour,
See your ladyship on her left hand, and make curtseys
When she nods on you, which you must receive
As a special favour.

LADY ALWORTH: When I know, Sir Giles,
Her state requires such ceremony, I shall pay it;
110 But in the meantime, as I am myself,

88. *took*: succeeded.
94. *sol fa*: beat.
109. *state*: rank.

I give you to understand, I neither know
Nor care where her honour is.

OVERREACH: When you once see her
Supported, and led by the lord her husband,
You'll be taught better. Nephew –

WELBORNE: Sir?

OVERREACH: No more?

WELBORNE: 'Tis all I owe you.

OVERREACH: Have your redeem'd rags
Made you thus insolent?

WELBORNE (*in scorn*):   Insolent to you?
Why, what are you, sir, unless in your years,
At the best more than myself?

OVERREACH: His fortune swells him,
'Tis rank he's married.

LADY ALWORTH: This is excellent!

OVERREACH: Sir, in calm language (though I seldom use it),   120
I am familiar with the cause that makes you
Bear up thus bravely; there's a certain buzz
Of a stol'n marriage – do you hear? – of a stol'n marriage,
In which 'tis said there's somebody hath been cozen'd.
I name no parties.

WELBORNE: Well, sir, and what follows?

OVERREACH: Marry this, since you are peremptory; remember
Upon mere hope of your great match, I lent you
A thousand pounds; put me in good security,
And suddenly, by mortgage or by statute
Of some of your new possessions, or I'll have you   130
Dragg'd in your lavender robes to the gaol. You know me,
And therefore do not trifle.

WELBORNE: Can you be
So cruel to your nephew now he's in
The way to rise? Was this the courtesy
You did me in pure love, and no ends else?

114. *No more*: i.e. 'No more deference in addressing me?'
119. *rank*: (i) obvious, (ii) dignity, title.
129. *statute*: see I, i, 50.
131. *lavender robes*: 'laid in lavender' = pawned.

OVERREACH: End me no ends. Engage the whole estate
    And force your spouse to sign it, you shall have
    Three or four thousand more to roar and swagger
    And revel in bawdy taverns.
WELBORNE: And beg after –
    Mean you not so?
140 OVERREACH: My thoughts are mine, and free.
    Shall I have security?
WELBORNE: No: indeed you shall not:
    Nor bond, nor bill, nor bare acknowledgement,
    Your great looks fright not me.
OVERREACH: But my deeds shall:
    Outbrav'd?
    (*They both draw; the servants enter.*)
LADY ALWORTH: Help, murder! Murder!
WELBORNE: Let him come on,
    With all his wrongs and injuries about him,
    Arm'd with his cutthroat practices to guard him;
    The right that I bring with me will defend me
    And punish his extortion.
OVERREACH: That I had thee
    But single in the field!
LADY ALWORTH: You may, but make not
    My house your quarrelling scene.
150 OVERREACH: Were't in a church
    By heaven and hell, I'll do't.
MARRALL [*to* WELBORNE]:   Now put him to
    The showing of the deed.
WELBORNE: This rage is vain, sir,
    For fighting fear not, you shall have your hands full
    Upon the least incitement; and whereas
    You charge me with a debt of a thousand pounds,
    If there be law (how e'er you have no conscience),
    Either restore my land, or I'll recover
    A debt that's truly due to me from you,
    In value ten times more than what you challenge.

159. *challenge*: claim.

OVERREACH: I in thy debt! O impudence! Did I not   160
    purchase
    The land left by thy father? That rich land,
    That had continued in Welborne's name
    Twenty descents; which like a riotous fool
    Thou did'st make sale of? Is not here enclos'd
    The deed that does confirm it mine?
MARRALL [to WELBORNE]:   Now, now!
WELBORNE: I do acknowledge none. I ne'er pass'd o'er
    Any such land. I grant for a year or two
    You had it in trust, which if you do discharge,
    Surrend'ring the possession, you shall ease
    Yourself and me of chargeable suits in law,   170
    Which if you prove not honest (as I doubt it)
    Must of necessity follow.
LADY ALWORTH: In my judgement
    He does advise you well.
OVERREACH: Good, good! Conspire
    With your new husband, lady; second him
    In his dishonest practices; but when
    This manor is extended to my use,
    You'll speak in an humbler key, and sue for favour.
LADY ALWORTH: Never; do not hope it.
WELBORNE: Let despair first seize me.
OVERREACH: Yet to shut up thy mouth, and make thee give
    Thyself the lie, the loud lie, I draw out   180
    The precious evidence; if thou canst, forswear
    Thy hand and seal, and make a forfeit of
    Thy ears to the pillory: see, here's that will make
    My interest clear. (*Opens the box.*) Ha!
LADY ALWORTH: A fair skin of parchment.
WELBORNE: Indented, I confess, and labels too,
    But neither wax, nor words. How? Thunder-struck?
    Not a syllable to insult with? My wise uncle,

    170. *chargeable*: costly.
    176. *extended*: seized for debt.
    185. *Indented*: see Additional Notes.
    185. *labels*: narrow strips for seals.
    186. *wax*: seals.

Is this your precious evidence? Is this that makes
Your interest clear?

OVERREACH: I am o'erwhelm'd with wonder!
190   What prodigy is this? What subtle devil
Hath raz'd out the inscription? The wax
Turn'd into dust! The rest of my deeds whole,
As when they were deliver'd, and this only
Made nothing! Do you deal with witches, rascal?
There is a statute for you which will bring
Your neck in a hempen circle, yes, there is!
And now 'tis better thought for, cheater, know
This juggling shall not save you.

WELBORNE: To save thee
Would beggar the stock of mercy.

OVERREACH: Marrall.

MARRALL: Sir?

OVERREACH (*flattering him*): Though the witnesses are dead,
200   your testimony
Help with an oath or two; and for thy master,
Thy liberal master, my good honest servant,
I know you will swear any thing to dash
This cunning sleight; besides, I know thou art
A public notary, and such stand in law
For a dozen witnesses; the deed being drawn too
By thee, my careful Marrall, and deliver'd
When thou wert present, will make good my title;
Wilt thou not swear this?

MARRALL: I? No, I assure you.
210   I have a conscience not sear'd up like yours.
I know no deeds.

OVERREACH: Wilt thou betray me?

MARRALL: Keep him
From using of his hands, I'll use my tongue
To his no little torment.

OVERREACH: Mine own varlet
Rebel against me?

---

195. *statute*: i.e. against witchcraft.

MARRALL: Yes, and uncase you too.
 The idiot, the patch, the slave, the booby,
 The property fit only to be beaten
 For your morning exercise, your football, or
 Th'unprofitable lump of flesh, your drudge,
 Can now anatomize you, and lay open
 All your black plots, and level with the earth   220
 Your hill of pride; and with these gabions guarded,
 Unload my great artillery and shake,
 Nay, pulverise the walls you think defend you.

LADY ALWORTH: How he foams at the mouth with rage!

WELBORNE: To him again.

OVERREACH: O that I had thee in my gripe! I would tear thee
 Joint after joint.

MARRALL: I know you are a tearer
 But I'll have first your fangs par'd off, and then
 Come nearer to you when I have discover'd
 And made it good before the judge, what ways
 And devilish practices you us'd to cozen   230
 With an army of whole families, who yet live,
 And but enroll'd for soldiers were able
 To take in Dunkirk.

WELBORNE: All will come out.

LADY ALWORTH: The better.

OVERREACH: But that I will live, rogue, to torture thee,
 And make thee wish, and kneel in vain, to die,
 These swords that keep thee from me should fix here
 Although they made my body but one wound,
 But I would reach thee.

LOVELL [*aside*]: Heav'n's hand is in this,
 One ban-dog worry the other.

OVERREACH: I play the fool
 And make my anger but ridiculous.   240

214. *uncase*: strip, expose.
221. *gabions*: earth-filled baskets used to strengthen fortifications.
228. *discover'd*: exposed.
232. *but*: if only.
233. *take in*: take.
239. *ban-dog*: fierce dog, kept chained up.

There will be a time and place, there will be, cowards,
When you shall feel what I dare do.

WELBORNE: I think so:
You dare do any ill, yet want true valour
To be honest, and repent.

OVERREACH: They are words I know not,
Nor e'er will learn. Patience, the beggar's virtue,
Shall find no harbour here; after these storms
At length a calm appears. –
    (*Enter* GREEDY *and Parson* WILL-DO.)
                      Welcome, most welcome;
There's comfort in thy looks. Is the deed done?
Is my daughter married? Say but so, my chaplain,
And I am tame.

250 WILL-DO: Married? Yes, I assure you.

OVERREACH: Then vanish all sad thoughts. There's more
    gold for thee.
My doubts and fears are in the titles drown'd
Of my right honourable, my right honourable daughter.

GREEDY: Here will I be feasting; at least for a month
I am provided: empty guts croak no more.
You shall be stuff'd like bagpipes, not with wind
But bearing dishes.

OVERREACH (*whisp'ring to* WILL-DO): Instantly be here?
To my wish, to my wish! Now, you that plot against me,
And hop'd to trip my heels up, that contemn'd me,
Think on't and tremble.
    (*Loud music.*)

260   They come, I hear the music.
A lane there for my lord!

WELBORNE: This sudden heat
May yet be cool'd, sir.

OVERREACH: Make way there for my lord!
    (*Enter* ALWORTH *and* MARGARET.)

MARGARET (*kneeling*): Sir, first your pardon, then your blessing
    with

        257. *bearing*: well-weighted.
        261. *lane*: passage, way.

Your full allowance of the choice I have made.
As ever you could make use of your reason,
Grow not in passion. Since you may as well
Call back the day that's past as untie the knot
Which is too strongly fasten'd, not to dwell
Too long on words, this's my husband.

OVERREACH: How!

ALWORTH: So I assure you; all the rites of marriage   270
With every circumstance are past. Alas, sir,
Although I am no lord, but a lord's page,
Your daughter and my lov'd wife mourns not for it.
And for right honourable son-in-law, you may say
Your dutiful daughter.

OVERREACH: Devil! Are they married?

WILL-DO: Do a father's part, and say heav'n give 'em joy.

OVERREACH: Confusion and ruin! Speak, and speak quickly,
Or thou art dead.

WILL-DO: They are married.

OVERREACH: Thou had'st better
Have made a contract with the king of fiends
Than these! My brain turns!

WILL-DO: Why this rage to me?   280
Is not this your letter, sir? And these the words?
'Marry her to this gentleman.'

OVERREACH: It cannot,
Nor will I e'er believe it – 'sdeath, I will not –
That I, that in all passages I touch'd
At worldly profit, have not left a print
Where I have trod for the most curious search
To trace my footsteps, should be gull'd by children,
Baffl'd and fool'd, and all my hopes and labours
Defeated and made void.

WELBORNE: As it appears,
You are so, my grave uncle.

OVERREACH: Village nurses   290
Revenge their wrongs with curses; I'll not waste

286. *curious*: painstaking.
288. *Baffl'd*: publicly disgraced.

A syllable, but thus I take the life
Which wretched I gave to thee!
   (*Offers to kill* MARGARET.)

LOVELL: Hold, for your own sake!
Though charity to your daughter hath quite left you,
Will you do an act, though in your hopes lost here,
Can leave no hope for peace or rest hereafter?
Consider: at the best you are but a man,
And cannot so create your aims, but that
They may be cross'd.

OVERREACH: Lord, thus I spit at thee
300 And at thy counsel! And again desire thee
And as thou art a soldier, if thy valour
Dares show itself where multitude and example
Lead not the way, let's quit the house, and change
Six words in private.

LOVELL: I am ready.

LADY ALWORTH: Stay, sir –
Contest with one distracted?

WELBORNE: You'll grow like him
Should you answer his vain challenge.

OVERREACH: Are you pale?
Borrow his help, though Hercules call it odds,
I'll stand against both. As I am hemm'd in thus,
Since like [a] Lybian lion in the toil
310 My fury cannot reach the coward hunters
And only spends itself, I'll quit the place.
Alone I can do nothing; but I have servants
And friends to second me, and if I make not
This house a heap of ashes (by my wrongs,
What I have spoke I will make good) or leave
One throat uncut, if it be possible
Hell add to my afflictions. (*Exit* OVERREACH.)

MARRALL: Is't not brave sport?

GREEDY: Brave sport? I am sure it has ta'en away my
    stomach;

309. *toil*: snare.
315. *or*: ere.

I do not like the sauce.

ALWORTH [*to* MARGARET]: Nay, weep not, dearest:
  Though it express your pity, what's decreed   320
  Above, we cannot alter.

LADY ALWORTH: His threats move me
  No scruple, madam.

MARRALL: Was it not a rare trick
  (An it please your worship) to make the deed nothing?
  I can do twenty neater, if you please
  To purchase, and grow rich, for I will be
  Such a solicitor and steward for you,
  As never worshipful had.

WELBORNE: I do believe thee.
  But first discover the quaint means you us'd
  To raze out the conveyance.

MARRALL: They are mysteries
  Not to be spoke in public: certain minerals   330
  Incorporated in the ink and wax.
  Besides, he gave me nothing, but still fed me
  With hopes, and blows; and that was the inducement
  To this conundrum. If it please your worship
  To call to memory, this mad beast once caus'd me
  To urge you, or to drown, or hang yourself;
  I'll do the like to him if you command me.

WELBORNE: You are a rascal. He that dares be false
  To a master, though unjust, will ne'er be true
  To any other. Look not for reward   340
  Or favour from me; I will shun thy sight
  As I would do a basilisk's. Thank my pity
  If thou keep thy ears. How e'er I will take order
  Your practice shall be silenc'd.

GREEDY: I'll commit him
  If you'll have me, sir.

WELBORNE: That were to little purpose;

320. *express*: squeeze out (as tears).
328. *quaint*: intricate, clever.
342. *basilisk*: mythical serpent whose glance killed.
343. *take order*: see to it.

His conscience be his prison. Not a word
But instantly begone.

ORDER: Take this kick with you.

AMBLE: And this.

FURNACE: If that I had my cleaver here
I would divide your knave's head.

MARRALL: This is the haven
False servants still arrive at. (*Exit* MARRALL.)
    (*Enter* OVERREACH.)

350 LADY ALWORTH: Come again?

LOVELL: Fear not, I am your guard.

WELBORNE: His looks are ghastly.

WILL-DO: Some little time I have spent under your favours
In physical studies, and if my judgement err not
He's mad beyond recovery: but observe him,
And look to yourselves.

OVERREACH: Why, is not the whole world
Included in myself? To what use then
Are friends, and servants? Say there were a squadron
Of pikes, lined through with shot; when I am mounted
Upon my injuries, shall I fear to charge 'em?
No: I'll through the battalia,
    (*Flourishing his sword unsheathed*)

360   and, that routed,
I'll fall to execution. Ha! I am feeble:
Some undone widow sits upon mine arm,
And takes away the use of't, and my sword,
Glued to my scabbard with wrong'd orphans' tears,
Will not be drawn. Ha! What are these? Sure, hangmen
That come to bind my hands, and then to drag me
Before the judgement seat; now they are new shapes
And do appear like furies with steel whips
To scourge my ulcerous soul! Shall I then fall
370 Ingloriously, and yield? No, spite of fate,
I will be forc'd to hell like to myself.

350. *still*: always.
354. *but*: only.
358. *pikes . . . shot*: pikemen reinforced with musketeers.

Though you were legions of accursed spirits,
Thus would I fly among you!
WELBORNE: There's no help –
Disarm him first, then bind him.
GREEDY: Take a mittimus
And carry him to Bedlam.
LOVELL: How he foams!
WELBORNE: And bites the earth.
WILL-DO: Carry him to some dark room,
There try what art can do for his recovery.
   (*They force* OVERREACH *off*.)
MARGARET: O my dear father!
ALWORTH: You must be patient, mistress.
LOVELL: Here is a precedent to teach wicked men
That when they leave religion and turn atheists,   380
Their own abilities leave 'em. Pray you, take comfort;
I will endeavour you shall be his guardians
In his distractions; and for your land, Master Welborne,
Be it good, or ill in law, I'll be an umpire,
Between you and this [*indicating* MARGARET], th'undoubted
   heir
Of Sir Giles Overreach. For me, here's the anchor
That I must fix on [*indicating* LADY ALWORTH].
ALWORTH: What you shall determine,
My lord, I will allow of.
WELBORNE: 'Tis the language
That I speak too; but there is something else
Beside the repossession of my land   390
And payment of my debts, that I must practise;
I had a reputation, but 'twas lost
In my loose course; and 'till I redeem it
Some noble way, I am but half made up.
It is a time of action; if your lordship

374. *mittimus*: justice's warrant for commitment.
375. *Bedlam*: Bethlehem Hospital, a lunatic asylum.
376. *dark room*: a common treatment for madness (cf. Malvolio in *Twelfth Night*).
388. *allow of*: approve.

Will please to confer a company upon me
In your command, I doubt not in my service
To my king and country, but I shall do something
That may make me right again.

LOVELL: Your suit is granted,
And you lov'd for the motion.

400 WELBORNE [*to audience*]:   Nothing wants then
But your allowance.
        [*Exeunt.*]

> 400. *motion*: proposal.
> 401. *allowance*: approval.

FINIS

THE EPILOGUE

But your allowance, and in that, our all
Is comprehended; it being known, nor we
Nor he that wrote the comedy can be free
Without your manumission, which if you
Grant willingly, as a fair favour due
To the poet's, and our labours (as you may,
For we despair not, gentlemen, of the play),
We jointly shall profess your grace hath might
To teach us action, and him how to write.

4. *manumission*: setting free (i.e. by applause).
9. *action*: acting.

ADDITIONAL NOTES

THE DUTCH COURTESAN

Act One

SCENE ONE

146–7 *Family of Love*: a sixteenth-century Dutch religious sect which spread to England (Mary Faugh and the Mulligrubs are adherents). They were supposed to have practised free love and desired the immortality of the soul.

SCENE TWO

8 *restitution is Catholic*: 'perhaps an allusion to Catholic demands for restitution of property seized under the reign of Henry VIII' (Walley). Cocledemoy wishes to keep the goblets because the Family of Love believed in communism.

92 *Curtian gulfs*: after Marcus Curtius, a Roman soldier who, to save Rome, leapt fully armed into a chasm in the Forum.

122 *So . . . nightingale*: in Renaissance iconography, the nightingale was represented sleeping against a thorn.

Act Two

SCENE ONE

79 *O . . . habent*: 'O miserable they, whose joys in fault we lay': Florio's translation of Maximianus (*Pseudo-Gallus*, I, 180), quoted by Montaigne. Marston in this play frequently echoes Florio's translation of Montaigne's *Essays*.

SCENE TWO

100 *Video . . . proboque*: 'The best I see and like' *deteriora sequor* – 'the worst I follow still'. Ovid, *Metamorphoses*, vii, 20 (Golding's translation, 1565–7).

SCENE THREE

55 *Paris Garden*: a well-known London landmark, the site of an amphitheatre for bull- and bear-baiting built during the reign of Henry VIII.

84 *Common Council*: governing body made up of city aldermen.

114 *'tis . . . Term*: i.e. the loss will be made up by one week's 'cutting' (adulterating wine and cooking the books) during the 'term' (period when payments fell due).

118 *Bid 'em play*: each act is separated from the others by a call for music, a feature of performances at the 'private' Blackfriars Theatre

Act Three

SCENE ONE

16 *ployden's*: the origin of the term is uncertain, though the sense is clear. A 'ploydenist' is a lawyer, and there may also be an allusion to Edmund Plowden (1518–85) the jurist, whose name was often spelt 'Ployden'.

42–3 *call'd in*: ordered to be withdrawn by the (ecclesiastical) censorship authorities; in 1599 they ordered the public burning of several books, including two of Marston's.

221 *In . . . formas*: 'In new situations the mind prompts the utterance of altered sentiments.' First line of Ovid's *Metamorphoses* (Walley's translation).

226 *Lindabrides*: heroine of a Spanish romance, translated in 1578 as *The First Part of the Mirror of Princely Deeds and Knighthood*.

SCENE TWO

36–9 *penurious . . . fortnight*: want of learning leads to a parish so poor that instead of a tithing pig the tithe consists only of pigs' tails. Infrequency of food leads to infrequent 'stools'.

39 *works of supererogation*: in Catholic doctrine, good deeds over and above what is needful for personal salvation.

Act Four

SCENE ONE

37 *unwholesome reversions*: depleted estates, with a possible allusion to sexual contamination from profligate husbands.

49 *Euphues and his England*: Lyly's sequel, published 1580, to his celebrated *Euphues: the Anatomy of Wit*.

49–50 *Palmerin de Oliva*: translated from Spanish by Anthony Munday.

50 *Legend of Lies*: probably, and appropriately, non-existent.

SCENE THREE

9–11 *Hadamoy . . . oteeston*: Greekish gibberish. The general idea is that Cocledemoy is trying to bribe Franceschina.

Act Five

SCENE THREE

143 *seven liberal sciences*: medieval curriculum: the *trivium* (grammar, logic, rhetoric) and *quadrivium* (arithmetic, geometry, music, astronomy).

143–4 *nine cardinal virtues*: traditionally seven: justice, prudence, temperance, fortitude (natural virtues); faith, hope, charity (theological virtues). Perhaps Cocledemoy means to add eating and drinking.

A MAD WORLD, MY MASTERS

The Actors in the Comedy

Inesse, Possibility: an estate *in esse* (in being) gave actual possession of land, as distinct from an estate in possibility which would give possession later.

Act One

SCENE ONE

35–6 *Lent . . . down*: flags flown from playhouse towers were taken down during Lent, when performances were forbidden.

59–60 *no . . . hundred*: in James I's reign, landholders worth forty pounds a year either had to receive (and pay for) knighthoods, or pay a fine. Follywit is saying that his uncle is wealthier than these newly made knights.

SCENE TWO

48 *Resolution*: a popular devotional work by the Jesuit Robert Parsons, *The First Book of the Christian Exercises pertaining to Resolution* (1582).

106 *th' master's side*: the master (governor) of a prison was allowed to let some rooms for his own profit (Bullen).

114 *to the third pile*: i.e. to the utmost. The third pile was the bottom (satin) layer above which, in heavy velvet, two further 'piles' were added.

Act Two

SCENE ONE

18 *free . . . mercers*: an honorary member of the cloth-sellers' guild. An allusion to the heavy debts for clothes incurred by gentlemen of fashion.

SCENE SIX

117–18 *speak . . . paid for't*: an allusion to the practice of bribing servants in order to obtain interviews and favours from their masters.

Act Three

SCENE TWO

25 *Rosamund . . . Harry*: Rosamund Clifford, the young mistress of Henry II, was forced to swallow poison by his queen.

56 *liquor of coral*: standard items of contemporary medicine, noted for cost and scarcity.

106 *Diversa . . . scabierum*: 'many kinds of scabs' (Pliny, Bk. XXVI, Ch. xiv.).

158 *Hercules' Pillars*: Gibraltar and Mount Abyla, traditional limits of known world.

Stage direction. Harebrain listening: the Courtesan's bed is in the inner stage area, with the curtains drawn, and therefore invisible to Harebrain.

230–32 *uncle . . . good cousins*: contemporary literature, doubtless basing itself on real-life exigencies, often presents the whore as having a variety of *ad hoc* relatives.

233 *Clerkenwell . . . St Johns*: the Priory of St Johns was in Clerkenwell, a notorious district.

Act Four

SCENE ONE

21 *German clock*: the earliest clocks from Germany were complicated and unreliable. Cf. Biron's speech in *Love's Labour's Lost*, III, i, 187–8.

38 *Feel . . . bone*: whether devils could be touched or not was a vexed contemporary question.

SCENE TWO

21 *Monsieur's days*: the Duke of Anjou, a hopeful suitor to Elizabeth I, came to England in 1581.

SCENE THREE

40–41 *onyx . . . silexque*: onyx (fingernail) and its compounds, and silex (flint). Part of a mnemonic quatrain from a widely used Latin grammar.

SCENE FIVE

106 *witness*: a witness to a marriage made it legally binding, though it had to be solemnized by a priest.

117 *All Hollantide*: All Saints' feast, 1 November.

Act Five

SCENE ONE

6 *Bartholomewtide*: Bartholomew Fair at Smithfield in August.

26 *interlude*: interludes were usually given during a break on festive occasions.

31–2 *fearful fools*: i.e. those fearing the plague, at the height of which playhouses were closed by order.

44 *whose men*: to avoid arrest for vagrancy, actors had to be under the official patronage of nobility or royalty.

SCENE TWO

21 *bold Beacham*: 'as bold as Beacham', after Thomas Beauchamp, first Earl of Warwick.

38–9 *stage ... gentlemen*: gallants often sat on the stage during a performance.

108 *Smug ... horse*: a scene (missing from extant version) of *The Merry Devil of Edmonton* showed Smug as St George riding a white horse.

197 *kneeling ... play*: a tradition of performances in noblemen's houses, which probably did not survive in the public theatres.

THE DEVIL IS AN ASS

The Prologue

26 *If this play ... the Devil is in't*: an allusion to Thomas Dekker's play *If it be not Good, the Devil is in it* (printed 1612).

Act One

SCENE ONE

32 *Lancashire*: fifteen women and four men were tried and condemned for witchcraft there on 19 August 1612.

61 *St Katherine's*: an area noted for ale houses, as the Dutch were noted for their drinking.

70 *shoot the Bridge*: the narrow arches of old London Bridge produced a fall under the bridge which it was dangerous, and at high tide impossible, to negotiate.

94 *Vennor*: Richard Vennor or Venner, who swindled the public by announcing an entertainment called *England's Joy* and absconding with the entrance money.

SCENE TWO

1–2 *Bretnor*: Thomas Bretnor, astrologer and almanac maker, as were Edward Gresham and 'Doctor' Forman (1552–1611).

3 *Franklin*: an apothecary, executed in 1615 for his part in the Overbury murder.

3 *Fiske*: Nicholas Fiske, self-taught astrologer and doctor.

3 *Savory*: Abraham Savory, an actor who may also have been involved in the Overbury poisoning.

92 *Devil's arse*: the Peak Cavern in Derbyshire. Jonson tells the legend in *The Gypsies Metamorphosed*, ll. 134–7.

SCENE THREE

111 *court-parliament*: an allusion to medieval courts of love. Cf. '*Love's Court of Requests*' in Jonson's *The New Inn*.

187 *roses ... ass*: in the Latin treatise *Lucius, sive Asinus*, the story is told of how Lucian, changed into an ass, was brought into a theatre to display his tricks; he regained his human shape by eating some roses he found there.

Act Two

SCENE ONE

84 *Harrington*: a brass farthing token, so-called after Lord Harrington, who obtained a patent for coining them in 1613.

120 *England ... dukes*: William the Conqueror and his successors, being themselves dukes, were apparently reluctant to create any. The first English duke was Edward, the Black Prince. There were no dukes in England between 1572, when the Duke of Norfolk was executed, till 1623, when James I created the Duke of Buckingham.

147 *Bermudas*: a district of London (approximately where Trafalgar Square stands) haunted by thieves, debtors and prostitutes; so-called, presumably, because the old name for the Bermudas was 'The Isle of Devils'.

178 *Good Fortune or God's Blessing*: an allusion to a folk-tale, of which there are several variants, in which a man puts by money saying it is 'for good luck' or 'God's blessing'; someone overhears him and comes to his door when the man is away, tells his wife he is 'Good Luck' or 'God's Blessing' and goes off with the money. Cf. Plautus, *Aulularia*, ll. 90–100.

SCENE TWO

128 *broker's block ... property*: Fitzdottrel, with his craze for showing off his cloak, is compared to a block for displaying clothes (property = stage prop).

SCENE THREE

85 *Dick Robinson*: Richard Robinson, who acted in Jonson's *Catiline*, also played female roles.

Act Three

SCENE ONE

64 *Plutarch's Lives*: North's translation of Plutarch's *Lives* was one of the chief Elizabethan sources for classical history.

80 *posture book*: there were several such works for soldiers, the standard one being Jacob de Cheyn's *The Exercise of Arms* (1607).

151 *Master of the Dependences*: bully boys who undertook, for money, to appear on behalf of a timid person in a quarrel (or 'dependence') were known as 'masters of the dependences'.

155 *writing ... against duels*: an edict of 1614 forbade duels and a proclamation of two years later prohibited the wearing of offensive weapons such as daggers and pistols.

275 *better fathers*: i.e. the Puritans are now better at equivocation than the Jesuits, who were traditionally noted for it.

Act Four

SCENE ONE

215 *alvagada*: modern spelling *albayalde*, white lead.

216 *argentata*: white ceruse.

218 *alum scagliola*: flaked gypsum.

218 *pol di pedra*: ? rock-alum.

219 *zuccarino*: confections of sugar.

219 *turpentine of Abezzo*: pitch-pine sap.

220 *soda di levante*: sodium carbonate.

221 *benjamin di gotta*: gum benzoin.

222 *Grasso di serpe*: snake's fat.

222 *porcelletto marino*: sturgeon.

223 *lentisco*: mastic.

223 *zucche mugia*: ? wash of sweet oils.

233 *carravic:ns*: ?

332 *Pastillos*: small 'pasties' or chewing sweets.

333 *Coquettas*: buns.

333 *almoiavanas*: cheese cakes.

333 *mantecadas*: wafers of lard and sugar.

334 *Alcoreas*: preserved lemon-rinds (*alcorcas*).

334 *mustaccioli*: marzipan.

335 *peladore*: depilatory.

336 *aqua nanfa*: orange-water.

340 *piveti*: clove-like spice.

SCENE THREE

117 *Duke of Shoreditch*: a mock-title, deriving from an alleged occasion when Henry VIII conferred the title on an inhabitant of Shoreditch for prowess in archery.

Act Five

SCENE ONE

27 *conduit-head*: there were nine conduits, erected in the early thirteenth century, for supplying the city with water. The one referred to was near the banqueting house on the site of Stratford Place in Oxford Street. Because the gallows at Tyburn were near by, 'to be invited to the Lord Mayor's banqueting house' became a euphemism for being hanged.

SCENE THREE

6 *Darrel's Tricks*: John Darrel, a Puritan preacher whose cures and exorcisms, began in 1586, were subsequently exposed.

7 *boy o' Burton*: Thomas Darling, for bewitching whom Alice Good-ridge was imprisoned in Derby jail, where she died in 1596.

7 *seven in Lancashire*: seven children, for bewitching whom Edmund Hartley was executed at Lancaster in 1597.

8 *Somers at Nottingham*: William Somers, who was supposed to be possessed. Darrel was imprisoned after two investigations into this affair, in 1599.

126 *boy o' thirteen*: Kittredge suggests that this was John Smith of Leicester, a pretended demoniac who caused nine women to be hanged there in July 1616.

SCENE FIVE

13 *his wife ... sorcerers*: the victim of witchcraft allegedly had fits when in the presence of his tormentors.

144 *mouse*: the boy of Burton was supposed to have pointed to a mouse that, he said, came out of his mouth.

A NEW WAY
TO PAY OLD DEBTS

Dedication

Robert Dormer (1610–43) was created Earl of Caernarvon in 1628. He died at the first battle of Newbury, 20 September 1643.

Prefatory Poems

Sir Henry Moody of Garesdon, Wiltshire, second baronet, died a bankrupt in Virginia in 1661 or 1662. Sir Thomas Jay, also of Wiltshire, graduated from Queen's College, Oxford, 1612–13, and was a member of Lincoln's Inn.

Dramatis Personae

term-driver: ? 'term-trotter, one who comes to the law courts for a term' (*N.E.D.*), or possibly one who insists on the letter of the law.

Act One

SCENE ONE

11 *Plimworth cloak*: cudgel. Travellers stranded at Plymouth apparently used to cut a stick and pretend to be on a walking tour.

SCENE TWO

29 *Spinola*: the Spanish commander, the Marquis of Spinola, captured Breda after a ten-week siege on 1 July 1625.

Act Two

SCENE ONE

130 *Abram-men*: real or pretended madmen (see *Cony-Catchers and Bawdy Baskets*, p. 108).

134 *Lady of the Lake*: the enchantress Vivian in the *Morte d'Arthur*.

Act Three

SCENE ONE

79 *Hippolytus ... Venus*: in Euripides' *Phaedra*, Hippolytus is a devotee of Diana, the chaste goddess of hunting, and shuns the love-goddess, Venus.

SCENE TWO

118 *Jupiter ... Semele*: Semele was destroyed when she saw Jupiter in his full splendour.

200 *tissues ... scarlet*: tissue was cloth made of interwoven gold and silver, scarlet a heavy material (not always red); thus the two are incompatible.

311–12 *dumpling, woodcock ... buttered toasts*: all these phrases possibly contain allusions to women: dumpling = plump lass; woodcock = fool; buttered bun or ? toast = harlot.

Act Four

SCENE ONE

124 *encloser*: the fencing off of common lands for sheep pasturing (enclosures) was a widespread grievance, though the practice had by this time long passed its peak.

155 *Olympus* Mount Parnassus had a double head, but Olympus, as the home of the gods, is probably intended. Boreas = north wind.

Act Five

SCENE ONE

185 *Indented*: contracts were written twice over on a single sheet, and the two copies separated by tearing; the indented edges fitted together to show that the separate copies were genuine.